KU-491-901

The Summer of Secrets

MARTINA REILLY

sphere

SPHERE

First published in Great Britain in 2007 by Sphere
Reprinted in 2007 (twice)
This paperback edition published in 2008 by Sphere
Reprinted in 2008 (twice)

Copyright © Martina Reilly 2007

The moral right of the author has been asserted.

*All characters and events in this publication, other than
those clearly in the public domain, are fictitious
and any resemblance to real persons,
living or dead, is purely coincidental.*

All rights reserved.
No part of this publication may be reproduced,
stored in a retrieval system, or transmitted, in any
form or by any means, without the prior
permission in writing of the publisher, nor be
otherwise circulated in any form of binding or
cover other than that in which it is published and
without a similar condition including this
condition being imposed on the subsequent purchaser.

A CIP catalogue record for this book
is available from the British Library.

ISBN 978-0-7515-3956-1

Typeset in Baskerville MT by
Palimpsest Book Production Limited, Grangemouth, Stirlingshire
Printed and bound in Great Britain by Clays Ltd, St Ives plc

Sphere
An imprint of
Little, Brown Book Group
100 Victoria Embankment
London EC4Y 0DY

An Hachette Livre UK Company
www.hachettelivre.co.uk

www.littlebrown.co.uk

Martina Reilly, formerly writing as Tina Reilly, is the author of a number of bestselling novels: *Flipside*, *The Onion Girl* and *Is This Love?* published by Poolbeg in Ireland and *Wedded Blitz*, *Wish Upon a Star*, *All I Want is You* and the Impac long-listed *Something Borrowed*, published by Sphere. She is also the author of a number of award-winning teenage books. She has worked as a columnist for the *Irish Evening Herald* and does freelance columns for the *Irish Independent* and the *Kildare Voice*. In her spare time she acts, teaches drama and writes plays.

For more information see www.martinareilly.info

'Martina has the wonderful knack of combining sensitivity for a serio[us] subject with a big dose of humour. She comes up trumps again [with] *The Summer of Secrets* . . . Strong on the bonds of friendship and [how] the past shapes our lives, it's the kind of book you can't stop reading even though you don't want it to end' *Irish Independent*

'A brilliant book' *Liffey Champion*

'This is one of the funniest books of the year . . . [will] have the most hard-hearted reader wiping tears – and not just of laughter – from their eyes' *Irish Evening Herald*

'Good, solid entertainment' *Irish Examiner*

More praise for Martina Reilly

'Hard to put down, laugh-out-loud funny . . . perfect holiday reading' *Woman's Way*

'Reilly is a star of the future' *Belfast Telegraph*

'Reilly has a wonderful comic touch, both in the way she draws her characters and in her dialogue . . . a brilliant read' *U Magazine*

'Martina Reilly's characters are so well observed . . . a substantial read' *She*

Also by Martina Reilly, writing as Tina Reilly

Flipside
The Onion Girl
Is This Love?
Wish Upon a Star
Wedded Blitz
Something Borrowed

Writing as Martina Reilly

All I Want is You

For Ali Gunn and Joanne Dickinson –
this is their book as much as it is mine.

Thanks to:

Gerry Kenneally, cognitive behavioural therapist, for all his help on PTSD. This book couldn't have been written without his input.

Thanks also to the staff of Irish Ferries for providing me with the times of ferries and plotting journeys from England to Ireland.

To all at Sphere – Jo Dickinson, brilliant editor, Louise Davies, Emma Stonex and Kirsteen Astor for making being a writer such a lovely experience.

To Dingle – the inspiration for the location of this book.

And finally to Colm, the ever patient, and Caoimhe and Conor, the best family in the world.

1

'ADAM?' I WHISPER.

    'Yeah?'

'I got the sack.'

'Bloody hell, Hope. Not again.'

His voice rises and someone behind tells him to 'shh'.

I giggle and Adam grins before remembering what I've just said and mouths 'You got the sack?'

I nod and turn my attention back to the stage. I've been trying to break the news to him and Julie all evening, but Julie is now ensconced behind the stage and Adam and I are unfortunately ensconced in front of it. We're surrounded by proud parents and school governors. I've taken advantage of the fact that the Wicked Witch of the West has once again forgotten her lines to break the news to Adam, my landlord and friend. The Wicked Witch has by now started shuffling from foot to foot and twiddling her broom in embarrassment.

'I'll kill you, Dorothy,' Julie's prompt comes loudly from somewhere backstage.

Dorothy, who has been glaring ferociously at the Wicked Witch, takes umbrage. 'Why kill me?' she says, marching towards the wings. 'I ain't the one that's forgot me lines!'

A titter ripples through the audience.

'Oh,' the Wicked Witch says delightedly, 'that's me line.' She assumes an aggressive pose. 'Yeah, I'll kill you, Dorothy!'

And the play starts to move on again.

'I thought you liked that job,' Adam mutters a few minutes later as Dorothy breaks into an out of tune song, accompanied by a miserable scarecrow, who looks more in need of dancing lessons than a brain.

'I did like it. But that web client, Michael Doyle, rejected my web text again.'

'Again? The tosser!' Adam is suitably aggrieved.

'Yeah, that's what I thought.'

'You didn't say that to him?'

I shrug. 'Well, what I –'

'Shh!'

Adam winces. 'Sorry!' he nods an apology to the woman behind. Then he mouths at me, 'Tell me later?'

'I'll have forgotten what happened by the time this play is over.'

Adam snorts with laughter then tries to turn it into a cough.

I wink at him and look demurely innocent.

Later is ninety minutes later, after the Wizard forgot all his lines and Julie had to shout them out while he opened and closed his mouth.

It was the funniest scene of the play.

Adam and I are in the half-empty school hall waiting for Julie to emerge. The only people left now are the organisers and assistants. Adam and I helped pick up the litter and are now hanging about like two spares. Adam hasn't asked me any more about my job, or lack thereof. I know he's waiting for Julie, so I can tell them both together. Julie works as a teacher in this school; it's a tough job but she loves it. Doing *The Wizard of Oz* with the children had been her idea, and she'd directed it too.

'Here she is,' Adam starts to clap as she comes towards us. Julie beams at us. 'Well?' she asks.

'Brilliant,' Adam pronounces. 'Best Wizard I've ever seen.'

'Totally.' I nod in agreement.

'Would you have noticed that anyone forgot their lines?' Julie looks from me to Adam.

'Hope lost her job again.' Adam deftly changes the subject, saving us some lies that we're bound to get caught out on.

'No!' Julie gawks at me. 'Hope!'

'No hope is right,' I joke.

She smiles briefly, before saying, 'But you liked that job!'

'The tosser rejected her web text again,' Adam says. 'How many times did you do it for him, Hope?'

'Twenty-five times in three weeks.'

'Tosser,' Julie agrees.

'So what happened?' Adam asks. He's leading the way towards the car park. There's still a queue of cars to get out. I don't answer until the three of us are sitting in Adam's monster car – a perk of his job as regional manager for a load of building supply companies. Out of the three of us, Adam is the rich one; he owns the house Julie and I live in, and two more besides. He works all the time and takes life very seriously, which is why Julie and I like to make him laugh. Before we came along, I wouldn't say Adam had much of a life. 'So?' Adam turns to me as I climb into the back seat, 'are you going to tell us what happened?'

'I know what happened,' Julie pronounces. 'You sent the muppet a really crappy draft, didn't you? Something along the lines of –' she thinks for a second – 'At Doyle Computers, we specialise in screwing up your computer system. We give your system viruses, bugs and, even better, we won't be able to repair the damage.'

Adam laughs.

'Damn!' I grin, 'That's what I should have done!'

'So what did you do?'

'I e-mailed the tosser my first draft again.'

'You didn't!' Julie laughs lightly. 'And he noticed? Is that why you got fired?'

I shake my head and say casually, 'Actually, he accepted it.'

'He accepted it? Your very first draft?'

'Yep.'

'But that was good.'

'Well, it would have been if I hadn't decided to take a taxi over to his office and ask him why he thought it was fun to waste my time.'

'Oh Hope, you didn't!' Adam looks at me in amused exasperation.

'I did.'

Julie begins to giggle.

'And naturally he was furious with me, but I just hopped back into the taxi and when I reached work, the taxi driver says –' I put on a terrible cockney accent – 'That'll be one 'undred pounds.'

'One hundred pounds,' Adam winces. 'Did you go via Mars?'

'That's what I asked and he got really stroppy and followed me upstairs into my office where my boss was waiting for me.'

Now they both start to laugh.

'And my boss is screaming at me that I'm fired and the taxi driver is looking for his hundred pounds, which I did not have so I turn to my boss and I ask him for my pay in advance.'

'Bloody hell, Hope!' Adam snorts.

'So then my boss starts yelling.'

'And what happened?' Julie giggles.

'I put up my hands, told the taxi driver that I would get the money out of the bank if he'd be good enough to trust me. And he says, how could he trust me when he's just seen me get fired. So I told him to take it or leave it. So he followed me to the bank and when he got back to his car it was clamped.'

They're laughing so hard now, I join in.

'Worst day of my life,' I pronounce.

'Aw, never mind,' Julie says and pats my arms, 'you'll get another job, you always do. Did you count to ten before you went over there?'

'I counted to fifty.'

Adam chortles.

'Anyway,' I continue, suddenly becoming serious, so they'll *know* I'm serious, 'I've enough money to cover the rent on my room for this month, Adam. And then, well,' I pause, before taking a deep breath and blurting out, 'you can rent out my room to someone else.'

Adam gawks at me in disbelief. 'Don't be stupid. You'll get another job.' He cracks a smile. 'I've never known anyone to get as many jobs as you.'

'Ha ha.' I poke his arm. 'No, I'm serious, Adam. I'm leaving.'

'Leaving?' the two say together.

'Well, just for a bit,' I clarify when I see their looks of dismay. 'I've decided, after all the excitement, to take a break and go away for a while. On a holiday.'

'A holiday?' Adam looks aghast. 'Hope, you've just lost your job!'

'Yeah and the shock of it makes me need a holiday far away.'

I'm gratified to see them smile.

'How long will you be gone?' Julie asks quietly, sounding slightly shocked.

I shrug. 'I don't know.'

'A month, two months, how long?' Her voice is a bit tearful now.

'Ju, don't.' I place my hand on her arm. 'I'll come back.' They're looking at me as if I'm bonkers. I try to explain the reasoning behind my decision, though I'm not sure I fully understand myself. 'Look,' I bite my lip, 'it's not normal to lose jobs all the time, is it?'

'You just haven't found the right job,' Julie says. 'That's all.'

'Ju,' I say, 'if I keep going, I'll have tried out every job in Britain by next year.'

She doesn't even smile.

'I just think that if I see a bit of the world, it might, you know, settle me down and I might be happy in a job.' So far, in London, I've lost about sixteen jobs in eight years. I truly don't know what's wrong with me. Most jobs I get, I quite enjoy. Give me a computer screen and some text and I'm happy. But unfortunately, for some reason, I also manage to get myself fired with alarming regularity. I've thought about why this might be and my problem it seems is that I don't like to be bossed around. I can be getting along great with everyone and then a boss will order me to do something and it's like another person inside me takes over. I FLIP. And that is meant to be capi-talised. I get on great with all my co-workers and they're always sad to see me leave, but the bosses are another matter.

'I'll pay your share of the rent,' Julie breaks into my thoughts. 'You can pay me back when you get a job.'

'That's not the issue, Ju.'

'Hope,' Adam says earnestly, 'you know I'd let you stay for free.'

I swallow hard at his kindness. 'I know.' I pause, touched. 'But you have to pay a mortgage, Adam and I'm a liability.'

'No!'

'Yeah,' I grin. 'I'm a disaster. You know it, I know it. I just think if I can get away and maybe get some perspective on it, things might make sense.'

'So go to Ireland,' Adam says. 'Go back to Dunport – you're always saying how much you love it. That's bound to be cheaper than going around the world. Bloody hell, Hope, just don't blow all your cash on a holiday.'

The mention of Dunport makes me flinch. I try out a smile. 'Yeah. Good idea. I'll check it out on the internet. Can I use your laptop when we get back?'

'Course.'

There is a silence. Neither of them knows what to say.

I feel a little guilty because I don't want to have spoiled Julie's night. I search for something to get us back on track. 'How many more nights is your show on for, Ju?'

And she's off. Haltingly at first, because she's shocked that I'm leaving, but it's not long before she's in full flow.

And as I listen to her, watching her face glow as she talks about her pupils, I realise, with a pang, that she has found what I so desperately crave.

2

I SPEND THE next few days on the internet looking for cheap flights. I have a bit of money saved, but I still need to be careful. I decide, mainly because I can afford it, that Boston will be destination number one. I book my flight and a motel and leave it at that. To be honest, I'm not exactly sure where to go from there.

But it's a start.

Julie and Adam are not so convinced. I think they reckon that I'm having a minor breakdown.

'Do you have enough money in case you might move on?' Julie asks.

'Yes.'

'And have you got your visa and passport and map?' That's Adam.

'Yes.'

'And have you changed your money to dollars?'

'Yes.'

'And have you checked your transport from the airport to your hotel?' Adam again.

'It's a motel and yes.'

After I satisfied them with these answers, they finally decided to leave me alone and accept the inevitable. And now, unbelievably, it's a week since I lost my job and our last day together before I go. Julie has pulled a sickie from work and brought me out for lunch and shopping. Later on, we're meeting Adam at his workplace, for a surprise night out. Neither of them will say where they are taking me.

It's going to be awful leaving them in the morning. So far, I've tried not to think about it.

'Here.' Lunch over, Julie places a small parcel on the table between us. 'Just a little good luck present.'

'Aw Ju, you've done enough.'

'Open it, will you!'

I smile and, forgoing all restraint, rip the paper off. 'A cap, cool.' It's pink and girly and the word *Tourist* is emblazoned across it in fake diamonds. I laugh and place it on top of my bouncy hair.

'Pink suits you,' Julie nods approvingly. 'And it's such a cute cap.'

'Yeah, isn't it? I'm going to wear this for the rest of the day!'

Julie gulps hard. 'Oh, Hope, I'm really going to miss you.'

'And I'll miss you too.'

We look at each other.

I turn away first.

We're in Topshop. Julie is busy examining the tops while I stand idly by. I can't afford anything new at the moment. And anyway, I hate buying clothes.

'White or off-white?' Julie puts both shades to her face.

'White,' I pronounce.

She frowns. I know she'll go for the off-white. She doesn't trust my judgement at all.

'Oh, I dunno. I think –' she stops mid-sentence and her eyes shift from me to a girl browsing a rack of expensive jeans. 'Oh shit!'

'What?' I lower my voice because she has lowered hers.

'See that girl over there?'

My head swivels around abruptly.

'Don't look,' she hisses, pulling me back.

'How can I see her if I don't look?'

'Don't make it so obvious.' Julie is still hissing. 'Turn around slowly, that's it. See the girl in the white top?'

'Yeah.'

'That's Angela.'

'Angela, your sister?'

Julie nods.

I've never met Angela, though I feel as if I know her from hearing Julie talk about her. They don't get on too well. According to Julie, Angela is the brainy one, the golden girl of the family. Julie, while not quite the black sheep, caused untold disappointment to her parents by becoming a teacher. Julie's parents sound a bit mad, to be honest. If I'd become a teacher, I'd imagine my mother would have been proud. Well, if she'd managed to forget her own life for a bit and thought about me, she would have been proud. As it was, it was maybe just as well she didn't know what I was up to. From this distance, Angela looks just like I thought she would.

'I suppose I'd better say hi,' Julie mutters.

'You don't have to. There's no law says you have to say hello to your sister when you meet her.'

'No.' Julie wrinkles up her pert nose and sighs. 'If I don't and she sees me, she'll think I'm jealous of her promotion. You'll come with me, will you?'

'Sure.'

I trail behind Julie as she walks towards the girl. Angela is even better dressed than Julie if that's possible. She's wearing a floaty white top that looks very feminine and a pair of wide trousers. A light loose cardigan hangs from her shoulders. Her hair is pinned back in a messy bun and little escaped ringlets, that look carefully positioned, trail along the back of her neck and on to her shoulders.

'Hi Ang,' Julie says, startling me with the false brightness in her voice. 'How's things?'

Angela freezes, her hand on a pair of dark navy denims. Then her shoulders relax and she turns to face us. She's like an older version of Julie, only I think Julie is prettier. She looks from Julie to me and back again. 'Julie, hi,' she stammers. 'Day off?'

Julie flushes. 'Eh, yeah,' she lies. 'School is shut today. Are you off too?'

Angela gawks from one to the other of us like a rabbit in headlights. She flushes too and pulls her cardigan around her in a defensive gesture. 'Yes!' It's very abrupt and sharp and makes me jump. 'Day's leave,' she shrugs. She tugs at a ringlet and winces. 'Eh . . .' she says haltingly, 'Mum was saying you were doing a show in your school?'

Julie sniffs. 'Was she?' she says. 'Surprised she remembered. Neither she nor Dad came to see it.'

'Well, they're busy people, I suppose.'

Julie rolls her eyes and makes a scoffing sound.

Angela flinches. 'Well, I hope the show went well.'

'Do you?' Julie gulps hard. 'You never came to see it either.'

Angela rubs her hand across her face. I can't figure out if she is annoyed or upset. But, I think, she could at least invent some excuse as to why she didn't bother going to Julie's show. Instead, to my disbelief, she says, 'I'm actually in a bit of a hurry Julie, so eh, bye now.'

It's like she can't get away fast enough. In silence, Julie

and I watch her disappear through a crowd of shoppers. I can't look at Julie, I feel so hurt for her.

'It's her loss,' I say eventually. 'She missed a bloody good show.'

'Yeah,' Julie lifts her chin, 'what do I care if she goes or not? I am finished with her. I even rang her to tell her about the show. She hardly ever rings me. In fact, I haven't heard from her in months. I'm never ringing her again.'

I don't like to hear that. I've done that and it hasn't made me feel any better. 'Don't be too hasty, Ju.'

'I'm not being hasty, this has gone on for long enough. Jesus, I could kill my family sometimes.' Then she flushes. 'Oh sorry, Hope, I didn't mean – well, I'm sure it's better than having no family.'

'Yeah, I'd imagine it is.' They think I've got no one, you see.

'So now,' Julie tries to get things back on track by smiling brightly. 'Let's go meet Adam and have a brilliant night.'

'Yeah, let's.' I don't care what they have planned for me, as long as it cheers her up.

An hour later, Julie and I are outside Adam's office. Well, I suppose it's not technically his office. Whichever store he happens to be regionally managing, that's where his office is. He's working out of south London today. We have to meet him at six.

By ten past six, he still hasn't arrived and the two of us are getting weird looks from builder-type men who are going in and out of the place.

'Hey girls,' an ugly leery fella quips, 'Would ya like anything laid, ey?'

'Yeah, you out on a mortuary slab,' I say back.

His builder friends laugh.

'How about a drink, gorgeous?' That's directed at Julie.

'No,' she says smartly, 'I might start seeing double and that wouldn't be nice.'

They clap at that and then wander off, but not before telling me that they love my hat.

'Did Adam say to meet him inside or outside the shop?' I ask Julie.

'I thought it was outside,' she says, stamping her feet up and down. 'Ohh, I'm freezing.'

'Let's just go in and get him, ten minutes' drinking time has been wasted with us just standing here.'

'Good thinking,' she says, falling in behind me.

We enter a huge warehouse cum shop. The ceilings are about a hundred feet high and the place is crammed with wood and tiles and flooring. And it's freezing. I don't know how people can work in it all day. The whole place has a frantic, tense air as staff rush here and there helping out customers or just for the sake of rushing about, it seems to me. Julie and I gaze around, not sure where to find Adam. This place is huge.

'Over there,' Julie points to a big sign saying INFORMA-TION DESK.

We cross the building towards the sign and are asked about a million times if we want assistance. Talk about a hard sell.

A cute-looking fella is behind the counter. Julie and I get into the queue and wait our chance to ask about Adam. Eventually the guy turns to us and bestows a gorgeous smile upon Julie. 'Ladies, what can I do you for?'

'Hi,' Julie bats her eyelashes. She looks at his blue shirt on which a name tag is pinned: 'Ben,' she says.

13

'Hi yourself,' he says back.

'We're looking for Adam Williams?'

'Adam Williams,' he repeats, frowning slightly. 'OK. Is he expecting you?'

'Yes. So he hasn't left the building yet?'

Ben looks as if Julie has just asked the most obvious question ever. 'Eh no, duh.' He waves his arm towards the heaving shop floor. 'Can't you guess?'

Julie and I look at each other. 'Guess?' Julie says. 'Is he on the floor? I can't see him.'

Ben frowns slightly. 'Eh – is this business?'

'No, we're his friends,' Julie says.

Ben glances from Julie to me and back again. The smile slides from his face and he sits back down in his chair. 'His friends?' he says. 'Oh, OK. I'll just give him a call.' He picks up the phone and dials a number. Then he tries another number. Finally he puts the phone down and says, 'I can't get through, do you mind waiting?'

'We'll go up to him,' I say. 'Just tell us where he is.'

Ben looks uncomfortable. 'Oh, I don't know – Adam, eh, Mr Williams, likes us to phone ahead with any visitors.'

'It's just us,' I say. 'He won't mind, honest.' I smile at Ben. Julie says my smile is my best feature. 'Please, Ben?'

Ben shifts uncomfortably.

'He's expecting us,' I say then more firmly.

'Right, well,' Ben licks his lips and points to his left. 'See those stairs over there. Go up to the top and Adam is in the office at the very end. A blue door, you can't miss it.'

'Great. Thanks.'

'Bye now.' Julie gives a flirty wave but Ben merely nods.

'Flirt,' I tease.

'Well, you smiled,' she jokes back.

Together we climb the stairs, Julie tucking her skirt in as all anyone would have to do from the ground floor is look upwards and they'd get a view they hadn't bargained for. When we reach the top, we hear voices. They seem to be coming from the office at the end. The nearer we get, the louder the voices become.

'Is that Adam shouting?' Julie asks.

'Nah,' I scoff. 'Adam never shouts.' Though I have to admit, it does sound like him. Outside the door we pause and look at each other. There is definitely a row of some sort going on inside. 'Will I knock?' Julie whispers.

I just rap hard on the door. If someone is shouting at Adam, well then they'll have Julie and me to contend with.

'What?' comes irritably from inside.

'We're looking for Adam Williams,' I say loudly. And a bit threateningly.

Silence.

Adam opens the door: he's red-faced but trying not to look it. 'Hi,' he smiles uncomfortably, 'who let you up?'

'The man on the information desk, we told him you were expecting us.' Julie tries to look over Adam's shoulder, but he's too tall. Then she points to her watch. 'It's after six,' she whispers.

'Yeah, I know, Ju. Just give me a second, all right?'

'Is this a bad time?' I ask.

'Nah,' Adam looks back into the office and then at us. 'Just give me a second.' He closes the door. This time there is no shouting. A few seconds later he comes out, pulling on his jacket. His face is still red. 'First thing Monday, OK?' he says over his shoulder to a man standing in the middle of the room.

'It means I'll have to come in on a Sunday,' the man says belligerently.

Adam pulls the zipper up on his jacket. 'Yeah,' he says, quite assertively, I think. I want to clap him. 'That's right.' Smiling at Julie and me, he pulls us from the office.

'What was going on there?' I ask as I climb into the back of Adam's car. 'Was there a row?'

'You could say that.' Adam fires the engine and then, pulling on his seatbelt, drives out of the car park. 'He hadn't half the invoices sorted and he thinks that was going to cut the ice with me. No bloody way, that's what I told him.'

His face is set in a hard grimace and Julie shoots me a look. Neither of us has ever seen Adam like this before. The guy must have really got to him. I hate that someone has upset him like this. 'Good for you,' I say and reach out from the back to pat his shoulder.

'Yeah, forget about it now,' Julie squeezes his arm. 'It's Hope's last night and we're going to have a blast.'

'Too right we are,' Adam is back to himself. It's like a light going on behind his eyes. 'We're going to give Hope the best night so she won't go away and leave us.'

'I'm not leaving you in spirit,' I say back. 'Just in body and mind.'

'Yeah, but we love your body and mind,' Julie pouts. 'It's your spirit that's the trouble. If it wasn't for that you might actually keep a job.'

'Ha bloody ha,' I sneer at her. Then I notice where we're headed. 'Hey, are we going back to the house for something?'

Neither of them answers me.

'Are we going back to the house for something?' I ask again.

There is a silence.

'We are, aren't we?'

'Aw, just for a party,' Julie says casually. 'You know, your surprise party for going away. The one that your friends have been arranging all day.'

'No way!' The shriek I give almost makes Adam crash his car.

The party is seriously wild. People I don't even know come. One of the bands from our local pub has set up in the sitting room and is playing tunelessly to anyone who will listen. Some of my old work colleagues arrive, and believe me there are quite a few of those. I'm good at keeping in contact with people. Well, most people. Adam spends his time drinking lots of beer and drunkenly chatting up the women while Julie does the same with the men. Neither of them scores.

I dance drunkenly to some of the band's tunes, around and around and around. Some time, in the early morning, Julie, Adam and I find ourselves together again. We're sitting on the sofa as the party winds down around us. People are asleep on the floor and others have gone home. I'm drunk and tearful.

'Thanks for this great surprise,' I mumble, my arms around the two of them. 'You are the bestest, brilliantest people I have ever met.'

'We are nice, aren't we,' Julie agrees. She is smashed. 'I really like myself.'

I laugh.

'I really like you too,' Adam says.

'I wish *he* liked me,' Julie points to a guy who is fast asleep on the other side of the room. 'He never even noticed me. He reminds me of the first man I ever slept with.'

'Why? Did he not notice you either?' I joke.

'Ha ha.' Julie sighs drunkenly. 'He did. Then I dumped him but then I wished I hadn't. He made loads of money afterwards.'

'So did the first guy I slept with,' I say to console her. 'He slept with me, told me he loved me and then dumped me. And then made a fortune running a hotel or something.' I sigh and say glumly, 'Stupid bastard.'

'You sound so over him,' Adam says drolly.

'I tell ya, I wish I'd never got over him.'

The two of them laugh loudly.

'Did your first girlfriend make loads of money?' Julie turns to Adam.

He flushes a little and coughs a bit and eventually mumbles, 'No, but she had a great time.'

We call him a liar and he tells us that if we want we can try him out for ourselves.

Julie rolls her eyes. 'Sleeping with you would be like sleeping with my brother or something.'

'Why? Is he a sexual magician too?' Adam asks.

They continue to banter, Julie replying that Adam probably was a sexual magician in that he could make all his girlfriends disappear, then she asks him how many girlfriends he ever had. He taps his nose and tells her to mind her own business. I take a sneaky glance at my watch.

It's after three. I really don't know how I'll get up in the morning but it's been worth it.

3

JULIE AND ADAM come to the airport to see me off despite the fact that they must be feeling horrendous. Adam is sporting a pair of dark glasses and he's been quite sick all morning. I don't think he can even remember the latter half of the party. He insists that he never got up and sang with the band. But he did, because Julie and I remember it. He made them sound even worse.

Julie looks quite fragile too.

I'm not too bad but it's only because I drank my pint of water before going to sleep. Still, I've a bit of a headache that won't shift.

We look an odd trio standing together at the departures gates. Adam, tall, skinny with over-long blond hair that he keeps pushing behind his ear, Julie, model thin, in skinny jeans and her new 'off-white' blouse, her thick blond hair shining under the artificial lights and me, average height, curly haired with a figure a basketball would be proud of. Anyway, I digress. Julie is making me promise to text her when I arrive. 'And you've definitely got your dollars and map and car booked from the airport to where you're going, have you?' she asks anxiously. Again.

'I've got the map,' I pat my shoulder bag.

'And you've got your phone and your bank book?'

'Yes, Mammy.'

She flaps her hand at me and adds defensively, 'Well, who knows how long you'll be gone?' She pauses, before enfolding me in a bear hug. 'Oh, Hope, we'll miss you.' Julie is an affectionate person. I think that's why I like her so much. I'm not really touchy feely. I wish I was. I'm never quite sure how hard to hug or how long to hold on for. Julie eventually lets me go.

Adam stands by awkwardly, looking at the pair of us. He's like me. He never hugs. He towers over everyone in the queue. 'Take care,' he says, patting me on the back. 'I'll keep your room free over the summer, just in case you decide to come back.'

I appreciate the gesture for the friendship that it is. Sometimes, like now, I feel almost guilty about how good they are to me. Sometimes, I think that if they really knew me, they wouldn't like me. The thought brings unexpected tears to my eyes.

'Aw,' Julie says, sniffing. 'Stop. Don't get me started.'

I try to smile. 'I'll keep you updated,' I tell them. 'Promise.'

'And I'll cut out all the jobs available in the newspapers,' Adam announces, 'and I'll send your CV in to them and if you get an interview, I'll let you know and you might come back.'

'Only jobs with no bosses,' I grin.

'No problem.' He smiles back. Adam really has a cute smile. 'There are loads of those about.' He pats me on the back again. 'Well, Hope-less, you'd better go.'

'Yeah.' And still I stand there, like an eejit.

'Yeah,' he says.

'Oh, for God's sake, give her a hug,' Julie mutters in exasperation. 'It's not that difficult.'

He flushes and I flush. Then he holds out his arms in an awkward way and I hold out mine and we embrace briefly. 'Now,' he says, his duty done. 'Off you go.'

'Off I go.' I hold up my small bag of hand luggage. 'Bye, you two. Take care of each other.'

'Bye!' they call out and I see that Julie is sniffing. She's buried her head in Adam's chest and he stands stiffly upright, rubbing her shoulder. His face has gone a weird colour and I think he's going to be sick again.

We wave and wave and wave.

Then they're out of sight and I'm left facing a long tunnel that'll take me into my holiday.

And something else, though I'm not sure what I want that something else to be.

The plane is a huge jumbo, all quite modern with cool green and beige décor. I find my seat beside a window, put my bag in the overhead locker and settle down to have a read of a magazine I've bought. There are a few articles in it on anger management. Well, I presume the one entitled 'Show your boss who's boss' is aimed at people like me.

A man plonks down beside me, breathing heavily.

'Nice cap,' he grins.

'Ta.' I turn back to my magazine.

'I nearly didn't make the flight,' he says in an unmistakably Dublin accent. 'I got up late.'

I smile at him politely. He's young and quite scrummy though very dishevelled. His hair is sticking out all over the place and his grey shirt looks as though he slept in it. 'Well, it wasn't that I got up late,' he continues, as he opens a packet of cheese and onion. 'It was more the fact that I never got to bed.'

Oh God, I think. I don't need some guy sitting beside me for hours droning on about his cool drunken sex-fuelled lifestyle. 'Really,' I say drily. 'Good for you.'

'Naw, it wasn't,' he says. 'I couldn't remember the name of the hotel I was staying in so I spent all night in a taxi while the driver helped me to look for it.'

'You're joking.'

'I wish I was. Feckin' taxi cost me a fortune. The wife is going to kill me when I get home.'

'Yeah, she probably will,' I smile. 'What was the hotel?'

'The Savoy.'

I start to laugh. 'How could you forget that?'

He shrugs, all wide-eyed bewilderment. 'I've never been in London before. I just went for business and even if the company was paying for everything, I could hardly charge an eight-hour taxi journey to every hotel in London to my expense account, sure I couldn't.' He offers me a crisp.

I take one and munch slowly as I say, 'Well, you could. Did your company actually forbid you from riding around in a taxi for eight hours?'

'Well, no but –'

'There you go so.'

He grins. I'd say he's a lovely husband. 'Right. Fine. So I'll charge them for the taxi and just lose my job, ey?'

'It's not a big deal – I lose jobs all the time.' What had been mortifying comes out as quite flippant as I talk to this stranger. It's a big act, of course – he doesn't know me and my very bad job reputation and so I can make a joke about it. Well, I suppose it would be funny, if it was someone else.

'Really.' He raises his eyebrows. He has lovely brown eyes, sort of twinkling. 'How many jobs exactly?'

'I've lost count.'

This makes him laugh. I used to laugh about it too, in the beginning before it became a habit I couldn't seem to break. Sort of the difference between biting my nails and biting my nails down to the quick. 'Maybe about sixteen.'

He whistles. 'How come?'

He has angled himself towards me now and I fold up my magazine, suddenly glad to be able to talk to someone for the duration of the flight. I don't like flying at the best of times. 'Well, I have a problem with authority figures,' I say with aplomb. 'At least that's what I think. I get on well in jobs until someone actually starts telling me what to do.'

'That would be a problem,' he acknowledges in mock seriousness. 'So what happens?'

'Various things.' I'm turning my life into a joke which I'm good at doing. I've been doing it for years. 'Sometimes I'll just not turn up for a few weeks and leave them in the lurch. Other times I've typed up letters with really offensive sentences in them.'

'Yeah?'

'Uh-huh. Things like . . .' I screw up my face: 'Dear sir, we regret to inform you that your application for a house has been turned down because we found you to be a wanker.'

The guy explodes with laughter. 'No way.'

'Yeah. Well, the boss didn't read the letters and he was supposed to. And my defence was that I'd meant to type banker. Which the man was. Still got fired, though. And just a week ago, I got fired for getting into an argument with a client of the firm I worked for.' And, as the plane taxis to the runway, I tell him that story.

'You were dead right,' he nods. 'He was power-tripping you.'

'I know.' I look at him. 'So what do you do?'

'I'm in marketing. I've been in London working on an angle to market this ironing board that's just been invented.'

'An ironing board? Was that not invented years ago?'

'Funny.' He crumples up his crisp bag and stuffs it in his equally dishevelled jacket. 'This is a special ironing board. It works with a special iron and irons both sides of a garment at once.'

'Fascinating,' I say drolly, as if he'd just explained the intricacies of algebra.

'It really is.' He's trying not to grin.

'Well, that sounds great.'

'Yeah. And it's my job to sort out the various campaigns. I was in London yesterday and now it's Boston and New York.'

'Great life.'

'Nah,' he shakes his head. 'I'm only married a year and it's hard on my wife. I'd prefer something where I didn't have to travel. But we need the cash.'

'Yeah?'

'My wife is expecting our first baby in a few months.'

'Congratulations.' He looks way too young to be a dad. He's got quite a boyish look about him, sort of like Adam only not as awkward.

'Ta. It's a bit of a surprise for us, though.' He rummages about in his plastic bag. 'I bought this for the baby.'

It's the most enormous rattle I've ever seen. Scary looking too. The child would want to be Hulk Hogan to hold it up, much less rattle it. 'Lovely.'

'Yeah, I thought so too. And it's not too boyish or girlish, so it's not?'

'Nope.'

As the plane takes off, he bends down and carefully puts the rattle away.

I hate the build-up to take-off. The trundling down the runway, the picking up of speed and finally the way the plane lifts up into the air. It doesn't seem to bother the guy beside me at all. 'Joe Ryan,' he introduces himself, just as we get airborne.

'Hope Gardner,' I say back.

'You're Irish, yeah?'

'Yeah.'

'Let me guess.' He screws up his face and says, 'Cork?'

'No.'

'Waterford?'

'Jesus, no.'

He then names about every county in Ireland, before I say, 'I'm from Kerry. And you're from Dublin.'

'Yeah. Well done.' He sounds impressed, obviously not aware that he has the thickest Dublin accent ever.

Just then the seatbelt sign, which had gone out, flicks back on again.

'Oh,' Joe rubs his hands together. 'Turbulence, I love a bit of turbulence.'

'Will passengers please return to their seats, we are experiencing some difficulties and may have to go back to Heathrow.'

Joe is still going on about turbulence, telling me of a trip he took once where the plane dropped hundreds of feet in seconds because it hit an air pocket.

'Did the captain say we're turning back?' I ask.

'Nah,' Joe shrugs. 'Why would he say that?'

I want to believe him but I'm sure that's what I heard. I take a quick glance up the aircraft and see the air hostesses belting themselves in. Is it my imagination or do they look a little freaked out?

'Sorry —' the woman who is on the other side of Joe

leans towards us. 'Are we turning back? Is that what he said?'

'That's what I thought.' I can barely get the words out. My mouth has gone dry. 'I hope everything is OK.'

'I was on a plane once where a lot of birds flew into the engine on take-off.' The woman nods. 'Apparently that's dangerous. Oh, my.' She grabs her seat as the plane banks sharply. It is turning back, and at speed. The overhead luggage slides about.

The murmuring from the other passengers grows louder. Someone at the back actually laughs.

'All passengers remain in your seats. Keep your seatbelts on. We are experiencing difficulties and are turning back to Heathrow.'

'Oh great.' Joe rolls his eyes and settles back in his seat. 'We'll be held up for hours now.'

His nonchalance reassures me. The noise level in the plane has decreased again. People are nervously glancing out their windows and whispering to each other.

'I don't mind telling you –' the woman leans over Joe to talk to me again – 'I always felt I'd die in a plane crash.'

Joe gives a guffaw of laughter and I manage a smile. 'You'll be fine,' I tell her. 'The pilot wants to get home to his wife and kids too.'

'It's probably a woman pilot,' Joe says. 'Panicking over nothing.'

The woman and I laugh a little but stop abruptly as the plane drops. It just falls straight down as if a huge weight has landed on top of it. Oxygen masks tumble and appear in front of us. People scream and a little girl behind starts to cry. Then just as suddenly the plane levels out again.

'Turbulence,' Joe says, though his voice is a little strained. 'That's all. That happened to me before.'

'Please fit on oxygen masks,' the Tannoy advises. 'Emergency strip lighting will now come on. We are experiencing some difficulties and for your own safety please keep your seatbelts on.'

Jesus. Jesus. Jesus. I feel sick. I fumble with my mask and Joe, his own in place, helps me with it. I am doing my best to stay calm.

POP!

POP!

POP!

Each bang is louder than the last.

'Oh God!' someone shrieks. 'Look!'

Smoke is pouring out of the wing on my side of the plane. I can only stare at it. I can't even scream or shout, just gawk at it in horrible fascination. It's as if I'm out of myself, just not quite able to believe this is happening.

POP-POP-POP.

More smoke.

The woman beside Joe starts saying prayers. She has her eyes closed and her hands are white on the grip of the seats. Silence in the cabin. Not one person is screaming and, save for the little girl behind, no one is crying. It's as if a weird fatalistic mood has overtaken people.

The plane lurches suddenly, left to right. The smoke is billowing out now but blessedly, I can see land. The smoke seems to stream back into the air at an incredible speed and I realise just how fast we are going.

'They've cleared a runway for us,' Joe says, in what I suppose is a reassuring voice. 'See, out there?'

I can't answer him. I wish I'd looked at what the air

hostess had done when she'd given her demonstration at the beginning of the flight. I fumble under the seat and pull out my life jacket.

'Are we going to die?' a little girl sobs.

'No,' her mother says, in a remarkably calm voice: 'the pilot knows what he's doing.'

Joe has his life jacket on and he turns to me and helps me on with mine.

'Thanks.'

POP-POP-POP.

The sound is louder.

The lights go off and the plane plummets. It's dark inside and bright outside. Overhead baggage starts to smash and thump. Some of it falls out. The plane is lurching about wildly.

Joe turns to me. His brown eyes are scared. I can only imagine what mine must look like. 'It was nice to meet you,' he says.

'You too.' I think I might cry. 'Will you hold my hand?'

'Sure.' He grasps my hand in his and I notice that he's holding the other lady's hand too. She's still praying.

'If you survive,' he says then, 'will you find my wife and tell her I'm sorry – Mary Ryan in Baltimore, West Cork – will you do that?'

'Tell her that you're sorry?'

'Yeah. She'll know what I mean.' He has to shout as the plane is screeching now. The poor child behind is bawling her eyes out in terror. 'Will you do it?'

'I will.' The noise is unbelievable. I clasp his hand tighter. 'And will you find my mother and tell her I'm sorry – Helen Gardner, Dunport, Kerry?'

'Will do.'

We hold each other as the plane careers downwards.

And I wonder if I'll see my life flash before my eyes.

4

I SEE BLACK shoes and I hear crying. I see a small girl jumping up and down, only wanting a little attention. I see her climbing into bed in her clothes and crying too.

I hear someone shouting. I feel a weight being lifted from me. Then I'm moving. Fast. The wailing of an ambulance.

Bright blue sky stretching on for ever. Bright blue sky and bright yellow sun. Down below I see a dark-haired girl, she must be nine or ten, climbing sulkily from a car, pulling a stumbling boy in her wake. She puts her arms about the boy, holding him to her and glaring defiantly up at a tall, lanky man in a grey suit. The little boy is crying. He doesn't like change, I know that.

I hear someone saying my name. Hope Gardner, the person is saying. Her name is Hope. Then the same voice says that I'm from Kerry and I've no next of kin. No next of kin? I think I do, though. Hope lives in London, the voice says. London? Am I not in Dunport?

I see a girl with black hair talking to a small boy. I see her handing the small boy a doll and he takes it and studies it and pushes it away. I see the small girl forcing it into his hand so hard that he pushes her off and tells her to 'go away'. I see the small girl dance and clap and laugh. I see an older woman smile a little.

The small boy smiles a bit too.

Two voices. A man's. He's saying that he should never have let me go. Jack? It doesn't sound like Jack. A woman's voice then. She's clasping my hand. She's begging me to open my eyes. But my eyes are open . . .

I see a dark-haired girl with a big black eye, smiling hugely. The small boy is bigger now and he's cheering. A girl, Amanda, is crying, because the dark-haired girl broke her nose. The dark-haired girl lets no one call her brother an idiot.

'Her eyes are open!'

Someone else says that's a normal thing. Coma patients sometimes do that.

The woman says in a whisper, into my ear, because I can feel it, 'I know you can hear me. I know you can, Hope. Please wake up. Please.'

The dark-haired girl and the small boy are cleaning. Cleaning so that things sparkle and shine.

The man is back. He's holding my hand now. He's saying that if I get better he'll take me on holiday. He doesn't care about work any more, he hates work, he says. Him and Julie will mind me, he says.

There is a telephone. Big and red and huge. It grows bigger and bigger and the little girl wants it and is afraid of it. She picks it up but it's too late now.

'She moved!' the man calls out. 'She moved and she squeezed my hand.'

I need to get away. It's too hard.

I see the dark-haired girl lose her smile and her sparkle and I see her run. Sometimes things leave her, sometimes they catch her up and when they catch her up, she runs some more. But she's tired now and needs to rest.

I see white and black and colours around the edges. I hear beeping and popping and voices. I hear someone say, 'Is she moving?' I hear someone else say, 'I dunno. Maybe.' I hear the first voice say, 'I think she is, look!' The second voice says nothing. I feel pressure on my hand. I turn my head and suddenly there is lots of noise.

Very slowly, I open my eyes. Two figures stand gawping at me. Blurs. Then a white blur taps my face gently. 'Hope? Hope? Can you hear me?'

My voice seems to come from somewhere very far away. 'Yes. Yes, I can.'

And somewhere someone laughs.

I like that sound.

5

I DON'T REMEMBER anything about the crash. Where once there must have been an experience, it's now a blank. Well, I do remember getting on to the plane, I remember sitting down with my magazine, but after that, everything is blurry. I can see the air hostesses looking anxiously at each other, but they would have done that so I don't know if it's an invented memory or not. And anyway, when I do start to think about it or ask questions, I shake and feel sick, so I just leave it alone. Like the way you would a wound, if touching it hurt. Apparently, the plane made it back to the airport but careered all over the place and smashed up and only seventeen people survived. Seventeen. I feel sick when I hear that. Seventeen people out of what must have been at least a hundred.

I was found hours into the search. I was unconscious and bleeding but I was alive. It has taken me almost two weeks to wake up.

Julie, who has spent those weeks mostly at my bedside, tells me of how she waited for news, of how, when they found my body, she and Adam thought I was dead.

'Take more than that to kill me,' I croak out. My voice is not my own. It's weak and it trembles and I hate it. My body is bruised and my head is encased in a bandage.

Apparently, I hit my head and my brain swelled and they had to operate on it to relieve pressure. I don't understand all the details but according to Julie, I am so lucky to be alive.

I suppose I am lucky, though my ribs are sore and my leg is lacerated and, hey, I have no hair. I don't know what my face is like, but Julie tells me that the bruising should clear up. I reach out and awkwardly pat Julie's hand. 'Thanks, Julie,' I mutter. 'Thanks for being here. I really appreciate it.'

'Yeah, I know you do.' Unexpectedly, tears glisten in her eyes. 'Oh, God, Hope, we were so worried. And all Adam kept saying was that he knew we shouldn't have let you go on your own and that he'd never forgive himself if you died.'

I roll my eyes a little and God, it hurts. My whole face feels like a swollen sore balloon. 'That's silly. It wasn't Adam's fault. I wanted to go.'

'Yeah, but even when you'd left to board the plane, Adam said he had a bad feeling about it.'

'Has he thought of going into the psychic business?' I kid gently. 'I believe there's a fortune going if you're any good.'

'Don't make a joke of it. He was serious.'

'Sorry.'

She squeezes my hand.

I find my thoughts drifting to everyone who must have died. I wonder why I'm alive and others are dead. What loss would I have been to the human race? The funny thing is, I can't even remember anyone on the plane.

The two of us sit for a few minutes in silence. I'm still clasping Julie's hand and she's rubbing my hand with her free one. No one has done that for me since I was tiny.

'Adam and I made a decision last night,' she says, unexpectedly breaking the silence.

'Yeah?'

'We're going to take you on your holiday!'

My heart lurches. I'm going to laugh. It's a nervous re-action. 'Julie, there is no way I'm getting on a plane again in a hurry.'

She giggles and then looks guilty about laughing. 'No. Sorry, I should have explained. We're taking you somewhere you'd like to go and yet you won't have to fly.'

'Where?'

'Dunport!'

She announces this triumphantly, as if it is the best surprise ever. I suppose, if I wanted to go back to where I'm from it would be a lovely surprise, but I don't. The thought of it makes my head reel.

'You're always saying how lovely it is and now me and Adam are taking you home.'

'No.'

She mistakes my 'no' for delighted disbelief. 'Yes!' She grasps my hands. 'Oh, Hope, it's a great idea. I mean, you so wanted to go on holiday and now . . . now, well,' she pauses delicately, 'well, you couldn't possibly look after yourself, or drive there or anything, so Adam and I decided that we'd take you.'

I stare at her. I can't speak. My throbbing head begins to throb some more. 'I, eh, can't let you do that,' I gulp out. 'That'd be too much.'

'Well, we already have. We've booked a cottage about two miles outside Dunport and paid for it in full.' She pauses and with shining eyes announces, 'for three whole months. That's how long the doctors said a complete recovery would take and it'd be so much better for you to recuperate in nice surroundings than in dirty old London.'

I always knew, that at some stage my lies would come

back to bite me. I just never thought it would be like this. I stare at Julie and feel as if I might cry. I don't want to lose my friend but I will. Oh God . . .

'Julie,' I say, and I can't look at her. 'I can't go back there.'

'Why?' She looks into my face. 'We're taking the ferry, we won't fly.'

'It's not that,' I whisper. 'It's just that, well, I can't go because . . .' I take a deep breath and say softly, 'my mother is still there.'

Julie doesn't move. The silence in the room is broken only by the monitors I'm wired to. Eventually she does speak, 'Your mother? But I thought –'

'I never said she was dead, Julie, I just, well, I just never talked about her.' My eyes meet hers.

'But you let me and Adam *think* she was dead.'

'I know.' I bite my lip, shame coursing through my body. I can't look at her. 'I know I did and I'm sorry.' I know she thinks I'm a freak. Well, wouldn't anyone? How many people go about pretending their mother is dead?

'And your father and brother, are they alive too?'

'No, they *are* dead.'

Her hand is still in mine, but she's not saying anything.

'We're not close,' I say at last. It's the first time in years I've spoken about her and it's like drawing back a rusty bolt. I don't know how to start or where to start. And like something that hasn't been unlocked in a long time, my words are stiff and creaky. 'It's my fault, I suppose. And hers too. She, well, she wasn't a great mother.'

'Why? Did she beat you?'

'No, nothing like that.'

'Did she keep comparing you to your sister the way my mother did?'

35

'I didn't have a sister, but no, she never did that.'

'So what then?' She is struggling to grasp it. 'Why should you pretend she was dead?'

'She, well, she was depressed a lot – OK?' Saying it makes me sound selfish and I know I am. I hate myself for it. But sometimes to survive you have to be selfish. 'I left Dunport when I was eighteen and I did keep in touch with her in the beginning, but Julie, you have no idea what it's like. Every time I rang her, it was like being dragged down a black hole, listening to her. And once I put the phone down I had to climb back out of the hole. So, after a while, I just stopped ringing. It was too hard. I was going mad myself.'

She doesn't say anything for a bit, then, softly, 'You could have told us.'

'I couldn't.' I shake my head, wondering how she can sound so calm about me deceiving her like that. 'I felt so bad about it. And, well,' I gulp, knowing I'll sound pathetic, 'I wanted you and Adam to like me.'

'Oh Hope,' she says and squeezes my hand. 'You're such a muppet. We would have liked you anyway.'

She looks at me as if I'm an idiot. Maybe I am. Slowly, hardly daring to believe it, I mouth, 'Would you?'

'Yes!' She laughs a little. 'And, anyway, I would have understood,' she goes on, surprising me once more. 'That's the way I feel when I talk to Angela or my parents on the phone. I ring them, feeling good cause I got a child maybe to understand and appreciate a poem or I got them to act on the stage and all I hear about is how Angela's inventing some huge world-famous thing or how they're too busy to go and see other people's kids on stage. It steals the good out of your life: it's hard to bounce back, I know.'

Her words seep into me, like medicine for my guilty feelings. 'You know?' is all I can manage.

'Yeah.' Her arm is about my shoulder and she says, softly joking, 'Only thing is, I don't go about pretending my sister and mother are dead.'

I manage a weak smile. 'I never said she was dead. I just omitted the fact she was alive.'

'Oh my God!' she shrieks, making me jump.

My head jars.

'I told the police you had no next of kin. I'm sure your mother would have wanted to know about your accident.'

'No, forget it. It'd only stress her out. It's better this way.'

Julie nods and gets up from the bed and walks to the window. My room overlooks the car park, which is not the best view for recuperation. I watch as she fiddles with the blinds and feigns interest in the comings and goings of various cars. 'You nearly died, Hope,' she says eventually.

'Nearly,' I nod. 'Isn't that a nice word?'

'The best word in the world,' she agrees. 'So wouldn't you like to make it up with your mother? Maybe this is your chance.'

I must admit, I'd been thinking about that in the last few days. Thinking about how unexpected life was and how you couldn't control it and that maybe it was best to be at peace with everyone. But the idea of seeing my mother now scared me, quite frankly. 'I don't know,' I stammer out. 'In theory yeah, I'd love to be able to talk to her, but Julie . . .' I can't continue. It means talking about stuff that I have shut away so firmly that to take it out now would be like releasing an emotional atom bomb. 'I just don't know if I can.'

Julie, I think, senses that there are things I'm not telling her but she doesn't push it and I'm grateful for that. 'You could come on holiday still,' she says, 'and make up your mind. You're fragile now, but in a couple of months you'll be a different person. I mean,' she presses on, sensing my weakening stance, 'I've already arranged for special leave and Adam is taking leave from his job for three months, so it's no problem. Plus we've paid for it.'

'Adam?' Now I am surprised. 'Three months?'

'Yeah,' Julie nods. 'He asked them yesterday and apparently it's cool.'

'I thought he was an important person in work.'

Julie giggles. 'He is. According to him, they let him go because they don't want to piss him off. But get this – he's still bringing his laptop and printer as he might need to work.'

'Oh yeah, that sounds like Adam – honestly, he's the only guy on the planet who could get leave and still have to work.'

'I know,' Julie smiles fondly. 'He's terrible, isn't he?'

'He's too soft,' I answer. Then I ask, 'Julie, have you seen Dunport?'

'No, but you make it sound gorgeous.'

'It is gorgeous.' It makes me smile a little, thinking about it. 'But there's no major night-life. It doesn't have a cinema and it's not like Ibiza or anything.'

'So? I'll be fine.'

'You'll go bonkers. And so will Adam.'

'This is for you. For you to get better.'

'I'll get better in London.'

'But it's paid for!'

'I'll pay you back.'

'No – you know you love the place, come on, it's two miles from Dunport anyway, so you don't even have to go into it if you don't want.'

'Two miles away? Is it up the mountains?'

'I think so, yeah. Adam booked it.'

The mountains. I'd like that. Once upon a time, I knew those mountains like the back of my hand. I'd climbed them, all over them. I knew the views from every angle. I could maybe climb them again – just once more. I could –

'How's the patient?' Adam bounds into the room. He's carrying the most enormous bunch of grapes I have ever seen and some magazines. Turning to Julie, he asks, 'Have you told her yet?' He actually sounds excited.

'Her mother is not dead. She's alive.'

'Bloody hell,' Adam drops the grapes on to the bed, his mouth agape. 'When did you find that out, Hope?'

Julie and I start to laugh. We're laughing so much, I can't even get the words out to explain.

I never thought I'd laugh about it.

In the end, I let them persuade me. Two miles outside Dunport isn't Dunport. I can avoid the town if I want. And if I do decide to see my mother, I can do that too.

And I need their help as I can't exactly walk very far or do too much and besides, they've paid for the place and can't get their money back. It was the only place left for the summer, apparently.

I find that, despite everything, I'm a little excited to be going back.

Later that week, a doctor comes in and offers me counselling. It's for the trauma I suffered during the crash, he says. I tell him that I can't remember the crash. I tell him that I don't think I need counselling. He gets a little stroppy about it, to be honest. 'I'll be fine,' I tell him in as firm a voice as I can muster. 'I survived the crash, I'll survive the life I've been given back.'

'So you haven't suffered from nightmares since?' he asks.

'No.'

'Or flashbacks?'

'No. I'm fine, honestly.'

'If you're sure . . .' He rises from the chair and his voice is laden with so much doubt, I could practically eat it.

'I'm sure,' I say.

'Well, I'm going to forward your files to the nearest hospital in Kerry and you can go there to have your leg cast removed and things like that. If you feel any need for counselling, or experience any strange sensations, just contact the hospital and they'll arrange it.' He leaves some papers beside my bed. 'They're just some notes on Post Traumatic Stress Disorder,' he says. 'People experience it to different degrees after a trauma like yours. If you have nightmares about the crash or feel in any way –' he pauses – 'different about things, please get counselling. Read the leaflets and try to recognise if any of it applies to you.'

'OK.'

I watch him walk out of the room and when he's out of sight, I glance through the leaflets. Then I bin them. Talking about the crash is not what I want to do. All I want is to get out of here and get better and go back to my life with my friends.

If I've learned anything from what happened, it's that life is short and you have to make the most of it.

I hold on to that as I drift into sleep.

6

THE DAY I get out of the hospital is the day we go on holiday. Adam picks me up. He's wearing, rather self-consciously, a pair of faded denims and a loose shirt. Despite their cool appearance, Adam still manages to give them an air of uptightness. I think it's his highly polished black shoes or something. I suppress a smile as he crosses towards me.

'All set?'

'Uh-huh.'

'Let's get you out of here then.' He picks up the small black bag that holds my hospital stuff. 'Julie's in the car and we're all packed. We decided that rather than take you back to the house, we'd drive straight to the ferry.'

'Oh, thanks.' I'm touched that they knew that returning to that house would be like taking a step back for me. I'd left it with the intention of going on a long holiday and that's what was going to happen. The hospital was merely a diversion on the road. If you can call a broken leg, swollen face and skull operation a diversion.

I hadn't realised how weak I was until I begin to walk alongside Adam. Being so tall, he strides ahead of me without even noticing. I'm too proud to tell him to slow down, and at the back of my mind I'm worried in case the nurses think I'm not fit enough to leave. They hadn't been too impressed when they'd heard I was going to recuperate out of the country.

'Bye. Good luck,' a nurse calls as I hobble by.

Another one holds up an enormous box of chocolates. 'There was no need,' she smiles.

'Yes there was,' Adam jokes back. 'Putting up with Hopeless is no mean feat.' They laugh and Adam blushes furiously. I belt him with my crutch and they laugh harder.

As we stand, waiting for the elevator, Adam gently lifts the hood of my sweatshirt up over my head. 'There are a couple of photographers out front, Hope. You might feel better with this up.'

'What?' Jesus, my one moment of fame and I'm going to look like a Hallowe'en reject. 'Oh God. Is there another way out of here?'

'I told them on the way in that you'd pose for one photo and to leave you alone after that. They seemed happy enough.'

'But, but, I've no make-up on.'

He looks surprised. 'You never wear make-up.'

'Yeah, and I never normally have the complete set of colours from the red spectrum on my face either.'

'Hope, you were in a plane crash – they want to see the bruises, it'll help them sell newspapers.'

'Well, thank you for your sensitive analysis of the situation.' I don't know if I should laugh or be annoyed with him.

'Look – you have bruises – big bloody deal. Your hair is gone – it'll grow back. You broke your leg – they were never much to look at anyway.'

That makes me laugh.

He grins. 'That's the Hopeless I know.' Then he awkwardly pats my back. 'You're alive – that's what matters.'

It takes a lot for him to say that; he starts to cough like mad and it's his excuse to turn away from me.

'Thanks, Adam,' I say and it takes a lot for me to say that.

As we get out of the lift and make our way to the front door, he puts his arm about my shoulders and says, 'Stand with me in the picture, that way you'll look good.'

'Can't argue with that!'

'Bitch.'

The photographers are as good as their word. They actually applaud me as I come through the door, which makes me feel like a complete fraud. I did nothing special. I just survived, which was pure luck. It was hardly a heroic act. I manage a weird sort of grimace as a smile for them and thank my lucky stars that I'll be out of the country when the photos are printed.

Adam ushers me towards his fancy car where Julie is waiting. She's munching crisps and turns to smile at me as I get in. 'Want one?'

I reach out to take one when suddenly I feel an overwhelming panic. I can't let them see it, so I lie back on the rear seat and close my eyes. 'No. Ta.' Something hard and pointy is pushing into my back and Adam pulls it from under me. 'Bloody car is crammed – Ju, did you bring everything you own?'

'It's three months, Adam,' Julie says, munching again. 'And I'm not planning on doing a whole load of washing.'

'Bloody hell.' Adam throws her little vanity case on to the floor and there is an immediate tinkling sound. Julie doesn't seem to notice as she's crunching like mad on her cheese and onion but Adam winces and I try out a smile. My panic is slowing, receding and I don't know what caused it.

'Julie packed for you too,' Adam says.

'Packed what? I brought most of my good stuff away the first time.'

'Mmm,' Julie agrees. 'I just bought you some new track-suits, you can't wear much else with that cast.'

'Thanks. I owe you.'

Adam starts up the car and we're off.

Julie turns to smile at me. 'Oh, isn't it great,' she announces delightedly, 'the three of us going away together?'

'Brilliant,' Adam agrees as he eases his monster of a car into the traffic. 'I've always wanted to go away with a couple of good-lookers for a few months.'

'Pity we can't say the same,' Julie snorts and Adam pinches her hard in the arm.

The sun is gone from the sky by the time we reach Kerry. The ferry crossing was OK but the drive from Rosslare to west Kerry has taken a while and Julie is now snoring loudly in the front seat of Adam's car.

Just the sight of the sign saying that we have crossed from Cork into Kerry makes my heart beat a little faster. Every stone on the road seems almost familiar. Not loved exactly, just familiar.

And then, another while later, the sign WELCOME TO DUNPORT appears.

'So, this is where you're from.' Adam peers out the window as he drives. It's grown dark and there really is not a lot to see. 'Do you want to call in on anyone?' The question is deliberately careless.

'No, it's fine.' I make my voice light. 'My mother is not

one for surprises. And anyway, like I said, we haven't talked in a while.'

'Well, maybe another time,' he says.

'In another life,' I joke and he doesn't smile. So I add, 'Maybe.'

Adam peers out the windscreen. 'Bloody hell, are there no directions?'

'Where's the cottage?'

'About two miles outside Dunport, on the Dingle road.'

'Straight on through the town,' I say. I know these roads like I know my name.

'Right.' Adam nods and doesn't say much more. After a bit, he begins to whistle tunelessly. We're on the main street now, if you could call Dunport's main street such a thing. There's a small shop that sells probably everything ever invented. It's run by an old Dunport family and has been there for generations. McCoys. Beside that is one of Dunport's three pubs. The biggest one and the one that normally has the entertainment – The Poitín Jar. It's run by the parents of a boy I went to school with. Then there is the massive church, way too big for the local population and freezing cold in winter. Then another pub and then a small shopping centre. The shopping centre is new, it must have bought over the old butcher shop. The entrance to the ruins of the Dunport castle I and some friends used to play in as kids, is bordered off. A big sign says, ACQUIRED AS HOTEL FOR THE GLEESON HOTEL GROUP. That's a step up – Dunport with its own hotel. And then, on the way out of the town there is a small garage selling overpriced petrol, the road to the small harbour that gets crowded in high season and another pub cum restaurant. They serve the best fish in west Kerry. Or so the sign says. The main street would be attractive in

45

daylight, I think, as I notice the big urns of flowers on the grass verges. It's a little deserted now and a little depressing. Growing up, I lived outside the town and as Adam passes the roadway leading to my old house, I involuntarily glance up as if maybe I could see a winking light from one of the windows, but of course it'd be impossible, what with the sharp bends in the road.

'Now keep going and you're on the Dingle road,' I tell him.

He does and the car begins to climb. Up and up and up. The road grows ever narrower. 'Bloody hell,' Adam mutters, half to himself.

'Look out the passenger window,' I say and smile.

It's dark but he gasps anyway. We're right on the edge of a mountain, with what looks like a shaky stone wall to keep us plunging to our death. Below us is sheer mountain rock and heaving black ocean.

'Is this safe?' he gulps.

'Are you worried about your car or us?' I joke. Then add, 'Of course it's not safe, that's why you have to drive carefully.' I point to a luminous sign. 'See.'

'Ha ha.' But he sounds ever so slightly nervous. 'Now,' he says, 'according to the directions given by the landlord, our house should be around here somewhere. It's just after a signpost that says "Dingle four kilometres". The cottage will be on the right.'

'OK.'

We both gawk intently out the window, before I make Adam jump by shouting out, 'There it is, there it is!'

Julie jerks awake. 'What? What?'

'We're nearly there.' I feel ridiculously excited. I can't wait to see the place. 'There's the signpost!'

'And here's the cottage,' Adam announces as he points

46

upwards to a small, run-down place with an unkempt piece of land and a broken stone wall about it.

The three of us stare at it, not quite in horror, but with something akin to it. Adam drops a gear to drive up the sheer driveway.

A man is standing in the lighted open doorway looking up and down. He's as grubby and as run-down as his property. He smiles slightly as Adam pulls the car into what is meant to be a driveway.

'*Fáilte*,' he calls, coming over to us. 'I thought you'd lost yerselves on the road.'

'No.' Adam gets out and slams his door. Julie does the same and both of them forget about me as they stare in dismay at their holiday home.

'Here,' I call from the back seat, trying to clamber out. 'Can I get out?'

Julie hands me my crutch as Adam asks the man, 'Are you Maurice?'

'Maurice Murphy, that's me.' He jangles his keys. 'Come and I'll show ye around. It's not that big but the three of you should fit.' He pats the top of his head for some reason and it's then I notice the oversized hairpiece. It's jet black and looks even more false than Jordan's boobs. In fact, it looks more like a rat than hair. Julie has noticed it too and she elbows me hard in the ribs as I join her at the door.

Ouch, it hurt.

'Oh,' Maurice spots me, and his jaw drops. 'What happened you, *a stór?*'

'Accident,' I say.

'Poor thing.' He shakes his head. 'Well, you couldn't be in a better place to recover.'

He turns his back and walks into the house. We follow

47

him into a small square room. A battered sofa and two chairs take up most of the space. The floor is stone and surprisingly clean. A fireplace with a fire laid. A huge window dominates the room. 'Wait until morning comes,' he points at the window. 'Lovely views.' There's also a small table and four chairs. He then leads us into a kitchen. Well, he leads Adam; Julie and I can't fit in. It's basic. There's a long wooden press holding cups and plates, an old gas cooker with an old-fashioned kettle sitting on top of it. 'As you can see, it's all gas,' Maurice points out. 'If you need a new cylinder, you can buy it in Dingle or Dunport. Which way did ye come?'

'Dunport,' I answer.

'Well, the local shop sells gas. The new shopping centre there is hopeless. They sell nothing but fancy wines and coleslaws.' Then he looks at Adam. 'Though maybe your sort are into all that.'

'I like a nice wine,' Adam answers pleasantly, unaware that he's just been insulted. The Kerry people have a funny way of insulting you. With their accent you never quite realise it's an insult until the last minute. But Adam is even slower than that. He goes on, 'I hope they do Australian wines, there's nothing like a good red from Australia to put me in good humour.'

Maurice looks him up and down. And again. Up and down. Then he nods. 'Right. I can believe that.' He gives a sort of grimace and pushes past him. 'Now here's the stairs to the bedrooms.' He indicates a set of steep wooden steps that lead from the living room. 'There's only two rooms, and whatever way you organise it is yer own business. Go on up and have a look if ye like.'

Getting up a set of steep stairs, almost narrower than

oneself, on a crutch, is no easy feat. I hold everyone up. When I eventually reach the top, I find myself on a landing, about two feet square. To my left is a door, and another to my right. I open the one to my right and am in a small bedroom with quirky sloping ceilings. A single bed is pushed over to the window. Besides that there is a small chair and a chest of drawers. The other room is the same.

'That chair folds down into a small bed,' Maurice informs us in the second bedroom.

'So you could sleep two in here.'

'Right.'

'There's no toilet in this house,' Julie says. Her face has fallen with everything she's seen. I reckon, if she lives to be a hundred, she'll never let Adam book a holiday for her ever again.

'It's outside,' Maurice explains. 'Sure when this place was built, toilets were a luxury. This house must be –' he screws up his face – 'oh, about one hundred years old. My grand-mother died in the room here.'

'No!' Julie sounds as if she's just seen the decayed remains for herself. 'She didn't.'

'She did.' Maurice mistakes her tone for amazement. 'She died roaring. That's what my mother told me. I never knew her. Some contagious disease she had that was rampant in those days. Oh, screaming and yelling, she was.'

'And she died here?' Julie repeats faintly.

'Right where you're standing.'

'Oh.' She turns anguished eyes on me and I have to look away or I'll laugh.

Maurice, undeterred, pushes past us and walks back down-stairs. I go last and hobble behind them all out into the pitch black of the night. The toilet is enclosed in a little shed about ten feet from the house. Maurice opens the door and, to our relief, it's modern and clean. It even has a power shower. 'So that's it,' he smiles around at us in the dark and we can really only see the gleam of his teeth. 'I'll leave the keys with ye and my number is on the fridge in the kitchen if you want to contact me. I'm in Dingle so I'm not too far away. Now, there's a few cottages around here, not too close, so you're fine really. The only one you'll have to be careful with is the one about a mile from here.' He points behind him, to his right. 'Now, the man moved in about a year ago and according to himself, he's an artist. A con artist, if you ask me. He doesn't talk that much and can be very grumpy. Mental, that's the only word for him. I've never seen him so much as draw a blade of grass never mind anything else.' He nods to us, pops the keys into Adam's hand and saunters confidently off in the dark.

The three of us lurch and stagger towards the house, tripping on bits of wood and tufts of grass that we can't see. In the distance, I hear a strange droning sound.

'Hope?' Julie says as I stop dead and start looking around.

'That noise, what is it?'

'What noise?'

'That!' I'm almost shouting. 'That noise, can't you hear it?'

They stop now too and listen. It's faint but growing louder. I can't move. I'm standing in the garden and my legs won't move. I mean, I'm trying to walk but I can't. I know what the noise is now, it's a plane, somewhere high above. I can feel a weird sort of panic taking me over, I don't want to be here when a plane goes by.

'Come on in,' Adam takes me gently by the arm and with him holding me, I stagger inside. 'You've gone pale,' he says as Julie shuts the door. 'Are you OK? It was just a plane or a helicopter or something.'

The noise is gone, blocked out by the shut door. I can breathe again. I shake my head and mumble, 'I'm fine. Thanks, Adam. It's just been a long day.'

I think the two of them are swapping glances, but they don't say anything. 'It has,' Julie agrees. 'A long day with an outside toilet at the end of it. Oh my God!'

'And a death in the bedroom,' I contribute, trying to smile.

'Yeah,' Julie agrees. 'How could you book this, Adam? Oh my God.'

Adam shrugs. 'Well, it was the only one left that wasn't booked.'

'And are you surprised?' Julie groans. 'Didn't you for one moment think, oh, I wonder why this cottage isn't booked?'

'I thought it wasn't booked because no one had booked it,' Adam says calmly, unfazed by Julie's hysterics.

'Did you know there was an outside toilet?'

'I didn't ask.'

'Imagine traipsing out there in the middle of the night – oh, God.'

'Buy a bucket for your room,' Adam suggests, jokingly. 'You can slop out in the morning.'

'Ha ha.' Julie glares at him. 'Well, just so you both know, I'm having the room that the grandmother didn't die in. Contagious disease,' she shudders. 'God knows what we can catch living here.'

'I'd imagine Maurice thought that it was a nice little piece of history he was imparting to you,' Adam grins. He turns to me. 'So, Hope, I'll be the gentleman, where would you like to sleep?'

I shrug. 'Down here. I'll take the chair bed from the bedroom,' I say. 'I can't make the climb up the stairs anyway.'

51

If I'm being perfectly honest, I don't particularly want a dead grandmother's bedroom either.

'Are you sure? I can help you up the stairs,' Adam says.

'Nope, I'm really sure,' I say and I've never, in my life, been more sure of anything.

'OK then,' Adam nods. 'Now, who's for a cuppa?'

Without waiting for an answer, he marches into the kitchen and begins washing out the kettle before filling it up. Julie and I plonk down on the sofa which groans under our combined weight. In the kitchen we hear Adam trying to turn on the gas. It finally gets going with an enormous bang.

'Almost blew my hand off.' Adam pokes his head out the kitchen door. 'But I've got the hang of it now.'

'Great,' Julie mutters. She's sitting very straight on the sofa, almost as if she's afraid of being contaminated by it. I don't blame her really, it's quite stained. But, to show my faith in our holiday, I lie back on it. It's not as if I have any hair that could be in contact with the dirty fabric. There is silence. The only sound is the bubbling of the kettle. It's a lovely silence, the kind you can only get in the heart of the country.

Julie shifts about uncomfortably.

'We'll make the best of it,' I say haltingly.

Julie sniffs and then flicks a glance at me. Her gaze softens slightly. 'Yeah. We will. And after all it's your holiday, Hope. And we're only here to help you.'

'So it's my fault, is it?' I nudge her.

'No, it's bloody his fault,' she hisses in an undertone. 'Honestly, why on earth did I ever let him book this? Sure, he's never been on a holiday in his life before, I bet.'

'Aw stop, he did his best.'

Julie rolls her eyes. 'Where's the tea?' she calls out, trying to inject some happiness into her voice.

'Only coffee.' Adam arrives in carrying three mugs of coffee. 'The tea was a little bit suspect.'

Jesus, why did he have to say that?

'Yeah?'

'A spider must have crawled in some time ago and rotted there.'

Both Julie and I look at him, our mouths open. Julie can't even reach to take the coffee from him.

'Joke?' Adam grins cheerfully. 'There was no tea!'

'Tosser!' Julie shrieks, belting him and he gives a huge guffaw of laughter, slopping coffee out on to the floor.

'Gotcha,' he says as we take our mugs. He raises his in the air. 'Cheers.'

'Cheers.'

'Cheers.'

7

IT'S DARK. OPPRESSIVELY dark. It's as if the dark is sitting on my lungs and pouring itself into my mouth. I try to fight it, to keep my mouth closed but it's fighting back and it's winning and it's –

'Hope, Hope.' Someone is calling out my name. And again, 'Hope. Hope. Wake up.'

Wake up?

I'm cold. I'm shivering. I try to open my eyes but I can't.

'Hope. Bloody hell, wake up!'

Now someone has their hands on my face. I can feel their touch through the cold. I know I'm dreaming now, but I can't wake up. In the dream, someone is holding me. Their hand is holding mine. Squeezing tight.

And my eyes shoot open and I'm gasping for air, almost as if I've been doing a David Blaine and holding my breath. I don't notice Adam at first, I'm so shaken, but as I calm down, I feel his breath on my face and I turn towards him. He's crouched down beside me. He's wearing these awful check pyjamas and he looks a little scared. 'Are you OK?' His voice is shaking.

I try to breathe normally. In. Out. In. Out. My forehead is beaded with sweat. 'Fine now.' Bits of my dream are floating away from me. 'Was I dreaming or something?'

'A nightmare more like,' Adam says. 'You were shouting and calling for help and saying that you promise to do it. And I couldn't wake you.'

'Really?' I wince. Nightmares? Wasn't that one of the symptoms –

'Really,' he nods.

I hoist myself up to a sitting position. 'Thanks for waking me.'

'No problem.' He still looks concerned. 'D'you want a glass of water or something?'

'Yeah.'

I rub my hand over my face and try to recall the dream and yet I'm afraid to.

Adam comes back in with two glasses of water and hands me one of them.

'What time is it?' I ask.

'Around five.'

'It's hot in here, isn't it?'

He doesn't answer. Maybe he doesn't think it's hot.

'I'll just get up and go outside and cool off.'

He helps me stand and hands me the crutch and I hobble out the back door. He follows me. Outside, it's still quite dark though the sky is streaked with crimson. The silence and stillness is so refreshing. A cool breeze is blowing very gently and it caresses my face. The sound of the ocean in the background calms me. When I moved away from here, it was that sound I missed the most. Hearing it now makes me feel quite emotional, the first real emotion I've felt since the accident, which is weird. Since coming out of the coma, I've been trying to get back to the Hope I was, I feel sort of detached somehow as if I can't quite connect with things. I mean, I joke and laugh, but it doesn't come as easy as before, it's as if I'm performing. I suppose it's normal; I mean, trivial things don't mean as much when you've almost died.

'Here,' Adam pats the back step for me to sit beside him. It's nice, just the two of us. It's like we're the only people awake in the whole world. We don't say anything for a bit and it occurs to me that I'm comfortable with that. I'm usually no good at silences, feeling as if I have to fill them. Eventually, I give in to old habits as I ask uncomfortably, 'Was I shouting very loudly?'

Adam shrugs. 'Yes, quite loudly. I woke up after hearing something – first I thought it was Julie snoring, but it wasn't. Anyway, it was you I heard. You were shouting and yelling for help.'

I don't know what to say to that, so I stare into my half-finished glass.

'Were you dreaming about the accident?' Adam asks it quietly, almost as if he's afraid of offending me.

I swirl the water about, clench the glass tighter in my hand. 'I dunno. I think maybe I was.'

'Do you want to talk about it?'

'It was only a dream.'

'A scary dream, though.'

I shrug, embarrassed.

'Hope,' he swallows nervously. 'Why didn't you get counselling after the accident?'

'I didn't think I would need it,' I say. 'They wanted me to talk about it. I didn't want to. I can't remember it anyway.'

'Well,' Adam seems to be choosing his words rather carefully, 'they mentioned to me and Julie that if you had flashbacks or nightmares you should see a doctor immediately.'

'One nightmare?' I make a face. 'I'm fine, Adam.'

'But maybe you need to remember, Hope. Maybe that's what the dreams are telling you.'

I don't reply. I wonder if maybe he's right. There was another time, years ago when I had nightmares and they eventually went but this nightmare was so real . . . I point to the sky which is lighting up a brilliant red and yellow. 'Look at that. Isn't it great?'

'Yes.' Adam says without interest as he takes a slug of water. 'Counselling works, Hope,' he says, then, 'It helps you deal with stuff.'

I wrap my arms about my legs, beginning to feel the chill in the early morning air. 'It helps only if you can talk about it,' I say. 'I don't think I can, Adam, I feel sick when I think of what happened. I can't even hear a plane in the sky any more without tensing up.'

'I noticed,' he says softly. 'You really should get help, Hope.'

I just stare at the dawn coming up.

'I got counselling when I was about sixteen, you know,' Adam says.

At first I don't believe I've heard correctly, so I turn to him and he flushes and looks quickly away. I put my hand on his arm. 'Why?' I ask quietly. 'Were you in an accident?'

'My whole life was an accident,' he says ruefully. He doesn't look at me as he says it; instead he stares at the brightening skyline. 'I've never really told anyone that before.' He laughs slightly.

I don't know if I should ask what for. After all, I haven't told him any of my secrets. I haven't told him that I've a fear of counselling. I'm afraid I'll be like my mother who never seemed to get cured no matter where she went. But at the same time, I don't want Adam to think that his telling me something so private is a thing to be dismissed. 'You're not a mess now,' I say and, without thinking, I link my arm through his. 'You're great.'

'I wish.' He gives another sad sort of smile. Then his blue eyes crinkling up, he says, 'You're great too, you know, and if you need to go to a counsellor, don't be ashamed.'

'It's not that,' I shrug, looking away from his steady gaze. 'I just, well, I don't want to end up like my mother, you know.'

'She was depressed,' Adam says. 'You're not.' He pauses. 'And it worked for me. I mean, I didn't think I needed it. But my mother made me go. She told me I was going to the doctor and instead I end up in a counsellor's office. I was furious; I didn't talk to her for months.'

He pauses and I wonder if he wants me to ask what he was there for. Instead, I surprise myself by saying wistfully, 'She cared about you. That was nice.'

'I'm sure your mother cared about you too.'

I shrug.

'Are you going to see your mother while we're here?'

'Perhaps.' The out-loud admission scares me slightly. Am I going to see her? And if I do, what will I say to her? 'Maybe,' I say.

'You should.' He sounds so confident. 'It's good to confront bad things.'

I think he knows what he's talking about. So I ask him. 'Why, did you?'

'I did.' Now he's looking at me. 'You'd never guess it, but in school I was the swotty one. The one with brains.'

I suppress a smile. How wouldn't I have guessed?

'I went to an all boys school and believe me, Hope, girls have nothing on blokes when they get their knife into you.'

'You were bullied?' I look at him and am not surprised.

Adam is kind and gentle and charmingly funny. He's also got a bewildered vibe about him and doesn't have the loud raucous sense of humour some guys have. The sense of humour guys tend to adopt when all together. He's probably too honourable for that.

'Yep.' He shrugs and winces. 'I hated sports. I was a good runner, quite fast, so I think that saved me at first. I pretended that I wanted to be on the sprint team and acted all macho for a while, but a macho guy that is into English and poetry and studies hard is soon found out.'

'I'll bet.'

'Anyway, I think you can always tell when someone isn't themselves and those blokes were like top-class sniffer dogs the way they hounded me down.'

His analogy makes me smile a little.

'They started off with name-calling and pushing and shoving and after a year or two, they started the physical stuff. I wasn't a complete wuss, mind, I did try to fight back and I could outrun them but my life was awful. In the end, I wouldn't get out of bed or go to school or do anything. My mother was in bits.'

'Yeah, I'd say so.' I snuggle into him. 'Poor you.'

'Poor me.' Cautiously he wraps his arm about my shoulder. It's nice. 'Apparently I was depressed and had no self-esteem and apparently I was also really angry. Anyway, it's true what they say – what doesn't kill you makes you stronger. I recovered, aced my A levels and now have a really good job. More than the rest of them have.'

His tone, slightly bitter, surprises me a little. Then, when I think about it, I'm not surprised. He should be bitter. 'Good for you.'

'And it'll be good for you too,' he says. He looks away

and says, in a practised casual tone, 'They gave Julie and me a list of counsellors over here, in case you decided to see one. And also the name of a doctor or two.'

'They gave or you asked?'

'Both.' His gaze meets mine. 'Anyway, you know they're there if you want.'

'Yeah. Thanks.'

'And there's something else, Hope –' He stops. 'No, no, forget it.'

'What?'

He studies me carefully and seems reluctant to go on. When he does, he speaks cautiously. 'It's about the accident, something you should know.'

'About the accident?'

'Yeah.'

He doesn't go on. I think he's waiting for me to give him permission; the only thing is, I can't even think about the accident, much less talk about it. 'Well?' My voice is quivering.

'You were buried underneath a lot of stuff when they found you.'

'I know.'

'A man was on top of you. They reckon he saved your life.'

'What?' I stare dumbly at him.

'They think that man saved your life.'

I turn away from Adam and stare at my hands. What can I say? I don't remember. I feel numb. 'Oh,' is all I can manage. I don't want to think about it.

We sit there for another while, saying nothing and watching the sun come up.

Later that day, after not thinking it through, but just going on instinct, I decide to go with the counselling. I suppose I made the decision because I don't want to have any more nightmares or feel sick whenever I see a packet of crisps. It was the crisps that had panicked me in the car, I realise now. Also, I suppose I'd like to know if my life was saved by a man I've never met and of course, I want Adam to think that his telling me about his bullying wasn't a complete waste of his time. I feel like killing those bullies for him. I was bullied too when I was a kid. Only bullied wouldn't be the right word, because I was a right vicious little thug myself. Our neighbour, Amanda Coonan, whose family ran the auctioneer business in Dingle, used to slag off my brother and me because we weren't as clean as she was. She poked fun at our house and our mother and everything. Most especially, however, she picked on Jamie, my little brother, because he wasn't able to defend himself as well as I could. Our mother kept telling us to ignore her, in the weary voice she used because she was depressed. But one day, I couldn't ignore Amanda any more. It started because she told Jamie he smelt. I remember throwing down my schoolbag, rolling up my sleeves and bursting into her cocoon of friends and demanding that she take her comment back. Of course she didn't, so I got into a fight with her. It was a real girly fight, pulling hair and scratching, until I gave her an enormous push. She ended up breaking her nose and it couldn't be reset. She left us alone after that. Even now when I think of her and of how she treated Jamie, my heart rate increases.

'Now Hope, soon to be cured person, this is your surprise!'

Julie has ordered Adam to drive to Dingle and now she's enquiring in an office about the three of us going out on a boat to see Fungi. Fungi is a dolphin that has lived in Dingle harbour for the last twenty years and Julie, ever since reading about him on the net, has been dying to see him. She, however, is trying to make out that she's doing it for me as a celebration of the fact that I'll soon be back to the Hope I was. Once I told her and Adam that I'd go for counselling, the floodgates had opened.

'Thank God,' Julie said. 'You really need it.'

'What?' I almost laughed at her bluntness.

'Well,' she shifted uncomfortably, 'you're not the person you were, you know. You snap a lot and are very jumpy. You were never like that before.'

Of course, I'd snapped and demanded to know what she meant, and she and Adam had exchanged wary but amused looks. Julie had just shrugged in a 'point proven' kind of way.

And according to them I also flinch a lot and don't laugh like I used to. So, today I'm making a conscious effort to be more like I was. If I can remember how I was.

Julie comes back out to Adam and me and tells us that if Fungi fails to show, we won't have to pay. I grin. The dolphin always shows up. We're directed to a waiting area at the harbour and the three of us sit down outside in the weak sunshine. If I had known we were going on a boat, I'd have worn something a lot warmer. Julie is dressed in light white trousers and a T-shirt.

'Julie, will you not be cold out on the boat?'

She looks down at herself. 'I don't think so, it's a nice day.'

I decide not to say any more.

'And I don't feel the cold anyway,' she states, before giving a delicious shiver. 'Oh, I can't wait to see the dolphin. Have you ever seen him, Hope?'

'No.'

'I've eaten dolphin, though,' Adam says.

His comment is met by a gasp from a few tourists. I laugh and Adam announces loudly that it was a joke.

'It's not funny,' Julie says piously. 'Dolphins are very nice animals.'

'Mammals,' Adam corrects her. 'Dolphins are mammals.'

Julie glares at him. I swear, the two of them seem to be constantly bickering; they're like some old married couple. Just then Julie's phone rings with an unusual *Jaws* ring tone.

Adam sniggers at its significance.

Julie glances at it before obviously flinching and rejecting the call. 'I hate people who use their mobiles when they're talking to others,' she says cheerfully. As if on cue, Adam's phone rings. His is playing some classical music. He looks at it, then looks desperately at Julie, then looks at it again. 'Work,' he winces. 'Sorry.' He flicks it open and goes, 'Hello?'

'So rude,' Julie says loudly, folding her arms.

'What?' Adam says sharply, causing people to look at him. 'You have got to be joking!'

'No I'm not,' Julie says.

'He's talking into the phone,' I tell her.

Adam walks away from us and then Julie's phone rings again. Once again she rejects the call.

'You can answer it if you want,' I say. 'I don't mind.'

'No, it's fine.' She doesn't sound as if it's fine. It starts to ring for a third time.

'It might be important,' I say. 'Obviously someone wants to speak to you.'

'Sorry about that,' Adam rejoins us, tucking his phone into his pocket. 'Bloody head office is going mental because one of the branches is down fifty grand. Some stupid mix-up or other. I said I'd sort it.'

'Sort it? How?' Julie almost laughs. 'Can you bi-locate? Anyway, you're on leave.'

Adam pauses. 'Eh, actually,' he begins, 'I'm not.'

'What?' both of us say together.

'I'm not on holiday, they refused me leave in work, so I just went anyway.'

'No!' Julie gawks at him, sounding a little impressed. 'Are you mad? You'll be fired.'

'Nah.' Adam shakes his head. 'I can work just as well from here anyway. It's no big deal. They'd never fire me. I'm too –' he pauses, seemingly arrested by what he was about to say – 'good,' he finishes off slowly.

'But –'

'Don't look so shocked,' he says and grins at us. 'You know me, I play things safe.'

That at least is true. He'd never risk his job.

'And as for bi-locating,' he continues, 'I don't need to, I have a computer. I can send horrible e-mails to the staff in the shop telling them to get their fingers out.'

'Oh yeah, I'd really worry getting an e-mail from you.' Julie rolls her eyes. 'What do you do, write them in capital letters so they know you're cross?'

'Hey,' Adam says, and I don't know if he's mocking her or serious, 'good idea. I'll do that.'

Just then, the few tourists who are waiting on the marina surge forward and we notice that the boat has arrived to take us to see Fungi. We climb aboard, everyone jostling for the seats at the edge, and within minutes we're bouncing about heading for just outside the harbour. Julie's phone continues to ring until it's out of coverage and I can't help noticing that something akin to panic crosses her face every time it buzzes. We soon forget about the phone as

Fungi makes his appearance. Adam, who has his state of the art camera with him, attempts to take a photograph but is thwarted by the fact that Fungi keeps appearing and disappearing and it's impossible to tell where he'll be next.

'It's like the KitKat ad,' he moans, as yet again he takes a picture of the heaving waves. 'You know the one where the bears do all their tricks when the people turn their back.'

'J-J-Just look at the dolphin and enjoy it,' Julie says, through chattering teeth. 'You'll miss him completely if you insist on taking a photo and what's t-t-t point in that. Y-y-you have to grab what's on offer.'

'G-g-good point,' Adam mimics her, as he flicks his camera off. 'V-v-very profound.'

Julie ignores him. 'I wish someone had told me it was going to be this cold,' she says. 'I can't feel my fingers. H-h-how much longer?'

'It's about an hour,' I tell her. 'So, another twenty minutes.'

'U-u-ugh.'

Adam, in a gallant gesture, wraps his jacket about her shoulders.

She smiles at him and he smiles back at her. They look nice, I suddenly think.

At last we disembark after what has been a brilliant hour. Julie's phone begins to ring again.

'Who is it?' Adam asks, as we make our way back to the car.

'My mother,' Julie winces. She's still shivering. 'I don't want to talk to her.'

'And why don't you want to talk to your mother?'

'Because if I talk to her she'll know I'm not in class. She'll know I've taken unpaid leave.'

'So?'

'She'll go bananas.'

'So do what I do,' Adam says. 'Just pretend you are in work.'

'How? Being here doesn't exactly sound like a playground, does it? No, I'll ring her tonight, find out what she wants.'

'It might be important,' I say. 'I mean, she really is trying hard to contact you.'

And her phone rings again.

'Go on,' I press, 'just in case something's happened.'

I swear, Julie pales as she flicks it open. Adam gives her the thumbs-up and she sticks her tongue out at him. 'Hello? Mother? Hi.' Her voice couldn't be any more nervous if she tried. 'What's up?'

Her mother says something.

'In school,' Julie says and I wince. She sounds as if she's lying. Then she says, 'Yes, I am in school.'

'Miss Adcock, can you come in a minute,' Adam says, in what is meant to be a schoolteacher's voice.

Julie glares at him to shut up.

'Well, yes,' she snaps suddenly, 'OK, Mother, I am on holiday. Are you satisfied?' Pause. 'No, I didn't feel I had to tell you. You're not interested. You didn't even come to my show. Anyway, my friend –' she stops and holds the phone away from her ear. Her mother is screaming at her now. 'Mother, you are not listening to me. My friend –'

Adam and I don't know what to do. Julie is shaking violently, though whether it's from the cold or her mother's ear-bashing, we don't know.

'Ju,' Adam begins, 'Are you –'

'That is Adam,' Julie says. She sounds really upset. 'No,

I have not gone away with a man. I am with two friends, one who almost died and another one who, well, who is my other friend who didn't almost die. Thank you.' Julie slams the phone closed and blinks rapidly.

'Maybe you shouldn't have answered it,' I say meekly. 'Sorry about that.'

I think Julie might cry. 'She rang me at work and found out I wasn't there. So when she heard I was on leave she just lost it.' She sounds as if she's just run a marathon. I can't imagine being that scared of a parent. Surely that's not the way it should be? 'Do you know what she said? Do you?'

Both of us shake our heads. We're blocking up the narrow street as we stand there in a small triangle, but people move on to the road to get by us.

'She told me that taking leave is not a good option if I want to get promoted. Can you imagine?' Her voice comes out on a small sob. 'Nothing I do is ever good enough for her.'

'Hey,' I put my arm about her. 'Don't cry. Come on. She's probably just angry you never told her you were coming over here.'

'I think –' Julie takes a sleeve of Adam's jacket and wipes her eyes. 'I think she wants me to become some famous revolutionary teacher – you know teaching kids by telepathic transference and, and, winning loads of awards.'

'And can you not do that?' I deadpan.

She chokes back a laugh and sniffs, 'I'll say Dad will be on now. She always gets him to call to back her up.'

'Well, definitely don't answer the phone any more.'

'I won't!'

After shopping for a few bits and pieces, including the local rag, we go back to the cottage, where Julie has the longest shower on record to try to get warm again and then later Adam offers to bring us out clubbing. 'We'll find somewhere, what do you say?' he says to us.

He really is so good. Julie loves dancing and she's still quite upset about the phone call from her mother. I don't think her father has rung yet.

She agrees and they turn to me.

'Sorry, guys, I'm tired.' And I am. I'm tired pretending to be myself and laughing and joking with the two of them when all I really want to do is – well, I don't even know.

So they bid me goodbye and I wave them off.

It's nice to be on my own, where I don't have to talk. I sit down, my leg sore from all the hobbling about, and something in the local paper, thrown across the sofa, catches my eye. It's in a column titled, DUNPORT'S SUCCESSES. A picture of a handsome man smiles out at me. My heart thumps so hard, I feel sick.

Jack.

Jack Dunleavy.

The Jack Dunleavy that I'd fallen for way back when I was eighteen. The Jack that had bunked off school with me, the Jack I'd told all my secrets to, the Jack I'd lost my virginity to and finally the Jack that had done brilliantly in his exams and gone to college and who I'd never heard from again. I pick up the paper and read:

Local man, Jack Dunleavy, is the managing director of the Gleeson Hotel Group. The newest hotel in the chain will be opened in Dunport in August. 'I'm very excited to be coming back and giving employment to the local area,' Jack said when interviewed. 'Dunport is a beautiful place and more people should get to know about it.' Jack will be in town in July for the official opening of the Hotel and promises us a famous mystery guest to do the honours. Well done, Jack, we're proud of you.

I stare at the picture some more, then very deliberately turn over the page. That is one man I do not want to see again. And yet . . .

8

T HE DAY OF my counselling session, I wake up early. I know that some time in the night I had another nightmare because I woke up suddenly, sweat pouring off my body and I had to hobble up and change my pyjamas. I found it hard to go back to sleep. Finally, at around six, I haul myself out of my sleeping bag and to my surprise find it's really warm in the cottage. Bright light is seeping in under the curtains and I pull them apart. Sunlight dances through the window, pouring over the tattered furniture and giving the room a beauty I didn't know it possessed. It is going to be a glorious day. I stand for a few seconds, just drinking in the view. It's by far the clearest day we've had so far. God, I think I had forgotten how beautiful the land-scape is. Blue sky meeting sun-drenched aquamarine sea. Blue mountains in the distance. Green trees, yellow gorse. It is a riot of fabulous splendour and in complete contrast to the duller days of the past two weeks.

I head into the kitchen and put on the kettle and while I'm waiting for it to boil, I butter a couple of slices of bread.

A few minutes later, I carry my mug of tea and my bread outside to the front of the house. It's not as easy as it sounds and it takes me a couple of trips due to the crutch. The sun is already warm on my face and I sit awkwardly down on the grass, one leg tucked under me, one leg splayed out, eating my breakfast and staring at the panoramic view. It's so peaceful. The only sound is the swish of the sea from far away and the occasional car going by on the road outside and someone shouting 'fuck' very loudly.

Fuck? Very loudly?

I turn and stare about. Striding along across the field, wearing faded, tattered jeans and a black T-shirt, is a man. He's about thirty with long tangled dark hair and dark stubble. As he gets closer, I can see his eyes are an angry flashing blue and his face is incredibly handsome except for the extraordinarily cross expression he seems to have adopted. 'I'm trying to sketch,' he says, standing about five feet away from me, legs apart, hands splayed in an exasperated manner.

'Excuse me?' I quirk an eyebrow, resenting his tone.

'I said –' he crosses towards me, hopping over the fence that separates his field from ours – 'that I am trying to paint.'

'And?' I stand up, scrabbling for my crutch and wondering if the tea I have is hot enough to throw at him if he's some kind of looney. 'What has that to do with me?'

'Nothing,' he states, snorting. 'Nothing at all. Thank you.' He continues to glare at me.

'Well then.' My hackles rise, my new bristliness coming in handy for dealing with this obnoxious man: 'don't confront me in that manner again. I am quietly having my breakfast and you decide to shout at me.'

'Yes,' he nods emphatically. 'You are in the way of my view.'

'It's not your view,' I state. 'Are you mad?' The question pops out without me thinking about it. As it does, it occurs to me what a stupid thing it is to ask someone who is obviously unhinged.

71

'Yes, I'm bloody mad,' he snaps. 'You are in my view.'

'Sorry, I don't know what you're on about.' I decide that it might be safer to go into the house than stay outside with this guy. 'I'm going in.'

'Good,' he says. 'Hurray!'

The nerve! 'Actually, I won't. I'm staying here.' I sit back down again.

He looks at me as if he can't quite believe what I've just done. 'You mean,' he splutters, 'you're just going to stay there and ruin my picture?'

'What picture?'

'The one I'm bloody trying to sketch.' He jabs in the direction he has come from and in the distance I see an artist's easel all set up. 'I'm sketching and you are blotting out the yellow gorse.'

The gorse stretches for miles. 'I'm not that big,' I say sarcastically. 'And if you'd come over and asked me politely to move, then maybe I would have. But seeing as you didn't, tough luck.' I give him a pleasant smile, only it's meant to annoy him. He stares at me for a few seconds, his blue eyes a combination of anger and confusion. Then he takes a few deep breaths and says in a strangled sort of way, 'Will you please move so that I can get on with painting my picture?'

'Move where?'

I think he thinks I'm being difficult. 'Any bloody where,' he snaps.

His snapping makes me cross again. I move two inches to my right. 'Here?'

'Oh, don't be ridiculous.' He glares at me. 'You're a very thorny person, aren't you?'

'Have you ever heard something along the lines of pot,

kettle and black?' I enquire. This guy has ceased to bother me. I think of him rather as I would an unpleasant boss.

'Have you ever heard something along the lines of silk purse and sow's ear?'

'What?'

'You are ruining my picture!'

'So move your easel.'

'Move your big round bulk!'

Oh. That hurt. 'No chance.'

More glares. He's moving his mouth but no words are coming out. Daintily I eat my bread, knowing I'm infuriating him. And glad that I can vent my anger on someone other than my best friends.

'Please,' he eventually spits out. 'Please will you move your, your, yourself?'

'All you had to do was ask,' I say sweetly as I hoist myself up, balancing on my crutch. 'Now, please can you tell me where I have permission to sit in my own garden?'

He's working inwardly. 'Maybe over there,' he answers evenly. 'Beside the wall.'

'That's in the shade.'

'Well, perhaps you can sit over there.' He points to the corner of the house.

'Fine.' I slowly stand up. 'I will sit there.'

'Thanks.'

I watch him as he turns his back and stomps off. He's got quite a nice bum and good broad shoulders. Pity about his personality. Still, I quite like the fact that despite my being on a crutch, with a bald head and a slowly healing face, he offered me no sympathy whatsoever. It's seems so long since I've been treated like a normal person.

*   *   *

At three o'clock precisely, I'm sitting in the counsellor's office. Apparently I have to be assessed to see if there is anything wrong with me. Julie and Adam have told me that they'll pick me up in an hour's time. They've spent the whole trip annoying each other. Adam chatted up a girl called Corina in a club the night before and Corina gave him her number. Julie keeps asking if he's going to ring her.

'Why? You jealous?'

'No,' Julie looked incredulously at him. 'Just curious.'

'Well, the answer is no,' Adam said. 'I am not going to ring her. I am here for a holiday. I'm not here to spend money on some girl I'll never see when it's over.'

'You tight-arse,' Julie snapped.

'Nothing wrong with having a tight arse,' Adam sniggered back at her.

And even though I'm terrified to be spending a whole hour in a doctor's office, it's better than listening to the two of them. I'm alone now, just sitting on the edge of a chair, waiting for the counsellor to come back in. His office is like any office anywhere. There are no fancy gadgets or machines bleeping away, unless you count a rather tatty ancient Dictaphone sitting on the desk.

'Hope, how's it going?'

I glance at the door where a man, surprisingly young, has just entered. He's tall, rangy and is wearing faded jeans and a white T-shirt. There's a tattoo of an angel on his wrist and on his finger he sports a bright and shiny wedding ring. His brown hair is long and he wears it in a ponytail. He really isn't what I was expecting and I feel a bit more relaxed. Just from looking at him, he gives off a vibe of living with a hippie girlfriend who spends her time cooking organic meals and wearing shoes spun out of hemp.

'Tim,' he says, holding out his hand.

'Hi.' I manage a smile.

'Well now,' Tim says, in a voice that conjures up lazy summer days, 'I was reading your file, Hope. Pretty bad experience for you?' He sits himself down in a chair opposite me, ignoring the chair behind his desk.

'Yeah.' I can't look at him now. Please don't make me talk about it, I silently pray.

'Well,' Tim says, 'First, I'm going to ask you some questions –'

'Not about the accident,' I blurt out. 'I can't remember it.'

Tim pauses and seems to be studying me. 'No,' he says softly, 'not about the accident. What I have to do first is get a picture of how you're coping since the accident. This will tell me how severe your symptoms are. It will also tell me if you do or don't have PTSD. Working on what I find, we can begin helping you – is that OK?'

'Yeah. I suppose.'

'Now, I've a form here,' he reaches behind him and retrieves a form from his desk, 'and I'd like you to answer these questions. Your answers can vary from none, which means no symptoms to a lot, which means –'

'A lot of symptoms.'

'Yeah.' Tim nods, grinning. 'OK?'

'OK.'

'Cool.' Now he begins to search for a pen. He finds one, bitten to bits and sticks it in his mouth. 'Right, let's start. Number one, do you have upsetting memories about what happened?'

'I try not to think about it.'

'But if you did think about it?' he presses.

I shrug. 'I suppose a lot,' I admit.

He ticks that answer off. 'How about nightmares?'

'A few but getting more frequent.'

'I'll put that down as moderate.' Another little tick. 'Flashbacks?'

'None.'

'Anything make you anxious that didn't before?'

'Planes,' I admit with a smile and he smiles too.

'Understandable. Anything else?'

'Crisps. Sudden noises.'

He ticks a box. I don't know what one. 'Have you lost interest in work or any other activity?'

'I don't like going out as much.'

'How about your relationship with other people? Has that changed?'

'I suppose a little. I find it hard to be interested in them. But,' I hesitate and decide to go on, 'well, mainly it's me. I feel I've lost myself. It's like I'm numb and all I can feel is anger now and again.'

'OK. Good.' He nods a little. 'That was my next question. How about imagining the future, do you have any thoughts on that? Is it hard to imagine?'

'Well, I kind of think there's no point really. I can't control it, can I? I mean, I could work my butt off and still die.'

'Did you always feel that way or is it just since the accident?'

I don't answer. Instead I swallow hard.

'Well,' he presses.

'I've felt like that, well, since,' I pause. I can remember the exact moment only I don't want to. 'Since I was about sixteen, I guess.'

'Sixteen, eh? Did something happen then?'

I shrug, aiming for casual but failing quite badly as my voice trembles. 'My brother died.'

'I see.' He pauses, writes a note down. 'Sleep? Is that hard?'

'Yeah.'

'Do you get angry more often? More irritable?'

'I suppose. I feel edgy or something, I can't explain it. It's like I don't feel safe.'

Tim relaxes into his seat and puts the form back on his desk. 'OK, Hope, well done. That wasn't so bad was it?'

'Nope.'

'OK,' he says again and nods. 'So now, you mentioned that your brother died?'

'Yeah.' I sound cautious.

'Can I ask you, Hope, if you've ever had any other trauma in your life? I feel that his death was a trauma, am I right?'

I blink and the silence seems to go on for ever.

'Trauma,' I eventually stammer out.

'Yes,' he smiles slightly and nods in an encouraging way. 'Trauma can mean different things to different folks. Basically, I'm asking if you've ever had anything unpleasant happen to you that changed the way you viewed things or that made you feel that the world was an unsafe place to be? Anything at all?'

'Everything?' I gulp out. 'Like all the bad stuff?'

Now it's his turn to blink. 'Has there been a lot?'

'Well, it was all a long time ago. I mean, stuff happened a long time ago. I'm over it all now.'

'Well, if you're over it, you should be able to talk about it. Tell me and we'll see.'

I start at the beginning. I can't quite make my voice work the way I want it to. It's as if it doesn't want to come out. I wonder if talking will oil it a bit. 'Well, my daddy died when I was six.'

'That would be scary for a little kid. That would make them rethink things.'

I hardly acknowledge that. I feel as if I'm talking about someone else. A stranger's life. 'Well, I wasn't there. He died in work from a sudden heart attack. I didn't understand at the time, not fully. I remember his funeral and me and my little brother playing among the black coats in the hall. And my mother crying all the time. That was scarier. I mean, you don't expect to see your parents cry, do you?'

Tim shakes his head.

'I remember thinking he was going to come back and make my mother happy again. But he didn't and that was awful. I couldn't understand that. I was angry at him then. And I thought, well, if he's gone, then other things can go too. Do you know?'

'Yes.'

'I became a bit of a worrier after that.'

'And did your mother not explain and reassure you?'

The question is like a well-aimed missile at my defences. The numb feeling I have when discussing it begins to crumble slightly. 'Well, you know, she did her best. Things sort of changed then.'

'How?'

I try to speak and can't. My mouth sort of opens up and some strangled word comes out. Tim holds up his hand. 'Don't, it's OK.'

I shake my head. Bloody hell. 'My mother just got sadder,' I state as matter-of-factly as I can.

'Sadder? As in depressed?'

'Yeah. Only I was six and didn't know it. Maybe I should have. I mean, she used to be so happy and all. She cried a lot at first and then she stopped. But after she stopped, she didn't get up or clean or cook or do anything. And we didn't go to school, we just played all day – me and my brother. And we never got washed or anything.' And that's when I really dry up. Well, my voice dries up but my forehead is coated in sweat.

Tim passes me a tissue and nods. 'That's OK, Hope,' he says gently. 'We don't have to go into it all now, anyway. We've loads of time. The whole summer.'

'I don't know if I can anyway.' I pat my forehead with the tissue. 'It was a long time ago, I never think of it. Never talk about it.'

He says nothing but I think I've just said too much.

'I'll book you in for next Friday morning,' Tim says. 'That's a week away. Does that suit you?'

I nod. There is no way I'm saying any more.

'I want you to fill in these forms over the next week.' He passes me three forms, which I take and feign interest in. I'm really sweating now. And breathing hard.

'Now Hope,' he says, 'between now and next week, you have a bit of work to do. I want you to fill that form out every time you find yourself in a situation that evokes trau- matic memories. That's the trigger. Like the crisps you mentioned or the planes. Then I want you to write how it affects you. Then I want to know if you deliberately avoid the trigger. And finally, I want you to record your anxiety level from one to ten. Ten is the worst – OK?'

I study the form. There are boxes and things to be filled in but it all seems easy enough. 'OK.'

'I'll see you back here next Friday then. And we'll talk about treatment and diagnosis.'

'Right.' I pocket the form and turn to go, before turning back to add 'Thanks.'

'No problem. See you next week.'

I don't know why, but I come out of the office feeling a little brighter than when I went in. I think it's the fact that with the forms in my hands, I feel a little in control. I haven't felt in control of my life for years.

9

'H EY,' JULIE IS peering out the window. 'There's a strange man in our garden.'

I'm struggling to fit into a pair of jeans. It's the first time I've worn them and they are not easy to get on, especially as I have to make them fit over the plaster on my leg. We're going out to a pub in Dunport and already I feel sick in case I meet someone I know. But I don't want Adam and Julie to think that I've gone all weird and hermit-like by refusing to go out. I want to try and get back to the pub girl I used to be.

'A strange man as in you don't know him or strange as in odd,' I ask, cutting my finger a little on the zip as I suck my stomach in as hard as it will go.

'Both,' Julie mutters.

'Here, let's have a look.' Zip still open, I peer out the curtains with her. When I see the easel going up, I realise who it is.

'That's the guy from the cottage across the way,' I say. 'He's horrible.'

We get a glimpse of profile.

'Mmm, not that horrible,' Julie nudges me. 'How'd you know him?'

'I met him yesterday morning. Trust me, he's horrible.'

I suck myself in, squeeze my eyes shut tight and hoist up the zip.

'What is he doing?' Julie is still staring out at him, albeit in a discreet way.

'Painting, apparently. But he really shouldn't be in the garden.'

'Maybe he'll knock and ask permission.'

From what I'd seen of him, I think this is highly unlikely.

And so it turns out. He sets up, adjusts his chair, sits down and begins to do whatever artists do.

'Jesus, he has a nerve,' I mutter. 'I'm going out to say it to him.'

'Maybe Adam should go out to him.' Julie attempts to pull me back as I make my slow way to the front door.

'Adam is busy sorting out his work problems,' I explain. 'And that guy shouldn't be in our garden. Besides,' I wave my crutch menacingly, 'I have this.'

Julie looks askance at me. 'Oh, Hope, I don't want a fight. Fighting with my mother is enough for me at the moment.'

'So stay here.'

She hops about from foot to foot, her fingers to her mouth. 'Ohhh, no, I'll go with you. I'll stand behind you, but I'll just tell Adam. Just hang on until I get Adam.' She flies up the stairs and I watch her go.

I don't need Adam. I hop towards the front door, fling it open and bellow, 'What are you doing?'

'Fuck. Shit!' He stands up and I note that he's somehow drawn a big brown line right through his picture. He glares at me. 'Do you know what you've just done?'

'No.' I hop towards him. 'Do you know you're spoiling our view?'

'You have just made me make a major mistake with this

painting. You've probably knocked me a month off schedule.'

He approaches me. Shit, I think, he's tall and menacing. He walks like a tiger, all loose-limbed and nonchalant. Though he's not very nonchalant at the moment. 'Have you any idea what this means?'

I stand my ground. 'Do you know that it's polite to knock and ask permission before you go setting yourself up in someone's garden?'

He glances about at the overgrown grass. 'It's hardly a garden.'

'Don't get personal.'

'It's not personal. It's not your garden.'

'At the moment it is and you have no permission to be here.'

That seems to throw him. 'I need to be here.'

'Hope,' Adam says, striding across the grass. 'All right?' Julie is tottering along on her high heels behind him.

'I'm just telling this guy that he shouldn't be in our garden.'

'Adam,' Adam holds out his hand. 'And you are?'

Ice blue eyes regard Adam angrily. 'Logan.'

Despite my annoyance, I explode in a laugh. 'Logan? Nobody is called Logan. What's your real name?'

He looks offended. 'Logan,' he says again.

'Oh. Sorry.' I bite my lip so I won't giggle.

He gives a 'hmph'.

'Well, Logan,' Adam says in a very reasonable tone of voice, 'are you planning on staying here long?'

Logan swallows hard. It's obvious he's not used to being reasonable. 'As long as it takes.' He glares at me. 'And it'll take longer now because she —' he says 'she' in an outraged tone — 'she has set me back about a month. Look,' he jabs at his strange-looking picture with his brush. 'I'll have to get rid of that line. See, look what she made me do.'

I roll my eyes. I feel a tiny bit guilty but not enough to apologise. Anyway, he shouldn't be here.

'And don't roll your eyes. It's obvious you have no idea of the finer things in life.'

'Well, I know what manners are,' I snort and fold my arms.

Julie giggles nervously and tries to make out she's coughing.

'Right, well,' Adam attempts to right the situation with a smile. 'It would have been nice if you'd asked to use the garden.'

No answer.

Adam cocks his head to one side. 'Otherwise, we'll have to inform the landlord that we have a trespasser.'

'Maurice won't do anything.'

'Oh he might,' Adam says casually, turning away. 'When we ask for our money back and he's left with an empty cottage until September.'

'It's only a garden,' Logan snaps.

'Exactly,' Adam nods. 'Our garden.'

'Ha ha.' I do a passable impression of Nelson from *The Simpsons*. I want to cheer and clap Adam on the back.

'You are getting on my nerves.' Logan jabs his brush at me now. Then he swallows hard and with major effort says, 'Can I use your garden to paint?'

'Yes.' Adam nods. 'Well, that's if the girls agree as well.'

'Oh,' Julie gives a bright, charming smile up into his sullen face. 'I don't mind. I'd love to see you paint. I love paintings.'

'I work alone,' he says. 'I need silence.'

'Oh.'

'Hope?' Adam asks.

I think he's got off too easily. I want to say no but Adam

84

would kill me. 'He has to move when I want to see the view,' I say instead.

Logan's eyes widen incredulously. 'Are you completely mad?'

'That's a yes.' Adam glares at me. 'So, we'll leave you to it.' He looks at me and Julie. 'Are you ready?'

'Yes we are,' Julie says.

The last I see of Logan, as we drive off is him staring at me in a way that I can't quite figure out. So I stick out my tongue and he gives me the two fingers and a scowl.

Charming.

Dunport is hopping. Any pretty fishing village on a sunny evening in June in one of the most beautiful places on earth is bound to be busy. The little harbour is all lit up with white twinkly lights that reflect on the black water. The slap and plash of water against the fibreglass boats is so rhythmic, you could fall asleep to it. The smell of chips and sea is a heady one, and always reminds me of home. And of summer. I begin to wonder why it's taken me so long to come home. But even as I'm wondering, I know it'll only be for a fleeting moment. And if I think harder, I'll wonder why on earth I've bothered to come. Julie and Adam had suggested Dingle as an alternative but I know they really wanted to try out Dunport.

It's a warm night and people have gathered along the harbour wall and outside the pubs and are drinking and laughing and chatting to each other. Mingling with the outside noise is the music from inside the pubs. A sign on a road leading from the harbour reads *Site for new Gleeson Hotel. Opening August.* I can just about see, in the half-light, the hulk of a new building in the distance.

'So, Hope,' Adam intrudes on my thoughts, looking expectantly at me, 'where to? Which pub is best?'

I turn from the sign. 'I don't know now,' I answer. 'Lynch's used to be.' I point to the Poitín Jar. 'It's also called Lynch's,' I explain. 'It was the only pub with entertainment but I suppose that's all changed.'

'Lynch's it is,' Julie links her arm in mine. 'Come on – let's go.'

Lynch's is the biggest pub in the town. We push past a crowd of people gathered about the front door and enter. It has changed but not too much. It's cleaner and airier but it doesn't have the modern minimalist décor that so many pubs are going for. It's still quite cosy and even though it's June, there is a turf fire burning merrily up at the back. Musicians are setting up and to Adam's delight it's a traditional Irish band. He plonks down on a seat almost in front of them. 'Come on, sit down.' He pats the seats beside him. Julie does as she's bid but I hesitate. I do not want to draw attention to myself and Adam certainly will if he insists on clapping and cheering along to the songs. 'Hope,' Adam says. 'Sit, before our seats are taken.'

I have no choice. I sit beside Adam, my jeans screaming in protest about my hips.

'So, my round.' Adam digs his hand into his pocket and asks what we want.

'Southern Comfort and red,' I say.

'Red?' Adam raises his eyebrow.

'Just ask,' I grin.

I've missed my southies and reds in London. There is no such thing as red lemonade over there. It's the first time I've had red in ages.

'Julie?'

'I'll have . . .' Julie screws up her face. She likes to try out different drinks all the time. She maintains that you can't have a favourite drink unless you've tried everything. 'I'll have the same as Hope,' she declares. 'I never had red before.'

'OK.' Adam saunters off, and is soon swallowed up by the crowd at the bar.

I focus my eyes on the wood grain on the table. I pretend to study the beer mats and my nails and anything really to avoid looking up and perhaps making eye contact with someone I knew. Though to be honest, it's unlikely. All my peers have probably left long ago. The opportunity for employment in Dunport wouldn't exactly be great, but I'm sure some of the older people would know me. Julie however is looking about. 'There aren't many great-looking fellas here, are there?'

'Most of the younger guys will probably have left for Dublin,' I answer. 'Or else they're sitting outside. No one with any cred is going to be listening to this band. It's only the auld wans in here.'

'Oh really.' Her eyes widen with disappointment. 'Maybe we should sit outside then.'

'And deprive Adam of the Shamrocks?' That's the name of the band.

'Well,' Julie lowers her voice and says, 'I think he's gay. That's probably why he likes hairy men.'

'Julie!' I don't find it funny. 'That's not nice. Adam is not gay and even if he was, so what?'

'Well then, why didn't he contact that girl he met the other night? She was mad into him.'

'Maybe he wasn't mad into her!'

'Have you ever known him to have a girlfriend?'

'That doesn't mean anything.'

'A guy like him should be straight,' Julie pouts. 'He's kind and considerate and knows how to treat a girl.'

Her phone starts to ring. She glances at it and turns it off. 'Your mother again?'

Julie nods glumly. 'Every time I turn it on, there's about six million messages from her. Dad hasn't rung at all, which is weird. She's obviously keeping him in reserve, like a machine-gun in a war.'

'And have you talked to her since?'

'No. She'll just have to let it go. When I became a teacher she was like this too, but she stopped eventually.'

Before we can say any more, Adam arrives back with the drinks in his hand. He's just bought orange for himself. 'I'll drink when we get home,' he says. 'I'm not leaving my car overnight.'

'Ohh,' Julie takes her drink from him. 'It'll be no fun being sober when Hope and I'll be drunk.'

'Well,' Adam says glumly, 'I need a clear head for tomorrow. That shop is sending me all their accounts for the last few months. I need to locate that missing fifty grand.'

'Oh, have they still not found it?' I'd forgotten about that.

'There's something they're not telling me,' Adam says grimly. 'So I've ordered all their files to be e-mailed to me. They're arriving in my mailbox as we speak.'

'Do you think they're on the fiddle?'

'I don't know,' Adam stares into his orange. 'But I have a week to sort it before my boss totally flips.'

'Poor Adam.' Julie pats his arm.

'But we all have tonight,' I say, then raise my glass. I take a gulp of my drink and savour the sweetness of the whiskey and red. Julie, on the other side of me, winces as she tastes hers. 'It's like lollipops.' Another cautious sip. 'Melted lollipops.'

Adam then has a try and he likes it. So he decides that as Julie doesn't want it, he'll drink it, then he says, aw bloody hell, he might as well get drunk with us. Drown his sorrows.

The Shamrocks have just begun playing and Adam is listening with rapt attention to the noise they're making as they sing about emigration and other general horror in an upbeat, bodhrán-beating way. The lead singer, if that's what he is, is doing some sort of an Irish jig about the stage, his heels clicking just ever so slightly out of rhythm with the music. His fuzzy grey hair is bouncing all over the place and he's yelling 'yahoo' in a very cowboyish way as he kicks his heels up as high as they will go. It's complete shite but Adam is lapping it up. He's not the only one. Some Americans behind us are clapping along and reading deep and sombre meanings into the man's performance and declaring loudly that the entertainment is 'so Irrrrrish'. I roll my eyes and think that Dermot Lynch, the guy that owns the pub, is a genius. And so are the Shamrocks. I wonder how much they get paid.

Eventually, it's my round. I dread going to the bar. So far, however, I haven't seen anyone I know. Mostly it's tourists. As Julie drains the dregs of her pint, I stand up. I hope that she or Adam will offer to go to the bar for me and I do a little stumble on my crutch, but Julie is attempting to make eye contact with some big bulky, bodybuilder fella she's spotted. She is such a flirt. Adam is so caught up in the music that he hardly registers I've stood up. And so, hopping slightly, I get out of my chair and make my way through the crowd. The good thing about being on a crutch is that people do let me through. I flirt with the idea of using it every time I walk into a pub. It's like the Red Sea parting before Moses. In no time, I'm tapping my fingers expectantly on the long polished wooden counter. The two barmen are flying about in a frenzy as if it's the last time anyone in the world will get a drink ever. That certainly has changed. Slow was the buzz word for a long time behind Lynch's bar. Unfortunately because I've no hair and my face is still slightly swollen, I don't exactly feel attractive enough to catch the barman's eye. I wait for a while. Beside me is a man sitting on a bar stool nursing a pint and he seems familiar. He's quite drunk and I spend the time trying to figure out who he is.

'Now, Mr D,' the barman says to him, ignoring me for the millionth time, 'what's it to be?'

Of course! It's Jack Dunleavy's dad. He has a look of Jack about him, though a much older, beer-bellied Jack. He mumbles out something and the barman goes to get it. When he comes back, the barman places a pint in front of Mr Dunleavy and ignores me again. 'Oy!' I finally shout. 'How long are you going to keep me waiting?'

One of the barmen turns to me. Looks at me and I look at him. And all I can think is, Oh shit. Oh balls. Or whatever curse word best describes attracting attention to yourself and then wishing you hadn't. It's Declan Lynch's son. The one who would have been a year behind me in school. To my absolute horror he crosses towards me, a hesitant grin on his face. I can only assume it's because he knows who I am. Normally people don't smile at others who have been complaining. 'Hey, *cé bhfuil tú*?' he says.

I feign a blank look at his Irish. He's asking how I am. A lot of people in Dunport would have Irish as their first language.

'Isn't it yourself?' he asks over the noise. His accent is as strong as mine used to be.

I decide there and then to draw on my meagre acting experience, which involved playing a tree in a primary school production of *Hansel and Gretel*. 'What sort of a question is that?' I ask archly, putting on an American accent. Well, it's a cross between a Kerry accent and an American accent.

'Hope?' the fella says. I can't remember his name. 'Are you Hope Gardner from beyond the cross?'

'I'll tell you who I am,' I say, 'I'm a customer and I want a drink.'

I notice uncertainty in his eyes. 'Are you not from around here?'

'Does every customer get a quiz before they order a drink?' I snap. I feel a bit mean as the semi-smile dies on his face. Another man behind me yells that he wants some service and he wants it now. He's a big loud Texan or something.

'I'm sorry,' the barman says. 'I thought you were a neighbour of ours come back. You look a lot like a girl that used to live around here.' Then he studies me, oblivious to the American, who's getting more annoyed. 'Or maybe you don't,' he says. 'The girl I knew had more hair for starters.'

I don't know if I should be offended.

'So what would you like?' he asks.

'Two Southern Comforts and red and a pint of Guinness.'

He looks again at me and too late I remember my accent.

'Pronto,' I Americanise.

'OK.'

The drinks arrive after a while. The Guinness takes ages to settle. As he brings them over, I notice him point me out to the other barman. I now see that he's the other brother, Greg, the one who had been in my class in school. He glances curiously in my direction. I dip my head so he can't see me properly. As the younger lad approaches with the drinks and takes my money, he says, 'My brother thinks you're the image of Hope too. Are you sure you're not a cousin or something?'

'I think I know who I am,' I scoff as I take two of the drinks. I'll send Adam up for the Guinness. 'Can you keep an eye on that pint until I come back and get it? I'm on a crutch see?'

'I'll bring it down for you if you like?'

'No, you're very busy, it's OK.'

I take the drinks and head down to the table.

'Adam,' I hiss, 'go up and get your Guinness, would you? The barman recognised me and I don't want him to.'

He and Julie look at me. 'My mother doesn't know I'm back yet,' I explain. 'It wouldn't be fair for her to hear it from someone else.'

Adam jumps up and heads to the bar.

'We could have gone somewhere else,' Julie says gently.

'I know.' I stare into my drink. 'Perhaps we should have.' I can't explain it. I think I came tonight because I needed to see the town from an observer's point of view before I go getting tangled up in it again. 'But I wanted to come tonight. To see if it's like I remembered.'

'And is it?' Julie asks.

'Yes and no,' I answer.

She looks at me a second more before I shrug and say again, 'Yes and no.' I lift my glass into the air. 'Cheers.'

'Cheers.'

I mean 'yes' because it's the same as I remember – the pubs, the *craic*, the noise. But I mean 'no' because it's not the same – the pubs are different, the *craic* is different and the noise is different. But it's down to interpretation, I think. As I look at Adam who is now carrying his pint down, being careful not to spill it, and Julie happily chatting up that bronzed, bodybuilder type, who is telling her that he's a self-employed businessman, which is impressing Julie a lot, I realise that Dunport is lovely, was always lovely, but when you're miserable and unhappy, nowhere ever seems good or safe and I'd blamed it on my home town.

I look at the Lynch boys behind the bar – well, glimpses of them, trading banter with the customers and laughing loudly at jokes – and I realise that I'd always felt threatened by their good humour, felt it was directed at me, instead of enjoying it as I might have done.

I find myself thinking of my mother. And that's when the lightness begins to leave me. How could I think of her differently? Maybe in order to do that, I'll have to see her. But in seeing her, I'll be looking back on myself. And that might just be too painful.

It's a strange night. We all drink too much. Through the haze, I see Julie writing her mobile number down on Mr Bodybuilder's arm. Then he kisses her briefly on the cheek and leaves with a load of mates. They all look like Action Man clones. They're shouting and laughing and back-slapping each other. Adam looks a bit miffed at the fella writing his number on Julie's arm but he soon forgets about it as he's invited up on stage by the Shamrocks to bang a bodhrán as accompaniment to some song. He dedicates his playing to his friends. He doesn't say our names. Julie, I and the Americans behind us all cheer loudly at him as he plays terribly but with passion.

And then the pub closes and we're all turfed out.

Night over.

10

THINGS WITH ADAM'S job must be in a very bad way because two days later he hands Julie the keys of his car and tells her to drive it into Dunport and get the shopping.

'But, Adam, your car,' Julie stammers as she stares at the car keys with disbelief, 'it's expensive and not for the faint hearted.'

That's what Adam always says about his car.

'It won't be my car for much longer if I don't sort this mess out,' Adam says without taking his eyes from the print-outs lying scattered over his tiny box room. 'So go on, knock yourself out.'

'D'you want a hand?' Julie asks. 'I'm good with figures.'

'And I'm good with words,' I offer.

They both shoot weird looks at me and don't comment.

'Buy me a nice Australian red,' Adam says, 'the one we had last week – that would help.'

'OK.' Julie jangles the keys: 'just don't blame me if I crash your car.'

The fact that he doesn't reply is a bit worrying.

Julie and I get the grocery shopping in Tralee and then divert to Dunport, to the gorgeous deli and wine shop, to buy Adam his Australian red. I hobble out of the car behind Julie and she holds the door of the shop open for me.

'Now, Australian wines,' she says as we enter. 'Where are they again?'

'Right at the –' my voice trails off.

Julie, oblivious, keeps going while I stand, completely frozen, my stomach somersaulting crazily as I look towards the deli counter. My mother. It has to be her. In fact, I know it's her because she's probably the only fifty-year-old woman in the whole of Kerry that still dresses like a hippie. Her grey hair is tied back with a patterned handkerchief and she's wearing long dangly earrings that touch the top of her shoulders. She has a grey, washed-out coat with tassels that reach to just below her calves and her feet are clad in brown leather sandals.

It is her.

I feel sick.

My mother is chatting to the woman on the deli, a Pole, and the words Warsaw and Pope John Paul the Second float across to me. She always liked talking to people from other countries, I remember suddenly.

I want to run, only I can't because I'm drinking in this first view of her in ten years. Maybe drinking is the wrong word. It's like I'm the scope of a gun, and I zeroed in on her and everything else is just background. Noises just seem to vanish. Julie has turned the corner and is now out of sight as I stand inside the door of the shop. Then, slowly, slowly, as if underwater, my mother turns towards me. I notice that she's still small and, despite the weird clothes, still beautiful. She's gazing at her coleslaw and she's smiling at it, for some reason, then she puts it into her basket where she already has a litre of milk and some rolls. Everything I see in the most amazing detail. And she looks younger than her years: maybe it's her clothes or the way she insists on bouncing along. She never bounced along when we were kids. Well, not that I can remember. And then, perhaps she's wondering why this practically bald woman is staring at her, but she looks in my direction and the smile freezes on her face for just the tiniest instant. Then it slides very slowly down it and her mouth opens a little. Almost protectively, she puts a hand on her coleslaw and now, now she's walking quickly towards me, a puzzled look on her face. I want to run away but I can't because my legs won't work.

'Hope?' My mother's voice breaks the spell I seem to have been under.

I flinch at her saying my name.

'Is it you?'

I don't know what to say. I try out a smile. 'Hi.' My voice is cracked.

She doesn't smile back. 'Oh my God.' Now her hand moves to her neck. Her mouth opens, then closes, then opens again. Her gaze travels the entire length of my body. 'Why . . . how . . . what?'

I'd forgotten what I must look like to her.

'Your hair.' She is staring, horrified, at me. 'And your leg?' She attempts to touch me, but I pull away. I don't know why. Her shoulders droop. 'What happened?' she asks softly.

'I was in an accident.' It hurts me to talk to her.

'What sort of an accident?'

I really don't want to discuss this, at least not here. 'Just an accident,' I say. 'I'm fine.'

'But your hair?'

'It'll grow back.'

'But, but . . .' she shakes her head and says with such hurt in her voice that I feel my stomach somersault all over again, 'you never told me.' Then she stops and says half tearfully, 'I'm OK now, Hope.'

I rub my face hard with my hand. 'Mammy, please . . .' It sounds like a plea. A woman going by stares at me.

'But I am. I can cope now.'

'Good. Good.' I can't seem to say anything else. And as the silence builds between us, I add in another 'good'.

'Just so you know,' she says. 'You can tell me what happened. You can tell me anything now and –' It's as if she realises that she's gabbling. She stops suddenly and shrugs. 'Sorry,' she mutters.

'No need.' My reply is terse. Please stop, I want to say. It's the first time since the accident that I've really felt anything and I wish I wasn't feeling it.

'Hope?' Julie's voice, anxious, is raised. 'Hope, where are you?' It's as if she's looking for a kid. 'Hope?' Julie slides to a halt beside me. 'What –?' She takes in the situation. 'Right. OK. I'm just . . .' she flaps her arm uselessly about and backs off. Then, from the corner of my eye, I see her taking out her mobile and phoning someone, probably Adam.

'Your friend?' my mother says.

I nod.

'Are you just, you know, passing through?' She tries to make it sound casual, but fails.

'I'm on holiday,' I answer.

'Oh.'

'I was going to call in,' I say. I wonder if it's a lie. 'Explain about –' I indicate my face and body – 'this. The accident.'

Is it my imagination or does her face brighten? 'Really?' It's as if she can't believe it. She moves her basket to her other hand. 'That'd be nice.' She pauses before saying fervently, 'I'd really like to see you, Hope.'

I wait for her to fix a date or something, but she doesn't. So I do. I feel I'm putting my hand close to a flame, one I'd told myself I'd never go near again. 'Maybe later this week?' I suggest.

'Any day is fine,' she nods. 'Any day at all. I have a mobile, you know.' Now, with a new purpose, she sets her basket on the floor and pulls out some paper from her pocket. 'Have you a pen?'

'No. Sorry.'

'Oh.' Disappointed, she slowly puts the paper back in her pocket. 'Right. Well, never mind, I'm in every day next week. I shop for things on a Monday,' she holds up her basket, 'but other than that . . .'

'OK.'

Neither of us moves. The distance between us is only a couple of feet but it might as well be miles. 'Where are you staying?'

'A cottage up the Dunport pass.'

She smiles at that. I remember suddenly how she used to smile years ago and I wonder how it all went so wrong.

'You always liked it up there. Is it Maurice's cottage?'

'Yeah.'

'I know his wife, she goes to flower arranging.'

'Oh.' I latch on to that. 'So you do flower arranging now, do you?'

'I teach it.' She's like a kid, boasting to a parent. 'Lots of people come to it.'

It knocks me sideways. My mother teaching? 'Wow,' I say. I feel, irrationally, a little angry. How dare she get better, I think, and here I am, a complete mess. And I know that sounds horrible and petty but in the second I think it, I take it back. I'm glad for her. 'That's good.'

Her lip trembles. 'I'm trying so hard, Hope. I really am. It'll never happen again, I swear.'

Oh God. I don't need this. Not in the middle of a tiny supermarket. I wish Julie would come back and rescue me. I think I might cry but not in front of her. Never in front of her. 'Better go.' I indicate Julie, who is being really good about not looking over, now that her phone call is finished.

'OK. Right.' Again she shifts her basket. 'Later in the week, so. Any day. I'll be there.'

'Right.'

And we step away from each other in a sort of dance, not wanting to draw closer than necessary.

It hurts.

Julie doesn't ask me anything as we get into the car. Instead, she squeezes my arm in a nice gesture of support.

'That's my mother,' I say unnecessarily.

'I guessed,' she says. She still hasn't started the car. 'She looks nice, Hope. Much nicer than my mother.'

I ignore that. 'I said I'd call in to her this week some time. Would you say Adam would mind driving me there?'

'No. Adam loves driving this horrible monster.' She hits the steering wheel with her hand. Julie hadn't liked driving it at all. It was too powerful and too big to park comfortably.

'I'll probably go Friday, after the counselling session.'

'Right.' Then she touches my arm again. 'Are you OK, Hope?'

'Yeah.' But my voice wobbles. I gulp hard to get it under control. I don't like the way this has made me feel. 'I'm fine, I'm fine.'

Julie doesn't seem to know what to do. If I was the old Hope, she'd cuddle me or crack some silly joke, but with this new brittle version, she doesn't know how I'll react. And I don't know either. So she just says, 'I remember once I ran into my sister Angela after she'd just got this gigantic promotion in work.' She smiles a little ruefully as she talks: 'and being the horrible sister I was, I was avoiding contacting her so I wouldn't have to congratulate her.'

'That is horrible,' I tease gently. 'Your own sister.'

'Yes, I know, thank you.' Julie sounds as if she couldn't care less. 'Anyway, I ran into her in Marks and Spencer's one Saturday and there she was and there I was and she says,' Julie puts on a very posh voice, 'Oh, Ju, did you hear about my promotion?' And I said, 'Yeah, congratulations.''

I look at her blankly.

'I found out I didn't care,' Julie beams at me. 'I was actually glad for her. I had my job, she had hers and that was it.'

'And that helps me – how, exactly?' I grin slightly. But I do know what she's trying to say. She's saying that maybe if you meet up with what you dread it won't be as bad as what you dread.

I hope she's right.

11

JULIE AND I are sitting in the front garden and it's truly summer. The ground is baking. Even the grass seems to have turned ever so slightly brown with the scorching heat. Julie has thrown caution to the wind and has donned her bikini top and tiny shorts and lathered herself with baby oil.

'You'll fry,' I say, horrified. 'Haven't you ever heard of skin cancer?'

'And haven't you ever heard of a tan? Besides, I have factor 50 on my face.'

I had factor 50 everywhere. I burn like a piece of dry paper. I go all red, then I peel and my tan never appears. I'm wearing a pair of rolled-up jeans; well, rolled up on one leg, the other is still in plaster. And I have a navy T-shirt. I think it's one of Adam's, I just took it off the line and put it on.

I lie back on the quilt Julie has taken off her bed and enjoy the feel of the sun caressing my body. We're supposed to be heading to the beach but Adam is beavering away on his laptop. He still hasn't figured out where the errant fifty thousand pounds has disappeared to. It's put him in foul humour and Julie and I have allowed him an hour before we give up on him coming with us.

'All we need now to ruin the day completely is for artist asshole to plonk down in front of us and start painting.'

'Oh,' Julie flaps at me lazily, 'he's not so bad once you talk to him. He smiled at me yesterday.'

'Every fella smiles at you.'

'Well, maybe if you smiled at him, he might smile back.'

'No chance.'

Logan has been coming all week to paint from our garden. He glowers at me every time I emerge from the house. And he stops painting and gets all guarded. I deliberately go out to annoy him, just to let him know he's there on my good will. Again, I know I'm being unreasonable but it helps me cope. It keeps me in touch with some sort of feeling.

Julie rolls over and looks down on me. 'Well, I hope my date tonight makes up for the lack of action in you and Adam. Honestly, I've never met two more boring people.'

Bodybuilder Boy rang her on Monday night and they arranged a date for tonight. The tragedy is she can't even remember his name.

'I like being boring.' I close my eyes and sigh contentedly. 'I'm going to stay here all night, slob out, drinking wine and eating chocolate, and you'll have to shower and dress and put on make-up and try hard to impress some guy you don't even know.'

'It's not like that.' I sense Julie rolling away from me and lying down now too. 'It's fun getting to know a new person, especially one like him.'

'Like him?'

'Yeah, well, he must be dynamic, mustn't he if he's got his own business. He runs a gym, I think.'

'I know, you told me.'

'People like that are always exciting.'

'Well, once you've convinced yourself, that's all that matters.'

'Piss off!'

We lie there for another while, listening to Adam curse every now and then from inside. He's sending e-mails all over the place and seems to be talking them through as he types. His bad mood is getting worse. I don't know if I fancy being with him on my own tonight. After a bit, it goes quiet again; the only sounds are of Julie shifting about beside me and insects humming and buzzing in the grass.

'*Julie!*'

Both of us jump. It's Adam: he's leaning out his window and beckoning Julie to come inside. 'Would you come in and have a look at this?' Then he glances at me. 'You too, Hope, if you like. I could do with a third opinion.' He's flushed, as if he's been out in the sun himself and got rather too much. 'Come on,' he says, disappearing from the window. 'Hurry.'

'Wonder what's got him so fired up?' Julie stands up and dusts herself down. 'I haven't seen him so excited since he was watching the paint dry in the house in London.'

'Stop!'

She grins.

Poor Adam, she's always on at him for being too boring.

Adam is pacing up and down his tiny room when we enter. As before, reams and reams of paper are strewn about the place. 'I'm in shit,' is all he says.

'What?' Julie sits on the bed, moving some of the paper out of the way. 'Have you found your fifty thousand?'

'Not exactly.' Adam sits down beside her. He picks up a sheaf of paper that looks like some kind of stock control sheet. 'But I know what happened to it. Just have a look yourself.' He pats the other side for me to sit.

With Julie and me sitting either side of him, he starts to explain. His voice is breathless, rushed and pathetically bewildered as he begins. 'A few months ago,' he says, 'I issued all the shops with a warning about fake bank drafts.'

'Right,' Julie nods.

'Anyway, in one week, this shop took in two bank drafts. One for ten thousand and the other for forty.' He shows us where they were lodged. 'They then give out stock to this company worth fifty grand. Only thing is, the bank drafts were fake.'

'But that was months ago,' Julie says.

Adam nods and half groans. 'Yeah. And ever since, they've been trying desperately to recover the money before I found out. So what they've been doing is this —' he points to another row of figures. 'See that bank draft, it was lodged in February, but they offset it against stock for January. They've basically used other people's money to cover the fifty grand originally swindled, leaving themselves fifty grand in debt going into the following month.'

'Clever,' I say, quite impressed.

Adam shoots me a look. 'Yeah. Until the boss decided to do a spot check and they hadn't finished up the accounts.' He groans. 'I should have noticed, but once the figures balanced, I didn't bother to check things.'

Julie picks up the statements and things and Adam shows her where the fiddling went on. After about half an hour, she nods. 'Yep, that's your money, all right. But what's the problem, isn't it insured?'

'Not if the bank warned us in advance and I issued letters to all the branches.'

'Are you in trouble, Adam?' I ask.

He sighs heavily and pushes himself up from the bed to

look out the window. 'I don't know,' he says, sinking his hands into the pockets of his jeans. He refuses to wear shorts. 'I suppose I am. If I'd been over there, I might have picked up on it, but I don't think so. Bastards,' he says bitterly. 'I'll kill them all.'

Julie joins him at the window and wraps her arm about his waist. 'Don't,' she says, 'don't be like that, Adam. It doesn't suit you. It'll be fine, you'll see.'

He rests his head on top of hers and snakes his arm about her waist. 'Hope so,' he says, sounding very despondent. 'I bloody well hope so.'

They look surprisingly nice together like that. I suddenly feel like an intruder, which is weird. I hop up off the bed and announce that I'm going to make a cuppa and does anyone want one.

Adam opts for wine and so we all join him.

Bodybuilder Boy arrives on time. He's way bigger than I remember from the pub. He pulls up to the cottage in a nifty sports car and after gazing at it lovingly for a few minutes turns towards the cottage, adjusts his cool denim jacket, which barely fits across his shoulders and, strutting in a cool sort of way, he arrives at the front door and hammers on it with his huge fist.

I open it as Julie has told me to pretend that she isn't ready – though of course she's been ready for ages. It's not a 'play-hard' tactic either, it's to see if there is any way I can find out his name.

'Hi,' BBB drawls, his thumbs resting in the loops on his jeans as he leans nonchalantly in the doorway. 'I'm here to pick up Julie.' His voice has a contrived American twang. God, he's such a stereotype.

'Oh,' I quip, 'I thought you'd done that already.'

It's lost on him. He winces, his coolness deserting him to be replaced by a Dublin accent, 'Eh, I haven't been here before, have I?'

'That's too philosophical a question for me at this time of the day.'

My witty repartee only succeeds in confusing him further. 'Is Julie here or not?' he asks.

'Yes. Come in,' I hold the door open a little wider. 'She's not quite ready yet. Who will I say is here?'

'Nelson,' he says as if it's obvious. Then his eyes narrow suspiciously. 'Why, is she seeing anyone else tonight?'

'No,' I give a passable laugh. 'Nelson? That's your name, right?'

'Eh – yes.'

I can't quite believe it. What a horrendous name. 'Nelson as in Mandela?'

'Pardon?' He's glancing about the room now. I know he's thinking how ugly it is and he's probably wondering if I'm unhinged.

'Like, is your name Nelson as in Battle of Trafalgar?'

He gawps. 'Huh?'

'Nelson as in *The Simpsons*?'

'Yes. My name is Nelson,' I notice that he's turned to the window and seems to be staring at his reflection in it. 'Now,' he spikes his hair and asks over his shoulder at me, 'is Julie here or not?'

'I'll just go get her.' I hobble to the end of the stairs. 'Julie!' I shout, though in reality she is sitting half-way down, 'Nelson is here! Are you ready?'

'Thank you.' Julie grins gratefully. Putting on her kilowatt smile, she stands up, marches on the spot for a few steps, to make like she's coming downstairs, before finally beginning to walk.

Nelson, who has been examining the manky sofa, gives a low whistle when he sees her. 'Wow, I thought you looked good the other night, but I was drunk then.' Julie's smile freezes ever so slightly. 'I was drunk too,' she says sweetly. 'Shall we go?'

'Yes, Julie, let's go.' He holds out an arm to her in an old-fashioned kind of way and she takes it. Only problem is, they won't both fit through the door together and so she has to let him go while he squeezes out in front of her.

I watch, like a mother hen, as he strides towards the car and with a fist the size of a rugby ball wrenches open the door for her. Julie is impressed by the car, I can tell. She slides into the front seat with a grace that belies her limited experience of bucket seats. He marches around the other side, eases his huge body into the driver's seat and the car roars into life, then stalls. He looks mortified and I try not to laugh. The car roars again and jumps about the place before taking off down the driveway.

And Julie is gone.

I feel a little lonely. Adam has promised to take me out tonight but he probably won't now, what with his work problems and everything. He hasn't been downstairs all day, except to grab a coffee now and again. I think he's composing a damage limitation e-mail to work. I'm good with putting stuff like that together, I suddenly think. I'm also good at telling lies that could be the truth, so I wonder if he'd like my help. It'd beat sitting on my own all evening. Plus, sorting out his problems will keep mine from skittering about in my head and popping up at the weirdest times. The form I'd got from the counsellor is pretty full at this stage. He's going to think I'm a basket case when I visit him in two days' time.

I hobble up the stairs and knock gently on Adam's door. 'Yes?'

I poke my head in. He's lying across his bed, a morose look on his face. His hair is dishevelled and his T-shirt is creased. He looks quite sexy, in fact, in a prim sort of way.

'You OK?'

He hauls himself up to sitting and shoves his feet into his bright trainers. 'Nope. Has Julie gone out with that ridiculous-looking man?'

'Yes. His name is Nelson.'

'Figures.' He glares at his shoes.

'Need a drink?'

'Aw, Jesus, Hope,' he says and rubs his hands over his face. 'I think I'm going to have to fly back for a week or so to sort this mess out.'

'D'you want me to help you compose an e-mail?'

'No. Thanks anyway. There are no words to describe the cock-up. It's a bloody mess,' he groans. 'I'll fire the lot of them.'

'You won't.' Adam firing people, what a laugh.

'And what do you suggest I do?' He looks crossly at me. 'I'm responsible for that branch. In fact, I'm responsible for all the branches in south England. If I let one guy off with losing me fifty thousand, what does that say to the rest of them?'

He's actually serious. I can't quite believe it. For the first time it dawns on me that Adam is a boss. He's in charge of others. He's a member of a club I seem to despise for what-ever reason. If I worked for him, I'd probably have been fired long ago. 'He made a mistake,' I mutter. 'He hardly set out to lose you fifty grand.'

'But he bloody well did!' Adam glares at me. 'And now my head is on the chopping block.'

'They can't fire you.'

'Really?' He raises his eyebrows. 'And how would you know?'

'Because you told us you were too important for them to fire you!'

'Yeah.' He rolls his eyes. 'Lesson, Hopeless: don't believe everything people tell you.'

I don't like his tone. 'Don't talk to me like that.' I sound cross myself now. 'I only came up to see if you were OK and obviously you're not, so I'll leave you!'

'Thanks.'

Ooooh. I slam the door really hard and give it the two fingers. And again.

I hop back downstairs, wishing heartily that I hadn't made the effort to climb up in the first place. Marching into the kitchen, I take a bottle of white wine from the fridge, uncork it and pour myself a large glass.

Then, just as I've begun to calm down – two glasses of wine in the garden would do that – Painter Boy comes along, complete with easel, paints and a scowl. Without saying a word, he begins moving about the garden, looking for the best place to set up, I suppose.

I stare at him, trying to make him uncomfortable. Trying to show him that really now is not a good time to be plodding about making a nuisance of himself. He ignores me. It's like I'm invisible. Each time it seems that he might have to look at me, he does so, but it's as if he can see right through me. Eventually, after consuming another half-glass of the most delicious wine, I say, 'A "hello" would be nice.'

His dark eyes flick across to me. 'Yes, it would,' he agrees.

'I meant from you,' I mutter darkly.

'Oh, right.'

He turns his back to me and continues. His easel is set up, he's doing something with his paints now. Mixing up colours, I think.

I can't bear his superior attitude; he treats me as if I'm dirt or something he trod on. Who does he think he is, I wonder? How dare he ignore me! What I should do is make a dignified exit. I should tell him calmly that he's the most ignorant man I've ever met and that I feel sorry for him. That's what Julie would do. But I don't. Of course I don't. Even as I know I'm losing it, I lose it. Part of it's at Adam but most of it is at him. 'One can only hope,' I say smartly, 'that your manners are in indirect proportion to your talent. I reckon you'd be the best painter in the world if it were true.'

He turns slowly about to face me. His eyes are narrowed and his lip curls dangerously. 'Firstly,' he says, taking a step towards me and brandishing a paintbrush, 'I'm not a painter, I'm an artist. Secondly, unlike your charmingless self, at least I have a talent.'

I'm gobsmacked. He's good. 'There is no such word as charmingless,' I retaliate weakly.

'There is in your case.'

The calm way he says it infuriates me. I think he's even smiling a little. I think he's enjoying himself. I think he wanted a row with someone and that's why he chose to come here, to row with me.

'If I were you,' I breathe heavily, 'I'd rather kill myself than have your kind of attitude.'

He eyes me up and down. Up and down. A small smile definitely curls about his lips. 'Looks like you already tried,' he says.

His aim is true. I blink once. Twice. Open my mouth and can't think of a thing to say. In fact, I think if I say anything, it'll be drowned in a sob. So I look like shit. So I've no hair. So I limp when I walk. My lip trembles. 'Thanks,' I gulp out before turning and legging it back inside. Well, as much as I can with a crutch.

'Hey –' he calls out after me. 'Hey!'

I slam the door and pull the curtain so he can't see how upset I am.

I try to be quiet. I drink and cry as quietly as I can but Adam obviously hears. Or maybe he was coming downstairs anyway, I don't know.

'Hey, why is it so dark in here?' he asks.

'I like it dark,' I snap.

'Hey, what's wrong?' He crosses towards me. 'Are you crying?' He sounds surprised. I suppose it's because he's never seen me cry before. I don't know if *I've* ever seen me cry before. This is a hiccuping sort of thing. Reluctant and sporadic. 'You are,' Adam says. 'Aw, don't cry. Come on. You know how useless I am with all that.' He sits opposite me and attempts to look up into my face. 'I'm sorry about earlier, Hope, I really am. I just had a gigantic shock.' He attempts a smile. 'Once I fire a few people I'll be OK.'

'I'm not crying over you. So, don't flatter yourself.'

'Oh.' He takes the bottle of wine from my hand. 'That's OK then.' He finds a glass and pours himself the remaining dregs. 'So what's up?'

It'd be too humiliating to tell him. So I just say, 'I had a fight with the painter guy.' Then I stop. 'Oh, sorry, artist.' I drawl out the word.

'Not again.' He sounds amused.

111

'It's not funny. He said dreadful things.'

Adam surveys me over his glass of wine. 'He's like you, Hope. Even Julie says it.'

'Says what?' Honestly, is Adam going all out to get at me tonight?

'He's kind of, I don't know, unhappy like you.'

'I'm not unhappy!' We both know it's a lie.

'Well, sorry, but you know what I mean. He seems to be, I don't know, a bit . . .' he pauses, then settles for 'unhappy' again. 'So give the guy a break, eh?'

'You can't be serious.' I stand up. 'Give him a break? He insulted me.'

'Hey,' Adam's eyes widen. 'You stood up without using your crutch.'

'Yes. I can do that now.'

A big stupid smile breaks out on his face. 'Well, good for you! That's great!'

And I suppose it is. Eight weeks ago, I'd been crippled. I look down at my leg. 'Isn't it?' I feel it should be but I don't know if I really care. Still, I manage a smile.

'Soon, you'll have your hair back and you'll be yourself again.'

I wish it was that easy but I nod anyway. 'Yeah.' It takes a second before I remember what we'd been talking about. 'But I'm not like that painter fella. And I won't be.'

Adam, his fifty grand momentarily forgotten, decides to open another bottle of wine in celebration.

12

ADAM TAKES US sightseeing the next afternoon. He'd spent the morning in his room, booking flights. He reckons he'll be away for at least a couple of days. His boss has been on the phone already, demanding to see him, having obviously found out that Adam's been running things from his laptop in Kerry.

Julie is quite impressed now by Adam's rebellious streak.

Anyway, Adam decided that he might as well get out and enjoy himself before the shit hits the fan. 'So,' he asks, as Julie, still sleepy from her late date, climbs into the front seat. 'How'd the date with Action Man go?'

'I'm more interested in how your meeting with your boss will go,' she says, lathering on the lipstick in the passenger mirror and fluffing up her hair.

'It'll be shit.' Adam winces as he puts the car in gear.

I close my eyes and clench my fists hard. Adam and Julie don't remark on me doing this every time he has to reverse the car down the driveway and out on to the road. I can't help it. It terrifies me.

'Maybe it'll be fine,' Julie says when the car is safely reversed.

'Nah, he's really mad. Technically, I'm supposed to visit all the branches at least once a month and give them pep talks and frighten them into working harder. And, in this case, warn them of bank draft forgeries. This branch is saying that they never got the bank draft e-mail I sent – well, that's their defence. So, it's all my fault.' He takes the Dingle road. I've recommended the Conor Pass as a scenic drive. It's the highest mountain drive in Ireland. 'I'm seeing the boss first thing Friday morning.'

Adam is flying out tonight. It's costing him a fortune at such short notice. He has no suits to wear, so he has to visit his house first.

'You'll be fine,' Julie says and pats his hand. 'You're able to talk complete shit so you'll wrangle your way out of it.'

'I'll need to talk a lot of shit to get out of this.'

We're silent for a bit as I direct Adam where to go. Once we're in Dingle, all he has to do is follow the road signs.

'So – Action Man – how'd it go?' Adam goes back to his previous question. 'I liked the car.'

'Yeah,' Julie nods. 'Car was nice.'

'So, where'd you go?'

'He took me for dinner and he knocked over a table on the way in. He's quite a bulky sort of a bloke.'

'I thought he looked very –' I try to think of a nice way of describing him – 'big.'

Julie is not impressed. 'He's not big,' she exclaims, 'he's *muscular*. He showed me his biceps last night. He rolled up his T-shirt and it was like he had a football bursting out of his arm.'

'Wow.' God, what a disgusting image.

'Apparently he co-owns a gym.'

'Oh, right.' That would make sense, the guy is way too muscled out for my liking.

'I thought he was self-employed,' Adam says. 'Co-owning something is not the same as being totally self-employed.'

'Yeah right,' Julie brushes his comment off with a wave of her hand. 'Anyway, he's picking me up tomorrow again.'

'Why not tonight?' Adam asks.

'Because my dear, you are leaving tonight,' Julie smiles at him. 'I have to be here to wave you on your way.'

Adam flushes. 'Oh. Thanks.' He smiles delightedly.

'And to make sure you're suitably dressed for your boss. If you project a Mr Cool image, you'll feel cool. What suit are you wearing for your meeting?'

Adam shrugs. 'A clean one, anyway.'

'We could buy you a new one today,' Julie says. 'Let's face it, Adam, your other suits scream "boring bastard". We could get you a dynamic one. A brighter one than your black ones.'

From the back, I see Adam's shoulders tense. 'I dunno. I think "boring bastard" is the image they want of me. Boring bastards don't take off to Kerry without telling anyone, do they?'

'Boring bastards can be replaced,' Julie says determinedly. 'Dynamic Dans can't.'

'I'm not a Dynamic Dan.'

'You are.' Julie is annoyed. 'Or at least you could be. You're quite good-looking, Adam, well, if you'd invest in a haircut. Your hair is altogether too long and floppy and girlish.'

'My hair is not girlish.' He flicks it off his face.

'And you need to be more assertive and powerful.'

'I am in my job.' Adam does sound a bit assertive now. 'They hate me in my job. Men quake when they hear I'm coming.'

'Yeah!' Julie and I laugh at the same time.

'Yeah.' Adam nods. 'This is what I do.' He coughs slightly before shouting out 'You!'

115

Julie and I jump.

'Show me last month's invoices!' Pause. 'Has this been paid? Why the bloody hell not? Are you a moron? Can't you read a date? Well, obviously you can't as it's not paid. Get that money by tomorrow. Well, I don't care how you get it, just do it. Got that?' And then he changes back to Adam again. 'See?'

'Oh, Adam, you're very sexy when you do that,' Julie teases. 'Who would have thought?'

He doesn't smile back.

The Conor Pass is a disaster. Julie freaks out because the roads are so narrow and we're going so high. I probably would too only I know the roads so well. She spends the entire journey with her eyes closed. That's when she isn't nagging Adam to get a haircut. In the end, to shut her up, I think, he agrees. Poor Adam, I reckon he was lying about what he's like in the job as he really can't stand up to Julie at all. Or maybe he doesn't want to stand up to her.

'I think quite short would suit you,' she muses.

'Do you?' Adam actually sounds interested. 'Do you go for guys with short hair?'

'Oh yeah,' Julie nods. 'I love that military look. It's really sexy.'

'Oh right,' Adam says. 'Maybe I'll get it chopped short.'

'Spiky would be nice,' Julie suggests and Adam nods. 'Let's go back to the cottage and get some money.'

Adam then freaks her out completely by attempting to turn the car on the narrow road.

I'm sitting in the car, waiting for the two of them to emerge from the cottage with cash when I see Painter Boy in the

116

next field. He seems to be debating whether to come into our garden or not. One minute he hops over the wall and the next he's back on his own side again. He doesn't have an easel but there is something in his hand. I watch, amused at his indecision and he must sense me, for his gaze flicks towards the car and he spots me.

'Great,' I mutter.

He starts to make his way towards me. He clothes are covered in splashes of red paint. He could do with a haircut himself, I think, as he comes closer.

'Hi,' he says hesitantly, bending down to look at me in the passenger seat.

I glare at him, remembering how he made me feel yesterday. 'Yes?'

He takes a deep breath. Then he stares at his feet and then up in the air.

'Is there something you want?' I ask. 'Besides unlimited use of our garden?'

'Oh, I see you've not sustained any lasting damage then,' he says back, 'after our verbal combating yesterday?'

He's good. Really good. Way better than Julie's guy yesterday. I narrow my eyes and glare at him. 'It'd take more than a few ill-chosen words to upset me,' I say with spirit. I toss my head, forgetting for a second that I have no hair. I'd look so much better if I had all my lovely curly hair swishing about my face.

'OK. Good,' Painter Boy says and I think he actually means it.

I notice for the first time that he has his hands behind his back. I also notice that he's hopping from foot to foot. His trainers are in a state. Old and falling apart. A bit like mine, actually.

'I thought,' he starts up, hunkering down suddenly, so he's at my eye level, 'Well, I thought, I just thought . . .'

He's like a car that can't quite go.

'Most people think,' I say. 'It's not something I'd go bragging about.'

'You're good,' he says.

His comment catches me by surprise and silences me.

'I just thought that I upset you yesterday,' he mutters then, really quickly. 'And well, I'm, I'm a bit sorry.'

'A bit sorry?' I hope he doesn't think that's an apology.

'And here,' he thrusts out his hand. In it is a small unframed picture. 'For you. To say that I'm a, well, a bit sorry.'

I'm amazed. I mean completely speechless. Totally stunned. Ashamed. Annoyed that he's made me feel ashamed. Slowly I take the picture from him. It's a picture of the sea. A stormy, black, blue, grey and white sea. Very powerful, quite abstract and quite disturbing. It's a weird picture to give someone to say sorry. 'Thanks,' I mutter. I want to add, 'I think' but I don't.

'Thought you might like it,' he says then.

'It's, eh, great.' I don't actually think I do like it. Imagine staring at that when feeling depressed or cold. It'd hardly cheer me up.

'Right. So, well – I'll, eh, go.' He stands back up again and thumbs in the direction of his cottage. He keeps staring at me, though.

'Hope,' Julie calls loudly, coming from the house, Adam in her wake. 'We're ready.' She smiles at Painter Boy. 'Oh, hi Logan.'

'Yeah, eh, hi.'

'We're going to Killarney. Adam is getting a haircut.'

'Thanks for telling everyone,' Adam says. 'Hey, Hope, what's that you have?'

'Picture.' I show it to them. 'Eh . . .' I can't say his name, 'eh, he gave it to me.' I point to Logan, who looks mortified.

'I was really horrible to her yesterday,' he says proudly, by way of explanation.

'Hey, cool,' Julie admires it. 'Wow, Logan, did you paint that?'

'Yep. It's an old one. No one wanted it.'

'Gee, thanks.' I sneer at him.

He ignores me. 'Are you going to Killarney, did you say?'

'Yep.' Adam jangles his car keys. 'Need a lift?'

'Well, yeah, if there's room. I need to get some paints and things. I normally book a taxi . . .'

To my dismay, my two friends insist that it's no problem, that there is loads of room and I find myself sitting as far apart as I can from him, in the back seat as Adam drives at his usual breakneck speed through the narrow country roads.

'So Logan,' Julie tosses him one of her flirtiest smiles, 'what is it you do?'

He looks a bit stunned at her question. 'I'm an artist,' he states as if talking to a moron.

'No,' Julie giggles a little. 'Like, is that your house, that little cottage or are you renting it like us?'

'Well, I rent it but I live there. It's a long-term rent thing.'

'Oh.' Julie nods politely. 'Must be lonely.'

Is it my imagination or does he flinch slightly? 'Well, it can be,' he acknowledges, 'but I have my sculptures and paintings.'

She snorts a little with laughter. 'Yes, but they can hardly talk, can they? You can't break open a bottle of wine with them, can you?'

'Well, at least I don't have to share the wine or listen to them moaning about the weather and the lack of job opportunities the way my ex did.'

No one quite knows what to say to that.

'Sorry,' Logan says after an uncomfortable silence has descended. 'Scratch that. My ex is a bit of a thorny subject. Yes, Julie, it's lonely.'

Julie and Adam manage a laugh as Logan, to make amends, offers, 'I'm working on a commission at the moment, so the loneliness is good for me.'

'A commission for what?' Julie asks.

'For the new hotel in Dunport.'

'The Gleeson Hotel?' I'm interested, despite myself. 'A guy I know – used to know –' I clarify, 'is in charge of that.'

'Yeah?' He's doing his best to sound interested, but the surprise in his voice at my civil tone is obvious.

'Jack Dunleavy?' My voice rises at just saying his name.

'Oh him,' he nods briefly. 'Yeah, I've talked to him. I don't think he's into my work that much. Anyway, I've to do a series of landscapes for the foyer and the main ballroom.'

'Great,' Adam says.

'It's money,' Logan clarifies. 'I'd prefer to be working on my own stuff. I'm not mad about doing what other people tell me to do, but it's money.'

'Hope hates doing what people tell her to do too,' Adam announces. 'You two have a lot in common.'

I bristle. I'll kill him for that. Logan looks as if he's bristling too. We move even further away from each other.

We all meet back at the car at four. I'm the first back and Logan is second. He's carrying enormous amounts of stuff and it's all large stuff. Big folders and bits of wood and huge boxes of paint. I'm carrying a big bag of toffees. I offer it to him and he attempts to take one but all his stuff falls on the ground.

'Shit!'

I'm tempted to leave him scrabbling about trying to rescue all his things, but that'd be horrible. I pick some art materials up and in silence load them into his arms.

'Thanks.' It's gruff.

'No problem.' I'm equally gruff.

Adam and Julie arrive back. They look as gruff with each other as Logan and I. Adam's hair has been butchered. That's the only way I can describe it. It's certainly short but instead of looking cool, he looks like a thug.

'I didn't mean that short,' Julie grouches as she gets into the car and pulls her seatbelt on. 'You know I didn't. You heard me tell the girl.'

'Well,' Adam starts up the car without looking in her direction. 'At least if I lose my job, I can enrol in the National Front.'

'It'll certainly frighten your employees,' I say, half jokingly. 'You won't have to do your tough act with them.'

'It's not an act,' Adam says shortly.

'Well,' Julie has the last word before we all lapse into silence, 'it's better than the girly cut.'

Adam takes a taxi to the airport that night with promises to ring us about the meeting. Julie hugs him hard as he leaves and, surprisingly, he hugs her back. 'Next time, I'll get to work on your hair,' he tells her. Then he turns to me. 'And you'll have met your mother when I get back and have your cast off. Sorry I won't be here. But you and Ju feel free to use the car, OK?'

121

'Yeah. Thanks.' God, I feel sorry for him heading over to a horrible meeting.

'Hug her, for God's sake,' Julie urges.

We do our awkward hugging thing that embarrasses everyone.

And then we watch as he drives off in a trail of dust.

13

JULIE DRIVES ME to the counsellor on Friday morning. She managed to infuriate everyone on the road as she refused to drive Adam's car faster than forty miles an hour. I swear, from the amount of abuse and horn-blaring we encountered, we both need counselling after it. As we pull up outside Tim's office, Julie's phone starts to ring. 'I'll just park here and answer my phone and when you come out, I'll be waiting,' she promises.

I climb out, holding my filled-in pages firmly in my hand.

'Good luck,' she calls.

I wave back in return.

Tim is sitting at his desk as I enter. He gives me a cheery smile and congratulates me on how diligently I've filled in the forms. He reads them and then looks at the notes he made last Friday. Then he ticks boxes and writes more notes and finally he clasps his hands together in front of him. 'Well, Hope,' he says, and he sounds less casual than he has done, 'at this point, from the information you've given me, I feel that a diagnosis of Post Traumatic Stress Disorder is probably the right one.'

'OK.' My mouth is dry, my mind reeling, but I manage somehow to sound calm and composed. 'Is that, you know, is it a big deal?'

Tim takes his time answering and when he does, I feel that every word he says is carefully chosen. 'Firstly, let me tell you that PTSD is a very understandable response to a traumatic event.' He pauses, to let that sink in. 'Are you following me, Hope?'

I nod. So what I have is understandable. The fury, the panic, the isolation.

'Basically, what happens is that you got on that plane with a certain belief system. You believed that planes were safe, that very little could happen; that there was a better chance of winning Miss World than being hurt on a plane.'

'Yeah, I always reckoned I had a good shot at the Miss World title.'

Tim laughs briefly before continuing. 'And then what? Those beliefs, the feeling that you had a certain amount of control over your life were shattered by what happened. Would this be about right?'

'I suppose, yeah.'

'So then, your poor old brain has to assimilate the experience into your life. It does this by trying to remind you of it, but your waking self can't comprehend the enormity of the change, it has no way of understanding the new belief system so it avoids thinking about it, because it's too scary to relive the trauma. As a result, the mind tries to assimilate your experience through nightmares, flashbacks and panic attacks. So you might avoid going to sleep or you avoid going out in case a panic attack happens. You can see, Hope, how it would lead to all sorts of problems.'

I nod.

'In some cases, like yours, you start numbing yourself to various emotions. You don't want to feel scared or threatened, so you avoid situations that would let you feel this way, you don't think about the accident, you don't put yourself in other scary situations, but it's impossible to cut just one emotion out; eventually it leads to the cutting out of others so that in the end you can't feel much of anything. And finally, a dissociation from other people can occur.' He paused and finished, 'That's what might happen if the PTSD was left untreated.'

That's what was happening.

'And does it make you angry too?' I ask. 'I feel edgy all the time.'

'Yes. When you're in a situation where you feel out of control, you react by getting angry. Because your experience has led you to believe that life itself is out of control and you don't like to feel that way. It's a vicious circle.'

'Oh.' I bite my lip. It's good to have a reason why I feel so bad. Almost a relief.

'And can I get cured? Can I feel like I used to?'

Tim pauses, which frightens me a bit. In fact, he seems hesitant to commit himself.

'Hope, I'll be honest with you. From talking to you the other day, it's obvious to me that this plane crash wasn't the only awful thing to happen in your life.'

'Yes but I never felt like this before.'

'Sometimes, when we have earlier trauma or repeated traumas, our view of the world changes anyway and then the latest trauma only strengthens this. It takes longer with someone like you. I can't cure you. You cure yourself. It means you'll have to work hard.'

Again, as before, my mind begins a slow internal spin. 'But will I be OK?' I ask. 'If I work hard.'

Tim nods. 'Yes. If you work at it. That's all I'm saying.'

'I will work. I promise.'

It seems to be the answer he's looking for. 'Good.' He nods. 'Now, let me explain what we'll be doing, so you'll be prepared for it. Basically, what I do is to tackle three things. First, I'll teach you how to cope with the feelings and tension that come with the memories you get: relaxation techniques, basically. The second thing I'm going to do is help you face the memories. Because you've had more than one trauma, we'll tackle the earlier ones first, the ones about your mother's depression. And from there we'll move on to the plane crash. This is called exposure. The more you talk, the less hold the memories have over you, does that make sense?'

No, it didn't, actually. How could I talk when I couldn't even let myself think?

'It's like, for instance . . . say someone is blackmailing you. They say to you if you don't do what I say, I will tell your great big secret. So you live in fear. You are basically in that person's control. But, say one day you turn around and tell that blackmailer to get lost. You say to him, do your worst, I don't care, I'll survive it. He immediately loses his control over you. You take back control.'

'Oh?'

'It's like that with the nightmares or the panic attacks. Just let them run their course. When you wake up at night, imagine a good ending to the nightmare. Write it down. It works. The same with the panic attacks. Just be aware that you can't die from them, they can actually do you no harm. Take back control.'

'Oh, I see.' It couldn't be as easy as that.

'Obviously, it's not as easy as that,' Tim says, 'but it's easier than you think. And thirdly,' he goes on, 'I'll be helping you change the way you think. For instance, you might say you can't control things so what's the point, and I might say in return, well, name me something you do have control over and how important is that or I might say list the advantages and disadvantages of that belief. You'll find that the advantages are not as compelling as the disadvantages. Things like that.'

'OK.'

'Is there anything you want to ask me?'

I'm sure there is but my mind is blank. There is so much stuff to understand.

'If you can't think of anything,' Tim smiles, 'you have my number, you can ring me any time.'

'OK.'

'So Hope, I'm going to ask you a question. What is it you expect to get out of this? What are your aims?'

'Normality.'

Tim allows himself a grin. His teeth are quite crooked, I notice.

'To feel that things aren't normal *is* normal, Hope, believe it or not. Just have a think during the next few days and decide what it is you want from this therapy. And we'll work at that.'

I don't need a few days to think about what I want. 'I want the nightmares to stop,' I say haltingly. 'I want to be able to relax. I want to hold down a job and not over-react. I want to see a plane in the sky and wave at it the way I did when I was a kid.' That last bit sounds stupid but it had just come out. Me and Jamie loved doing that. I used to pretend I could see into the plane and would drive him mad by telling him that all the passengers were waving at me and not him. 'Just those things for the moment,' I mutter.

Tim nods. 'Cool, yeah. Well, for next week, Hope, I want you to keep filling out the forms. Keep monitoring your triggers. Most importantly, I need you to stay off the drink. And when you see a plane in the sky, look up for maybe a second and wave. Just a second. Just remember, it can't do you any harm.'

If it fell out of the sky, it would do me a lot of harm, I think. Then immediately I have the thought: how likely is that?

'And if you manage to hold it for one second, the next time you see a plane, hold it for two seconds and wave. Just keep building on it and let me know by next –' he consults his diary – 'Friday how you get on. And let your friends know what you're doing, they might help you.'

'OK. I'll try.' I take the fresh forms he's proffering me.

'And have a think about next Friday, Hope,' he says, just as I've opened the door. 'We're going to talk a little about your mother – OK?'

I nod. Little does he know I'm on my way to see her. Maybe by my next session, my slant on my mother will be very different.

'. . . and I have to start looking at planes in the sky and wave at them,' I say finally to Julie, who has asked how my session went.

She doesn't respond. It dawns on me suddenly that she hasn't responded to a thing I've said. In fact, she hasn't even looked at me since I started to speak.

'And he told me that what I had was incurable.'

'Really?' Julie turns to me and I nod. 'Oh, Hope, that's fantastic.'

Her eyes look a bit red, but it's hard to be sure because she seems to have plastered on fresh make-up. 'Julie, have you been crying or something?'

'No.' She doesn't look at me; instead she fires the engine.

'So you think it's good that I'm dying?'

'You're dying?' Now her eyes widen in horror. The car splutters to a standstill. 'Dying?'

'No, no I'm not,' I say hastily as her eyes fill up. 'It's just when I said I was, you told me it was fantastic.' I attempt a smile.

'Did I?' She still sounds weepy. 'Sorry about that.'

'That's OK.' I study her. She definitely was crying. 'What's wrong, Ju?' What could have happened in the last hour? 'Has Nelson cancelled or something?'

She flaps a hand in my direction. 'Nothing.' She sniffs. 'You don't need my problems. You've got to see your mother now.' She makes another attempt to start the car.

'She isn't expecting me at a particular time.'

The car judders and jumps and eventually stalls. 'Damn!' Julie says in frustration. 'Damn! Damn!'

'Come on.' I take the car keys from her and give her a gentle shove, 'Tell me. I'll probably make it a whole lot worse for you, but I'm listening.'

She rewards me with a half-hearted smile.

'Well?'

She sighs and looks at me despondently. 'That phone call, just before you went, remember?'

I nod.

'Well, it was Dad.'

'Oh, so he rang at last, did he?'

'Yeah,' she nods. 'They have this bad cop, good cop routine going. He's generally the good cop. He told me how terribly disappointed he was at the way I'd treated my mother.'

'What?!'

129

'I reckon if I'd murdered someone, they'd forgive me easier.'

'Julie, you took early leave to go on holiday, it's no big deal. People do it all the time.'

'Not the Adcocks,' she says in a tart voice. 'The Adcocks value their careers.'

Poor Julie, I'm thinking. But the scary thing is I'm not feeling it. I can't let her see that. 'Well, you're an adult now. You can do what you like. You're an adult Adcock.' And for some reason, that sets us giggling.

Then just as I think Julie has cheered up, she says, 'He told me how terrible it was that I had upset my mother so much. She's devastated that I took off without telling her, she felt like a fool when she rang my school and I wasn't there, and if that was all the appreciation I could show them for the years of sacrifice they had made for me, I was no daughter of theirs.' Her voice cracks a little. 'Imagine.'

'Bloody hell,' I borrow Adam's favourite phrase.

'Well, he didn't say it in an angry way,' Julie said, 'he was all mournful and disappointed, which is worse than anything. I think he expected me to apologise.'

'I hope you didn't!'

'I'm not that pathetic,' she says with some spirit and I give a little cheer.

'Then he goes on about how upset she is that I'm not taking her calls any more and then he started on about how Angela never takes holidays and that's why she's advanced so much in her career and that maybe I should think about it.'

'Saint Angela.'

'Exactly. And then,' Julie gulps, 'worst of all, he got to saying how he'd be in Ireland on business next weekend and that we should meet up. Oh God, Hope, what will I do?'

'He's coming to the cottage?'

She shakes her head. 'No, he wouldn't find that. He'll be in Killarney, he said and he'd love to see me.'

'Well, that's understandable.'

'No, I know he's going to give me a parent heart to heart. If I refuse to see him, it'll cause war. If I see him . . .' She doesn't finish; instead she says, 'Hope, why can't they let go?'

I think of my mother who let me go a long time ago, probably not deliberately, but it had happened, and I don't know which is worse. 'He just maybe loves you too much?' I suggest.

'No,' Julie says bitterly, 'he loves what he thinks I am too much.'

'So see him,' I say. 'If you want, maybe Adam and I will go too. That'll wrongfoot him.'

She gives a horrified giggle. 'Yeah, it would, wouldn't it?'

'Yeah, we'll hang about with the two of you all day and he won't get a word in.'

'Brill!' She smiles.

And I'm glad I've made her smile so I make myself smile too.

131

14

THE JOURNEY FROM Tim's office to the cottage on the outskirts of Dunport only seems to take seconds. One minute I'm looking at streets and shops, the next we're driving by the sea with shops and pubs to our right.

'This turn,' I say to Julie and she dutifully indicates left and begins the short drive up the road to my mother's house. I get her to stop just a stroll away from it. I don't need my mother quizzing me on Julie. I'm not ready to tell her things yet. And I'm not ready for Julie to see where I grew up. I was always half ashamed of our house – my mother never cut the grass or washed the windows like other people's mothers. She never painted the door or swept the footpath. Our net curtains were a dirty white and were never changed. Once, when she was feeling well, she did take them down and wash them, but she never hung them back up. I did that, months later, when I eventually located them. She liked growing things, though, and we had a passable garden, but that was it. Most of the time, our house looked unloved and reeked of decay. It was in direct contrast to Amanda Coonan's house which was a little down the road from ours. They had landscaped gardens and waterfalls and rockeries. They were the first people in Dunport to have venetian blinds and their brass doorknob was always sparkling.

'Good luck,' Julie calls, her good mood restored by the massive ice-creams and large cappuccinos we'd had before leaving the vicinity of the office.

I hold up my mobile. 'I'll ring you when I want you to come, OK. I shouldn't be more than twenty minutes.'

'Yeah, I'll go for a walk along the beach.' Julie does a three point turn, which takes ten attempts, and heads off back in the direction of the main road. I watch until the car is out of sight and then, taking deep breaths, I begin to walk towards home.

The Coonans' is immaculate as always and I scurry past it, not wanting them to see me. I don't know how I'll feel about Amanda Coonan now; I'll probably still hate her. I get safely by and in the distance I see the white gable wall of my mother's house. My step slows and I almost stop and flee but something inside makes me go on. Step by step by step I advance towards the house until soon I'm standing at the end of the short driveway. The garden is still unkempt but amazingly in a nice sort of way. Summer flowers sprout from unexpected places. Poppies and daisies flutter alongside the cultivated ones. The windows are clean and she has bought roller blinds. I take all this in as I walk towards the front door. There is no handle. It must have fallen off, but there is a bell. I stare at it a while before reaching up to press it. A dull buzzing sounds inside the house.

No one comes.

I press it again.

And still no one comes.

I can't believe this. Surely she has to be there. Surely she wouldn't leave when she knows that there is a chance I'm going to call? And so I press it a third time.

Inside, I hear footsteps coming up the hallway. My breath quickens as the door is slowly pulled open. And she stands in front of me, smaller than me, her tiny-boned hand holding the door ajar.

'Hello,' I say, rather formally. 'It's eh, me.'

'Hope,' she says back, pulling the door wider to allow me in. She gives me a smile which I half-heartedly return. 'Come on in.'

Her voice is as soft as ever and her eyes follow me as I walk by her into the hall. It has been transformed. Wooden floors and painted doors. Pictures on the walls. One of me, I notice, smiling out of the frame and holding a little boy. I was probably about five in the picture. And Jamie would have been only one or so. He's struggling to get out of my arms. I had a habit, when he was a baby, of picking him up and cuddling him really hard. There is another one of the four of us. My mother and father, arms around each other, gazing at me and Jamie with pride. Jamie's slightly slanted eyes glitter with mischief. And yet a third, of me and Jamie when we were older. At my twelfth birthday party. Jamie has his arms around me and is hugging me tight. I can't look at that one. In fact, I don't realise I'm looking at all until she says, 'They're my favourite pictures and one of the local lads framed them for me.'

'Lovely,' I croak out.

'Would you like a coffee? Or a tea?' She sounds anxious.

'Tea, please.' I don't really want one but I think it will be better to be holding something or sipping something when I can't think of things to say.

My mother moves towards the kitchen and, as I enter, I notice again, how much improved it is on what I remember. Clean. Bright. For some reason, there are flower arrangements everywhere. Half-finished ones and ones only begun. My mother waves her hands at them as she picks up the kettle. 'I'm always working out what arrangements to do at the evening class, I like to keep things different.'

I go around examining the flowers as she pulls out biscuits and sugar from the press. 'They look great,' I say. I point to a pretty spray of white orchids. 'This is like something you'd see at a wedding.'

'Yes, I'm doing a wedding in a few months.'

'Really?' I'm impressed. 'A wedding. Is that not a big job?'

She turns to face me and her steady gaze unnerves me a little. 'I can cope with big jobs like that,' she says and her tone is faintly chastising.

'Oh.' I flush. 'I didn't mean . . .' my voice trails off, but of course, I had meant it and we both know it. I leave the flowers and sit at the table.

'I've been working hard to keep it together,' she tells me in a gentle voice. 'It was difficult at first but it's getting easier.' She sits opposite me at the table. 'I know I let you and Jamie down, Hope.' Her voice falters and her eyes water and I turn away. I'm not able to cope with her emotion. 'I can't say anything to make it better. But at the time, I couldn't help the way I was.'

Yes she could have, I feel like saying. How come she works hard at it now and she couldn't when Jamie and I were there? I want to say it, to shout it at her, to demand an answer. Instead, I find I'm staring at the table, unable to meet her gaze and unable to take her apology. I think I'm afraid to row, I'm afraid of the emotion and I'm afraid that it will set her back in her own recovery. I learned early never to argue with my mother, it only left me feeling guilty when she cried for days. And angry that I had to bottle it all up.

So, looking at the table, I notice that it's new and scrubbed and clean. Not like the brown stained thing we grew up with. In fact, its cleanness seems to mock me. Did we not matter enough for her to pull herself together for us?

The kettle clicks off and she stands up to make the tea.

I just want to go now. I feel more hurt than I ever thought I could. But I sit there and watch as she stirs the teapot and pours the tea into two bright yellow mugs. I even mutter 'thanks' as she places mine before me.

'So, what happened to you?' she asks. I get the impression that that's all she's wanted to know since I came in.

'I was in an –' I gulp slightly as I find I'm unable to speak about the accident without choking up – 'well, it was an accident. In a plane.'

'In a plane?'

'Yes. It crashed. Lots of people died.' I give what I hope is a laconic smile. 'I didn't.'

Her face pales. It's ages before she speaks. 'Oh God.' Then something clicks, 'Was that the London plane last May?'

'Yeah.'

Her expression swings between bewilderment and hurt. 'And how come no one contacted me?'

I can't tell her that my friends thought she was dead. 'A mix-up, I suppose. Anyway, I'm telling you now and I'm fine so –'

'But you might not have been!'

'But I am.' I say it firmly. Let's not go that route, is what I mean. I half expect her to keep going. To ask if maybe I didn't want her there or for her to say how upset she feels that she wasn't there.

But to my surprise, she says instead, 'They shaved your head.'

'Yeah.' I explain about the operation and the fact that my hair will grow back and that I'm getting the cast off my leg in the next week. That cheers her up. 'Good.' She nods. 'That's good.' Then she asks a little about my life in London and I tell her and she asks if I'm working and I lie and say that I am. I don't tell her about all my job losses and my PTSD. I guess I'm doing what I always did, filtering out the bad bits of information to protect her.

Just then the front-door bell rings. My mother motions for me to stay sitting. 'It's probably just Amanda to look at an arrangement I've done, I'll tell her to call back later.'

She hops up from the table and closes the kitchen door behind her. As she opens the front door, I hear an unmistakable nasal voice and my heart tightens. My mother laughs at something this Amanda says and then the Amanda says goodbye and that she'll call later and my mother closes the door and comes back into the kitchen. She sits back down, oblivious to my shock.

'Who was that?' I dip a finger into my cold tea.

'Just Amanda, I'm doing her wedding for her. She's marrying –'

'Amanda? Amanda Coonan?'

'Yes. Why, would you have liked to meet her?'

I flinch from the insensitivity of the question. 'No!' My voice cracks. 'No I would not!'

She knows something is wrong but to my disbelief she doesn't know what. 'Oh,' she says.

'Amanda Coonan?' I say in disbelief, again. '*The* Amanda Coonan?'

She winces at my change in temper. I can see it but I can't control it. I'm an onlooker to my own anger. But, I think, even if I hadn't had the PTSD, I'd have been fuming.

My mother nods and then says in an unfamiliarly steely voice, 'Yes. Amanda.'

'Amanda that used to call me a dirt bag and say we were all descended from rats? Amanda that picked on . . . Jamie?' My voice catches as I say his name and I notice the way my mother balks. 'That Amanda?'

My mother swallows hard. 'Yes, Hope,' she says evenly. 'That Amanda. The girl you punched so hard she had to stay overnight in hospital. And whose parents very nicely made her apologise for what she'd said to make you hit her. The Amanda that for the past few years always offers to get my shopping when I can't make it to the shops. Or when I'm feeling down.'

'Oh, good for her!' Now I'm fighting. I've never fought with my mother before. 'Good for her.' I stand up. 'Well, maybe she should be here drinking tea with you instead of me.'

'No.' My mother sounds distressed. 'No. I'm glad it's you. I'm so glad it's you, Hope.'

I can't answer. I can't say anything or it'll sound petty and mean, but I so desperately want to lash out. To tell her how I felt all those years ago. To tell her how I still feel, I suppose. But instead, I do what Julie advises and count to ten. At the end of the count I stand up and say, 'Well, anyway, I have to go now. I have some shopping and stuff to do.'

'Hope?'

I hold up my hands to fend her off.

'Hope, please –'

I shake my head.

We stare at each other. I can't go until she lets me. But I can't stay either.

'OK,' she says and if she's disappointed, she doesn't let it show. 'Will you call again?'

'I don't know.' I start to back out of the kitchen. 'I might have to go back. I don't know.'

She crosses towards me and I pull back. I can't have her touch me. I don't know what I'll do.

'OK,' she says. Her shoulders sag. 'Well, I'm glad we met, Hope.'

I can only nod.

'And please keep in touch with me. Let me know how you're getting on.' A pause. 'And I'm sorry about Amanda. I'm glad you're fine. You are fine, aren't you?'

'Yes, Mammy, I'm fine,' I say firmly. I'm right back to my childhood when she'd awaken, half crazy in the afternoon and ask me if things were fine. And assuming my teacher's voice or whoever else impressed me back then, I'd lie and say things were fine. Me and Jamie were fine, the house was fine, and school was fine. Lies, lies, lies until I was sick of them. 'I'm fine now. And I have to go now.'

'But you'll be back?' Her eyes look pleadingly at me. 'Won't you?'

I'm not going to lie to her. Instead I shrug.

'Oh.'

We look at each other for a few long seconds. Finally, she says, 'All I can say is sorry, Hope. If I could turn back time, you know I would.'

I would too, I want to say. If I could turn back time, I might just have done things differently. 'Bye, Mammy.'

'Bye, alannah.'

That term of endearment spears me. I don't say anything, just walk as quickly as I can away from the place.

15

IT'S THREE DAYS later. I'm sitting with Julie in the hospital, awaiting the doctor who will, at last, take my cast off. It's over four days since Adam left for London and we still haven't heard from him. He should have had his meeting by now and Julie and I are beginning to get very worried. Julie has just tried to ring him again and all she has got is Adam's voicemail.

'Say he's done something stupid,' she says, redialling. 'I mean, he really liked his job and say he's lost it.'

'Did he really like his job?' I must say, I'd never noticed that about him.

'Well, if you had a job that enabled you to buy three houses and boss people about, wouldn't you like it?' Julie asks as if it's a no-brainer. 'He loved that job.'

There is something flawed in her logic but I don't bother pointing it out. I can't wait to get the cast off as my leg is so itchy. I just want to scratch and scratch it. The hospital in London has sent my file over and apparently after getting my cast off, I've to go and get my head examined. Julie thinks that's funny.

'Oh, I do hope he's OK.' Julie flicks off her mobile and stares at me with big anxious blue eyes. 'Would you say he's OK, Hope?'

'Well, he's not the sort to do something stupid,' I answer. I'd thought about this a lot in the last couple of days and didn't quite know how to say it delicately. 'Like that's kind of a spontaneous thing to do, isn't it, and he's not like that.'

Julie gives a horrified laugh. 'Oh, when you put it that way . . .'

'Hope Gardner?' someone calls, interrupting us. 'You can see the doctor now.'

'So, he'll be OK,' I say over my shoulder to Julie as I pick up my crutch and hobble down the corridor into the doctor's office. I reckon I could have taken the cast off myself but Julie had shrieked at the idea. The doctor is a youngish man, probably a trainee or whatever you call them. He has my cast off in no time and he asks me to do various things with my leg and then asks me if I feel any pain.

'None. It's just a little weak,' I say. It's also pale and hairy, which horrifies me. The minute I get back, it's out with the razor.

'Gentle exercise will soon have you as right as rain,' he says. 'You're a lucky girl.'

'Isn't she?' Julie beams at me like a proud mother. 'She was in a plane crash, you know.'

'And how is that lucky exactly?' I deadpan.

The doctor smiles. 'Well the best of luck with the rest of your life, Hope,' he says, as I stand up and automatically reach for the crutch. 'You don't need it any more,' he says and grins.

And I don't. Suddenly I have two free hands. It's weird, but I hardly know what to do with them as I leave the office. I settle for swinging them back and forward and gazing in admiration at my leg.

My head is healing well too and I'm congratulated on

141

the fact that my hair has grown an inch. 'You're a survivor,' the surgeon tells me. 'And whoever operated on you did a wonderful job.'

Aren't doctors great? Whoever invented medicine was a genius.

Nelson arrives to take Julie out that evening. It's the last night of his holiday and he's going back to Dublin the next day. However, he has promised to keep in touch with her and to call down every weekend until she goes back.

When Nelson pulls up in his little car, Julie and I watch amused as he huffs and puffs and pulls and tugs and eventually emerges from it and plants his enormous feet on the ground.

'Hi, Nelson.' Julie hammers on the window and he waves a big shovel of a hand in greeting.

She beckons him to come on in.

He enters and nods hello at me before turning to Julie. I reckon that first-night conversation with me frightened him off. He has hardly said two words to me since and apparently asked Julie if the accident affected me mentally.

'Hope got her cast off today,' Julie says to him. She's busy applying a deep red lipstick to her rosebud lips.

'Oh yeah,' Nelson nods, eyeing me. He has dropped his twang, but still stands like some extra from a cowboy movie. 'Nice one. So you can walk proper and all now, can you?'

'I can.'

'Great.'

'And her hair is growing back,' Julie announces.

'Fantastic,' Nelson nods. 'Women always look nicer with a bit of hair.'

I smile. It's impossible to feel offended. The poor guy hasn't a clue what to say to me.

'Indeed. Have a good night now.'

'Will you be OK on your own?' Julie turns to me. 'I thought Adam would be back by now and I don't like leaving you. Do you want to come with us?'

Nelson shoots her a panicked look but fair play, he refrains from refusing outright. Instead, he says, in a phoney, regretful voice, 'I've only booked a table for two.'

'Sure cancel it and we'll go to a pub,' Julie says.

He looks hurt. 'It's the best table in the restaurant.'

'I'll be fine,' I say. 'Go on, enjoy yourself. I'll probably go for a walk or something.'

'You can't go for a walk on your own,' Julie exclaims. 'It's so lonely around here – anything could happen.'

'I should be so lucky!'

'Promise me you won't go for a walk.'

'Promise me you won't snog Nelson!'

'That's hardly fair.'

'Bye now.' And before she can say any more, I close the door on both of them.

Of course I'm going for a walk. I know this area like the back of my hand. Still, with my leg only just out of plaster, I don't think I'll go too far. Maybe just to Painter Boy's house and back. I'll go across country as well, rather than sticking to the main road. It'll be nice to stroll through the warm early evening air and maybe sit down and just drink in the view. Julie and Adam are great company but neither of them is that interested in walking. They're pub and club people. When I was in London, I was like that too. I think I'd let myself forget the way I used to be.

Before I leave, I check my phone for messages. None.

Adam still hasn't rung. I shove my mobile into my pocket, pull on a raincoat and gingerly push my feet into my trainers. It's weird wearing shoes again. My leg feels weak and heavy at the same time. I close all the windows, though it's highly unlikely we'd have a break-in, take the key and lock the front door. Shoving my hands into my pockets, I begin to walk.

It takes a lot longer than I anticipate to get to Logan's cottage. I approach it from the side and when I get there, I'm exhausted. I sit on his wall and admire the lovely bunch of wild flowers I have picked and then I find my eyes drawn to his house. To my surprise, it's in good nick. The white-washed walls gleam brightly, the dying sunlight making them look a sort of rosy red. And the windows are cleaner than ours at the cottage. His garden is a bit untamed though, but in a nice way. Wild flowers – poppies, buttercups, daisies, dandelions and some blue ones that I don't know the name of – are in bloom and sway about in the light breeze. I lean over the wall and take a few of the blue ones to add to my posy. A big fat ginger cat sits in the shade of the porch, eyeing me malevolently. I like cats but this one seems a bit too much like its owner for comfort. It stares at me, before getting to its feet and arching its back. Then it hisses a little at me, making me jump.

'Piss off,' I hiss back.

The cat hisses a little more.

I hiss back and give it the two fingers.

'Have you permission to be here?' a voice behind asks, making me fall off the wall. It's him. With a stupid grin on his face and his hands in his pockets.

'Your cat is a danger.' I scramble to my feet, mortified to be caught hissing back at his stupid cat.

'Here, Ginger,' Logan says, calling the cat, his hand outstretched. 'Here, Ginger.'

Ginger. What an inspired name.

The cat eyes me, then eyes Logan and finally comes towards us, its tail in the air. With a nimble leap, it hops on to the wall and from there on to Logan's shoulder.

'Ginger, meet Hope. Hope, this is Ginger.'

The cat and I grimace at each other.

'She's very unfriendly and aggressive, but you'll get used to her.'

I'm about to say that I have no intention of getting used to his cat, when it strikes me that he's talking about me to his cat.

'I could say the same about you,' I retort. I brush myself down. 'Now, sorry for trespassing, but I knew you'd understand, being a superior trespasser yourself. I'll go now.'

When I turn to leave he exclaims, 'Hey, you've no crutch.'

'No.' I feel shy at his look of delight. 'I, eh, got my plaster off today.'

'Brill. I broke my leg once, the itch nearly killed me.'

'Me too.' I smile briefly before turning away again.

'So how'd you break it – fall from some high moral ground, did ya?'

I'll show him and his very smart comments. 'Actually, I was in an aeroplane accident.'

My heart lurches at the words. I wonder will I ever get used to saying it.

'Ha ha.'

'It's true.'

Doubt clouds his black eyes. 'Really? When?'

'May.'

'That London plane – the one that crashed on landing?'

'The very one.'

That silences him. He looks at me with something akin to awe. 'Wow.'

His look silences me. In fact, I very nearly feel tears in the back of my eyes. I don't know why, I can't explain it. Anyway, I blink them back hard and again attempt to leave.

'I know when I broke my leg, it hurt like hell when I walked any distance on it.'

I smirk slightly, unable to resist. 'Well, that's not surprising; it was probably hard for it, having to support your inflated ego.'

He laughs. 'Good one. Still, your leg must be sore now. D'you fancy –' he shrugs, pets his cat, which has curled itself about his shoulders and is rubbing the side of his face with its nose – 'well, d'you fancy a cuppa or a can of beer to help you on your way home?' His eyes slide away from his cat and meet mine.

I suppose it's a kind of peace gesture. Like the way his stormy painting was. I'm not sure if I need another peace gesture, though. There is something about this guy that sends prickles of irritation up my skin. It's the way he won't let me win, I think.

'Well?' he asks.

'I suppose I could spare a moment to keep you company,' I answer airily. 'Do you not have many friends then?'

He flinches a bit but rallies. 'Well, most people with a life probably are doing something tonight. I just thought, seeing as you weren't . . .' He gives a cocky grin, puts the cat down and strides into the cottage.

I allow myself a smile now before following him inside.

The first thing that strikes me is that it's so cool. Not cool as in trendy, cool as in it could be freezing in winter.

It's surprisingly bright too. The big window at the front floods the front room with light. He uses this as a studio: large canvases are stacked against the wall, smaller ones beside them. Some paintings are hung, to help them dry, I suppose. The stench of oil paint is everywhere. I remember the smell from art class at school. I don't get much of a chance to stare at them; all I get is the impression of lots of green and blue and red before Logan calls me from the kitchen.

His kitchen is bigger than ours and there is a small room leading off it – a sort of den where I notice a TV and DVD recorder.

'Tea? Coffee? Beer?'

I opt for the coffee. He gets a beer for himself from the fridge then puts on the kettle and leans against a counter top as we wait for it to boil. I don't know what to say now I'm standing in front of him on his own territory. He's taller than I realised and leaner and better looking. In a mean, rangy sort of way. His hair is mussed up, standing in spikes all over his head and he needs a shave. His eyes are an intense blue and he has the sort of mouth that seems to wear a permanent sardonic grin. Or at least it does whenever I see him. He's grinning at me now.

'So you don't drink beer,' he says, breaking the silence.

'Nope. I don't drink.' A complete lie and I have no idea why I'm saying it. 'I hate drink.'

'I love it. Cheers.' He raises his can and takes a big long slug. 'Ahhhh,' he says then. 'That's good.'

'Your cottage is bigger than ours.' It comes out like an accusation.

'Yep. Nice, isn't it? I hope to buy it from the landlord one day – I only have the money to rent it at the moment. When

I get the cash from the hotel commission, I might be able to make a deposit on it.'

'Oh. Good.' I study my ragged nails. I really would like to sit down, I think. My leg is aching. 'How's that coming along?'

'Well, aside from a mishap here and there –' he grins a little – 'pretty good.'

'Good.'

More silence.

He breaks it again. He coughs a bit and says awkwardly, 'Look, Hope, I know we got off to a bad start. To be frank, you really pissed me off when you sat in the middle of my sketch, but I was having a bad day overall, anyway.' The kettle clicks off and he turns to fill my cup. 'Sorry about that.'

It's a nice apology, I think. 'It's fine. I can barely remember it.'

'Yeah. Right.' He rolls his eyes and hands me the cup.

'Thanks.'

'Come on,' he indicates the sitting room. 'Let's sit down.'

The room is small and cosy. I make for a battered but comfy orange chair and sink into it with relief.

Logan sits opposite.

'So, can we start over?' he asks, hunching forward towards me.

There's a surprise. I half smile at him. 'OK,' I shrug, 'why not?'

'I mean,' he goes on, smiling back at me, 'it's important to quit when you're ahead.'

'You're not ahead,' I say. 'You surrendered.'

'Yeah, I suppose, you're better at it than I am.'

'Thank you.'

'You must have had a hard and bitter childhood to get so good.'

Bastard. If it wasn't so true, I'd admire him for that one. 'You mustn't have had a childhood at all to act so childishly when I met you,' I say sweetly.

He grins slightly. I realise that I too am smiling. That's a bit of a shocker. We smile at each other for a few seconds until we both realise that we're doing it and avert our eyes.

'I'm Logan,' he says after a bit, standing over me. 'Logan Jones. I'm from Dublin. I'm twenty-eight and I sculpt. At the moment, I'm stuck doing a bloody commission for a new hotel as last year I won a prize for my work. I earn fuck all, love this part of the world and have a mean temper when someone ruins a picture on me. I don't get to talk to many people and I like it that way. You?'

He's got a nice voice when he talks conversationally. It's warm and sweet and friendly. Despite my reservations, I'm warming to him. I don't know if I want to.

'I'm Hope Gardner,' I begin. 'I'm from Dunport. My mother still lives here. I'm twenty-seven and at the moment I'm between jobs, having been fired from my sixteenth job a couple of months ago, don't even go there. I, too, as you can guess, am earning fuck all. I live in London and share a house with Adam and Julie. And I have a mean temper when people shout at me.'

'And why did you lose your sixteenth job?'

'Piss off.' I take a gulp of coffee. It's not so hot now and tastes great.

'How'd you ever swap here for London?'

I smile at him. 'London is great. Mad night-life. Good fun.'

'Yeah, but you love it here, I know you do. I saw you that

149

day when you were in the garden, you just drank in the view. Just like I do.'

'What do you sculpt?' Not that I'm interested, but I don't want to think about how I love this place.

'Mainly wood.' He regards me for a bit before asking, almost shyly, 'D'you want to see some stuff I've done this summer?'

'Sure, yeah.'

'Come this way.' He pulls open his back door and strides ahead of me into the field. He has a small shed behind his house, which he unlocks. Flicking on a light, I am amazed to see a workshop with various kinds of wood all lying about the place. The smell of the shaved wood is gorgeous too. Logan picks his way through the mess and, beckoning me over, he holds up a beautiful bird, in full flight, all carved in meticulous detail. Its feathers actually seem real. The whole thing gleams from the inside out, almost as if it had a spirit. 'I finished this last night. What d'you think?'

Reverently, I touch it. It's warm. 'You did that?'

'Yep.' He gently puts it down. 'It just appeared out of the wood. You like it?'

'Yeah.' It touches me somehow, that bird. The freedom of it. Of course I don't say this. 'It's really good. Beautiful.'

'I like birds,' he says. Then grinning a little, he adds, 'The human variety especially.'

'How original,' I say drily. 'You should stick to the sculpting. Or carving or whatever you call it.'

'I figured that out myself a long time ago,' he says back. 'Nothing but heartbreak otherwise.'

'You said it.'

'So, d'you want another coffee?'

It's getting quite dusky out. It'll be dark if I stay any longer. 'I'd better head off.'

'Don't be a stranger now – call over again, eh?'

I don't really think I will. Still, it hasn't been as bad as I thought and he actually does seem nice. 'Thanks for the coffee,' I say.

'No problem. Safe home.'

We nod to each other, then he turns to his workbench and I make my exit.

It takes me what feels like hours to walk home. I have definitely overdone the whole leg bit. By the time I reach the front door, I'm feeling so sorry for myself that I barely register Adam sitting on the doorstep.

'Hey!' He startles me out of my reverie and I jump about ten feet in the air. 'Sorry, Hope.'

'Nah, it's fine. God, it's good to see you.' He looks totally dishevelled, despite the fact that he has a suit and tie on. His tie is pulled loose and his shirt is hanging out over his trousers. 'Where have you been?' Without giving him time to answer, I unlock the front door, saying, 'Julie and I were so worried. We left about a hundred messages on your phone. In fact, I wouldn't be surprised if Julie is ringing you even now and ruining her date.'

'Oh,' Adam plonks wearily down on to the sofa and pinches the bridge of his nose with two fingers. 'So she's still seeing Gym Boy.'

'Yep.'

He heaves a great big sigh, closes his eyes and leans his head back. Something is wrong. Something awful. 'Hey,' I sit down beside him and catch his arm. 'Was it really bad?'

He doesn't answer for a second. Then, he gulps and says, 'Yep. Any wine?'

I jump up, grab a bottle of red and uncork it. All the time, he sits, staring at his hands and his feet until, after I hand him an enormous glass of red, his eyes meet mine. His hand is shaking as he lifts the glass to his lips and takes a huge gulp of the drink. I wish I could join him. 'So?' I probe gently.

'I'm, eh, suspended,' he mutters, looking into his glass.

'Suspended?'

'Surprisingly, they didn't like the fact that I took off to Kerry and never told them,' he tries to make a joke about it. 'Nor did they like the fact that the fifty grand was missing for months.'

'But that bit wasn't your fault!'

'I'm in charge. And anyway, the guys in the stores said they never got the memo.'

'But you sent it!' Oh, I'm full of indignation for him. 'And did you tell them that your friend was at death's door and that's why you came to Kerry!'

'Nope.' He grins a little now. 'With all due respect, Hope, whether you live or die is of no importance to them.'

'Huh – that's bloody businessmen for you.'

'Yeah.' He nods in agreement but I don't think he really means it.

'So, how long are you suspended for?'

He winces. Swirls his drink about in his glass. 'Until September, then they'll review the situation.'

I think that's great, though I don't say it. He's got all summer with me and Julie now. He won't have to go upstairs to his laptop any more. We can have a blast together and then he can resume work when we all go back to London.

'That long?' I say, trying to sound sympathetic. 'How'll you manage for money?'

'I do have savings,' he says as if it's obvious. 'And if the worst comes to the worst, I can always sell the houses. In fact, I'll probably have to sell one of them as the mortgage is huge on it. And I won't be getting paid.'

'Oh no!'

'Oh yeah.' He takes another gulp of wine and clears his glass. He really is turning into a bit of an alco. I pour him half a glass and he raises his eyebrows so I fill it. 'So, where were you tonight?'

I welcome the change of subject. To be honest, it's a bit rich me sympathising with him over his job. I'd never stand to be suspended. I'd probably tell them that if they didn't trust me they could shove their stupid job. In fact that's what Adam should have done. I flirt with telling him this but he asks again where I've been. For some reason, I don't want to mention Logan so I just stick out my plasterless leg and say airily, 'Oh, just exercising my completely healed leg.'

He doesn't say anything for a bit, just smiles at me affectionately. Then he nods. 'I'm so proud of you. You're such a fighter.'

'Yeah, going into battle with all my bosses over the years has stood me well, eh?'

He laughs. It's good to see him laugh. 'So, did you go far?'

'About two miles in all.'

'Isn't that a bit far?'

'Yeah. I know that *now*.'

Another laugh, and then he asks, 'And Julie, how's she getting on with Gym Boy?'

'OK, I think.'

'Does she like him a lot?'

He asks the question in a casual manner but by the way he looks at me, I think he really wants to know. Jesus, I wonder if he fancies her. I hope not, I don't want our friendship to be ruined by him liking her and her turning him down. I shrug and decide to opt for a casual tone. 'I don't know. I think he likes *her* a lot. He's a bit phoney, to be honest. It's like he's trying to be something he's not.'

He doesn't say much to that, just drinks another large mouthful. 'And your mother?'

And so I spend the next forty minutes or so telling him about the meeting with my mother. 'So it didn't go well?' he asks at last.

'Not brilliantly,' I admit. 'If only Amanda hadn't called, it might have been better.'

'Yeah, but Hope, how can you let her have this hold over you? So she picked on you, maybe you should just let it go. Move on. Try and rebuild.' He's slurring his words now, he's quite drunk I think. I wonder if he's been drinking at the airport.

'She bullied me,' I say.

Adam laughs at that. 'Hope, she didn't bully you, believe me, you don't know how bad real bullying can get.' He laughs again, half to himself, and pours the dregs of the bottle into his glass. 'And Julie? What's the story with her folks, have they rung yet?'

I tell him about that and about my counselling until at last I dry up. It's just as well, because he seems to be falling asleep.

'Maybe you should go to bed?' I suggest gently.

'Yep.' He puts his glass on the table and, swaying quite a bit, stands up. 'Night.'

I swallow hard and almost lose my nerve, but just as he turns to the stairs, I say in a rush, 'Sorry for being partly responsible for you being suspended.'

He freezes and turns back to me. To my relief, he looks incredulous. 'It's not your fault,' he says and shakes his head in amazement. 'I chose to come. I wanted to be with you both. I wanted a holiday. You having that accident opened my eyes, you know? You can't think like that, Hope.' He says all this in a drunken way, but he means it. He crosses towards me. 'You getting better is worth losing my job for.'

'Losing?'

'Yeah.' He nods vigorously, his face red. 'You know, if I did lose it.'

'You won't lose it.'

'Come here.' He attempts to enfold me in a hug but ends up missing me and walloping his hip off the side of the table.

'Bloody hell, that hurts.'

I'm so glad he's back.

16

JULIE GIVES ADAM a huge hug when she sees him the next day. He and I are up early and munching on some stale bread. He looks tired and hungover, as if he hasn't slept and I probably look the same. I awoke at some weird hour in the morning after having the most horrendous dream about the crash. This time, I was being shoved away and pushed hard and things were hurtling towards me and falling down on top of me. I woke up, sweating, right down at the bottom of the sleeping bag. I'd been a bit afraid to go back to sleep after it.

So, I'd done what Tim suggested. I'd got up, found a stray piece of paper and a pen and written down an alternative ending to the dream. Even recalling the dream had left me quite shaken, but I had. Then, I'd changed it. In my imaginary dream, the things falling on top of me were soft and gentle and weren't hurting me. They were pillows, things that would give me a good night's sleep.

Adam manages a pretty convincing smile when Julie waltzes downstairs. She's tired looking too and her hair is messed up. 'Hey,' he grins. 'Good night?'

'Adam!' She flings her arms about him and then, holding him away from her, she scolds, 'Why didn't you return any of my calls?'

'I had a lot on, sorry.'

'That's not good enough.' She sounds quite cross. 'Hope and I, we thought you'd done something stupid.'

'Yeah, I took off to Kerry and didn't tell my boss.'

'No. You know what I mean. We were so worried.' She sits down beside him and stares up at him. 'Only for the fact that I'm so glad to see you, I'd ignore you for the rest of the holiday.'

'Sounds tempting.'

I excuse myself as Adam starts to tell Julie what he'd told me last night.

I'm just emerging from the shower when I see him. Logan is tramping across our garden and to my horror I see he has a bunch of wild flowers in his hand. *My* wild flowers. I'd forgotten all about them and now he's going to present me with them and Julie and Adam will know that I've been in his house.

Then I think, so what? What's wrong with me being in his house?

The answer of course is nothing, but if there was nothing wrong with it, then why didn't I mention it? That's what they'll ask. Why didn't you tell us, Hope? Why did you forget to tell us that you'd been in Logan's house? I thought you hated him.

Oh God! I watch hopelessly as he gets nearer and nearer the back door. I want to call out but as I'm standing in nothing but my tracksuit trousers and bra, I can't. My clean T-shirt is blowing about on the line and I never brought it in with me. It had still been damp and I thought that maybe another ten minutes in the sun would dry it.

Fool, I curse myself.

Frantically, I scrabble about for my pyjama top and can't find the stupid thing. I poke my head out again and he's about three feet from the door.

Shit! Shit! Shit!

'Logan!' I yell. 'Over here!'

He stops and turns towards my voice.

'Over here,' I call. I still can't find my top. How far can it go in a bathroom?

Logan begins to walk towards me and I hastily slam the bathroom door closed.

'Hello?' he says hesitantly.

'Out in a minute.' I force the panic from my voice.

And there it is, drowning in a pool of water. I pick it up, squeeze it out and pull it over my head. Yeuch.

'Hi,' I say breezily, opening the door and running my fingers through my hair. It's a bit embarrassing, emerging from a bathroom to talk to a guy you hardly know. I'm a bit anally retentive like that, so I say, 'I was just having a shower.'

'Yeah . . .' his upper lip rises in a smirk: 'with your clothes on and everything.' And then he looks at my clothes and he grins a bit more. 'Wow, is that true then?' He nods at the slogan on my pyjamas.

Honestly, why do pyjama manufacturers do that? Why do they think it's cute or funny to have messages scrawled over pyjama tops? Mine says, *I think this is hot*, with the 'hot' written in big tall letters. There is a picture of a chilli beside it. And I'd bought the pyjamas in the mistaken belief that it was an innocent message about chillis. But Julie, ever the wise one and always looking for the unsaid in the English language, pointed out to me that the chilli was in fact a very phallic symbol and that it also rhymed with *that* particular part of the male anatomy. I'd been a little shocked but mostly disbelieving and had continued to wear my suggestive attire. Logan's mind obviously worked on the same one track as Julie's.

'Have you never tasted a chilli then?' I ask innocently, looking at Logan.

'Nope.' His grin has broadened out. 'But I did hear that women prefer the bigger ones.'

I'm left with my mouth open. I can't think of a reply. Logan reaches out his free hand and gently puts his finger under my chin and before I'm aware of it, he's closing my mouth! 'Your flowers from yesterday.' He holds them out to me with an exaggerated gallantry.

'You didn't have to.' But I take them from him all the same. My face is flaming red, I'm sure of it.

'Oh I did,' Logan nods in an infuriatingly smug way. 'I also heard that when a woman leaves something behind her, it's a signal that she wants it brought back as an excuse to see the person again.'

'You're listening to the wrong people,' I scoff as I attempt to march by him.

'I added a few flowers of my own to the bouquet,' he calls after me. 'Yours was a bit pathetic – the colours were all wrong.'

'I was wondering what the pansies were doing in it all right,' I retaliate. 'Now I know.'

'They're not pansies,' he says patronisingly. 'They're –'

'Who's out there?' Julie pokes her head out the kitchen door. 'Oh, hi Logan,' she beams. 'Come to paint?'

'No he hasn't.' I attempt to go by her and close the door on him.

'Just came to bring Hope back the flowers she left at my place yesterday.'

Now Julie's mouth is open. She gawps at me as I stalk in past her.

'She was in your place yesterday,' she says. 'When?'

'I wasn't actually *in* it,' I attempt to explain before he can make matters worse. 'I more or less had to go in as I was tired from my walk.'

'That's it,' Logan spreads his arms wide. 'She was tired and so she had a cup of coffee and a chat, and what an entertaining companion she is. Full of put-downs and *joie de vivre.*'

Julie giggles and then at my expression stops and starts up again. 'She's great really,' she says, flustered.

'Yeah, I thought that too,' Logan nods. 'I'm a bit upset as I only gave her a cup of coffee. I would have given her a chilli if I'd known she liked them,' he goes on in a mock-regretful voice.

Julie guffaws loudly.

'It depends on whose chilli it is,' I say, grinning. 'Yours would probably be too small.'

Julie laughs again.

'I can work on growing it bigger.'

'Oh,' I say, feigning disgust as I move from the door. Julie thinks he's hilarious altogether and I leave her to talk to him while I busy myself looking for a mug to put the flowers in. They do look nice with the extra ones he has added and when I put them on the windowsill they add a lovely splash of much-needed colour to the kitchen.

A couple of hours later, after Julie and Adam had become completely juvenile about my visit to Logan's, we head to the beach at Inch.

It's one of the nicest beaches in the area. You'd swear a

kid got a box of crayons and painted the sky bright blue, the sand pure gold and the cliffs bright green.

'I wonder if Logan's chilli is an Inch,' Julie says airily, as she spreads the rug from Adam's car on the sand.

I ignore her and plonk down, an edition of the *Dunport News* in my hand. Adam and Julie change into swimming gear and while Adam heads off down the beach to the water, Julie plasters herself in factor 2 and lies down. I put on sunglasses and start to read the paper. There's a big piece about the progress of the new hotel and of how Jack Dunleavy has commissioned lots of Irish companies to supply things for it. Suddenly, a drone in the distance causes me to freeze. It's an aeroplane. It's coming in across the sea and I see it without even looking for it. The sun glints on the steel and immediately, behind my sunglasses, I close my eyes. I can't help but think of all those people up there, staring down at me. I want to run but there is nowhere I can go. I'm out in the open. I shove my hands into my ears but Julie must have heard the plane too.

'Hope, it's a plane,' she says.

Since the session with Tim, I haven't actually seen any planes. This is the first one. But I wrote about my nightmare, I tell myself. I can't be expected to do everything all at once.

'I have to get out of here,' I breathe heavily. My eyes are still closed. 'Please Julie, let's go.'

'But Hope, you –'

'Julie!'

'Look up, Hope,' Adam says. He must have come back up from the sea. 'Look up and I'll count one second and you can look down.'

'I can't.' I stare fiercely downwards.

'Yes you can.' He takes off my sunglasses. 'Come on.'

'No.' I try to push past him.

I'm sure people are looking at the three of us. I don't care.

He grabs me by both arms. 'One second. Pretend it's something else you're looking at.'

'I can't.' The drone is getting louder; the plane is more or less overhead now. I'm sweating. 'Let me go!'

'I'll buy the wine for tomorrow night?'

'I can't drink. Please let me –'

'We'll stop teasing you about Logan?' Julie offers.

I don't think even that will tempt me.

'If you don't look you'll think, why didn't I do it? It was only one second. Come on, Hope.'

Adam sounds as if he thinks I can do it. And he's right, I will regret it. Steeling myself, I ask him to count. Slowly I drag my gaze away from the rug, up to Adam's legs, up to his blue swimming shorts and his encouraging gaze. Up past his butchered hair and on to the blue sky and the wispy clouds.

'There,' Adam points to the plane as it trails smoke in its wake. 'See it.'

I glance up, he counts to one and my gaze shoots down. I am wrecked.

'Well done!' It's as if I've won the lotto. 'Good girl!' He cheers a little and says, 'Next time two seconds.'

Julie claps her hands.

I have to take deep breaths. But I force myself to listen to its drone until I can't hear it any more. And I feel proud of myself. Probably for the first time ever.

Two more planes fly over that day and with Adam and Julie by my side, I steel my nerve and look at them. The third time, I don't feel as apprehensive. In fact, I manage to gaze at it for three seconds as Adam waves away at it like a loon, making me laugh. 'You're such a kid,' I joke.

'Don't remind me,' he smiles back, then says, 'I'll have you waving by the end of the holiday.'

In fact what happens is that when the fourth plane goes over, some kids beside us think it's a game and they join in waving. Then the little girl says to her brother, 'They're waving at me, not at you!'

And I laugh out loud.

17

ANOTHER WEEK, ANOTHER counselling session. Adam drives me this time and he's under instructions from Julie to buy some nice wine as she has decided to cook dinner for us on our return. Neither Adam nor I is too excited at that prospect.

I stand outside Tim's office, half afraid to go in. He seems to be shouting at someone. I knock and he yells out something; I think it's a 'come in', so I open the door. He's got his back to me and is on the phone. 'You are such a stubborn cow,' he hisses before turning to me and reddening. 'Eh, have to go, talk later.' He slams the phone down on a shrieking voice.

'I hope that's not the last person you treated,' I joke feebly.

He gives an equally feeble laugh and doesn't answer. Instead, he sits down and beckons me to do the same. Then he begins by asking me how I've got on in the past week. I find myself telling him that despite all my hard work, I have continued to wake up screaming at nights. I can't recall the dreams, I only remember the feeling of utter terror that I'm being suffocated.

'Did you try and change the ending of the dream?'
'Yes.'
'OK, well, keep reviewing your ending over and over

before you go to sleep, visualise it, tell yourself that you don't care if you have the nightmare, that you will deal with it. Get your mind into that sort of mode.' He flashes me a quick smile. 'It's like brainwashing yourself.'

I nod, then tell him about the work I've done listening to the planes. He's very pleased with that. 'OK,' Tim nods. 'You've done well, Hope. You can listen to a plane without running inside. I know it's still scary, but can't you see how well you're getting on?'

'Yeah.'

'What I want you to do for next week then is to work on the crisps. Try and see if you can just look at a packet without getting panicky. Then maybe get someone to rustle them. Then open them. Then smell them. Do it in small stages. If the anxiety for one step goes away, go on to the next step. If you find that you get very agitated, slow it down, come and talk to me about it, OK?'

'OK.'

'Now what I'm going to do with you this week –'

He is interrupted by the phone ringing. 'Sorry about this.' He picks it up and immediately I hear an angry voice yelling at him. Tim doesn't reply. He listens until the voice has run out of energy then says as pleasantly as he can, 'Thank you for your call. Your comments have been noted.' With that, he hangs up the phone.

Offering me no explanation, he re-starts his sentence but, as before, the phone rings. Tim flushes, then says, 'I'm just going to disconnect this, Hope, if you don't mind.' He pulls the lead out of the phone and looks very satisfied with himself. Then he continues as if nothing out of the ordinary has happened. 'As I was saying, what we're going to do this week is to work on relaxation exercises. I'm going to give you techniques you can use whenever you feel panicky or agitated. You can use these during your homework exercises and also during the exposure therapy I will carry out here.'

'OK.'

Tim looks like he could do with some relaxation himself, I think.

'Now you have to practise these exercises,' he continues, somewhat sternly.

'I will.'

He then proceeds to show me different ways of relaxing both my body and mind. 'You'll use these the next time you come,' he tells me. 'What I'm going to do in the next session is to create your first exposure tape. It'll be you describing your early memories of your mother's depression and as you talk about it, you will get anxious. If your anxiety reaches a level of ten, we'll stop and try to get you relaxed before beginning again. Does that make sense?'

'Yes.' I'm tempted now to cancel the next session but I know Julie and Adam won't let me. And I suppose, if push came to shove, I wouldn't let myself either. It's strange, but being able to conquer my fear of the aeroplanes has brought me back in touch just a little. By facing the fear, I know I can face other things.

Tim goes over and over the relaxation techniques with me and then makes out a step by step chart of how I should deal with the 'crisp' issue. God, it sounds so trivial but it's not. Everywhere I go, people munch on cheese and onion. I can't stop going out just because of the smell of them, can I?

The hour ends very quickly and as I leave, Tim tells me that the next time we will have an hour and a half. 'This day next week,' he says.

I see him reconnect the phone and immediately it rings. He looks furious as he answers it.

Julie has invited Logan to dinner. 'He was passing and he looked hungry,' she says.

And, as dinner progresses, I realise that he is hungry. Starving, in fact. Any man that can ingest meat that looks like the remains of an abattoir fire has got to be ravenous.

'Nice one,' Logan says, polishing off his last potato. 'God, it's ages since I had a decent meal.'

'And after today, it'll be even longer,' Adam chortles as he cracks open more wine. Julie throws a spoon at him from across the table.

Adam pours wine for everyone as I get up to fill my glass with water.

'So you really don't drink,' Logan calls after me. 'I thought you were fooling me that day in my house.'

'No challenge in fooling a fool,' I say back as the water splashes into my glass. The water up here is lovely.

'Hope drinks all right,' Julie says. 'She just can't at the moment.'

I freeze. Water runs over the top of the glass and on to my hand. What did she have to say that for?

'Why not at the moment?'

A pause before Julie babbles, 'Oh, well, eh . . .' Her voice dies out to be replaced by an awkward silence.

'Did I just put my foot in it?' I hear Logan ask.

'No,' I call from the kitchen, turning off the tap. I steel myself and come back into the room. All three look at me. 'I can't drink because I'm having counselling about the accident.'

'Yeah?'

'Yeah. I'm still a bit freaked out by certain things, so the counsellor told me that it was best not to drink.'

'That's rough,' Logan nods sympathetically and for once there is no joke behind his remarks.

'Yeah,' I stare at my hands. 'But it'll get better.'

'Of course it will,' Julie gushes. 'No doubt about it!' I think she's trying to make up for her lack of discretion. 'Hope is a fighter! Isn't she, Adam?'

Adam nods silently.

'So, what things freak you out?' Logan asks.

God, I hadn't banked on him being quite so frank. 'Mainly guys shouting at me first thing in the morning,' I joke.

Logan smiles, tipping me a half-salute, '*Touché!*'

'You don't have to be in counselling for things to freak you out,' Julie says, over-compensating again for her remarks. 'It's normal, Hope, to be freaked out by certain things. Adam,' she pounces on him, 'what would freak you out?'

'Dunno.'

'Well, who would freak you out?'

Adam is pretty well on. Again. He thinks deeply before saying, 'Well, when I was sixteen, I had a breakdown.'

'Where?' Julie says. 'On the motorway or something?'

'A mental breakdown,' Adam says without a trace of his usual discomfiture. He's going to die in the morning, I think. And it won't be from a hangover. 'I had a breakdown and my mother took me to counselling. And I told that guy everything. I'd hate to meet him again. It'd be so embarrassing.'

Julie looks gobsmacked. I don't think she was expecting that. 'Right – OK – Logan?'

'I'm not finished,' Adam says grumpily. 'I'd also hate to meet his secretary, I had a crush on his secretary and made a fool of myself. I'd also hate to meet the blokes in the store who said I didn't send on that e-mail and I'd also hate to meet –'

'That's a lot of people,' Julie says uneasily.

'Mmm.' Adam nods and nods and fills up his glass again.

He's been in a strange mood since he got back from London.

'Logan?' Julie asks.

Logan is not so drunk as the other two but he's getting there. He's got no respect for wine, tossing it back as if it's water. 'My ex,' he grins a little but it doesn't quite meet his eyes.

'Why?' Julie asks.

'Well, because she's my ex,' Logan shrugs. 'Not a nice business meeting your ex.'

'Oh I dunno,' Julie says airily. 'I always like to meet my exes when I'm done up and show them what they missed out on. I quite like that, actually.'

'Well, my ex only missed out on a rented bungalow in the middle of nowhere.'

'Ah, but what a nowhere,' I say. 'Best nowhere view in the world.'

'True,' Logan agrees. 'But unlike your good and intelligent self, Hope, my ex thought it was the dingiest, most horrible place she'd ever been. We owned a house in Dublin and she wanted to move back but I didn't. She missed her beauty salons and her shops.' He's smiling but he sounds incredibly hurt.

'So you split up?'

'Yep. Acrimoniously.'

'That's awful,' Julie remarks.

'It was. But life goes on.' He doesn't sound as if he believes it.

'And now, me,' Julie says. 'Who would I hate to meet?' Another frown. Then a shrug. 'I can't think of anyone. God,' she smiles, 'I like everyone.'

'What about your dad?' Adam drawls.

Julie's face clouds over. 'Oh yeah.'

'And your mother?'

'Yes.' Julie sounds uncomfortable now.

'And your sister?'

'Yes, Adam, thank you. I think Logan has got the picture.'

I don't think Logan was even listening. He's swirling his wine about in his glass with a sad look on his face.

Later that evening, Julie whispers to me, 'Adam isn't gay after all.'

'Yeah? How do you know?'

'Well, he said he fancied his shrink's secretary, didn't he?'

'You can have a male secretary,' I answer. 'You're very sexist.'

'Oh yeah.' Her face falls. 'Never thought of that. Damn.'

18

'THERE,' JULIE POINTS him out to us. 'See that man by the gift shop, with the briefcase, that's him.'

Adam and I gape at this first glimpse of Julie's dad. He's tall, thin and grey haired. That's all we can see, for he has his back to us. He is peering into the gift shop window, oblivious to the three of us staring at him. He's carrying a brown leather briefcase which he is swinging from side to side.

'Oh God,' Julie starts to chew on a nail. 'Oh God, I feel sick.'

I slap Julie's hand away from her mouth. I know she can't bear ragged nails mainly because mine are in bits and she gives me awful grief over them. 'He looks fine,' I say, cocking my head to one side, 'and he seems quite calm.'

'It's always calm before a storm.' Julie hops from foot to foot. 'Oooh, I think I'll ring him and say I'm sick.'

'Come on.' Adam grasps a reluctant Julie by the elbow and steers her towards her dad. When we get close, he drops her arm and hoists himself up to his skinny six foot two. Julie's father looks suddenly shorter.

'Hi, Dad,' Julie says to his back, a fake smile failing to illuminate her face. 'I see you found the shop.'

He turns to face us. He doesn't look so bad, I think. He's quite a handsome man in an older person type of way.

Tanned, rugged features, bit of a beaky nose, but with Julie's sparkling slate grey eyes.

'Hello Juliet.' His smile is curt and efficient, his voice brisk and to the point. It's as if he's talking to a business partner. It makes me recoil slightly. His gaze flicks to me and Adam.

'My friends.' Julie indicates me. 'This is Hope. She was injured in the plane crash, the London to Boston one – remember?'

'Yes,' he nods at me. 'You're a lucky girl. Nice to meet you.'

His handshake is reassuring. Nice and firm.

'And this is Adam,' Julie says. 'He's another friend.'

'Hello, Adam,' Mr Adcock says. 'Are you the man with all the houses?'

'Mortgaged to the hilt, you mean,' Adam says pleasantly.

'No matter. Initiative, I like that. Don't I like that, Juliet?'

'Yes,' Julie says wearily. 'Initiative equals success.'

'Initiative equals success,' Mr Adcock repeats as he rocks back and forward on his heels. 'Well, it was nice to meet you two. I hope you don't mind if I take Juliet off you for lunch.'

We'd rehearsed this. Unfortunately acting isn't my strong point.

'Lunch?' Adam says. He sounds so natural. I'm impressed. 'We haven't had lunch either. D'you fancy lunch, Hope?'

'Yes I do,' I say. I sound like a five-year-old repeating a poem she has learned. 'I – am – starving.'

'Maybe we can join you?' Adam says. 'I bet Julie is taking you to the Store, because if she is, that's our favourite place to go too.'

Mr Adcock visibly balks. 'Well,' he tries to say pleasantly, 'I had hoped to have my daughter to myself. I haven't seen her in a while.'

'Aw, that's great,' Adam ignores Mr Adcock's last comment and grins. 'Let's go.'

He strides ahead of the man and I scamper to catch up with him.

'Shit, he made it clear he doesn't want us there. Julie assured us that that wouldn't happen,' Adam hisses at me from the side of his mouth.

'And you made it clear that we're going anyway,' I say back out of the side of my mouth. 'Well done.'

He doesn't look so sure.

The Store is madly expensive. It's OK for Julie, her dad is paying for her, but for Adam and me, it's a different story. I think I can just about afford a lettuce leaf, while Adam's funds stretch to a sandwich.

'I thought you said you were both starving.' Mr Adcock looks sourly at our meagre plates.

'I am.' Adam rubs his stomach and says with a forced joviality, 'My favourite food is sandwiches.'

I'd laugh only Mr Adcock is making me nervous. No wonder Julie is scared of him.

'And Hope can only eat small portions at a time,' Julie chimes in, obviously not trusting me to come up with my own lie. 'Because of the operation.'

'What operation?' Julie's dad asks me.

'On my head,' I say.

Julie rolls her eyes. It's obviously the wrong answer.

'How would an operation on your head stop you from eating?' He seems genuinely interested. 'I've never heard of that before.'

'Oh,' I stare at my minuscule lunch. 'I can't remember all the details. It's all a bit fuzzy.'

'Mmm.' Mr Adcock stares at me for a moment, making me even more uncomfortable. Then he turns his attention to his dinner and attacks it with relish. Julie barely touches hers; she keeps giving him sideways glances and she can't seem to sit still.

The minutes tick past and no one says a word. Adam finishes his sandwich and I finish my tiny salad. Mr Adcock clears his plate and Julie plays with her food. More minutes pass and eventually the four of us are staring at each other and no one is saying anything. Mr Adcock has begun to look at Adam and me expectantly, as if he'd like us to leave, which I'm sure he would. Only Julie is almost imperceptibly shaking her head at us.

'So, eh, Mr Adcock, what are you doing over here?' My voice is a squeak. I fiddle with my fork.

'Attempting to have lunch with my daughter,' he says back. Quite rudely, I think.

'Oh,' I flush. 'I meant, work wise. Julie said you were over on business.'

'Medical conference,' he says abruptly.

'Dad is a surgeon,' Julie offers. 'Very well known. Very successful.'

'Oh, good for you,' I say lamely.

Mr Adcock acknowledges the compliment.

More silence.

Adam shuffles a bit. For all his brave talk, he doesn't seem to know what to say now. I cough and tell myself that I will not be the first to break. I will not be the first to break. I will not be the first to break.

'Oh Dad, just tell me why you're here!'

Adam and I jump.

Julie is staring desperately at her father. 'Go on, tell me.'

'To see you,' her father says evenly. 'To talk to you.'

'Well, talk then,' she says and I think she has decided to dive right in, for which I am secretly relieved. We could have been sitting there all afternoon otherwise. 'You can say what you want in front of Adam and Hope,' Julie continues. 'They're my friends.'

Mr Adcock shifts uncomfortably in his seat and fixes Julie with a steely glare. 'I don't think I want to discuss this in front of them.'

'Really?' Julie raises her eyebrows. 'Were you planning on discussing how I threw my career away?'

'If you want to put it like that, yes!' Her father nods, his gaze sweeping the table. 'Yes, I was.'

'Newsflash: I didn't throw anything away.' I have to admire Julie. Her voice shakes only slightly and she's maintaining the semblance of a smile as she speaks. 'I am a teacher, Dad. I teach children. I will always teach children because it's what I want to do.' She pauses and her voice rises a little. 'I do not want to be Angela.'

'Will you keep your voice down,' he snaps. 'No one is asking you to be Angela. And why didn't you tell your mother you were going away if you thought there was nothing wrong with it?'

'Because of this!' Julie spreads her hands wide. 'You. Your reaction.'

'I have done nothing bar have lunch with you and your friends.'

'Oh come on,' Julie's voice rises some more. 'You're only here because Mum sent you.'

'I am here because I am on business,' her dad matches her. 'But yes, your mother is upset. She feels that she has sacrificed herself to give you and your sister the best education she could, and how do you repay her? You take off without telling her.'

'And what about what I sacrificed for you,' Julie says and throws her knife down on the table where it bounces a little before landing in front of me. I don't know where to look and neither does Adam. Everyone else does: they are all staring over at us. From the corner of my eye I see a little man bustling across the room. 'I sacrificed my friends so I could study and be what you both wanted. I sacrificed my childhood to be a bloody swot and for what? For nothing.'

'Excuse me,' the manager tries to intervene. 'You can't really argue in here. We are trying to create a special ambience —'

'It's nothing because you didn't go for it,' her dad says back. He doesn't look so handsome now. A big cross line has appeared between his eyebrows. 'You could have been anything and you chose teaching so don't blame us for your nothing.'

'An ambience of calm, an oasis of —'

'The nothing is the fact that I have nothing from you. No childhood memories, no holidays unless they were to educational places, no funny times, no joy.'

'Folks,' Adam stands up.

'— peace. And we ask all our customers to —'

'I'm not sitting here taking this from you!' Mr Adcock bellows furiously, all composure gone now. 'How dare you speak to me like that!'

'Dad, I'm not scared of you or Mum any more. Another reason I never told her I was gone was because I was scared. I was scared of your reaction. Well, now I've had it, it's not so scary.'

'— respect that. So please —'

'Oh shut up,' Mr Adcock snarls at the manager. He throws a pile of notes down on the table and then jabbing his finger at Julie, says, 'We never scared you, don't try and put that on us.' He starts to leave the table.

'Oh yes you did! Do you know when you couldn't figure out how your car had the big scratch on it? Well, Dad, it was me. I accidentally scraped it with my bike, but I couldn't tell you because I was so bloody scared. Do you remember the time when –'

But he has gone.

Julie stands there for a second before swaying and bursting into tears.

'If I'd known your dad was going to pay, I'd have had a bigger dinner,' Adam says a little later, as we sit in a dark, old-man's pub. 'I'm so hungry, I could even eat something that you've cooked, Ju.'

Julie slaps him absently and picks up a beer mat. She begins tearing it to pieces. 'I'm sorry about the scene,' her voice wobbles. 'I didn't know that was going to happen. I thought, I don't know, that he'd,' she crumbles the cardboard between her fingers, 'well, I don't know what I thought.'

Adam looks at me over her head.

'You did the right thing, Ju,' I say. 'Only thing is, what happens now?'

Julie shrugs. 'Well, I'm not apologising. I did nothing wrong.'

'Just, you know, don't lose contact.'

'Are you joking?' Adam says playfully. 'If that was my dad, I'd run very fast in the opposite direction.'

Julie's giggles turn into sniffs and soon she's crying again.

'He's not so bad,' she says tearfully. 'But I just, well I just can't put up with it any more. Their rules, their expectations. I just can't.'

'Aw, come on, Ju.' I watch, in a sort of detached way that scares me, as Adam takes her face between his hands and wipes her tears away with his thumb. Then he lays her head against his chest and runs his long hands up and down her hair while making drinking signals with his free arm.

I head up to the bar, glad to be able to do something to help. Adam is a lot better at the touchy-feely stuff now for some reason, while I, who was never fantastic but who would have been able to hug a friend, am floundering.

As I look at him murmuring gently to her and her smiling back at him, I vow that I will get back to the land of the living if it kills me. For no matter how bad Julie is feeling, it's a hell of a lot better than not feeling anything at all.

I bring the drinks down to the table. Three oranges. Julie is still snuggled up in Adam's arms and they look nice together, in a friendly sort of way. 'D'you know something, Ju, your dad can give out all he wants about you, but he really can't afford to. He's not exactly a hot-shot doctor himself, is he?'

'Isn't he? Why?'

'Well,' I sit down and take a sip of my orange, 'he'd never heard of the "eat-less-head-operation", had he? I mean, come on, who hasn't heard of that?'

Her laughter is definitely my best medicine.

19

TIM IS NOT pleased with me at all. 'So you haven't exposed yourself to crisps?' he says.

I'm not in the habit of exposing myself to packets of crisps, I could say, but I haven't the nerve. He really isn't impressed with me and I feel a little ashamed of myself too. 'It's just that some friends of mine have been upset recently and I kind of forgot about it.'

Tim raises his eyebrows. 'Now look, Hope –'

'I'm sorry, OK. I'll try it for the next week.'

Tim nods. 'Make sure you do. I really can't work with you if you're not going to put in the effort, Hope.'

'I've practised all the relaxation.' I attempt to gain some Brownie points. 'I'm ready to talk or whatever today.' Actually, I've been terrified of it, but now I'm afraid to admit that.

This at least elicits a small smile. 'Good.' Tim turns to his Dictaphone. 'Now Hope, I'll ask you questions as you talk. If you feel anxious, stop and relax. Let me know the quality of anxiety you are experiencing on a scale of one to ten, all right?'

I can only nod. Tim talks me through some relaxation so that by the time he switches on the recorder, I'm feeling very chilled.

'Right, Hope,' Tim talks slowly, 'you told me that when your father died your mother began to get depressed. What age were you?'

'Six, almost seven. My brother was about three.'

'And you also said,' he consults his notes, 'that you never got washed or went to school or anything. What was your mother doing?'

'Just lying in bed all day. She didn't sleep, I don't think, and she hardly ate.'

'And did anyone notice?'

'Eventually, yeah. I don't know how long later. It could have been days or weeks. I was only a kid, time meant nothing to us. I think it was because I wasn't turning up in school so they sent someone to the house. No one really called in on us after the first few weeks after the funeral so none of the neighbours knew, or maybe they did and they sent the woman who came, I never really found out.'

'And what happened then?'

I stop and take deep breaths. What happened then is vague, an impression mainly of people's reactions to me and Jamie.

'Take your time,' Tim says, 'you're doing really well. Are you feeling anxious?'

'A little.' I concentrate on my breath, listening to it go in and out. 'Sorry,' I mutter. 'It's not so much what happened, it's the way I remember it. It was so confusing, so weird and no one explained anything to us. And I don't know how Jamie felt, he was only three.'

'Take your time.'

'OK.' I let a long slow breath out and continue: 'People came and talked to us. They took my mother away, they brought me and Jamie to a centre somewhere, they weighed us, washed us, talked about us. Next thing we know, we're in a new house with a new family.'

'And did no one explain that it was temporary or tell you what was happening?'

I shrug. 'They probably did, but all I could focus on was that they'd taken Mammy away. And Jamie . . .' My eyes fill up, I blink my tears away. I try to breathe again. 'Well, Jamie, he cried a lot and wouldn't talk. It went on for weeks, so one day I kept pretending to think he was a girl and giving him a doll to play with and he eventually got really mad and told me to go away or something. It was the happiest day of my life.'

'That must have been awful.'

I shrug.

'And did you see your mother during this time?'

'After a while, they let us visit her. I don't know if it was a good idea. Jamie cried for hours when he had to go back to the foster home. I was the only one who could comfort him.'

'Big responsibility?'

'I didn't mind.' My voice is sharp. 'He was a good boy. I didn't mind at all.'

'You're doing well, Hope. So what happened then? Did your mother come home?'

'Yeah.' Suddenly I feel really numb. 'My mother was cured then and we went home and my brother was thrilled.'

'And you?'

'I, well,' I run my tongue around my lips, he's going to think I'm awful now. Here it comes. 'I was happy but not happy.'

'Can you tell me why?'

'Do I have to?'

'If you think it'll help.'

I scrunch up my eyes and try to explain it better. 'I was angry at her for making me ashamed, for not being like other mothers and I was furious and jealous too. Jealous of the way my brother loved her. I'd been the one who minded him.' I bite my lip. 'Though it wasn't her fault, I suppose. She couldn't help it.'

'Neither could you.'

'I could have been happier. I don't think I talked to her for a week.'

'You couldn't help the way you felt and it's healthier to express it. Look what's happening now when you're trying to avoid feeling.'

I'd never thought of it like that before. It's a kind of relief. 'I suppose so.'

'So your relationship with your mother changed, did it?'

'Yeah. I couldn't trust her not to leave us again. My whole childhood was spent trying to keep her from feeling sad. To keep her with us. I tried to control everything. I thought if I kept her happy, we'd all be happy and I was stupid enough to think it would work.' The bitterness in my voice surprises me.

'You were a child. That's the way children think. It's too scary for them otherwise.'

'Well,' I glare at Tim, though I don't know why I'm doing it. 'When she got sick again, I ignored it for ages.'

'She got depressed again?'

Jesus, I think. My life sounds awful. He must think I'm a real sad case.

'After a good few years. Like, we were OK for ages.'

'And what happened then?'

I swallow hard. Without even realising I'm doing it, I start

182

rubbing my hand really hard across my face. 'She got sick,' is all I can manage.

'Is this upsetting you?' he asks gently.

I can't even talk or react. I'm sweating now. And breathing hard. 'I'll be fine in a minute.'

'It's OK. You can leave it for now. Relax, OK. Take deep breaths. It's fine.'

He waits for a little while and I feel myself return to normal. I don't know what happened there, I was doing great, telling him about my life. Relaxing. I manage a grin of sorts.

'What's the anxiety like now?' he probes.

'It's bad, at least an eleven.'

Tim allows himself a small smile. 'OK, we'll leave it there for today. Now Hope,' he says as he ejects the tape from the recorder, 'I want you to listen to this over the weekend as many times as you can. The idea is that you become almost immune to it, that instead of it upsetting you so much, it just becomes a memory. A sad memory, but just a memory. I think you'll be fine with it: despite your anxiety, you've coped well. I want you to come back to me on Monday, we'll gauge how you're getting on and maybe take it a bit further, if that's OK? And I want you, in your mind, to replay the next part of your story, even the beginning of it, just to help you get a handle on telling it. We can take as long as you want over it. Just remember, it's a memory, it can do you no harm. Yes, it seems to have upset you but you have survived.'

Surviving is a lot more than just being alive, I feel like saying.

'Of course, surviving is a lot more than existing,' he says. 'We all get damaged as we go through life, our perception changes. Yours unfortunately changed radically at a very young age, we have to address that.'

'OK.' I take the tape from the desk and put it in the pocket of my jacket.

'And here?' Tim pulls out another recorder from a drawer in his desk. 'I don't suppose you packed a Dictaphone when you decided to come on holiday.'

I grin. 'No, and I forgot I'd need one to listen to the tape.'

'Very disturbed thinking,' Tim teases gently. He checks that the Dictaphone is working and shows me how to operate it. 'Now, see you Monday and I want to hear some progress on the crisps.'

'I promise,' I say.

Julie is determined to help me with the whole crisp issue. I think she needs a diversion; she's been so miserable since she met her father. Nelson is only visiting at weekends, so she doesn't even have him to escape with and Adam and I are just a reminder of what happened that day. I think it's awful that her parents haven't been in touch since, but then again, she hasn't rung them either.

'So I just show you a packet of crisps, is that it?' she asks.

'Basically yes. That's the first step.' I feel good. Calm.

Adam bids us goodbye as he trots upstairs to his laptop. Julie has taken to christening it his lapdog because she says that Adam is pathetic to be working still for a company that has suspended him. Adam never bothers to defend himself, but I think she hurts him.

'One packet of crisps.' Julie duly waves a packet of Tayto Cheese and Onion in front of me.

I feel surprisingly OK. A slight increase in heart rate but

that's only nerves. 'Now shake them, make them make a noise,' I say, consulting the steps Tim has drawn up for me. Julie shakes them, scrunches the packet between her hands. 'All right?'

'Yeah.' My heart is hammering now. I don't want her to see it. If I can only get over this, I think, I'll definitely get better. 'Now,' my voice trembles as I look at the list, 'open the crisps.'

It's like looking at a soon to be car crash. Even if I wanted to I couldn't tear my eyes away. As Julie pulls open the crisps I see every little tear along the opening slowly revealing what's inside the packet. Deep breaths, I tell myself, deep breaths. They're only bloody crisps, for God's sake. But it's no use. I can't stand it. I think I'm going to die. In. Out. In. Out. My breath is coming too fast.

'Hope?' Julie's voice comes from far away. 'Hope?'

I bolt for the door, wrench it open and run right into the centre of the front garden, Julie following behind. 'Are you OK? Hope?'

The terror is receding now. The urge to run seems ridiculous when looked at logically. 'I'll be fine.' I sit down on the grass. It's warm. 'Sorry.' I rub my hands through my hair, pulling it, feeling the pain of it. It helps bring me back. 'Sorry.'

Julie sits beside me. 'No need to be sorry. We just did too much too soon, I reckon.' Breathe. In. Out. In. Out.

'Like, imagine you were scared of water, would you go from the shallow end to the deep in under three minutes?'

Her perception pulls me right back. 'No, I guess not.'

'Well then,' she nudges me. 'We'll start over. Take out the crisps for about two days and when you feel you can really cope with that, we'll move on – how about it?'

She's so good. There she is with massive family problems and she still cares about me. What did I ever do right to deserve her?

'Sounds good to me.'

20

I T'S SATURDAY NIGHT, early July, and the three of us are getting ready to go out. We're only going to Lynch's in Dunport. I haven't been there since I pretended to be an American, but tonight, whatever happens, I'm determined to be Hope Gardner.

To be honest, I don't really want to go out, but Adam has persuaded me to come along as he doesn't want to be on his own with just Julie and Nelson and all Nelson's friends that he's bringing down from Dublin. I tell him that Logan is going, but he says he still needs me there. I think it's a ploy to get me out; the two are afraid to leave me on my own. Julie was more freaked out by my panic attack than she let on.

She comes into the front room now and surveys me in my casual attire of jeans and a T-shirt. 'Are you putting any make-up on, Hope?' she asks almost accusingly. She looks amazing. Yes, she is wearing jeans and a shirt too, but on Julie the clothes look like they're celebrating. And her make-up is cool. She's lathering on lip gloss now and the result is fabulous shiny pouty lips.

'D'you want some?' She sees me gawking and holds the lipstick out to me. 'Go on, you've nice lips, they're kind of like Angelina Jolie's.'

I take the gloss from her and copy what she has done. It's hard, as she's hogging the hand mirror.

Julie looks at me with narrowed eyes. Gently she takes the gloss from me and studies my face. 'Eye shadow,' she pronounces, 'you need brown eye shadow – let me do it, would you?'

'Aw no, I'm not wearing make-up, I just wanted to try it out.' I go to wipe my lips clean but she squeals and grabs at my hand.

'Don't rub it off, it's made a huge difference to you,' she chastises. 'No, come on, a bit of eye shadow won't hurt.'

I suppose it won't and anyway, I don't want to be the only girl not wearing make-up. If Nelson is anything to go by, the whole lot of his friends, men and women, will be image conscious. Plus Julie is discreetly plastered in the stuff. 'Right.' I sit down on the sofa and Julie gives a little cheer that makes me smile. She scrabbles about in her well worn make-up bag and with the air of a pro scrutinises millions of shades of eye shadow. She chooses a smoky brown and a grey.

'You seem in better form,' I remark as I close my eyes.

'A little.' She smudges some colour on my lids. 'It's awful what happened, but I'm free now to an extent. And I've got you and my other friends in London. What is it they say? Friends are the family you'd choose for yourself?'

I like that. It's true. Me, Julie and Adam are a family of sorts.

Julie begins to mix the colours on my lids.

'I don't think your mam and dad would like me much.'

'Are you joking?' Julie says a little bitterly. 'They'd love you!'

'Yeah?'

'Yeah! Against you I look great. You're unemployed. They'd encourage our friendship, that's for certain.' She stands back and surveys me. 'Some eyeliner now,' she says, searching her bag again. 'When my parents tried to make me into this showpiece daughter, they were damn lucky I didn't go in completely the opposite direction and learn nothing.'

'Why didn't you?' I had learned nothing in school but that was because my mother took no interest in me. I thought maybe I'd get her attention that way. And there was Julie with an abundance of attention and she hated it.

'Because I knew what I wanted to do, that's why. And I wasn't going to let them with all their pretence and snobbery put me off. Now, eyes up.'

I look upward and feel her pencilling my eyelids. It's a horrible sensation.

'You should think about what you want, Hope. I haven't heard you talk about your mother since, but you should really keep up the contact now it's been re-established.'

I shrug and Julie squeals as her pencil veers off course.

'Sorry.' I wait while she fixes up my eyes before saying, 'I probably will. I mean, I don't know if I'll visit her again but I'll call and write. I need time. It's funny, I find it hard to see her as, you know, *capable*. It's like she's a different person.'

'Yeah well, she probably is. A better, stronger person. You should give her another chance. It's important to make the best of things, for you.'

'Did you practise that speech?' I tease, feeling a little touched.

'Look.' She holds up the mirror for me to look at myself and I have to say, it is a bit of a transformation. My eyes

189

look huge in my round face. In fact they look so big, my face actually looks smaller. And my lips are fab.

'Use whatever you have to make the best of things,' Julie says, patting her make-up bag. 'You know what I'm saying.'

Then she turns towards the stairs and yells for Adam to come down.

How did she ever become so bloody wise and clever?

The Shamrocks are playing really loudly as we enter. Nelson and his friends have taken over a corner of the pub and have a major amount of drink lined up in front of them. As we enter a huge cheer goes up and Julie waves back at them.

'Oh, everyone is looking at us!' she laughs.

I keep my head down as the bar staff look over. Still, with the crowd jammed into the pub it'd be hard for them to spot me. I manoeuvre myself in between Logan, who has come with us in the taxi, and Adam so that they block me from view.

'Hiya babe.' Nelson pats the seat beside him for Julie to sit down.

Babe? Oh God. The man gets worse.

'Hiya.' Julie plants a kiss on his lips and he ruffles her hair. I don't know what she sees in Nelson really – he's kind of false looking with his massive arms and his huge bulk. He's not that friendly to Adam and me either, though, I think, surveying the crowd around the table, he must have something going for him to have so many friends of his own. There are at least five men, none of whom look as beefy as Nelson. Some are passably good-looking, and all seem quite friendly. There's a few women too, as done up as they can possibly be, and I see one or two of them eye up Adam as he sits down. Or maybe it's Logan, I can't be sure. Nelson introduces us and they all shout out a hello before turning back to their drinks and the music. I sit in beside Julie and Logan sits beside me. Adam sits opposite us. Then a girl, quite pretty, joins the table, having bought some drinks at the bar. She hands them around before searching for a place to sit. I think we must have taken her seat. She ends up squeezing beside Adam. 'Hi, we haven't met,' she says, holding out her hand. 'I'm Kate.'

'Great,' Adam shakes her hand.

'And you are?' Kate looks at him with amused eyes.

'Oh, yes, sorry. Adam. I'm Adam.'

'Oh, I love that accent,' Kate says pleasantly. 'All sort of posh. Are you posh?'

'Eh,' Adam actually ponders this. 'I suppose if you call growing up in Kensington posh, then I could be considered such, yes. But I don't feel posh.'

'No, that's David Beckham's job,' the girl jokes.

Adam doesn't get it. I cringe for the poor girl as her laughter splutters out like a dying car engine.

'Good joke,' I offer feebly.

She smiles at me and stares into her glass. Adam looks away from her, seeming very uneasy. Kate asks him something else and he makes a tepid reply. I can't bear to look, so I turn to Logan, who's watching the exchange with amusement.

'He could be in there,' Logan whispers to me. 'What's wrong with him?'

'He's not himself in the last while,' I defend him. I remember suddenly what Julie said all those weeks ago, about Adam being gay. Maybe he is. He's dying a death in front of that poor girl. He just can't seem to be his funny, charming self and I can't even think of a way to intervene and save him. But aren't gay men good with women? Nah, I dismiss that as a pathetic stereotype.

'Is that Nelson, the guy Julie was on about on the way here?' Logan's breath is warm on my ear.

'Yes,' I say back. 'Quite a specimen, eh?'

'Christ!'

'He'd like to think so,' I joke and Logan laughs, showing me his even white teeth.

'Hey, Hope, Nelson is buying,' Julie calls. 'What are you having?'

'An orange, thanks, Nelson.'

'Logan?' Julie asks.

'Carlsberg.'

'And Adam?'

Adam jumps and wipes a hand over his face. 'Sorry, what?'

'If we can tear you away from Kate,' Julie smiles, 'what are you having?'

'Kate hopes he's having her, isn't that right, Kate?' Nelson booms out heartily.

'Oh shut up, Nelson,' Kate snaps. 'I'm only being friendly.' She gets up and finds a spot among her other friends.

'I'll eh, have a Guinness,' Adam says, sounding despondent.

Nelson glares at Kate as he stands up. Almost upending the table, he squeezes his way past us to the bar.

'So, that's the famous Nelson,' Logan says to Julie.

'No, that's not him,' I say. 'He was killed years ago. That's Julie's Nelson.'

'Ha! Ha!' Julie makes a face at me. 'Yes Logan,' she clarifies, 'that's him.'

'Big bloke.'

Julie nods. 'That's because he owns a gym, he does a lot of weights.'

'What gym?' Logan asks. 'My sister has worked in loads of gyms in Dublin – she's a fitness instructor.'

Julie shrugs, 'I don't know, he showed me photos of it, but he didn't tell me the name.' She turns to his friends, 'Hey, what's the name of Nelson's gym?'

There follows a bit of a debate, which is odd, you'd imagine they'd know the name of their friend's business. But then again, maybe they're his football buddies or something. Eventually they settle on 'Northsiders Gym'.

'Ring a bell?'

Logan shrugs. 'Nah. But maybe he knows her. Debbie Jones.'

Just then, the Shamrocks begin to play again, drowning out all conversation.

'Adam, you love this song,' I say and kick him under the table.

'Yeah.'

Nelson bangs my orange down in front of me.

'Thanks, Nelson.'

'No problem.' He gives out the rest of the drinks and then goes and sits beside Julie again.

'Did a Debbie Jones ever work at your gym?' Julie asks Nelson. 'She's Logan's sister.'

'A fitness instructor?' Logan offers.

Nelson shakes his head and I miss his reply because abruptly Adam stands up from the table, taking his drink with him, and disappears into the crowd.

'Where's he gone?' I ask.

No one bothers to reply. I wonder if I should go after him, but maybe he's just gone to get a better view of the woeful Shamrocks. That's the sort of anorak thing Adam would do.

After about twenty minutes, Adam still hasn't come back. I'm a little worried about him now, which is stupid, I suppose, he's a grown man, but he really hasn't been himself since he got suspended from his job. In order to have a look for him without being too obvious about it, I offer to go to the bar for drinks.

'Anyone want a drink?'

No one answers, they're all too busy chatting so I say it a bit louder and I'm met with a series of 'no's'.

'Right, excuse me.'

Logan has started to chat to one of Nelson's mates. They follow the same football team or something ridiculous like that. Anyway, they're bonding really well. Both of them are wearing the exact same T-shirts, red and white. That's how they found out, apparently.

I wish I followed something that I could bond with someone over but no one really chats about designing text for a website, do they? And even if they did, it would only mean that they're about as exciting as I am, which might not be a good thing. Thinking these saddo thoughts, I push my way to the bar, only to remember that I don't want either of the barmen brothers to see me. There are three barmen on tonight and I only hope the third one serves me. Every time Davey or Greg Lynch goes by, I dip my head. But of course, Greg eventually asks me what I want. I flirt with doing the whole American thing again and eventually chicken out.

'Orange,' I say as casually as I can.

'Hope Gardner,' he says, grinning widely in recognition

as he rests his hands on the bar top. 'I heard you were back – how you doing?'

'Fine.' Please don't ask about the last time I was in here, I silently pray. Please don't. 'Are you going to pretend to be an American tonight?' he asks. 'I can play along if you want me to.'

'No, no it's fine,' I laugh a little over the raucous roar of the Shamrocks, trying to pretend that disguising my voice and acting as if I'm someone else is perfectly normal. 'I only did it because I hadn't seen my mother and I didn't want her to hear I was about before I'd called in to her.'

'You could have just told Davey to keep it to himself,' Greg says, smiling.

'Yeah well,' I shrug, 'that wouldn't have been any fun, would it?'

'True,' he grins. I know he thinks I'm a total freak-head but sure so what? Nothing will have changed. 'So what are you having again?'

'An orange juice.'

'Wow. We'll make our fortune out of you,' he jokes as he gets a glass.

'Yep.'

'D'you want anything else?'

'No thanks.'

'You're not in on your own, are you?'

'No, I'm with a crowd.' I indicate the corner we're in.

'Oh. Right. It's great to see you again. I've a break coming up in a few minutes, can we catch up?'

Catch up? On what? What had I done except be in a plane crash? Still, Greg was a decent enough guy. 'OK. That'd be fun.'

I hand him the money for the drink but he waves it away. 'On the house!'

'Thanks.' I smile at him and just as I turn to leave, I spot Adam sitting on his own on a bar stool. He's gazing into his pint and looking as if he's just been told that he has PTSD or something.

'Hi, handsome.' I sidle up to him.

It's like I've electrocuted him. He jumps about a mile out of his seat. 'Oh you,' he mutters. 'Hi.'

The guy is smashed.

'How much have you drunk?'

'Not as much as I'm going to drink.' He grins wickedly and lifts his pint to his lips.

'And what are you doing here, why aren't you sitting with us?'

'Too many people there. That Nelson fella is like . . .' he frowns and thinks for a while, 'he's like King of the Friends.'

'What?'

Adam waves a hand at me and says a bit narkily, 'Go on, go away back to the table. I'll join you when we're going home.'

'What the hell is wrong with you?'

He lifts his face about an inch sideways and says with slurred deliberation, 'Go down to the table, see you later.'

'Fine.' I take my orange and leave. At least I know where he is. That's a relief of sorts.

Fifteen minutes later Greg comes down to the table. I stand up to let him in. 'Sit in, do,' I say and he sits in between Logan and me. Logan glances curiously at him, before ignoring him completely and resuming his boring chat about 'what's the greatest goal you've ever seen?'

196

'This is Greg,' I tell Julie and Nelson, who are the only inquisitive ones, it seems, 'he was in school with me.'

'When she bothered to come into school!' Greg jokes and I manage a laugh.

'Just cause you were a big swot,' I joke back.

'Well you were too up until about fifth year,' Greg says. He thumbs to me. 'I'm telling ye, this girl was the best one for English ever. You did everyone's English homework, d'you remember?'

'Yeah,' I nod. 'Two quid a shot.'

'You charged?' Julie sounds impressed. 'I would never have figured you for a businesswoman, Hope.'

'I'm good at English,' Nelson says. 'I speak it all the time.'

There's a bit of a silence as no one knows if Nelson is joking or not.

'Joke?' he quirks his eyebrow and then we laugh. In relief more than anything.

'This one here,' Greg nods at me. 'She went down in school folklore, didn't you?'

'Did I?' God, I hope he's not going to tell about the time I got thrown out of class for arguing with the history teacher. That was in sixth year, I'd been a bit mental that time.

'Yeah!' Greg says it as if I should know what he's talking about. 'The charity Countdown gig?'

God, I'd forgotten that.

'What happened?' Julie asks.

Greg looks at me and I shrug, 'You tell them.'

'You may not know it,' Greg says, as if he's building up to some big climactic story, 'but Hope is brilliant with words, right. I mean, totally freakily brilliant.'

I flush, embarrassed. 'Don't mind him.'

'Anyway, one year, they had this charity Countdown

competition in school based on the *Countdown* show on TV. Anyone could enter, it was mostly sixth-years and teachers. No one could believe it when Hope entered. What age were you?'

'I dunno. About fifteen, I think.'

'The idea was that everyone had to place a bet on who they thought would win before the competition started. Of course, everyone was betting on the teachers. So Hope told our class to bet on her, didn't you, Hope?'

I wince. This isn't exactly my proudest moment in life. 'I told my class to bet on me and if I won, they were to give me 50 per cent of their winnings and if they lost, I'd pay them back their initial bet.'

'We couldn't lose,' Greg grins at me. 'So we bet all we had on her. And she stormed into the final, didn't you?'

I shrug.

'And she was up against some geek from sixth year and she just blew him out of the water, she got two nine letter words, *two*, and because we'd all bet a pile of money on her, we cleaned out the bookies.'

I giggle in embarrassment at the memory. 'Fifty to one was the odds on me.'

Greg laughs. 'They had to use the charity money to pay us and Hope made a fortune.'

'And the charity?' Julie asks.

'Made nothing,' I flush, ashamed.

'Aw, God, Hope!' Julie doesn't know whether to laugh or be shocked.

'I didn't know that would happen,' I defend myself. 'I mean, the greedy little feckers put loads of money on me.'

'I had ten on her,' Greg nods. 'And I won five hundred.'

I don't tell them, but guilt had made me give back some

of the money I won. 'Two hundred and fifty of which you had to give to me,' I say sweetly to Greg. 'All in all I made over a grand.'

'You must have been really good,' Julie looks at me with admiration.

'Genius,' Greg confirms. 'I mean, give the girl a nine-letter word all jumbled up and she can guess it like that!' He clicks his fingers.

'Any number of letters,' I tell him, trying to sound modest.

'When did you discover you could do that?' the girl, Kate, asks.

'When I used to watch *Countdown* as a kid. I kept beating the contestants.'

'You must be very clever.'

'No, I was as thick as that,' I hammer the table. 'But I was big into Scrabble as a kid. In fact –' a memory pops into my head, a lovely happy image that makes me smile – 'My dad and mam played it a lot and I'd watch them. I could read really early too. I was just good like that.'

'Hey, hey,' Julie claps her hands. 'Anyone got a pen and paper?'

'Oh yeah,' Logan looks over from his riveting conversation, 'I always bring a pen and paper to the pub.'

Everyone laughs.

'Naw, serious,' Logan pulls a pen and paper from his pocket. 'I bring them everywhere.'

'Nerd' and 'anorak' are flung at him but he just grins good-naturedly.

Julie, much to my embarrassment, passes the pen and paper around and asks everyone to write down the longest word they can think of. 'I'm going to jumble up the letters and see if you can guess them,' she announces. As an afterthought, she says, 'And it's two euro a word which Hope can win. Anyone who catches her out, gets the kitty.'

'Aw, Julie,' I groan. 'I want to talk to Greg here.'

'I don't mind,' Greg says amicably. 'Let's see if you're as good as you were.'

'She's good at something?' Logan asks jokingly, suddenly giving us his attention. I notice that his conversation partner has left the table. 'And what would that be?' his eyes sparkle, 'besides colonic irrigation.'

'Ha ha,' I sneer, knowing what he's going to say.

'Colonic irrigation?' Julie asks. 'Are you, Hope?'

'Yeah,' Logan nods. 'You know, she can annoy the shit out of just about everyone.'

More laughter. Logan grins cockily at me. I have to smile.

'So what is it you're good at?' he asks again.

Julie tells him and he smirks. 'OK,' he says, putting a two euro coin on the table in front of me, 'I got one.'

I realise I'm the centre of attention. Everyone is looking at me. I try not to squirm.

'You want to take it?' Logan asks.

'Go on,' I say coolly. 'But it better be good and hard.'

'That's a bit personal, isn't it?'

'Ha ha.'

'Garden-sou.'

The letters rearrange themselves in my head. I make a face and say in an anguished voice, 'Oh God, it's so difficult.' I see him smile a bit before I quash it by adding, 'and DANGEROUS!'

Now he looks a little impressed. Someone claps. I smile triumphantly at him and take his two euros up from the table, waving the coin tantalisingly before his eyes. 'Ha ha,' I half sing. 'Up yours.'

He gives me a devastating grin. I say devastating because it is. It knocks me for six, it's so wide and sunny and friendly. It's the nicest smile I've ever seen, quite frankly. My own smile transforms itself into a jaw-drop.

'Here you are, Lo,' Logan's new best friend arrives back at the table with a drink for each of them and he forgets about me again.

I can't believe that he had that effect on me. I'd blame the drink if I was drinking.

'OK,' Julie breaks into my thoughts. 'How about C-I-I-O-U-E-S-L-D?'

'I need to see it written down.'

She passes me the paper on which the letters are written.

Unlike Logan, Julie doesn't realise that the hardest way for me to spot the words is by putting the letters into some kind of logical arrangement. 'Delicious?'

Nelson cheers. It had been his word.

After a few more futile attempts to catch me out, everyone makes admiring noises and conversation starts back up again.

Greg asks me what I'm doing these days. I give him a sanitised version of events and tell him briefly about the plane crash and then quickly steer the conversation on to him. He's been working in the bar since he left school and now he's officially the manager.

'And do you mind being tied to the business here?' I ask.

He shrugs. 'I used to but now I don't.'

'How come?'

'Well, it was expected that I'd work here. It's not so bad, though. But I still think that you were lucky you could get away.'

I shrug and admit, 'Sure I sort of had to get away, the way things were.'

Greg smiles sympathetically at me. Everyone in Dunport knows the story of my life. It had been splashed all over the *Dunport News* at the time. 'Yeah, it must have been tough on you.'

'Horrible.' I look at my hands. I really don't want the conversation to go down this road.

Greg senses it I think. 'Well, things always work out. They did for me. I'm happy now. I'm marrying Amanda Coonan in September, she works in Dingle, so we're both here for life. D'you remember Amanda?'

Amanda. I can't believe a nice guy like Greg would marry her. It seems that she's going to haunt me for the duration of my stay here. I force myself to smile. 'Oh yeah, I remember her. Congratulations.'

'Thanks.' He looks at me. 'So, are you seeing anyone?'

'I'm single,' I answer lightly. I don't admit that I've never really been serious about anyone since Jack.

'You won't stay that way for too long,' Greg, ever the gentleman says. 'Anyway,' he stands up, 'I better get back. Nice seeing you again, Hope. Sure no doubt you'll be in again.'

'No doubt at all,' I say, smiling up at him. 'Great to see you too.'

'Oh yeah, and do you know who's coming back to Dunport next month?' Without waiting for my reply, he says, 'Jack Dunleavy.'

Jack's name makes my heart flutter. 'I heard,' I try to say with as much nonchalance as I can.

'You and him had a thing going in sixth year, didn't you? We used to wonder what ye got up to on your days off.' Greg laughs at his humour.

'Believe me, it wasn't very exciting.'

Greg laughs again. Then with a general goodbye to the table he's off.

'He's lovely,' Julie says. Then, as if it's just occurred to her, she asks, 'Where is Adam? I don't think I've seen him all night.'

'He's up at the bar, completely smashed.'

'Why?' Julie looks in concern at me.

'I have no idea. He just got up and left the table.'

So then Julie gets up to see if Adam is OK. She arrives back with a face like thunder. 'Bastard,' she sniffs and she looks like she might cry. 'Well, there is no way I'm looking after him.'

Great!

21

I T'S THE END of the night and Logan and I are on each side of a completely hammered Adam. The guy can barely walk and he staggers between us as we make our way towards a taxi.

'Eh, I hope now he won't be sick in here,' the taxi driver says with justifiable concern. 'I'm telling ye now, I won't be the one cleaning it out.'

'He'll be fine,' I bluster. 'He's not as drunk as he looks.'

Logan gets in and I push Adam in after him, like a delicate parcel. 'Now to find Julie,' I say.

'Is she not going off with Nelson?' Logan asks.

'I don't know, I'll just find out, I don't want to leave her behind.'

I walk back through the throng of people milling about outside the pub. Julie sees me and waves. 'Hey, hiya Hope.'

'Are you coming with us or what?' I drag her to one side.

Julie smiles a little uneasily. 'Well, would it be OK if I brought Nelson back?'

'What?'

'Well, he's in a B&B and he's sharing with someone, it's hardly ideal.' Julie looks pleadingly at me. 'Please.'

'Julie, you don't really know this guy, and besides, I sleep downstairs and I don't want him tripping over me and everything. Come on, it's hardly fair.'

'Well where are we supposed to go then?' she says grumpily.

I feel like telling her that if Nelson wanted to advance things further, he should have taken out a room for himself in the B&B. Why should we have to accommodate them?

'I'll ask Adam, see if it's OK with him,' I mutter, hoping that she'll blame Adam instead of me. 'Come on.'

'But Adam is so drunk, he won't know what he's saying,' Julie pouts. 'He told me, when I went to see him at the bar, that he didn't want to sit at the same table as Nelson. I mean, what has Nelson done to him? Nothing, that's what. And you think he's going to be happy that Nelson is staying over.'

'Let's just see,' I try to say reasonably. I'm not used to being the sensible one in our relationship. 'Come on.'

Julie stomps behind me towards the car, Nelson calling after her.

'Hey, Adam,' I say brightly, 'have you any objection to Nelson staying over?'

Adam opens bleary eyes. 'Nelson?' he drawls. 'I hate Nelson. Why didn't someone kill him at Waterloo?'

'Because he wasn't bloody at Waterloo, that's why!' Julie folds her arms and glares at us, though why she's glaring at me, I don't know. 'Well, Nelson and I are getting a taxi back to the cottage. I have paid for my room and I can bring anyone back I want. So I will and I am.'

'Fine,' I say narkily. 'You do that.' I hop into the taxi and close the door on her.

'Ouch,' Logan says in amusement.

'You might not want to,' Logan says, as we near the cottage, 'but there's a spare bed in my place.' He looks from me to

Adam. 'The sofa converts, if you like. And one of you can take the floor.'

'I paid for my room, I'm using my room,' Adam says stubbornly. 'I'm using my room as I paid for my room.'

'Hope?' Logan looks at me. 'What about you? Did you pay for the floor downstairs?'

'Eh, no, as it happens.' I smile. 'Adam and Julie paid for the cottage. I buy the food as much as I can.'

'Anyway, you know the offer is there,' Logan says. He smiles that smile again.

'I hope,' Adam says, 'that she snores and he can't get to sleep.'

'Hate to break it to you, mate,' Logan winks at me, 'but I don't think Nelson is planning on getting any sleep.'

'Shit. Yeah.' Adam nods.

That's it. What with Adam being completely drunk and probably in a bad temper and Julie and Nelson not getting any sleep, I decide that I want out. 'Logan, d'you know what, I think I will join you in your cottage.'

'Fine.' Another smile. 'I would have done the same.'

We arrive at the cottage before Julie and Nelson and although Logan and I try to get Adam upstairs, he refuses to go. 'I'm going to sit here,' he says, plonking himself down at the table. 'Sit here and wait.'

'And I'm going to sit in the taxi and wait,' Logan says, giving up.

'Yeah, see you in five,' I say to him.

When he goes, I grab my toothbrush, pyjamas, underwear and some fresh clothes. Just before I turn to go, I try to talk to Adam again.

'What on earth is wrong with you tonight, Adam?'

'I'm drunk,' he says. 'I'm a failure as a human being, I'm terribly terribly cross.' He lays his head on his hands and declares, 'Oh God, the world is spinning and I forgot to get on the roundabout.'

There's no point in talking when he's like this. I don't even know if I should leave him. He really is acting very weird.

'Go,' he waves me away, his head still buried in his arms, like a kid falling asleep in school. 'Go!'

Maybe I'll talk to him tomorrow, when he's back to himself. 'Well, try and get some sleep,' is the last thing I say as I close the door.

The five-minute drive to Logan's is done in silence. It's a bit weird actually to be spending the night under the roof of a guy I hardly know. I imagine he feels the same way. The driver lets us out at the cottage and Logan's horrible cat springs out from somewhere to greet us. It's quite taken aback to see me there and hisses at me for a bit as Logan laughs.

'He's the jealous type,' he grins as he scoops the cat up in his arms. Unlocking the door of the cottage, he tells me to come on in. He flicks on the lights in his studio and saunters on into the kitchen where he grabs some cat food from a press, opens it and puts it into a bowl for the cat. It's soon purring loudly. Logan opens the door to the small sitting room and, pulling on the orange sofa, changes it into a bed.

'Now.' He surveys it for a second. 'I have a quilt, I think, and a sheet or two. Is that OK?'

'Great. Yeah.' I put my overnight bag on the floor. Well, it's a plastic shopping bag, really. I don't possess anything like an overnight bag, hardly ever having done this sort of thing.

Logan goes out of the room and I'm left standing like a spare in the middle of it. I can't sit down as I'll be sitting on my bed, which would be a bit weird. But of course, there's another chair in the room, so I perch on the edge of that. From somewhere in the small house, I hear Logan pulling at stuff and he soon comes back in with a duvet and one sheet. 'Now, I'll just put this on for you and that'll be you all set up.'

'Thanks for this.'

'No probs.' He makes up the bed with the air of someone who has never made a bed before. 'I'd offer you my bed only the cat normally sleeps on it. He'd probably attack you.'

'No, this is fine.'

He gives up trying to get the sheet straight and just dumps the duvet over it. Then he stands back to survey his work. 'There.'

'Great.'

Neither of us knows what to do next.

'I have an opened bottle of wine in the fridge, d'you want to help me finish it off before we call it a night?'

'I, eh, can't drink,' I say.

'Oh right, well d'you want some tea?'

'Yeah. That sounds good.'

It isn't good, though. Logan, I think, would win a prize for the worst tea in the universe. It's so black, even when milk is added, that I fancy he actually burnt it.

Logan wisely has the bottle of wine for himself. He looks around for somewhere to sit and realises that the only place available is the newly made up bed. I feel like laughing with the awkwardness of it all. It's like the sofa bed had suddenly become enormous in the room.

He smiles sheepishly and indicates the bed. 'D'you mind?'

I shrug, feeling in control. 'Why should I? It's really only a chair.'

'That's right.' Logan sits on it. Right at the edge. He takes a mouthful of wine and swallows.

We look at each other.

'So,' I swirl my tea about, trying not to look at him sitting on my soon to be bed, 'did you enjoy yourself tonight?'

'Aw yeah.' He nods. 'It's nice to go out with a crowd, it's ages since I've done that.'

'So you don't get out much?'

'Naw,' he shrugs. 'Maria, my ex, she was the social one.' He looks a little wistful as he talks about her. 'If there was a party anywhere, she'd be at it.'

'She sounds like fun?' My voice is a bit strangled. I wish he didn't look so sad, as if he missed her.

'Yeah, she was.'

'And did she like art?' I can't help it now, I have to nose.

'Yeah. She especially liked my art.'

'Really?'

'Yeah, when it sold for a lot of money.' He laughs at his own joke. 'Naw, Hope, she wasn't into stuff like that, which was why I liked her and why I guess she drove me nuts, too. She was into movies and rock music and shopping and clothes and hair.'

'Oh. Right.'

Logan's smile fades slightly. 'Nope,' he says, half to himself, 'it was all wrong.' He pours himself more wine and nods at my teacup. 'D'you want some more?'

'Eh – no, thanks.'

We sit a while in silence, sipping our drinks and gazing at everything bar each other. I can't look at him because he's obviously forgotten he's on a bed and he is now lying on it, with his head against the wall. Long lean denim-clad legs with bare feet, his red and white T-shirt creased. He looks quite desirable if you like your men dark and sombre. I normally prefer blond hair myself. Anyway, eventually he finishes his drink and hauls himself off my bed, the duvet creased from where he has been lying on it. 'Bathroom is at the top of the stairs,' he says, sounding a little embarrassed. 'I'll leave you now.'

'OK. Thanks.' I can't look at him.

And he's gone.

Once I'm sure he's safely upstairs, I dump my tea down the kitchen sink.

There is someone shaking me. I grab an arm, gasping, and wallop – snap awake. Logan is standing over me. 'What the hell –?'

Oh God. Oh God. I let him go abruptly. 'Bad dream,' I say. My pyjama top is soaked with sweat. I shake it slightly. 'Sorry if I woke you.' I can't look at him.

'That was some dream.' He sits down beside me. 'D'you want a glass of water or tea or anything?'

'No, honest, I'll be fine.'

He looks doubtful. 'Does it happen often, dreams like that?'

'Logan, just stop. I'm fine. OK?' It's typical, my dreams have been easing off and then I have to have a horrendous one in a strange house with a strange man living in it. 'Just leave me,' I say again, 'I'm fine.'

Usually that stroppy tone would have people running for cover. Not him.

'You are not fine,' he says back equally stroppily. 'That

wasn't an ordinary dream. Jesus. You scared the hell out of me for one. I couldn't wake you.'

'I said I was sorry!'

He sounds taken aback. 'I don't want apologies, Hope. Dreaming like that is not a sign of someone that's fine.'

'Yes it is. I've always had vivid dreams.'

'Was it about the plane crash?'

He's not going to go away, I realise. Logan is not like Adam, he's oblivious to the rules of normal society. 'Yes, it was,' I admit reluctantly. 'I mean, if you nearly died, wouldn't you dream of it too?'

'I guess so.'

'See?'

He sits down beside me on the bed and asks, 'Is this the sort of stuff you're getting counselling for?'

'Yes.' I sound abrupt, but it's only because I am completely mortified. I lie back down and turn my back to him. 'Logan, just let me go back to sleep.'

'OK. Once you're all right.'

'It's only a dream.'

Despite the fact that I have my back to him, I sense that he has not left the room. 'Only a dream to you,' he says, and I think he sounds a little cross and upset, 'but Jesus, I thought you were being attacked.'

I turn towards him. For the first time I notice how pale he is. I've been so caught up in how I feel that his feelings didn't really register. He must have got a horrible shock. I'm ashamed of being so selfish. When did I become like this? I sit up in the bed and, wrapping my arms about my knees, I give what I hope is an apologetic smile.

'I never thought of that, Logan,' I admit softly. 'I'm sorry for scaring you.'

He looks at me and I become aware that I'm wearing my chilli pyjamas.

'I'll treasure that apology.' He half smiles. Then, standing up, he says, 'And I'm sorry if I embarrassed you about the counselling.'

I stare at the quilt he's thrown on my bed. It's a kids' one, showing Superman saving Lois Lane from a burning building. Jamie had loved Superman. 'My mother was depressed a lot of her life,' I say. I don't know why I'm telling him this. It's easier than talking about me, I suppose. My finger traces the outline of Superman's face. 'And I'm, you know, scared that I might have something like that. Or some branch of it.' I look up at him. 'Counselling is scary for me, I react accordingly.'

A small silence, before he says cautiously, 'Depressed people don't have brilliant comebacks like you do.' A pause. 'And I don't think if you were depressed that I'd enjoy your company as much.'

That's a nice thing for him to say. 'You enjoy my company?'

'Well, I've always had a thing for thorny objects.'

'Ha ha.'

We look at each other. 'Thanks, Logan.'

'You OK, then?'

'Better than I was, thanks.'

'Good.'

He switches off the light and the last thing I see is his lovely smile.

22

I'M AWOKEN THE next day by the sounds of Logan pottering around outside. He's talking to his cat. I lie for a while and listen to him, grinning a little. I suppose being alone on a hill in the middle of nowhere would make anyone a bit mad. Well, I smile until I remember the night before. It's all like a bad dream now – ha ha. Eventually, I swallow my embarrassment and get up, pulling on my jeans and sweatshirt, before running a brush through my hair. Then it's out to the kitchen to locate some strong coffee.

'Hey,' Logan spots me and comes into the kitchen. 'How are you today?' He looks good.

'Fine. Sorry again about last night.'

He ignores that, for which I'm grateful; instead he reaches up into the press, pulls out the coffee and tea and bread. 'Here, you look like you could do with a bit of a feed.'

Is he telling me I look awful? Or maybe he's telling me I look skinny, which would be a first. 'Thanks.'

'OK.' He holds up the bread. 'Toast? Bread?'

'Toast. Two please.'

He switches on a gas grill and puts the bread underneath. 'You're welcome to stay as long as you like. Only thing is, you'll have to walk back to your place unless you want me to call you a taxi.'

'I'll walk.'

'Thought you might.' Pointing to various presses, he says, 'Butter in there, Coco Pops in that press and marmalade beside it.'

'Marmalade?' I half giggle. I can't help it. 'I thought only old people ate marmalade.'

'I'll have you know, Dunport marmalade is the best you can buy. Full of whiskey.'

'Right,' I make a face. 'I'll stick to the butter.'

'You don't know what you're missing.'

'Yeah, I do.'

He holds my gaze and I hold his and then flush a little. To break the moment, I gabble, 'Well, you go on, I'll find my way about. Thanks for letting me stay the night.'

'No problem. Now, when you leave, just pull the door behind you. I'll have the key.'

'Why, are you going somewhere today?'

'Yeah. I'm spending the day walking the mountains to try and find the best place to sketch from. I want a spectacular sea view, or rather, that's what bloody Jack Dunleavy wants for the foyer of his hotel.'

'A sea view?' I pull the grill pan out and flip over the bread. 'Have you gone up by Kinsella's waterfall?'

'Kinsella's waterfall?' He frowns. 'I've been here a year, I've never seen a waterfall.'

'Ah, but I grew up here. I know all the best places.'

'So where is it? Are you having me on?'

'As if.' I'm indignant that he would think I'd sabotage his work. 'It's . . .' I try to describe how he could get there and then I think, damn it, I haven't been up there in such a long time, it'd be nice to go. 'If you want, I'll show you. I'd enjoy the walk.'

'And it really is a good sea view?' Logan sounds doubtful. 'I was hoping to head away towards Dingle, to the highest place there.'

'Amateur,' I scoff. I pull the bread from the grill, I like my toast, like my tea, very un-brown. 'Let me eat this and I'll give you a visual experience you will never forget.'

Too late, I realise how it sounds. Logan opens his mouth to make a quip and I hold my finger up. 'Ah, ah.'

So, without any smart comments, he sits beside me and joins me in a coffee.

We leave about twenty minutes later. I've told him it'll take about an hour to reach the waterfall. Logan looks at my footwear. 'D'you want some boots or anything?' he says. He opens a press in the corner of the kitchen that I hadn't noticed and some wellies fall out.

'Maria left these behind when she left,' he says, holding up a fancy pair of pink ones with a picture of a pig on the front. Maria, I think, might have loved clothes, but these wellies were a bit on the pathetic side. Still, it'll save my trainers. I slip my feet into the boots, which are a perfect fit. Logan hands me my trainers in a plastic bag. 'You could leave your clothes here,' he says, 'pick them up on the way back. It'd save you carrying them.'

'Naw, I'll head back once we get there,' I tell him. 'I need to see how Adam is.'

Logan packs a sketch pad and some charcoal and pencils into a small rucksack and hoists it over his shoulder. 'OK, lead on, this had better be good.'

It's so long since I've really walked the hills that I'm sure I bore Logan by pointing stuff out to him. Still, give him his due, he doesn't seem bored. And even if he was, I wouldn't be able to stop myself.

'Wow, David Attenborough has nothing on you,' Logan grins as I identify some birds by their calls. He's staring at me in a way I can't quite fathom. 'You really love it around here, don't you?'

'I used to,' I admit. 'Now, it's like seeing a friend that I haven't met for ages.'

'Well, obviously that friend hasn't changed too much,' he says back.

I shrug. 'Some things you just don't forget,' I mutter.

But my friend *has* changed, I find out, or else my memory has altered drastically. The climb gets suddenly steeper. I'd forgotten that. It comes rushing back to me how, when I was a teenager, I could scamper up this hill. I was used to it, I suppose. Now, not having climbed it in a decade, the backs of my legs start to ache and the boots, the ones I thought were a perfect fit, have begun to chafe my heels. Still, I've told Logan where we're going and go there we will.

'Wow,' he pants, behind me, 'this is some climb.'

'It's worth it,' I pant back, wondering indeed if it is worth having a major heart attack for. Or even worse, sweaty stinky clothes for. Thank God I have very little hair, as it would be in bits at this stage.

The climb seems endless. In fact, gazing upwards, I begin to feel that it will be endless. How could I have thought it only took an hour?

'Are you sure we're going in the right direction?' Logan asks a few minutes later. 'We've been climbing now for the last forty minutes. I thought you said it was only an hour away.'

'Slight mistake about the time,' I admit sheepishly, 'but no mistake about the direction.'

'Well, Hope, I'm going to have to sit down, I'm totally wrecked.'

'Weakling,' I tease, but half-heartedly. Wrecked doesn't even describe how I feel. I think if I sit down, I'll never get up again. But I sink to the ground beside Logan and gratefully take a chocolate bar from him.

'Drink?' He pulls a bottle of water from his haversack. 'I bought one each. Just as well, eh?'

I take it and try to act like I'm only a little thirsty. I wish I'd brought sunscreen as the day is beginning to heat up and my face is burning, though whether it's from exhaustion or the sun, I'm not quite sure.

After about ten minutes, Logan stands up and stretches. 'Right,' he looks up at the hill, 'onwards and upwards. Up you get.'

My legs are stiff. My broken one is on the verge of rebellion, I think, as I try and fail to get up.

'Here.' Logan thrusts a hand out. 'Come on, my Kerry guide.'

The touch of his hand in mine as he yanks me to a stand makes my insides feel as if I've just done a loop the loop on a particularly dangerous rollercoaster. His grip is so strong and firm that he seems to have a problem letting go.

'Thanks,' I mutter, as he releases me. 'My bad leg is having a bad day.'

'And what about your good leg?'

'That's having a bad day too,' I admit reluctantly. 'It's trying to make up for the bad leg.'

'Oh dear.' Logan eyes me up and down with a speculative

grin. 'Well, my legs, though tired, are having a pretty good day overall.'

'Show-off.' I give a brisk, dismissive smile as he laughs. 'Let's get on.'

He gives a mock-salute and falls in behind me.

Ten minutes of excruciating pain later, Logan stops, cocks his head to one side and asks, 'What is that noise?'

'That,' I grin triumphantly, 'is the waterfall. Not long now.'

Pushing past trees and climbing rocks and squelching through damp earth, we emerge, at last on a plateau above the waterfall. The sound of it is fantastic in itself, just the roar of the water.

'Now look,' I say as I beckon Logan forward.

We have ascended the hill on the less steep side. The waterfall is to our right and a little further right is a sheer drop down to the ocean.

Logan stands beside me, totally speechless.

'Well?' I know I sound smug, but I can't help it.

'I'd never have found this myself,' he admits delightedly. 'Hope, it's brilliant. Just what I need. Thanks.'

'No problem.' I have to sit down or else I'll collapse. 'I'll just forward you on the doctor's bills.'

'I'd pay them a hundred times over for what you've given me,' he says seriously. He rummages about in his rucksack and finds some chocolate. 'Here, eat this.' Then he pulls out his sketch pad.

I wonder if he wants me to leave. After all, he seems to get very narky when he's working. But the truth is, I can't start walking again, even if it is downhill. My legs are too sore.

'Logan,' I say as I break off a square of chocolate. 'Like, it's not that I love your company or anything, but I'm staying here for a while. I'm too knackered to move. I'll try not to disturb you.'

'No worries,' he nods. 'You eat that and I'll work. These pictures are going to be great.' So saying, he begins sketching.

I find a shady tree and, legs outstretched, I munch on the chocolate while watching him. Head bent in concentration, his hand flies over the pages. There's something incredibly sexy about a man absorbed in his work. The more I look at him, the more turned on I feel. It's just because he's working, nothing to do with *him*. Every so often he turns and grins at me, almost as if he's making sure I'm still there. So, to avoid his gaze, I close my eyes.

I wake up, I don't know how long later, and Logan is still sketching away. The sun has begun to dip in the sky but it's stayed warm, and even at this height insects are buzzing about. I shift a bit and immediately groan.

Logan flinches.

Oops, I think I've just messed up another piece of art.

'Sorry,' I call out, feeling a lot more sorry for myself than him.

He puts down the sketch pad and shrugs. 'Naw, it's fine, I was just doing a few extra ones and letting you sleep. How are you?'

'Great,' I lie. I attempt to get up but the pain in my legs is unreal. 'Oh my God.'

'Sore, huh?'

'You could put it like that or,' I gaze heavenwards, 'you could say that someone has shoved hot pokers into my leg joints.'

'Not guilty,' he grins, 'much as I was tempted.'

'God, Logan, you should be in stand-up.'

'Well, I'd do better than you, that's for sure: you can't even stand, for starters.'

'I can,' I say, rising to the bait and with a superhuman effort I clutch the tree and, trembling, haul myself up.

'So, will we go?' he asks.

If someone had offered me a stretcher, I would have gladly climbed on to it. 'We can try,' I answer. I'm a bit sorry that the day is ending for us now. It's been surprisingly enjoyable and it's nice to share my favourite places with someone who genuinely appreciates them. 'Jack won't believe you found the waterfall,' I remark as I gingerly put one foot in front of the other. 'Not a lot of people know how to get to it. It's a well-kept local secret.'

'You knew Jack well, huh?'

'Yep.' I answer. Then add on with a laugh, 'my first love.'

'Well, at least you learned some sense. He's a pain in the arse to work for. I think he regrets employing me, he doesn't much like my pictures.'

'Jack never had much taste.'

'So that's why he went out with you, was it?'

'That's not nice.' I belt him one but before the blow can land, he catches my arm.

'Neither is that,' he says, grinning. 'If you do it again, I'll be forced to hold your hand all the way down to protect myself.' He lets me go.

I'm tempted to hit him though why I'm not quite sure. I don't want to find out.

'And you should, in all fairness, apologise for trying to hit me. I was only wondering about Jack's bad taste.'

'My arse, I'll apologise.'

'Well, you do generally tend to speak out of it, so off you go.'

'Oh feck off!'

His laughter scares all the birds away, but it makes me smile.

It doesn't take as long to get down. I think I confused the time it took to climb up with the time it took to climb down.

'Well,' I say, once we reach the road, 'I'll go on.' His place is to the left, mine to the right.

'OK.' He seems at a loss for what to say. 'See you.'

'Yeah.' I stand, unable to move.

'Thanks for today. One of the best days I've had here.'

'Me too.'

'Maybe,' he shrugs and says in an offhand manner, 'maybe you'd like to show me some more places I should see?'

I nod in an equally casual way. 'Sure, just let me know. You bring the chocolate and I'll bring the intelligence.'

'Great. It's a date then.'

I roll my eyes. 'A date to me, Logan is fine wine, fancy food and a decent companion, not sore legs, midge bites and severe sunburn.'

He laughs, lifts his hand in a wave and walks off.

I walk on quite painfully, though for the first time in ages I feel as if I'm actually alive. Maybe it is the jolting pain in my legs that keeps me focused on the world, or maybe it's the breeze in my face, or the sun on my back or the colours of the grass. And the freedom of the open space and knowing that I can go anywhere and do anything I want. And yes, Logan too, who made me laugh and shared his chocolate with me. To be able to enjoy the company of someone other than Julie and Adam and let them enjoy my company. I'm in touch with a small part of myself that I thought might be gone and it's the most wonderful feeling, as if I'm coming home, back to myself after a terrible separation. I am, I realise with a jolt, content. Content just being here, in this tiny moment of time. Awareness of that makes me feel even better. And then my bad leg stumbles on something and I almost fall. And boom! I realise that being happy never really lasts. I could have slipped and banged my head on a rock and died. Or someone close to me could die. Which has happened twice already. Or someone connected to me could have a car accident. Or get on a plane. Or be run over by a drunk driver. The whole uncertainty of life hits me like a bowling ball smashing into a skittle and my happy thoughts shatter into the ether and this whole void of black emptiness opens up before me. Sucking me in and pulling me down. I think that if I don't run, if I don't get away, I too will shatter and break up and fall away. But my legs are sore and my breath becomes all uneven and my heart speeds up and my head swirls and I really do feel as if I'm going to die. I'm afraid to sit down as I can't think of where exactly I am. My breath is ragged. I try to control it. Tim's voice comes into my head and he's telling me that this won't kill me. It's a panic attack. So I don't run. I stand and breathe in and out instead. In and out. Breathe in and out slowly. Focus on it. I do this and it takes a while and I feel I'm swimming through black until, at last, I can see the end and the shimmering world waiting for me when I finally crash through the surface. I feel the edges of the panic ebbing away as the world comes back to me. I'm shivering, but OK. I hear the sound of the birds and the sea. I'm feeling the breeze on my face. But I find I can't enjoy it now. Being unguarded like I was lets the other thoughts in too. And I can't let that happen. I have to control myself.

But I've beaten it. I've got through it, another part of me says. In a way, haven't I been controlling myself all my life? And trying to control others? I've never been spontaneous. Except for the times when I lost my jobs. But even that was a sort of control, because I didn't want anyone controlling me by telling me what to do.

Maybe it had been my only way of breaking out, but it had only imprisoned me all the more.

Maybe – I let the positive thought through – maybe I'm finally beginning to understand something.

I'm fairly OK when I get back to the cottage about forty minutes later.

'Hi,' I call, wondering how last night had gone. It strikes me that I haven't thought about my friends all day and I find that kind of amazing.

Julie and Nelson don't seem to be around and a very sick looking Adam is sitting at the table, pretending to read the newspaper. I know he's pretending because it's open at the gossip pages and Adam never reads those.

'How's the head?' I ask.

He looks up at me shamefaced. 'Yeah, sorry about last night. I wasn't exactly good company, was I?'

'Well, it would have been hard for you to be, seeing as you spent all night up at the bar and we were at a table.'

'Yeah. Sorry.'

He doesn't seem inclined to say any more. In fact he doesn't even ask me where I've been all day, which is unlike him. 'Where's Julie?'

'I don't know. We had a row.'

'Oh, Adam.'

'Apparently, I ruined her night,' he says. 'I kept getting sick and I ruined her night.'

'Yes,' I agree, 'that would ruin anyone's night.'

He gives a bitter sort of a scoff before turning back to the paper.

'D'you want a cuppa?' I ask as I cross into the kitchen. 'I'm making one for myself.'

'Yeah. Go on.'

I take my time making the tea, wondering if I should ask him what the matter is. I carry his tea in to him and sit beside him at the table. 'Adam,' I ask carefully, 'can you please tell me what the problem is?'

'I don't have a problem.'

'You were in quite good form until we went out last night and then, for some reason, you left the table and got completely smashed and fought with Julie.'

There is a long silence. Adam stares into his tea morosely.

'Did that girl Kate say something to you?' It's the only thing I can think of; he left right after she talked to him. 'Did she hurt you or anything?'

'Hope, stop, OK?' He buries his head in his hands. 'Just leave me.'

'But I can't. Look, you helped me feel a lot better after the accident, now for God's sake let me help you.' I'm a little worried about him. It's awful but fabulously brilliant. 'I'm worried about you, Adam.'

More morose tea-staring.

'Is it,' I bite my lip, the thought I had last night flitting through my head, 'well, you're not gay, are you?'

I've got his attention now. 'What?' He stares at me incredulously. 'What?'

'You know, it's OK if you are. Me and Julie won't mind.'

'You think I'm gay?' He looks at me, shell-shocked. 'I'm like your –' he makes quote signs with his fingers as he says savagely, making me flinch – 'gay friend?'

'No!' God, this was all wrong. I was only trying to help him if he was. 'No. I don't see you like that.'

'Good.' He shakes his head. 'Jesus!'

'Sorry, Adam.'

He shrugs, then mutters something.

'What?'

'I said,' he raises his bloodshot eyes to meet mine, 'I said, that I can't blame you for thinking it.'

I don't know what he means by that, so I say nothing.

'After all,' he says bitterly, 'I'm hardly a Don Juan, am I?'

'Don Juan was a cad, you're not like that.'

Another scoff. 'No, I'm just a saddo who can't even talk to a woman without practically vomiting.'

'What? That's not true. Julie and I are women.'

He laughs a little, though it's not a nice sounding laugh.

'Is there something wrong with that?'

'You and Julie,' Adam says, deliberately slowly, 'are women who rent a house from me. It's easy to feel good about the two of you.'

I think I should be annoyed. But I'm too stunned to reply. And hurt. He can hardly mean it. He's our *friend*, for God's sake.

'Shit! Sorry!' Adam says in frustration. I think he's still a bit drunk. 'In the beginning, Hope, it was like that.'

'Oh, thanks.' I want to belt him. Stupid tears threaten to spill over.

'I'm sorry, but it was.' Adam looks at me. 'It's not like that now.' He manages to take my hands in his. 'But Hope, being your landlord gave me confidence with you and Julie.' He bites his lip. 'I'm such a total fucking loser.'

'What? You're saying that unless you feel superior to a girl you get terrified of her.'

'Basically, in a nutshell, that would be about right.' He can't look at me and his flippant tone belies the desolation on his face.

'So, what are you telling me, that you've only had relationships with girls you considered beneath you?'

He looks at me for a long time. Then he turns away. 'Hope,' he says softly, 'when you have zero confidence, there's not a lot of people below your level.'

'What?' I try not to sound taken aback. 'You've never had a girlfriend?'

He shrugs.

'Never?'

'Nothing serious.' He bites his lip. 'One could almost say my relationships were a joke.'

I don't know how to respond.

He shakes his head. 'When that girl Kate talked to me last night, I started to tremble, for fuck sake. I broke out in a sweat.'

'So that's why you left the table.'

'Yep.' He manages a sad sort of grin. 'There am I, looking over at Nelson, the weirdest bloke you ever saw and he's got Julie. How? I could never pull a bird like her in a million years. It just hit me, sitting at that table, looking around, how totally screwed up my life is.'

I don't answer. Instead, I do what comes totally unnaturally to me, I reach out and ruffle his hair and rest my head on his shoulder. 'I don't know why,' I whisper. 'You're not a bad-looking bloke for an Englishman.'

He laughs a little miserably. 'Ta.'

'But I've seen you talk to girls in London, in the pub and stuff?'

'No one else our age goes into Joe's pub in London. And when we go out, I'm usually drunk.'

That's true, actually only I'd never noticed it before.

'D'you remember a few weeks ago, Ju and I went out?'

I nod.

'Well, I got totally smashed and talked to this girl. A lovely-looking girl. She even gave me her number. I couldn't ring her, though. I tried for days afterwards to dial her but I kept hanging up at the last minute. I panic around women the way you panic around crisps.'

'Well then,' I say, nudging close to him. 'We'll do exposure therapy on you. The first thing we'll do is to –' I think hard – 'we'll get you to go up to a girl and ask her the time. Easy peasy. But you have to be sober and presentable.'

'Aw no, I don't think so.'

'It'll work, Adam. Give it a try.' God, I feel desperately sorry for him. 'We'll take it step by step, Julie will help.'

'Julie won't help,' Adam groans. 'She hates me.'

'Julie doesn't hate you.'

He allows himself a dejected smile. 'Oh, yes she does,' he nods. 'Truly.'

'Look,' I say forcefully, 'just let go this holiday. Chat up a few girls while sober, I'll help you out. You'll see it's not so bad.' I study him. 'You should have told us this before, Adam. We never knew you had so little confidence.'

To my surprise, he looks more miserable than ever. 'There is a lot you don't know about me, Hope. I'm a terrible person.'

'No you're not.'

He doesn't look like he believes me but he manages a smile of sorts.

Who on earth, I think, would have thought that a guy with three houses and a big job would be so insecure? But then again, the smart part of my brain tells me, maybe that's why he has the three houses and the big job. Which means that I must be supremely confident. Which is crap.

Julie of course spoils any good I might have done Adam by completely ignoring him when she comes back. She waltzes into the house, humming some irritating tune and talking over to me as I sit on the couch trying to find a comfortable position for my aching joints.

'Hi, Ju,' Adam says, trying to be friendly. 'How's Nelson?'

Julie makes a face at me that he can't see. 'As if you care,' she sneers. 'Do you know what that idiot sitting over there did last night, Hope? Do you?'

'Let's just let it go,' I say. 'You're sorry, aren't you, Adam?'

He makes a face at me that she can't see. 'Sort of,' he concedes.

'Sort of?' Julie whirls on him. 'Sort of? You bloody well sat up in here last night until we came back, then you told Nelson that you were mystified as to how any woman went out with him, then you came over to me and asked if my taste was up my arse.'

Adam winces. 'Did I?'

'You know you did.' Julie folds her arms and stalks over to the table where he is still sitting, nursing what must be a massive hangover. 'Then you told Nelson to watch out for my plays. My plays are crap, you said. *The Wizard of Oz* was more the Wizened of Odd, you said.'

Adam opens his mouth to say something but Julie snaps,

'Just because you were a total loser with Kate last night, don't try and wreck my relationships! Kate said you were a weirdo!'

Oh Christ!

Adam shoves his tea away and stands up. He's gone quite pale. He shrugs and says in a remarkably composed voice, 'Fact, Julie: Nelson is the weirdo. Fact: you shouldn't have brought him back last night. Fact: if I behaved appallingly and said stuff, I'm sorry.'

'If?!'

'Julie, he's apologised.'

'Fact,' Adam turns around: 'you can do better than Nelson.' Then he stumbles towards the stairs. At the top, he slams his bedroom door really hard.

'Oh Ju,' I whisper, quite horrified, 'you shouldn't have said that.'

I'm about to tell her about Adam when she snaps, 'So my play was crap, was it?'

'That's not really that important now,' I say. 'If you'll just –'

'And were you and him,' she stabs a finger towards Adam's room, 'laughing over it? Was he sniggering away?' She turns her face to the ceiling and bellows at full volume, 'Toerag!'

'Julie, will you just let me explain –'

'Don't bloody bother.'

And she stomps upstairs and slams her door.

'Will you both cop on!' I shout.

Neither of them answers.

The whole night alone stretches before me. I take out my tape, put it in my ears and continue at least trying to make myself better.

23

J ULIE DIDN'T GET up this morning at all. Despite the fact that Adam and I made a lot of noise shouting at each other, she didn't come down.

Yes, I rowed with Adam today.

I asked him why did he think it was necessary to inflame an already bad situation by not apologising to Julie. He told me that though he regretted ruining her night, he was not going to say sorry for stuff that he'd said that was true. Mainly the things about Nelson. I told him that he'd want to cop on and apologise or the rest of the holiday would be ruined.

He said his holiday was ruined anyway.

I asked him why so.

He clammed up on me and snapped, 'Do you want a lift or not?'

So we travelled to Tim's office in silence.

Just before I climbed out of the car he did mutter 'Good luck.'

Unfortunately I told him to get lost.

And now I'm sweating as Tim sets up the recorder again so that I can relate to him details of my miserable existence. He's quizzed me on my exposure therapy and I spoofed a little about the crisps. Since Julie scared me stupid, we haven't attempted it again. But I tell him with pride about my panic attack and how I handled it and he's pleased with that.

'So, you see, Hope,' he grins. 'By accepting that sometimes we have no control, that gives us a certain amount of control. And I'm sure you found out that there were things you could control – for instance your response to the panic attack.'

I nod. 'Yeah.'

Tim then asks me for the tape and I hand it to him. 'Now you've been listening to this over the weekend – how did it go?'

'OK, I think.'

As he replays it for me, I have my eyes closed and I have to visualise the situation as far as I can remember it. At various points he asks me how I feel. Because I've listened to it a few times now, I don't feel too anxious at all.

'How does not feeling anxious make you feel?' Tim asks.

I want to tell him that it makes me feel great, but instead I blurt out, 'Guilty.'

'OK,' he nods. 'Can you tell me why?'

'Because it was a horrible time and it got worse and if I let it go, does that mean that I don't care about what happened any more?' I have to swallow hard after saying that.

'If you care, you care,' Tim says. 'Carrying a big stone of guilt around with you doesn't make you care any more or less, does it?'

I shrug. I don't know.

'Well?' Tim presses, 'does it?'

'Maybe not.'

'Maybe not,' he repeats in a more positive tone than I had used. 'Now, Hope, seeing as you've done so well this week, we'll move on with the next part of the story. I'll slot this tape back in.' He pops the tape in and begins to speak. 'OK, so you were saying about your mother getting sick again, Hope. Take your time with this. Relax as you talk. Now close your eyes and visualise it.'

I was about fourteen. Jamie was ten. And it wasn't noticeable at first. She just stopped checking our homework. Instead, she'd sit in at the television and look at it but not look at it. Then maybe a couple of months later, I noticed that nothing was being done in the house when we were in school. I'd come home and wash up the breakfast dishes and put a wash on and tell Jamie to take a bath and make some dinner for us. She wouldn't eat.

'And did she talk to you at all?' Tim asks. 'What would she say?'

I shrug. 'She was always polite. She'd ask us about our day in school but she wouldn't listen. I don't know if Jamie noticed anything. It was all so gradual. But I worried.'

'Can you tell me how you used to feel?'

'I'd go to school in the morning and I'd spend my time praying that when I got home she'd have done some little something in the house to give me hope that she was all right. But she never did. I'd walk up towards the house after school, with my stomach clenched and a sick feeling right at the back of my throat. And I could never invite friends over and as a result I could never go to friends' houses either. There was so much to do at home.'

'OK,' Tim says, 'what happened then?'

She stopped talking. She stopped getting out of bed and she stopped eating. I used to go in to her and make up lies to try and jolt her back

232

to us. I told her all sorts of crazy stuff. I made up one day that some
boys had tried to attack me on the way home from school. That got
her sitting up but then she just looked at me and shook her head and
said I was a liar. I told her about exciting things like funfairs and
stuff that was happening in school. I remember once winning piles of
money in a school charity thing, a Countdown competition, and she
didn't even say 'well done'.

'And how did that make you feel?'

'Hurt. Angry. Scared. I didn't know what to do.'

'Did you think of ringing a doctor?'

I feel a small tear trickle down my cheek. 'I wish I had now,' is all I manage. 'Everything that happened was my fault.'

'How are you feeling, what's the anxiety level like?'

'About an eight.'

'OK,' Tim says, 'I'm going to switch the tape off and you're going to start over. Then we'll see if you can continue.'

I start from my mother getting sick the second time. This time I remember more detail. How the curtains were always closed. How I was afraid the neighbours would notice. How I pulled open all the curtains before I left for school as I knew my mother wouldn't bother getting up to close hers again. How I bought the shopping in different places every week so people wouldn't notice; how I lodged money that came for her in the bank and how I forged her signature on withdrawal forms. Lots of little deceptions that I couldn't break. That became a comforting habit. That eventually led me into fooling Julie and Adam into thinking that my mother was dead.

Tim nods. 'OK, we've a half-hour left, do you think you can continue?'

The worst part is coming, I want to tell him, but I can only nod.

I wanted to call the doctor. It was the day when she hardly moved at all. The only thing to tell she was alive was that she was breathing. She didn't talk to us or look at us. I told Jamie I was going to have to ring the doctor and he started to cry. Jamie was all I had left. He was my most precious thing. I couldn't bear to see him cry. He didn't want to go and live in a stranger's house, he said. Imagine, he still remembered how he'd hated it. All he wanted was for us to be together. If I rang the doctor, they'd take Mammy away and put us in a new family and maybe a new school for a bit and he didn't want that. He didn't want Mammy to go. And so I fooled myself into thinking we'd cope.

Tim stops me. Gets me to relax and hands me a tissue. He tells me that it's good I'm upset. Some people can't even get in touch with their long-ago feelings, he says. But he doesn't want me to get too upset.

I tell him I want to go on.

He nods and presses the record button.

We did OK for a few months. I even thought at one stage that my mother was improving because she started to eat a little more though she was so thin. It was like some weird self-preservation thing kicked in, as if she wanted to disappear but not to die.

But then, the horrible thing happened, Jamie –

Tim holds up his hand.

I'm hyperventilating.

'Let's leave it there, Hope. Just listen.' He presses the tape and I hear myself talking about that time. And then he does it again. Each time, my anxiety levels rise.

But the third time, I can visualise and listen and I feel a slight shift.

'Good.' Tim takes out the tape and hands it to me. 'Listen to this for at least forty-five minutes a day between now and next week, Monday, OK?'

I slip the tape into my pocket.

Then he gets me to close my eyes and he relaxes me. When I get up to go, twenty minutes later, I'm calm and relaxed again.

'Good girl.' Tim smiles at me. 'You're doing great, you really are.'

His smile gives me confidence. 'Thanks.' But he still hasn't heard the worst part. I haven't talked about that yet.

'See you next Monday, Hope.'

I'm just at the door when I pause. I wonder if I dare. I probably shouldn't but he can only say no. 'Tim, can I ask your advice?'

'Shoot.' He's tidying up his desk, putting all my files away.

'Well, it's not about me, it's about a friend I have.'

'Go on.' He allows himself an amused smile.

'No, it really *is* about a friend of mine,' I stress. 'The thing is, he panics around women. Is there anything I could get him to do to make him more confident?'

To my surprise, Tim guffaws. 'Hope, if the guy has any sense he'll stay well away.'

'What?'

Tim makes a small gesture of surrender as he says, 'Sorry, I shouldn't have joked like that.' He frowns a little. 'Your friend needs what you're doing, exposure therapy. Just get him to relax and then approach a woman and ask her something, it might be the time or it might be for a match or whatever. That's step one. The next step would be to get him to prepare a sort of chat-up line. You know, a "hello" followed by a "do I know you from somewhere". Things like that.'

'That's what I told him!' I'm chuffed.

'Aw, you'll put me out of business, so you will. Go on.' He flaps his hand at me to leave.

As I close the door, I suddenly remember that I'm fighting with Adam.

Great.

To my surprise, Adam smiles at me as I climb into his car.

'Oh, hi,' is all I can manage.

'I was going to get lost,' he says, jangling his car keys, 'but I was afraid you wouldn't be able to get your big mouth into a normal size car.'

I take this for the peace gesture it is and smile.

'I'm sorry, Hope,' he says as he eases the car into traffic. 'I've been a complete jerk, especially to you. You were great to me yesterday.'

'Yeah, I was,' I smile back. 'You big fool.'

'And I'll apologise to Julie when I get back, OK? I should never have gone on about her snoring.'

'Yeah, but she should never have said you were a weirdo.' As he opens his mouth to agree, I hold up my hand. 'But you started it. You should never have ruined her and Nelson's night.'

'She's too good for him.' He glares straight ahead as he manoeuvres the car into the right lane.

'That's not your business. He seems OK and he must be pretty successful, running a gym.'

'I'm successful but she doesn't make a fool of herself over me, does she? No. What has he got that I haven't? I've got a cool car.'

'You've got a big car, Adam. There is a difference.'

'Ha.'

I look curiously at him. 'Adam, is there something you want to tell me? Do you fancy her for yourself?' It would certainly fit; his behaviour was pretty bad.

'As if!' Adam snorts.

I don't know if I believe that but I let it drop. 'So,' I say, 'we'll all say sorry to each other and then we'll all go out for lunch. And maybe head to the beach.'

'Yeah. Good idea.'

It's just what I need after the morning I've had.

There's no need to apologise to Julie when we get back because she has gone. There is a note on the table saying that she taken a taxi to the train station and that she's spending the rest of the week in Dublin with Nelson. She'll be back on Monday and there's no 'goodbye' or 'take care'.

'Ouch,' Adam says. He sounds ever so slightly devastated. Tossing the note into the bin, he snaps, 'Well, let's hope she'll have calmed down by Monday.' He looks at me. 'So, disturbed cognitive therapy patient, what do you want to do? Grab a towel and head to the beach?'

And that's what we do.

There's a girl on the beach, looking in Adam's direction. He doesn't look half bad in swimming shorts actually. For one thing, he doesn't seem to have an awful lot of body hair and his skin is surprisingly smooth and tanned.

'Adam,' I kick him gently, 'see that girl over there, the one with the blue togs.'

Adam hoists himself up on to an elbow. 'Yeah?'

'Walk over to her and ask her the time.'

He pales. 'No. Not on a beach.' He attempts to lie back down again.

'Where is more ideal?' I kick him again. 'I don't see any massive clocks hanging about in the sky, do you?'

He ignores this.

'Look, do you remember when you got me to look at the aeroplane and I was terrified and you told me I'd regret it if I didn't? Well that's exactly how scared I was. Just go for it.'

I don't think he's going to bother, but then he sighs and hoists himself up. 'OK. I'll just ask her the time.'

'Yes and say please and thank you and just make believe it's me or Julie.'

I pretend not to notice the sheen of sweat that breaks out on his forehead. He lopes self-consciously towards the girl and I lie back down and watch him through half-closed eyes. Please don't chicken out, please don't chicken out, I pray. I can't hear the exchange but he arrives back a minute or so later, flops down beside me and says, 'Well, that was embarrassing.'

'How so?'

He holds out his wrist on which his big expensive watch resides.

'Oh shit!'

'Yeah.' He lies down beside me and says casually, 'So I told her it wasn't working and she believed me.'

He's breathing heavily but he sounds thrilled with himself. 'Good man!'

His hand catches mine. 'Thanks, Hope.'

'Now you have to keep doing that until you're not so anxious about it. Then we'll work on harder stuff.'

'Yeah. Yeah. Fine.'

We both lie there and fall asleep.

24

TUESDAY MORNING. AGAIN, the sun is warming the room through the curtains; outside, I can hear birds singing and the faint drone of a car on the road. I'm a bit burnt from the sun yesterday and I groan as I climb out of the sleeping bag.

Adam and I had stayed on the beach for hours, not having had anything else to do, and while he read an important-looking literary book, and asked two more women for the time, I lay back on my beach towel and fell asleep. Luckily I wasn't wearing a bikini or togs or I would have been fried. Instead, my arms are a purplish colour, as are my shins. I'm half afraid to look in the mirror at my face but as I wash myself, I take a quick glance.

'Oh no!'

I look as if I'm about to have a major heart attack. If post traumatic stress doesn't get me, skin cancer will. I've never been one to get a tan and I've always used sun cream before but yesterday I'd only put it on once before falling asleep. And I'd slept for six hours.

I lather on some aftersun, but it dissolves on contact, making my face gleam.

I wonder if I have sunstroke.

I wander glumly back inside and meet Adam in the kitchen.

'I think I have sunstroke,' I say, leaning against the counter as he fills the kettle.

'Well, you look as if you're going to have a stroke OK,' he chortles, dodging a belt from me. He dumps two tea-bags into two mugs and shoves some bread under the grill.

'Any plans for today?' I ask.

'I might drive into Killarney and buy some trinkets to take home; you know, souvenirs for my mum. I might even ask a few more women what the time is, I'm getting good at that.'

'Brilliant.' I'm glad he's in better form. The morose, bad-tempered Adam of the last couple of days was not someone I'd like to meet again. 'But before that,' he continues, 'I'm just going to do some work on the net.'

'Adam, you're mad. You're suspended.'

He pours out the tea. 'So if you want to tag along to Killarney you're welcome,' he says. Then, with a mug in his hand and a slice of toast between his teeth he wanders back upstairs.

I sit outside in the shade of the house, my cup of tea balanced on the overgrown path. Taking my mobile phone from the pocket of my jeans, I dial Julie's number. It goes straight to voicemail. 'Hi Ju,' I whisper, not wanting Adam to hear, 'hope Dublin is going well. When you come back, we'll all talk. Just so you know, Adam confessed to me that he's afraid of women. I think seeing you and Nelson and other couples together just got to him that night. Please ring me back.' I hang up. It's a little weird she didn't answer, I muse. Surely she'd want to gloat about what a brilliant time she was having, if nothing else. Or maybe she is still really mad at both of us. I sigh and settle back against the hard wall of the house. Really, I think, Maurice should have

240

supplied the cottage with some patio furniture. And a clean sofa. And some new chairs. But the state of the place had lost its importance. It was all surface.

'Hey, knew you'd be waiting for me!'

It's Logan, striding across the field, haversack on his back and a smartarse grin on his face. He's wearing his football T-shirt and a pair of tracksuit bottoms that frankly have seen better days. In fact, all of Logan's clothes have seen better days.

'Would you be totally devastated if I said I wasn't waiting for you?'

'Absolutely, yep.'

'Well, then, I wasn't waiting for you.'

'Aw, you can lie, but your eyes tell me a different story.'

'Really? You can see "feck off" written in my eyes?'

He laughs and plonks down beside me. 'Any plans for today?'

'You are the second man to ask me that,' I say. 'I'm flattered. And the answer is no, no plans as yet. Adam is going into Killarney to buy some ridiculously expensive touristy rubbish and I'm not sure if I want to accompany him.'

'So accompany me.' Logan is so close, I can smell the minty smell from his breath. 'I'm heading cross country to Dingle. I was wondering if you could show me a good place, midway up, for getting the whole landscape?'

My legs are still quite stiff, but I don't tell him that. 'Midway up,' I say, thinking of all the nicest places along the mountainside. 'Yeah, I reckon I can manage that.'

'You might want to bring some sunscreen,' Logan nods at my face. 'It's meant to be a scorcher today. And here —' he hands me a plastic bag. Maria's wellies are inside. 'A gift to you from me. I don't use them at all.'

'Wow, your generosity knows no bounds! A pair of your ex's second-hand wellies, fab!' I pull off my trainers, but before slipping on the boots I say, 'Back in a sec, I'll just let Adam know.'

'No rush.'

I go back inside, run up the stairs in my stockinged feet and burst into Adam's room. As he said, he's on the computer, but he's in a Job search page.

'Job search?'

'Yeah,' he smiles sheepishly. 'Well, if those idiots at my place think I'm going back with my tail between my legs after the summer, they can think again. I mightn't go back at all.'

'Good for you!'

'I might even resign.'

'Oh no, I wouldn't do that, not until you have another job.'

Adam flushes and nods. 'Yeah. Maybe. So?'

I tell him that I'm heading off with Logan to show him a few scenic spots to paint from. Adam grins. 'Wow, very friendly, aren't you?'

'Don't be stupid. Look, if a blow-in is going to be painting my county, I want him to do a good job, right?'

'Oh yeah,' Adam sniggers, 'that's very important. And I'm sure Logan, who has been living here a year, wouldn't have a clue where to paint from.'

'As a matter of fact, he doesn't.'

I ignore Adam's juvenile laughter as I go back downstairs.

'Right,' I say in a very businesslike tone to Logan, 'come on then.'

'Hadn't you better put on your wellies first?'

'Your ex's wellies.'

'No, I gifted them to you.' He smiles munificently. 'They are now yours.'

'Sorry, how could I have forgotten?' I pull them on and, with Logan running to catch up, stride away from the house.

We walk for most of the day. It's not so tough this time as we're not going too far up the mountain. Logan has, as promised, brought along some chocolate. And a bottle of Club Orange. The man seems to live on sweet things. 'Don't you ever eat anything that's fresh?' I ask.

He looks puzzled. 'Why? Is that chocolate out of date?'

'I mean fresh fruit and vegetables?'

'Boring!' He rolls his eyes. 'You sound like Maria. She was a big one for organic things. She spent a fortune on organic bananas one time. Organic bananas!' He says it with the wonder of someone who has just seen a spaceship landing. 'I told her if she grew some stuff in the garden, that'd be better. I told her that the amount of greenhouse gases emitted by the plane that carried those bananas to Ireland probably deleted any organic benefits of them.'

'Fresh fruit is good for you.'

'Do I look like I'm suffering?' He holds his arms wide away from his body and grins.

He looks pretty damn good, I have to admit, faded track-suit and all.

'More chocolate?' his eyes sparkle.

'Go on so.'

We trudge another while in silence. The only sounds are the birds and the grasshoppers.

'She'd never have come walking with me like this,' Logan says out of the blue. 'Not in a million years.'

'Who?'

'Maria.'

'Oh.'

He spends a lot of his time thinking about Maria, I think. And his voice is quite bitter when he mentions her name. Things must have ended very badly.

'How's the counselling going?' he asks.

I have to admit, I'm a bit taken aback by that. 'Eh, OK,' I mutter.

'Sorry, should I not have asked?'

I shrug.

'It's just that I don't want you to think I don't care. Or that I wouldn't ask.'

He sounds uncomfortable but not as uncomfortable as I'm feeling.

'Tell you what, if you want to tell me, you just tell me, I won't ask again. Deal?'

'Counselling is going well. It's slow but OK.'

'Oh.' He shifts his haversack to his other shoulder. 'Do you have to talk a lot about the crash?'

'We haven't even got to that yet,' I say.

'Really?' His jaw drops. 'So what else is there? Like, is that not why you went in the first place?'

And so I explain to him about my reaction to the crash being so much worse because of other stuff that happened before. Wisely, he doesn't go there. Instead he just nods and smiles and says that his first impression of me was obviously right and that I did need help.

'Not as much help as you'll need if you say something like that again.'

'Point taken.'

We smile at each other and it dawns on me that I'm falling for this guy. I'm falling for him because he's funny in the same sarcastic way that I am. I'm falling for him because he loves living here, which I did once upon a time. I'm falling for him because he doesn't treat me as a victim. And I'm falling for him because he's so bloody gorgeous.

But I wonder if he's falling for me.

I take him to a midway point above Dingle and he hums and haws and doesn't seem all that impressed with it. 'It's just that the view to the sea is blocked by all the heather,' he says.

'Can you not just paint in the sea,' I grouch. I'd been looking forward to a sit-down. 'Just pretend that it's there.'

He looks faintly shocked. 'Eh, no.'

'Right, come on.' I start marching again. 'You're a hard man to please.'

'Would you prefer if I lied?' He runs in front of me. 'Would you prefer if I said, Oh yeah, Hope, that's a fantastic view of the ocean there. Hang on now while I paint the sea.'

'Yes, I would, actually. I would prefer if you lied.'

'No you wouldn't. If I lied about that, how could you trust me again?'

'I don't trust you anyway.'

'Liar,' he jokes cheerfully.

At last we get to a place that he likes. I sit down, as before in the shade, and plaster my face with sun cream. It's quite sore but not as sore as my legs have got. Being with Logan is pretty torturous on my poor body.

'Hey, stay like that,' Logan instructs.

'What, like this?' My hand is putting cream on my neck.

'Yeah, I love the curve of a woman's neck.' Logan begins a quick sketch.

245

'You can't draw me!' Immediately I take my hand away and he groans.

'Aw come on, Hope. You're totally gorgeous.'

That comment floors the both of us.

'In that pose,' Logan clarifies. He looks appealingly at me. 'Please?'

And so, semi-flattered and with my heart beating fit to burst, I sit like that for another twenty minutes until he's satisfied.

'Can I see?'

'Nope.' He holds the sketches to his chest. 'One day I'll show you, OK?'

'I have a right to look.'

'No you don't.' He turns away from me then and begins sketching the surrounding countryside.

I don't pursue it. I think maybe it's that I don't want to see how he perceives me. I want to hold on to the 'totally gorgeous' comment. If he's drawn me in some weird way or in some pose that I consider unflattering, I'll be disappointed. I've never let any man close enough to me since Jack told me I was gorgeous. I've gone out with some nice guys since, but only about once or twice. I just didn't want to get left again, I suppose.

Logan finishes up pretty quickly. He puts all his stuff away and turns to where I'm sitting on the grass. 'We must be near enough to Dingle now,' he says.

'Yeah, about a mile.'

'What say we walk into it and grab something to eat? My treat.'

I'd been thinking along the same lines myself. Logan's chocolate isn't doing it for me, I want something a bit more substantial. 'Yeah, why not, but I'll pay my way.'

'No, I insist.' Logan crosses towards me: 'you've been great today, so it's like a payment.'

I don't bother to argue. My funds are depleting rapidly, what with all the food the three of us eat. 'OK,' I smile. 'Thanks.'

We arrive in Dingle about half an hour later. The two of us are quite scruffy compared to all the fresh-looking tourists milling about the place. There's a big queue for Fungi, the dolphin. Logan asks me if I've ever seen him.

'Yeah, Julie, Adam and I came last month.'

'Me and Maria went one day. It was right before our relationship broke up and Fungi never appeared and she blamed me.'

I laugh.

He laughs too. 'So, where would you like to go?'

I shrug. 'Don't mind.'

We go into a small restaurant. Logan orders beef with vegetables and I order a big plate of seafood pasta. Then we find seats outside in the sunshine.

'Well,' Logan says, biting his lip, 'it's not fancy food, it's not a fancy place and I'm probably not your ideal companion, but hey, I'm not complaining.'

He's smiling but there is an anxious look on his face.

'Neither am I,' I say back.

'Good,' he nods.

'Well –' a plate of dinner is put down before each of us – 'I hope ye'll think your dinner is good.'

We both laugh, but as we begin to eat I become aware that the moment has been lost. I wonder where that conversation might have led.

* * *

We catch a taxi back to Dunport and the silence stretches between us. I desperately want to ask him what he meant by saying that he wasn't complaining. Maybe he likes me? But chances are that that's all he does – like me. What a bloody fool I'd feel then.

Logan chit-chats about various things with the taxi driver and as we reach my place first, I have to go.

'Thanks again for today,' Logan says. 'I'll be in touch.'

'Yeah. OK.' Just before I close the door, I screw up the courage to say, 'And I enjoyed dinner.'

'Great.'

There is nothing else I can say. He won't let me pay for the taxi either and I don't want to add to his bill, so I slam the door and wave them off.

25

IT'S EIGHT O'CLOCK. Adam is showing me what he bought in Killarney and it is just as I feared. Horrendous leprechauns with big bright gaudy pots of gold and Irish dancing dolls with flaming red hair and freckles.

'Adam, how much did you pay for all this?' I ask, but before he can answer, I hold up my hand. 'No, please, don't tell me. It's best if you don't.' As he puts them back in the bag, I ask, 'And how did you get on with the girls of Killarney? Did they have the *time* for you?'

He grins at my pathetic pun. 'Yep, no problems there. That was an easy step.' He dumps his bags on the floor. 'So, what comes next? I'm up for it.'

'Let me have a think and I'll let you know.'

He's about to say something else when we hear the crunch of tyres on the gravel outside as a car pulls up.

'That's a bit odd,' Adam remarks. He glances out the window. 'It's a taxi, hey, it's Julie. What's she doing back?'

We get to the front door in time to see the driver pop the boot and hand Julie a large case. She takes it and pays him and turns to see us standing silent in the doorway. She looks at us and we look at her. She doesn't look happy.

'Ju?' Adam breaks the silence as he asks uncertainly, 'Are you OK?'

At his voice she glares at us, though her eyes are watery. 'Oh, you'll be gloating now, the two of you,' she sniffs, pushing past us and running inside.

'Julie!' I run after her but she's only gone as far as the sitting room. She plonks down on the sofa and scrubs her eyes with the sleeve of her gorgeous white jacket. She must have been crying in the taxi, I think, as her face is a mess, full of splodgy make-up and streaked lipstick.

'Julie?' I ask gently, 'What happened?' I sit beside her.

Adam comes in carrying her case. Depositing it on the floor, he shuts the door and looks down at us. Then he sits on the other side of her. 'Ju?' he says tentatively. 'What's wrong? Come on, I rang you and apologised.'

'You rang her?' I look at him. 'So did I.'

Then we both look at Julie. 'I turned my phone off because I didn't want any messages from *him*.'

'Who? Nelson?'

At the mention of his name, her eyes fill up with more tears but she blinks rapidly to stem their flow. Hesitantly, I put my arm about her shoulder.

Neither of us says anything.

Her eyes fill up again. A tear plops on to her hand. 'He's a liar, that's what happened,' she sniffs. 'He's a big, fat, testosteroned, bulky liar and I hate him. And you were right, Adam, my taste was up my arse.'

'I was horribly drunk when I said that,' Adam mutters.

'You were still right.'

'What did he do?' I ask. I'm not surprised, really. There was something suspicious about him. I can spot a liar because I was one myself.

Julie sniffs again but sits up straight in a state of righteous indignation. 'Well, firstly, he doesn't own any gyms.

250

None. Oh God, I feel so stuuuupid.' She bites her lip. 'I stood, like a, like a stupid prat, inside the gym he said he owns. I asked to see him. The owner, I said to the girl behind the desk, Nelson Curry, I'd like to see him. They said that he wasn't the owner but they recognised his name as one of their members. I thought there must be a mistake. So I ring him. I tell him I'm in Dublin, outside his gym. I don't tell him what the receptionist said on the desk. And he tells me to wait outside, that he'll meet me.' She pauses for a bit. 'Anyway, he comes in a taxi to meet me. He pulls me into the taxi and starts chatting away about stuff. Stupid stuff, like what's in the papers and what he heard on the radio and then he tells the taxi driver to stop and out we get. Then he asks how you and Adam are and then I know he doesn't own the gym.'

'How?' The story is a bit meandering but I'm getting the gist of it.

'Well, I knew he didn't like Adam much after the other night, so why should he care about how he is?'

'Good point,' Adam says wryly.

'And suddenly, I hate that he doesn't like Adam, even though I was finding it hard to like him myself. So I say, why didn't you introduce me to your staff. And he says, oh they're all very busy and they don't like all that sort of thing. And I say, you don't own a gym, do you, and he says no. And I say, what else don't you own. And he says, I'm a milkman and I own a milk float.'

'What?' Jesus, I think, Nelson a milkman.

'Bloody hell,' Adam says.

'Yeah. Now, I've nothing against milkmen. But I do have a grudge against lying tossers who make a fool out of me and get their friends to do the same. So I told him that and

I left him shouting after me, telling me that he was self-employed, that he hadn't lied about that. Anyway, I booked into a hotel and ignored all his calls and then I came back here.'

'Wanker,' I say.

Adam doesn't say anything.

'Isn't he a complete wanker, Adam?'

He shrugs. 'Stupid, maybe.' He shifts uncomfortably. 'But, you know, understandable.'

'What?'

'What?!' That's Julie and she is not happy. 'Do you have some kind of an anti-Julie agenda?' she says, half crying. 'I tell you that this guy has made a complete fool out of me and you say it's understandable. Thanks!'

'Adam?' I hold out my hands in a for-fuck's-sake-what-are-you-playing-at-here gesture.

'No, Ju,' Adam says, in a hopeless kind of way, 'I'm not trying to get at you, but what was the guy meant to do?'

'Eh,' I make a face, 'maybe, oh, I dunno, tell the truth?'

Adam gulps hard. He starts to chew his lower lip. 'Look,' he says, as if talking to two morons. 'Nelson sees Julie. He thinks she's hot. She tells him she's a teacher. So a hot babe who's obviously clever, what is he meant to do? Say, "hey, I'm Nelson the milkman"?'

'Yes.' Julie can't believe she's hearing this and neither can I. 'What's wrong with that?'

'Nothing, except he thinks he mightn't stand a chance with you.'

'That's ridiculous!'

'And maybe,' Adam says over her, 'when he told the lie, he just wanted a bit of a one-night stand. Like, what's sexier – a guy who owns a gym or a milkman?'

252

'So it's OK to lie to get someone into bed, is it?' Julie asks tearfully.

'No!' Adam shakes his head. 'It's not about getting someone into bed,' he explains desperately, 'it's about, I suppose, trying to be better than you really are to impress someone you think is better than yourself.'

'Crap,' Julie pronounces. 'It's a sicko who'd do that.'

'I've done it,' Adam says softly.

What is Adam playing at tonight? We both glare at him.

'I did it to impress you two,' Adam says. He stands up and shoves his hands into his pockets. He fixes his gaze firmly on his grey socks. One of his toes is poking out.

'What, do you not have a big fancy job then?' Julie asks hotly. 'Did you steal your big fancy car and your three houses?'

'No,' Adam shakes his head. 'No, I had all that.' He takes a deep breath. 'I don't have it now, though.'

'Adam?'

'They let me go in my old job, OK? They fired me.'

'No!' That's Julie. 'Oh Adam, that's awful!'

'Suppose it is,' he agrees.

'But that's not the same as Nelson,' I point out. 'You never told us because you didn't want to ruin the summer.'

Adam gives that strange laugh, the one he'd given the day after he'd got really drunk. It's a horrible sound. As if he almost hates himself. 'I never told you because,' he pauses, and raises his gaze to our eye level, 'because you would have hated me.'

'Don't be stupid!' Julie stands up beside him, her own drama momentarily forgotten. 'How could we hate you?'

He smiles bleakly. 'Because –' he looks at Julie – 'because you'd find out what a bastard I was at work.'

We look blankly at him.

'The blokes hated me,' Adam goes on, startling us. 'They informed management that I was away. Yes, the fifty thousand was a mistake but it might have been OK if they hadn't hated me enough to squeal on me.'

'Why did they hate you?'

Adam pales and gulps hard. It's obvious he's finding it difficult to admit why. Taking a deep breath, he says quietly, 'I bullied them.'

Julie and I recoil.

Julie recovers first. 'You?' she gawps at him. 'You?'

'Yes.' Adam nods, looking ashamed. 'I spent my life being picked on,' he says bitterly. 'I was this scrawny, girly-looking boy and great fodder for abuse. So when I got working, I just said to myself, there is no bloody way these blokes are going to get one over on me. So I stamped over everyone to get to the top. I didn't let anyone away with anything. I quizzed them about their sick days, their days off. Blokes resigned because of me. Had breakdowns because of me.' He pauses and looks at both of us, then says slowly, 'And it suddenly hit me, when I was fired, I'd turned into the one thing I despised. I guess I was ashamed. I couldn't tell you – not then. That's why I never rang in the day or so afterwards.'

There is silence after this speech. Adam won't meet our gaze; instead he focuses on his socks.

'So why now?' I ask, breaking the silence.

'Because . . . I don't know . . . because we'll be going back and I'm tired of lying.' He pauses. 'I've been lying for so long now, I barely know who I am any more.'

'I, eh, can't imagine anyone being afraid of you,' Julie ventures.

'Me neither.'

Adam shakes his head. 'You and Hope were the only ones that kept the nice part of me alive.'

More silence.

'Look,' Julie says, her fingertips brushing his arm, 'this is your chance to start over, Adam.' She links her arm in his. 'To be the nice guy you know you are. You are not like Nelson.'

Adam pulls his arm from her grasp and walks away from her. 'I'm not a nice guy,' he says almost savagely.

'You are, isn't he, Hope?'

'A very nice guy,' I confirm.

He turns to face us. Bows his head and says nothing.

'Come here.' Julie crosses to him and enfolds him in a hug.

He wraps his arms about her. His eyes are suspiciously shiny.

'Ta,' he mumbles.

26

THE WHOLE HOUSE is awoken by the squeal of tyres on gravel the next day. In fact, a spray of stones clatters against the dining-room window, waking me up quite suddenly. The dream I'd been having slides away. It had been horrible, I know that much, for my forehead is filmed with sweat. Of course that could be a result of the sunburn too.

A furious banging starts up at the front door and peering out, I see Nelson, with yet another fancy car, standing in front of the house and hollering up at Julie's window. 'Julie,' he's saying. 'I'm sorry! Please, listen to me!'

Julie doesn't seem to be reacting at all. I don't know whether to let him in or not. I stand, in all my glory, in a pair of cotton pyjamas with teddy bears printed all over them.

'Julie, I've been a fool. I know I have. Please, just give me a chance to explain.'

I take a step towards the door.

'If you let me explain, I'll give you free milk for life!'

'What on earth –' Adam has come downstairs without me hearing him. He looks wretched, as if he hasn't slept.

'Nelson,' I say.

'Let him in,' Adam says.

'But Julie –'

'Will have to sort it out herself.' He strides determinedly towards the door.

'Is she here?' Nelson steps inside and looks wildly around. 'Did she tell you?'

Both of us look at the ground.

Nelson sighs. 'I've been a twit,' he mutters. 'I don't know how I thought I'd get away with it. And I wouldn't mind, but coming down here every weekend has lost me a few customers. They don't like getting all their milk on a Thursday. I gave them up for Julie.' He plonks down on the sofa, which shakes violently.

'Pity about you,' Julie's voice, ice cold, comes from the stairway.

Nelson stands up again. 'Just let me explain?'

'Don't you dare upset her,' Adam says quietly. 'Just say your piece and leave her.'

'Eh, I was talking to Julie,' Nelson says a bit snottily.

'Yeah, and I was talking to you,' Adam says. 'Now Ju –' He walks back to her and his hand caresses her shoulder – 'me and Hope will get out of your way, the place is all yours.'

I pull some stuff from the jumble of clothes on the floor. 'I'll just get changed and I'll be gone.' I shoot a look of solidarity at Julie but she's glaring at Nelson. I don't know how he can stand there and face her, I'd be terrified.

'You were so hot,' is the last thing I hear as I leave the room.

Adam and I stroll through the streets of Dingle, licking some rapidly melting ice-cream cones.

'I hope she doesn't take him back,' I mutter.

'Me too,' Adam says. 'She's better than that.'

'Yeah.'

'Had any luck on the job front?' I ask.

He flushes. 'Thanks for being so decent last night.'

'Only because you are,' I smile. 'So go on, any luck?'

'I've sent my CV out to a few places all right,' he admits. 'I'm hoping to hear back soon. I've sent yours out too.' He pauses. 'Are you coming back to London with us?'

'Of course I am.'

'Oh, it's just that I thought with your mother and every-thing —'

'I haven't seen her since that day in her house,' I admit. I dump my ice-cream into a bin. It's dripping all over my fingers. 'I mean, I think I'd like to, you know, because it's the normal thing to do, but for me, I, well, I think my life would be easier without her in it. Does that sound horrible?'

'Nothing is horrible if the reasons are right,' Adam says. He dumps his ice-cream too and begins licking his fingers, one by one. 'It's just a question, I suppose, of under-standing the reasons. And you, Hope Gardner, are not horrible.'

'Thanks.'

'Just like I'm not horrible.' He grins suddenly. 'Isn't that right?'

'Yeah.'

We pass a small shop selling pictures. One in the window catches my attention. It's the colours. Bright and vibrant. Then I notice that it's by Logan. Wow. He does have talent.

'Let's go in here.' I take Adam by the arm and guide him into the shop. 'I want to see what else Logan has done.'

His pictures dominate the shop. Oh, there are others, but

his are so loud that I'm drawn to them. Adam follows me about exclaiming over them too.

Two girls come in some minutes later. They look nice, I decide.

'Now Adam,' I whisper, 'this is your chance. Walk up there and tell those two women that you know the artist.'

'What?'

He says it loudly and the two girls look over at the commotion and then turn away again.

'Are you mad,' he hisses, looking in desperation at me. 'I can't do that.'

'Why not? You're sober, you do know the artist and there are two girls there who look like a bit of a laugh – go up and talk to them.'

'No.'

'Adam, think of me –'

'With the planes, yadda, yadda. I'm sick of you and the bloody planes.'

'Go on,' I laugh and give him a gentle shove in the back. 'Pretend that you're thinking of buying the picture, ask them what they think of it.'

'What if they think I'm weird?'

'So, they think you're weird. Big deal.'

He considers this. 'OK, Right. OK.' He starts to psych himself up. I wish he'd worn nicer clothes than his cords and cream T-shirt. Not exactly babe magnet stuff. Still, as he makes a slow walk towards them, I think that his one saving grace is his ass. He has a class A ass.

I see him study the picture the girls are looking at, then, as casual as anything, he turns to them and says, 'I'm thinking of buying you, think of the picture, yes?'

They look at him.

He flushes and I want to die for him.

Then one of the girls laughs. 'Pardon?' she giggles. 'What was that?'

'Yes,' Adam nods, trying to grin, 'I probably should rephrase that.'

That makes them both smile.

And he begins to chat to them, talking about the picture he's going to buy. I can see his shoulders hunch up and he starts that nervous thing with his hand through his hair, but the girls don't seem to notice. In fact, they agree that his choice is a good one.

And then, after about five minutes he excuses himself and comes back to me. 'I'm going to have to buy it now,' he says. 'Thanks.' But he's grinning.

Two hours later and two hundred quid down, Adam and I make our way back to the cottage. Adam has the number of one of the girls; they'd joined us for a coffee at my instigation. He has promised to call her, but I don't think he will. He's not ready to go there just yet, I don't think.

'Hey,' he says as we drive up, 'Nelson is gone.'

'Well, we have been away for hours,' I answer.

The back door is open and we shove it in. Though neither of us will admit it, we're both a bit nervous.

'Hello?'

I wonder if Julie has gone out. I'm just putting the kettle on for coffee when she comes into the kitchen. 'Hi,' she says quietly. She looks pale and sort of shocked. Even though she's dry eyed, she still manages to look ten times more upset than she had been.

'How did it go with Nelson?' I ask.

'What did he say?' Adam says.

Her lip quivers and she looks like a five-year-old. Leaning against the back door, she says as she wraps her arms about herself, 'I'm so shallow, I really am.'

'You? Shallow? Never?!' I make my voice sort of jokey. Of course she's shallow, everyone is shallow sometimes.

'I know you're joking, Hope, but it's true.' She shakes her head and says, 'I'm shallower than . . .' she tries to think of a comparison, 'shallower than a baby's paddling pool.'

'Did that muppet Nelson say you were shallow?' Adam sounds furious. 'Did he?'

'No.' Julie heaves a great big sigh. 'But he made me see that I was. Thanks.' I hand her a mug of coffee and, wrapping her hands around it, she takes a noisy slurp. 'When Nelson was here today, I realised that I'm a whole lot shallower than I even thought.'

'How come?'

'Well, when he stood here, telling me how he thought I was "hot". God, I hate that word, well, when he stood here today, I looked at him. I mean, really looked at him.' She stresses the 'really looked at him'.

'And?'

'Well, I realised that,' she swallows hard, 'that yes, I was only going out with him because I thought he owned a gym.'

God, I think, that is shallow, but I don't say it.

Adam does, though. 'That is a bit shallow all right.'

'Adam!' I nudge him furiously.

'He's right,' Julie says without any anger. 'I mean, without the gym, Nelson is just a ridiculous-looking man, isn't he? All horrible muscle and massive thighs. D'you know, Hope, his thigh is as big as your head.'

'Too much information.' I wave my free hand about.

She smiles briefly. 'Sorry. Anyhow, I looked at him today

261

and realised that I actually didn't like him. I didn't like him at all.' She sounds as if she can't believe that she went out with him. 'I didn't like the way he was always giving off about Adam. I think he was jealous of you, Adam. Imagine.' She rolls her eyes.

'Yeah, imagine,' Adam repeats, though he doesn't sound as convinced.

'We had a row once about you, Adam. And I didn't like the way he loved himself, I didn't like his pathetic lies. I wonder why I bothered with him.' She bites her lower lip. 'I mean, how could I have been so stupid?'

I don't know, myself.

'I don't know,' Adam says.

'And it was his gyms.' She pauses. 'But it wasn't only that.'

'No? What else?' I ask.

'You'll both think I'm pathetic. I know you will.' She points at herself, '*I* think I'm pathetic.'

Neither of us says anything.

'I went out with him because he owned those gyms and I thought –' for the first time her composure cracks slightly, her voice wobbles as she goes on – 'well, I thought, it'd impress my parents, didn't I? And I thought that it'd make Angela half crazy with jealousy. I mean, her boyfriend is only a professor of something or other.' She swallows hard. 'Isn't that awful of me?'

I borrow Adam's line of the night before. 'Awful but understandable.'

'Yes, understandable because I'm so superficial.'

'No.' I put my coffee down and try to choose my words. It's strange, me counselling Julie; it's normally the other way around. And it's nice that she's upset, it sort of makes me feel more connected to the world. 'It's understandable because no matter what, everyone cares about what their parents think.' Even me, funnily enough. 'I mean, I rebelled because I wanted my mother's attention. You conformed because you wanted to please them. It's all down to them, in the end.'

Julie is silent for a bit, then she says, in a surprisingly surprised voice, 'That's really good, Hope.'

'So,' I pat her hand, 'you can blame your folks. I blame my mother for everything.'

She grins. Then says, 'But I thought I'd outgrown all that. I did what I wanted by going into teaching. I gave my dad what for when we went for lunch that day. It's such a shock to realise that I still want their approval.'

'Yeah well . . .' I shrug. 'It's nice to have your folks' approval.'

'And I was trying to get one over on Angela. I'm pathetic, aren't I?'

'No, Nelson was pathetic.'

'We suited each other.'

'No. Never.'

'Never.' Adam nods vigorously. 'I told you you could do better, remember?'

'Yeah, Adam, I remember.'

The two of them smile at each other.

'You can do so much better,' he says intensely. 'And,' hesitantly he holds out his new purchase, 'if Logan can give a picture to Hope to say sorry, then I can give one to you. Sorry for all the stuff I said, about your play and everything. It was a brilliant play.'

I'm stunned. What an apology. The picture cost a fortune.

Julie looks at the picture and then at Adam. 'Thanks,' she says, taking it from him. 'But I knew you didn't mean it.'

Adam flicks me an amused glance but I keep my face straight.

27

THE DAY I'VE put off thinking about for the past week arrives. I've begun to dread the thought of the weekly counselling session, mainly because I'm knackered for about two days afterwards and today will be the worst day so far. Today will be the day I have to talk about Jamie. Really talk about Jamie. Talk about the day Jamie died. I think it's the day I died too, in a way.

'Hiya,' Tim beckons me in.

'See you eleven-thirty,' Adam and Julie say simultaneously.

It's all a bit embarrassing, everyone knowing I have to go to therapy.

Tim's office doesn't look as neat as before. It's messy with files everywhere. Something like Tim, actually. He looks a bit rough too.

'Sorry.' Tim scoops up some files and dumps them into an open cabinet. 'I'm hopeless at keeping the place clean.' To my surprise, he lifts a sleeping bag off the floor and, opening the messiest filing cabinet I have ever seen, shoves it inside and slams the drawer shut. 'Now,' he surveys his office, scratches his hair and pulls at his ponytail. 'Now, where is the recorder?'

'On the desk.'

'Sure. Of course.' He flashes me a smile and busies himself

looking for batteries for it. 'You're doing well, Hope,' he mutters from under the table where he is rummaging about in a box. 'Someone with your background can be very difficult to work with.' When he pops his head back up, I glimpse two new batteries in his hand.

'Really?' I don't know whether to feel proud or not.

'So now . . .' he assumes his position in the chair, inserts the batteries into the recorder, and looks at me. 'How have you got on with the other tape?'

'Good.' I think about how to say what I want to say. 'I mean, I can listen to it and it isn't as horrible each time but it makes me feel, I dunno,' I gulp hard, 'well, really sad, I suppose.' I sound defensive.

'Well, you told me your brother died,' Tim says gently. 'Of course you should be sad. Maybe at the time you weren't sad enough.'

'Maybe.'

He takes me through some relaxation and finally asks if I'm ready to talk. 'Just stop if the anxiety gets too much.'

'OK,' I gulp hard and decide to jump straight in. 'One day, Jamie didn't feel too good.'

I stop.

'Hope?' Tim looks at me quizzically.

'I, I can't.'

'How anxious are you now?'

'Ten.'

Tim switches off the recorder. 'OK. Now here's what I want you to do.' He talks me through another relaxation technique that he has made me practise. It takes a while but eventually I calm down.

'Now, I want you to imagine what happened when Jamie felt sick. Just think about it.'

I do. I feel sick.

'And again. Think about it again. What happened when Jamie felt sick.'

I do. I still feel sick. But Tim gets me to keep at it. When my anxiety level is at an eight, he asks me to go on.

I close my eyes. I'd talked about this only once before. With another counsellor. I can still see that day. In all its horror. The horror of a child who is powerless. And the horror of unforgiving time. I would have sold my soul to turn back time that day. To take back the choices I made.

I've been making the wrong choices ever since, I think.

He felt sick, he said, and he was pale. A funny blotchy pale. But he got out of bed and said that he would go to school, otherwise I'd have to forge a note for him and he knew I hated doing that in case we got caught. So he climbed out of bed and stood swaying for a second before getting sick all over the place. I made him climb back in. He felt hot. I cleaned up his sick and said that I'd take the day off school too. I could say we both had a tummy bug. Jamie nodded and closed his eyes. They were sore, he said. Turn off the light.

I did what I was told and tiptoed out of the room.

I spent the morning trying to get Mammy to eat some toast and doing the washing. About two hours later, I checked on Jamie. He had a headache. He was delirious. For the first time I felt uneasy. 'Will I get a doctor?' I asked him.

I made out a 'no'. Or at least I thought I did.

I thought he said 'no'.

'Hope, relax,' Tim says. 'Just relax. It's a memory. A bad memory but you can't change it now. You have to live with it. Relax.'

I breathe deeply. Oh God, how I wish I didn't have to

live with it. All the lies I'd told came back to haunt me that day.

'So,' Tim says when he sees I'm relaxed, 'what happened then?'

I told Mammy that Jamie seemed to be very sick. But she told me to stop lying and to leave her alone. I kept insisting. Crying and insisting and asking what could I do? I told her I was going to call the doctor. I don't think she answered.

I sat for the next hour with Jamie, holding his hand, trying to talk to him. He didn't respond, I watched him sleep, only he wasn't sleeping, not really.

Then I noticed the rash.

I'm crying. Tim switches off the tape. 'Let's leave it there, OK?' His voice is soft and caring. 'OK, Hope? Take a little break.'

I can only nod.

But the memories are sweeping in now that the door has been opened a crack.

The blue of the sky that day. The red quilt on Jamie's bed. The way my mother looked like a skeleton, though I hadn't noticed at the time. The dirt in the house, the washing piled high. The way I shook constantly.

The red-purple rash on Jamie's hand.

If only I'd made other choices.

Tim plays the tape for me. I listen to it and I cry my eyes out. I haven't even got to the worst part. And Tim plays it again. And again. And again. And again. I don't think I'll ever stop crying. There's a hole in my belly that's heaving with all the tears I want to cry. But amazingly, after a while, I don't know how long, they dry up. I listen to the tape for what must be about the tenth time and I hear the sadness in my voice and I feel like crying for me instead.

Tim waits a second or two before asking me if I want to continue. 'We can stop now if you like.'

But I'll have to face it again next week and I'm not sure if I can do that. I might chicken out. There's a very high percentage of that. 'I'll go on,' I say. 'There's not a lot more to tell.'

'OK, in your own time.'

I saw the rash. Purple. Spreading as I looked.

'Mammy!' I screamed. 'Mammy!'

Jamie hardly stirred.

In my mother's room, I heard a low moan. I ran in, screaming and crying and telling her what the matter was. Screaming as loud as I could. Screaming so that everyone would hear. I shook her so hard, her bones seemed to rattle under her skin. I shook her so that maybe something could happen to change things. In the end, when she'd pulled herself up in the bed, I didn't even wait for her to say anything, instead I half fell, half tripped down the stairs to the red telephone. For seconds I stared at it, knowing that the world was now going to come crashing into our lives. Knowing that Jamie didn't want that but having no choice. I rang an ambulance.

Jamie died in his bed with his mother cradling him and me sobbing in the doorway.

I sob again as I tell the story. Cry as if my heart is breaking. It seems so long since I've cried. It *is* so long since I've cried like this. I'm not good at it. I heave and almost retch. 'All he needed to be happy was his family and we let him down.'

Tim lets me cry. I cry for ages. Eventually he passes me a suspect-looking handkerchief which I try to look as if I'm using.

'Are you ready to go on?'

He was buried. Meningitis, they said. My mother was let out of the hospital for the funeral but was brought back in again and she stayed for a long time. I was sent to a foster home in the area but kept at the same school. Everyone knew and nobody talked about it. When they tried to get me to counselling, I went missing. What was the point? I'd told so many lies to so many people that I hardly knew what the truth was any more. And facing the truth would be hard. And Jamie would still be dead at the end of it.

'What's the worst thing about that story for you, Hope?'

'That my brother died.'

'Did you feel guilty? How did you think? How do you think now?'

His questions come at me like bullets. He probably isn't talking so fast, but to me, it seems overwhelming.

'Of course I felt guilty. I still live with the "if-onlys".' I clench the handkerchief hard in my hand and lean towards Tim. 'If I'd only rung earlier, if only I hadn't let my mother get into such a state, if only I'd told someone. But we didn't want to be sent away. And Jamie trusted me. And depended on me.'

'You did the best you could at the time, didn't you?'

'I was a kid. I had no power. I just tried to keep all the people with power out of our lives. And by doing that, I killed Jamie.'

'You did the best you could at the time, didn't you?' he repeats. 'You made him happy in the months before that.

270

He might still have got sick and died and you'd still blame yourself – wouldn't you?'

Those words halt the other words I'm about to say. I think about what Tim has said. I think about me and Jamie with a foster mother and him getting sick. Yes, I realise, I would have blamed myself. I'd have thought it was something he picked up at the foster mother's or something.

'No matter what happened, you would have blamed yourself. Hope, you did your best.'

I did my best. I blink.

'You did what you felt had to be done. OK, it ended sadly, but if you could turn back time, would you really have done it differently?'

I think back. I feel the fear creeping over me of being sent to a stranger's house. Even now, I can never sleep when I go somewhere new. I feel the pity for my mother and for Jamie and I think that maybe I would do the exact same thing again. Maybe.

'Thanks,' is all I can whisper. And it's the most heartfelt thanks I have ever uttered.

Tim plays the tape for me. I listen to my halting words. That girl on the tape is me, I think. The real, hurt me. Not the smartass woman I present to the world. Not the kid that lied her way from childhood to adulthood. For a long time, I despised the child in me that had messed up so badly. Now, I just feel glad that I was once her and that I once felt so deeply and cared so deeply. The new me and the London me too, I realise, just gets angry when stuff doesn't go her way. It's the easiest thing to do. I can't bear to feel power-less so I give myself power. I walk out of jobs when someone makes me feel less than valuable. I walk out of jobs rather than accept my lack of power.

I listen to that tape and suddenly I understand myself a little better. I make sense to myself.

'Hey, what happened in there?' Julie asks when I emerge. 'You've been crying.'

'Yeah.' I wipe a hasty fist across my eye. 'It's been a bit of a rollercoaster.'

'Is it working?'

'I think it is.'

'Have you remembered the accident yet?'

'We haven't even gone there yet.'

She looks surprised. 'But, you've been going for weeks now.'

I stare at her. My best friend. Oh, I have other mates, but none like Julie. I wonder how I let her get so close. Maybe because she was so different to me, I just never figured that I would get to like her so much. And they've been so good, bringing me to therapy and never pressing for information. Adam is behind her, smiling at me in his lovely gentle way. I imagine him living his lie of a working life and I feel that I have to explain to them. To let them see the real me.

'Can we go for a coffee?'

They've never yet refused that invitation.

It's Adam's idea. He suggests it and I probably would never have thought of it myself, but once he says it, I know it's the right thing to do. So we hop into his car and twenty minutes later I find myself outside a graveyard that I haven't visited in a decade. I've bought a bunch of roses at the entrance and Julie and Adam have bought some flowers too, which is lovely of them, I think.

I lead the way to the grave. The direction is burnt into my memory the way a farmer brands an animal, hot and painful and always there. To the right, straight on and finally we stop at a surprisingly well tended grave marked with a simple white headstone.

In loving memory of Frank Gardner, loving husband, sadly missed by his wife Helen and children Hope and Jamie and also our precious little boy, Jamie, who died age 12. Missed by his loving mother and sister.
Rest in Peace.

A picture of Jamie sits on top of the grave and Julie picks it up. Her face softens and I think she might cry. 'Oh Hope, was he –?'

'Yes, he was.'

I take the picture and study my little brother. He's about eight in it. Dressed in shorts and a T-shirt with a big banana-shaped smile. His happiness in the picture is palpable. Jamie was a very happy kid. 'Hi Jamie,' I whisper. 'It's Hope.'

Adam and Julie lay their flowers beside some others that have been left on the grave, then, squeezing me on the shoulder, they move off.

I sit down on the grass and place my flowers alongside my friends'. 'Just came to say hi,' I mutter and then I don't say anything else, just sit there, feeling peaceful and sad all at the one time. Every so often I hear Julie exclaim aloud over what she's reading on the various headstones. Things along the lines of, 'Oh God, three brothers in this one, isn't that terrible?' And another time, 'Wow, imagine being that old!'

The two of them arrive back, Julie red-eyed and Adam

looking at her in faint amusement. 'Well,' he half grins, 'there's nothing like a graveyard for a bit of fun.'

'Stop!' Julie thumps him. 'It just makes you realise, when you read all those headstones, how lucky you are.'

And she's right, it really does.

28

I TAKE THE Dictaphone around the back of the house. It's the eighth time I've listened to the tape since it was recorded. It's a cool enough day, with more cloud in the sky than in the last month. It looks like the heat wave is nearing an end. The thought depresses me slightly. I sit down in my usual spot, my back against the wall of the cottage, plug in the earphones and listen to a voice that I barely recognise as mine, talking about an event that shattered whatever hope I'd ever had.

To my amazement, it doesn't hurt as much listening now. I mean, my heart speeds up and I break out in a sweat, but instead of it consuming me whole, I can half recognise the real emotion underneath the terror. And when I recognise the emotion, I feel more terror. It's like a huge black grief-ridden hole inside me. I think that if I get too near, I'll fall in and never come out. But each day the terror of the event diminishes is a day I get nearer the grief. Which is scary enough. Each time I listen, I remember things in a little more detail. This time I recall Jamie saying, 'I just want us all to be together, Hope.' He didn't speak really well, Jamie, but I could understand him. And I could understand why he'd say that.

Going to his grave has taken the edge off the grief too. It helps, knowing that it's neat and tidy and remembered.

'Hey.' Adam, smiling, comes out into the garden about ten minutes later, just as I'm pressing the rewind button to listen again. 'I got some good news at last.'

'What?'

'He's got a job interview,' Julie answers, following behind him. 'What's it for again, Adam?'

'Manager of a small hardware store.'

'Oh, yeah, great,' I try to sound enthusiastic. 'Good for you.'

'Yes,' Adam reads my mind, 'it is a bit of a comedown.' He doesn't sound too unhappy about it, though. 'But I have to start somewhere. I have to think positive.'

'But what will you say when they ask why you're interested in that job when you've had a bigger and better job?'

Adam shrugs, unperturbed. 'I don't know. I'll cross that bridge when I come to it.'

'Well, if it's a half-decent hardware store, you'll probably build the bridge too,' Julie says, giggling.

'Awful joke.' Adam makes an anguished face.

'So when is the interview?'

'Two days' time. I have a suit in London, so I'll fly over tomorrow night and pick that up. I should be back the next day then. I'll just go up to the computer and book my flights.'

He bounds inside, full of enthusiastic energy.

Julie looks at me, her eyebrows raised questioningly. 'What if he doesn't get it?' she whispers. 'Like a piddling little job like that – what if they turn him down? It'll dent his confidence horribly.'

'Hopefully they'll see how good he is,' I say. 'Let's just wait and see.' I wrap the earplugs around the Dictaphone and lay it on the ground beside me. Julie is just about to sit down too when a shout makes us both look up.

It's Logan. I don't know how we didn't spot him before this. I wonder if he wants me to go walking with him again. I haven't seen him in a good few days and just looking at him now, I realise that I've missed the unpredictable creature. One-handed, Logan jumps over the low stone wall dividing our garden from the field next door and strides towards us.

'Cor,' Julie whispers in an undertone to me. 'Get a load of that. A bit of all right or what?'

Logan has had his hair cut. It's now very short and very shiny. It shows off his fine arched eyebrows and wide-set blue eyes. But his clothes are still on the manky side. 'Hi, girls,' he greets us with a big sunny smile. 'Enjoying the clouds?' He indicates the sky, which is getting more sullen looking by the minute.

'Fabulous,' I smirk. 'I come here for the clouds every year.'

'I like the hair,' Julie says admiringly.

'Lack of hair, you mean,' Logan says, running a paint-splattered hand through it. 'Got it done yesterday.'

'Suits you,' Julie nods. 'Doesn't he look much nicer, Hope?'

I can feel myself flushing. 'Yeah,' I mutter, reluctant to say any more.

'Go easy on the praise now, Hope, don't go overboard or anything.'

'I wish someone would throw you overboard,' I retaliate, grinning.

Logan laughs. 'Anyhow, witty and all as you are, Hope, I was looking for Adam. I need a favour.'

'In his room,' Julie says. 'Go on up.'

Logan disappears into the house. 'Wonder what he wants?' Julie muses.

I shrug, pretending not to care. I'm disappointed that he hadn't wanted me because I would have liked to go on a walk. Adam and Julie hate walking. They can't see the point of having a car if you're going to walk. The environment doesn't stand a chance with the two of them. From Adam's room, I can hear murmured voices. Adam arrives down a few seconds later, with Logan in tow.

'Just heading to Logan's to help him move some furniture and stuff,' Adam announces. 'Back in a while.'

They jump into Adam's car and are gone.

For some reason, I feel a weird sense of foreboding.

About three hours later they arrive back. Adam is in bits. He's obviously not used to any sort of major physical work. 'Just going to have a quick shower,' he says as he lopes by us. He grabs some fresh clothes from the line and disappears into the shower room.

Logan has obviously showered at home. He's also changed into a gorgeous sparkling white T-shirt and a cool pair of denims. All in all, the effect is sexual heaven.

'New clothes?' Julie asks.

'Was I that bad before?' Logan grins. Without waiting for an answer, he says, 'I've just ordered some food from the Chinese in Dunport, do you eat Chinese?'

The three of us are Chinese addicts.

'Yummy.' Julie immediately begins setting the table. She pulls out a bottle of wine and uncorks it. 'Hope, get some forks, would you?'

I do as I'm bid as Logan stands there, his hands in his pockets, watching us.

'Adam was a great help today,' Logan says, 'so I decided that I'd better treat you. And what with Hope doing her guided tours for free too, I really owe you one.' He winks over at me.

I'm not exactly happy with my help being in the same class as Adam's.

'You don't owe me anything,' I say, shyly. 'I like the walks, I told you that.'

'Aw well, I've finished the commission now. Tell ya one thing, I'd never work for that fecker Jack again.'

Finished? Is he telling me he won't need me to walk with him any more? To show him new places and new sights? Did he really only want my help with his art or did he want my company too? I don't know, and the disappointment of not knowing comes as a big surprise. I feel that if we'd even had one more day together, things might have got off the ground a bit more. That instead of him telling me he liked me, he might have kissed me. Oh, the thought of him kissing me sends shivers right through my body.

'Are you cold, Hope?' Julie asks.

I jump. 'No. Why?' My face has flushed again.

'You shivered and now you've gone all red. I hope you're not coming down with something. Do you feel poorly?'

'I feel fine.'

The fact that I'm in counselling, I think, might be a factor against going out with someone. But how would I feel if someone else moved in on him while I was faffing about? Then again, I'm going home in a few weeks, so a relationship is definitely out. No, I decide, I won't make a move on him, it wouldn't be fair. If he, however, made a move on me . . .

'Move up there, Hope,' Adam says, reappearing, his hair damp from the shower, but looking a lot less wrecked. 'Make some space at the table.'

The bell rings, announcing the arrival of our dinner. Logan answers the door and arrives back in, his arms laden with boxes and packets. That's the great thing about Chinese, there are so many *bits* to it. Little dips and different types of rice.

'Hope ya can eat all this,' Logan says as he dumps the food on the table. 'I'm totally starving. I haven't eaten dinner for about a week, trying to get myself organised.'

'Organised for what?' I ask, helping myself to some fried rice.

'The pictures had to be ready for the Gleeson Hotel opening by tomorrow, so I've been working flat out.'

'And his ex is coming down as well,' Adam says, heaping his plate high with chow mein, 'so he had to do a bit of a clean-up.'

Logan chortles. 'Yeah, that's why I got the new clothes and the haircut, she's a hard girl to impress, so she is.'

His ex? I glance up at him. He smiles back at me. His ex is coming and he's trying to impress her. His ex is coming. But he'd told *me* I was gorgeous.

'Your ex?' Julie is agog. She loves relationship stuff. 'But if she's your ex, why is she coming? I thought the word ex meant you never saw them again.'

'She's coming to sort things out,' Logan says with a big smile. 'At last she sees sense.'

They're going to sort things out. I bite my lip and I don't think I can eat anything else. I feel ill. I think of what might have happened if I'd told him I liked him. Thank God I didn't. But he made me vulnerable. He *almost* made a fool out of me. He reminds me of Jack suddenly, of how I fell for Jack and he left me. And thinking like that makes me angry. I haven't felt the white searing anger since I started counselling, but I can feel it now.

'But she's not coming till tomorrow evening,' Logan

continues, oblivious to my mounting anger. 'As I'm away tomorrow afternoon.'

'So where are you off to tomorrow?' Julie asks.

'Probably getting a facial done to impress his ex,' I say, with only a hint of anger in my voice.

Logan laughs. 'God,' he mock-groans, 'I should have thought of that when I was buying the new clothes.'

I feel sadder than ever.

'Naw, no facial, Hope,' he grins that grin at me and I feel the loss of him so keenly it hurts. 'I've to bring the pictures down to the hotel and tell them how I want them hung. There's a van coming tomorrow to load them up. I'll probably be there until tea time.'

'How you want your pictures hung?' I say. My nasty tone is stronger now. I wish I could stop it, I know I should stop it, but it's either that or cry. 'Does it really matter? They're only pictures.'

He doesn't seem to take offence. 'Yeah, course it matters. You can't have a big picture on a small wall unless you want it to cover the wall. You need light to show off some pictures to their best. It all matters. Some pictures have to be hung in sequence. All that kind of thing.'

'Most people wouldn't notice.'

'You'd be surprised.' He grins at me.

'Yeah, I would, actually.'

He stares at me, not sure how exactly I mean that comment. I think he's a little thrown. 'Maybe you wouldn't notice,' he concedes, 'but if they were hung wrongly, you wouldn't think the pictures were as good.'

'I suppose with the way you paint, you need all the help you can get.'

'Hope!' Julie exclaims.

'Joke.' I raise my eyebrows and don't smile.

Logan looks at me, confused, I think. When I still don't smile, he spears a piece of chicken. 'Well,' he says, chewing carefully, 'I think your jokes are about as crappy as you obviously think my painting is.'

And with that comment, the evening is ruined. It's his sour voice and his morose expression combined with my sneering tone and my morose expression. Never before have I deliberately hurt him. But he has hurt me too. Or at the very least, he led me on. And he did lead me on. It wasn't my imagination. Still, I do feel like a heel. But to apologise would be like saying to him, Oh yeah, it's OK to hurt me, go right ahead. And I can't do that.

He doesn't stay long after that. And when he goes, Adam and Julie turn on me. I'm stacking the plates, pretending that things are fine, but Julie surprises me by grabbing them off me and slamming them down on the table. 'What the hell did you have to go and ruin the night for?' she demands. 'I thought you liked Logan.'

I bite my lip. 'I just don't like his paintings.' It comes out sounding defensive.

'So, you decide to tell him that? You think that's nice after he's just spent ages painting stuff for the local hotel?'

'Can we just clean the kitchen?'

'No, Hope, we can't. How would you feel if I told you what I don't like about you?'

'Fire ahead.'

Of course, she doesn't. Instead she looks at me, all concerned, 'Hope, why did you do it? It just came out of nowhere.'

I can't tell her. I just can't, the humiliation would be too much to bear.

Adam surveys me from his position on the sofa. 'I don't know,' he says cagily, 'I thought there was a nice little fling blooming there for a while. Him calling for you with little picnics, bringing you for coffee, you showing him around.'

'I was just helping him out. And anyway, he and his ex are sorting things out: why would you think we'd have a fling?'

'Because the guy liked you, Hope. It was as obvious as the nose on your face.'

'Well, if he liked me so much, why is he going back to his ex?'

Silence.

'Rewind,' Adam says quietly. 'Logan is going back to his ex, is that what you said?'

'No, it's what he said. Sorting things out, he said.'

'Yeah,' Adam glares at me, but he's smiling, albeit in an incredulous way, 'they owned a house in Dublin, she sold it, she wouldn't pay him his half and now she's coming to sort things out.'

Oh shit!

'But he got his hair done and moved furniture and –'

'To show her he was doing fine without her.'

I am the world's biggest mouth. Biggest idiot. Biggest bitch. I can't even react.

'Julie,' I turn to her for some support, 'didn't you think he was getting back with his ex?'

'No,' Julie shakes her head. 'I got the impression that she hurt him too much for that.'

I look from one to the other of them and suddenly want to get out. I don't want to discuss what I just did, how I ruined what could have been a lovely friendship by my stupid insecurities. Blindly, I push past Julie.

'Hope, come back.'

But I leave.

I arrive back at about three in the morning. I spent the time sitting and looking at the ocean, until it became too cold for me. I think about what I did. How I felt out of control again and how I lashed out. Have I learned nothing from all my previous experiences? Before, though, it was bosses who got the brunt of it. Now it was someone I'd come to care about. Why hadn't I clarified things?

I owe him a huge apology.

I sneak back in and all is quiet. Though I do hear Julie moving about upstairs. I think she's been waiting up for me. As silently as I can, I pull out my sleeping bag and without undressing or washing, I crawl inside.

I will do the right thing, this time, I swear to myself.

29

'W ELL,' JULIE SHAKES me awake the next day, 'did you go and apologise to him last night?'

I groan, pretending not to be fully awake and crawl further down in the sleeping bag. Last night uncoils itself from my memory like a rattlesnake.

'Hope! Did you apologise or not!' Julie almost deafens me; her mouth is so close to the side of my face.

'Ouch!' I sit up and rub my ear. 'Do you mind, I was asleep!' Then at her unrelenting stare, I shake my head and mutter 'No'.

'So where did you get to?' she asks, sitting back on her hunkers. 'I thought you'd jumped into the sea or something, I was about to call out rescue services. It was Adam's idea that maybe you'd gone over to Logan's.'

I probably should have, I realise then. That would have been a good idea. 'Well I didn't,' I say back. I pull the sleeping bag up to my chin, like a comfort blanket. 'Sorry if I worried you, I just went for a walk and had a bit of a think. It's not easy to hang around when you've just made a big fool out of yourself.'

'You fancy him, don't you?' It's a statement.

I squirm under her gaze and mutter, 'I'm not sure.'

'Oh, Hope, come on, be honest with yourself. You light up

when the bloke walks into the room. And you had a big hissy fit last night because you thought he was getting back with his ex. That must mean you at least want him for yourself.'

I think about this. I know one thing: I don't want anyone else to have him. 'Well, yes, I do like him,' I admit.

'Fancy him,' Julie interjects.

I ignore that. 'But I don't know if he likes me, and after last night I'm sure he'll never want to talk to me again.'

'Well, regardless of whether he does or not, you still owe him an apology.' Julie surveys me. 'And I hope you're going to give him one.'

'I could make a rude comment just there.' I crack a smile.

'Don't joke your way out of it, Hope.'

'I know,' I heave a big sigh. 'You're right. I'll call over this morning.'

'He's busy this morning, moving all his pictures. You'll have to leave it until tomorrow.'

That's right. Shit! And then his ex is coming and who knows what might happen there. I just hope he remembers all that he said was wrong with her. 'First thing tomorrow morning, I'll be outside his place.'

'Good.' Julie nods approvingly. 'Only thing is, you'll have to walk over because Adam will have the car and won't be able to drive you.'

'Yeah, I don't mind walking.' It'll help build up my courage.

'I'll go with you if you like.'

'No thanks, Ju.'

'Are you sure, because you know you might die of shock having to apologise.'

'Ha bloody ha.' I reach out from my sleeping bag and grab the sofa cushion which is lying on the floor. Julie hates that cushion as it's so manky. Aiming it, I fire it at her retreating body. Laughing a little, I lie back down. It dawns on me, slowly, that I was upset last night. I actually felt upset. OK, I was angry but I was upset too. I almost wanted to cry when I heard Logan going on about his ex. And it's scary having to apologise for being so horrible to him, but I feel scared, and I feel regret and I feel guilt and now, Julie has made me smile.

It dawns on me slowly that I can *feel* again.

Some part of the old Hope is back.

At last.

Later that day, Adam drives off, but not before he gives me a lecture on how badly I behaved last night and how I really should apologise. I agree with everything he says and promise him faithfully that I will. He tells me that he thinks Logan really likes me and that if I liked him I'd be mad to blow it over a stupid misunderstanding. 'I'd just like to see you with someone nice,' he says.

I get a lump in my throat at his concern. 'And I'd like to see you with someone nice too,' I tell him. 'So, after the interview, I want you to go into a coffee shop and buy a coffee for a girl on her own, OK.'

'Yeah. OK.'

We hug each other without any awkwardness. 'Give 'em hell at the interview!'

'Will do.' He turns to Julie. 'Bye.'

'Yeah. See you. And don't buy coffee for a really good-looking girl,' she says. 'They're always the bitches.'

'You must get a lot of coffee bought for you then, eh?' Adam jokes.

'Oh, go get lost.' Julie pushes him into the car. 'Go on, safe driving!'

With a beep of his horn, he's gone.

Julie and I run out into the road after him and wave until he's out of sight.

We're in Dunport, having walked there from the cottage. Julie is in bits, she's never walked as far in her life. And no one has ever walked as far in high-heeled sandals either.

'It's my mother's birthday next week,' she says as she sits down on the small harbour wall to examine her feet. 'I don't know if I should ring her.'

'You should ring her,' I say. I sit down beside her and wince at the massive blister on the ball of her foot, 'but what you really want to know is, do you want to ring her?'

'Yep. That's it exactly. She'll probably rip my head off.'

'So? Just do it, at least you won't regret it.'

'Mmm.' Her blond hair falls across her face as she gazes at her foot. 'Is there a chemist here at all?'

'McCoys will probably do a plaster.' I stand up. 'You wait here.' And then I spot him. Striding along the main street, bigger and more mature than I remember, but still with the ability to make me weak at the sight of him. My heart lurches and I sit back down on the wall, hoping like hell he won't spot me. The last time I'd seen this guy was when I was eighteen.

'Oh God.'

I feel suddenly ill.

'What? What?' Julie looks up at me.

'That guy, coming towards us, I know him.' I gulp hard. 'Julie, how do I look? Quick, tell me how I look?'

'Just normal.' She looks at me, puzzled and then at Jack, who is getting closer and who seems to be heading in our direction.

'Ohhh.' I wish I'd worn my nice jeans instead of my tracksuit this morning, but it's too late now. I want to get up and race across the street, but that'll only draw attention to us. I just have to sit tight and hope he walks on by.

'Julie,' I hiss, 'that's Jack!'

Julie is looking in bewilderment from me to the man. 'Jack who?' she hisses back.

'Jack, the, the, fecking guy I used to go out with. The one who owns the hotels now.'

'Oh God!' She looks me up and down. 'You don't want to look like that when you meet an ex.'

'I know,' I groan.

He's getting nearer.

'Quick, put your head down,' I say to Julie.

I pretend to be looking at her foot. She pretends she wants me looking at her foot.

'Hey, Hope? Hope Gardner?'

He's stopped and is standing over us.

I take a deep breath. Fuck it, I suddenly think. What the hell does it matter what this guy thinks? Why should I have to look good in front of him? So what if he thinks I'm a slob. So. Bloody. What. At least my hair is OK. There's not much of it to be in a mess.

'Hello?' Slowly I look up. I try out a puzzled look as if I don't know who it is.

Jack stands, hands in his pockets, trying, I think, to look relaxed and casual. 'Hiya, Hope.' He smiles a tad nervously. 'I thought it was you. It's me. Jack. D'you remember?'

How could I fucking forget, I want to snap. But I don't. I'm very proud of myself as I smile and nod and say, admittedly through gritted teeth, 'Hey, Jack. Yes I remember you. How's things?' If only I could have been so calm with Logan yesterday, I would have been better off. But better late than never. I stand up so I'm on his level.

'Things are good.' Jack nods, trying out a smile. 'I heard you were back. Greg Lynch told me, so when I saw you walking along, I thought I'd catch up and say hi. I was going to call in to see you in Maurice's cottage tomorrow.'

'Oh, were you?' Jack looks, well, without exaggeration, totally great. Nice faded denims, expensive ones. Expensive trainers and a white grandfather shirt with the crocodile label. 'Oh, by the way, this is Julie. She's a friend of mine.' I indicate Julie who has been looking at us anxiously, unsure what to do.

'Hi, Julie,' Jack proffers a clean hand, his nails shaped and in better condition than mine. 'I'm an old friend of Hope's from school.' He winces as he catches a glimpse of her foot, 'Ouch, that looks nasty.'

'We walked a long way,' Julie smiles, taking his hand in hers.

Jack smiles back. 'That's Hope for you. D'you need a plaster?'

'I'm getting her one,' I say, thinking how ridiculous this whole conversation is.

'Good,' Jack grins. Then he says, 'I was going to call on you tomorrow, Hope, to ask you if you'd like to come to the hotel opening Saturday week.'

I'm stunned. Behind me I can hear Julie suck in her breath. Anything remotely glamorous and she's up for it.

'Hotel opening?' I can't resist pretending that I don't know what he's talking about. 'What hotel opening?'

Julie hops up and pokes me in the back.

'Oh,' Jack flushes. 'Well,' he tries to say modestly, 'I don't know if you know, but I'm in charge of the big new hotel there,' he points to the entrance gate, 'and we're having an opening night on the twenty-eighth of July for friends and business people and anyone associated with the hotel. And when I heard you were about, I just wanted to invite you.' He pauses. 'It'd be nice if you could come. It should be a good night and it'd be great to catch up.'

He sounds as if he means it. A small part of me thinks he wants to show off to me, which is a little flattering.

'Oh right,' I nod. 'That sounds good.'

'So the opening is Saturday week. And everyone who comes gets to stay over in the hotel too. It'll be fun.'

'I'm sure it will,' I say, and my voice has grown steadier and more pleasant as I go on. 'But I might be doing something, I'll have to check and get back to you.'

He looks slightly taken aback. 'Well, yeah, of course. Sure, I tell you what, I'll reserve the room anyway, how about that?'

'OK,' I nod. 'But I actually have two friends staying here so –'

He doesn't let me finish. 'You can all come.' He looks beyond me to Julie, who is barely able to contain her delight, there is this massive smile on her face about to break out. 'Would you like to?'

Julie shoots a look at me before nodding and going 'mmm' in a really high-pitched way.

'That would be great, thanks for thinking of us, Jack.'

'No probs.' He smiles again and seems about to say something else but then nods and indicates the street. 'Anyway, I'll go. Nice to see you, Hope.'

We watch as he saunters off.

Julie turns to me and squeals. 'Yes! Yes! Yes!'

'Well, I'm glad you're happy,' I say to her, amused.

'I'm more happy for you,' she says, her hands grabbing my arms. 'You were magnificent! Oh, I'm so proud of you! God, I thought you were going to chew him up and spit him out, I really did! And you didn't. You were great!'

'Was I?' I know I was, but I want her to say it again.

'You. Were. Fab.' Julie shakes her head. 'I think I could learn a thing or two from you, you were so, so . . .' she scrunches up her cute face as she tries to find the right word, 'so mature,' she finishes.

'I just didn't want another Logan scene,' I admit. 'It was totally the wrong thing to do last night.'

Julie nods. 'He'll be all over you when you apologise,' she says. 'I think he's mad about you.'

'He's mad at me, more like.'

She ignores that. 'And wow! Oh, Hope, we're going to the big opening, how cool is that?' She does a one-legged dance and her excitement makes me laugh. Then she frowns. 'But we've nothing to wear. We're going to have to go shopping!'

Shit! I hadn't thought of that.

30

I'M UP EARLY the next morning. The apology to Logan is hanging over me like a swarm of midges. Just when the worry has disappeared, a little part of my memory gets stung again and I quake at the thought of what I should say. Over and over in my head I've played out various scenarios. 'Sorry about the other night, I got the wrong end of the stick.' Of course, then he'll want to know what the wrong end of the stick was and I'll be forced to admit that yes, I was jealous and annoyed because I thought he was going back to his ex. That would be embarrassing. I'm not an up-front girl that can just grab a man. For one thing, I don't feel attractive enough to do that, especially now with only an inch of hair on my head. It's typical: if only my waistline was as slow growing, I'd be thrilled. So no, I cannot confess that I like him. It's OK for Julie to tell me she thinks he's mad about me, but so far, apart from him saying he *likes* me, which is not in the same league at all, I have no proof of that.

Some time in the early hours, I had the, quite frankly heinous, thought of blaming my outburst on my unstable mind. 'It's the counselling, Logan, I can't help it.' Yes, it's a cop-out but I don't care.

Later on, I decide to plumb for a wait and see what

happens tactic: going in totally unprepared and just letting the dialogue take its course. That way I don't have time to be nervous. Maybe a simple 'sorry' will suffice.

At seven, before Julie even turns over for her second sleep, I am washed and dressed and ready to leave the cottage. Logan is generally up early and I just want to get the apology over with and be able to enjoy the rest of the day. As the morning is damp and misty, I pull on the horrible pink pig boots over my jeans and stride off across the field.

There is a car outside his house.

A blue car with teddies strewn all over the back seat. It can only be *hers*! She must have stayed the night. I feel sick. For some reason I thought she'd be staying in a B&B somewhere.

I think about leaving. Yes, I still owe him an apology, but I never banked on his ex being there to witness it. I stare at the car for a few more minutes and decide to turn back. I'll talk to him another day, when she has gone, assuming she *is* going to leave.

The cat crawls out from under the car and glares at me with malevolent green eyes. It starts to hiss so I hiss back. It arches its back and spits. 'Go away, you mangy thing,' I say, making big whooshing motions with my hands. 'Go away.'

The cat is not intimidated. Hissing and spitting, it crouches down, back legs ready to leap into the air and attack me. I let out a scream. And another one.

Logan comes running from his workshop and stops, hands on hips, and snaps, 'Ginger!'

Immediately the cat does a complete schizophrenic. It's as if it smiles, then it starts to purr and rub itself along Logan's legs, all the while glaring balefully at me.

'I'll thank you not to frighten my cat,' Logan says.

Shit! His voice is as cold as the ocean that provides the backdrop to our exchange.

'You should keep your cat under better control,' I retort, trying not to sound confrontational. 'It was going to attack me.'

'Yeah, well . . .' he shrugs.

My heart plummets. Now that he's in front of me I will apologise, but his icy manner tells me that this apology will probably not be easy.

'He just doesn't like you,' Logan continues as he scoops the cat up into his arms and they both glare at me. 'I wonder why?'

He doesn't say it in the joking way of before. I feel as hurt as he must have done the other night.

'I didn't come here to talk about your cat,' I stammer.

'No?' He widens his very cold blue eyes at me. 'Come to give me some more of your expert opinions on art?'

'Logan, stop.'

He does and we both stand there like combatants.

'I'm sorry, OK.' My voice trembles.

'OK.' He shrugs.

'I really mean it.'

'Just like you meant all that stuff you said the other night?'

'I didn't mean that. I was being . . . well,' my face flushes. I can't tell him how I feel, not like this, not with his ex in residence. 'I was nasty.'

'You got that right.' He nods and says, 'Fine. Thanks. Good.' Then he walks away from me, still cradling the cat in his arms.

At first I can't believe it. Then I feel dreadfully hurt. OK, it wasn't exactly the apology of the century. But I did apologise. Before I know what I'm doing, I call, 'Logan?'

He turns.

'Is that it?' I say. 'Is that all you're going to say?'

'What else is there?'

He is being deliberately horrible. I blink. In my scenarios, it had all ended really well. I'd never envisioned this. 'Well, you could mean it when you say it's fine.' A touch of belligerence has crept into my voice.

'I do mean it. It's fine. Thanks for the apology. You should get back now, I've work to do.'

'Well, don't walk away from me. Did I walk away when you apologised to me before, did I? No, I was very nice to you.' I sound like a four-year-old.

'I gave you a picture.' He sounds like a three-year-old. It gives me a bit of comfort.

'Yeah, well unlike you, I don't have to bring a gift to say sorry to someone. I hope I sound sincere.'

'I accepted your apology.'

'So that's it,' I say. 'You accept my apology and we never speak again.'

'Why would you want to speak to me?' he asks. The cat is squirming in his arms now. I think it's feeling a little uncomfortable with his master's palpable annoyance. 'You obviously can't stand me. You know, I thought we were getting along OK. I sort of liked being with you. I liked our bickering. I didn't mean half of it.'

'Neither did I. You'd better watch that cat.'

'Oh yeah.' He drops it to the ground and it takes off. He looks at me. 'So why? Why were you so horrible to me then, the other night?'

The insanity excuse would be a lie. I'm not going to tell lies, I've told lies my whole life. But can I tell the truth? The only truth I know at this moment is that I can't tell him how I feel. Maybe he's back with Maria. I'm scared to have this cold man reject me even more than he has my apology. 'I . . . I, I don't know.' I stare at Logan's feet. He has new trainers on. He must really have tried to impress the ex.

Logan stays completely still, not saying anything.

'I'm just sorry.' My voice is contrite. 'Really sorry. I do like your paintings. I have no idea why I was such a cow.' I chance a quick peek up at him. There is a funny look on his face. Sad or tender or what, I don't quite know. 'Logan,' I blurt out, 'I really thought we had something.'

It's exactly the wrong thing to say. His face shuts down and he nods. 'Yeah,' he says, slowly, and every word is like a knife, 'so did I.'

And then, just as the humiliation is working its humiliating way from my feet up through the rest of my body, a woman pokes her head out the back door. Long and lean, dark haired and dark eyed, tanned, smooth skin, her very being everything mine isn't. 'Logan,' she says, and her voice is pure golden honey, 'where do you keep the shower gel?'

She's dressed in one of his T-shirts. It barely covers her.

'In the shower,' Logan says and I'm comforted that he doesn't glance in her direction.

'Fine,' she says a little snottily. Then she turns to me and is about to ask me my name or something, when she notices my footwear. 'Are they my boots you're wearing?'

Double humiliation.

Every single humble bone in my body evaporates at her accusatory tone. OK, I still want to cry at the fact that Logan is obviously no longer my friend but there is no way his ex-girlfriend is going to look down on me. 'Well,' I say, my voice wobbling at what I'm about to do, 'fair exchange is no robbery.'

'Pardon?' She arches her already arched eyebrows at me.

'You slept in my bed, I wore your boots.'

And I turn my back on the two of them.

'Logan!' I hear her screech as I walk off. 'Who is that woman?'

'She slept in the spare bed,' I hear Logan tell her and I think he's laughing.

I hope Maria slept there too.

Julie laughs too when I tell her, though she can't believe Logan was so horrible to me. 'Well,' she says supportively, 'the least he could have done was accept your apology.'

'He did.'

We're sitting in the beer garden in Lynch's, waiting for Adam. He's meeting us there on his way back from the airport.

'No,' Julie shakes her head, 'he didn't. Not really. If he had, he would have been friendlier. I think he has a nerve. You accepted his when he gave you the painting.'

'I told him that.'

'Good for you!'

We clink glasses and drink. Despite my cheery demeanour, I'm gutted. I'm trying not to think about it. I'm trying not to get too upset over it. I let Logan in and that's why it hurts. It's part of life, Tim would say, and he's right. At least it showed I cared. I haven't cared for a man in ages. So it's a horrible sort of progress, I suppose.

'I wonder did he sleep with her?' Julie asks. 'Do you think he did?'

'I don't know.' I don't want to think about that either.

'Are you going to ring your mother?' I ask instead, changing the subject.

'Boo!' I jump as Adam squeezes my shoulders.

'Fecker!' I belt him and he laughs. 'You gave me a fright!'

He's dressed in a suit and carries a bag. 'Sorry,' he grins.

'Hey,' Julie asks. 'How'd it go?'

Adam plops down into a seat beside us and rolls his eyes, 'Bloody awful,' he smirks triumphantly.

'It can't have been that bad,' I murmur.

'No, everyone always thinks that,' Julie agrees.

'Oh believe me, it was bad.' Adam is still smirking. 'In fact, can I just say that that interview was the low point of my professional life.'

Julie and I exchange a look. She asks the obvious question, 'So why are you so happy?'

I think she thinks he's having a kind of a breakdown. It must be great to have a breakdown and feel happy about it.

'I am happy because,' Adam says easily, 'for the first time in my professional life, I was myself.'

'What?' Julie is baffled. 'Adam, are you OK?' She touches him on the sleeve. 'Are you OK, really?' she asks.

Adam kisses her hand extravagantly. Then he sighs deeply and contentedly, while still keeping hold of her hand. 'Hope, run up to the bar and get a Guinness for me, would you?'

'Get it yourself, you lazy git,' I chastise him but I go, and return a few minutes later with a pint for him. Greg has given it to me on the house.

'So, go on.' I place it in front of him. 'Tell us.'

Adam lets Julie's hand go, lifts his pint and drinks deeply. 'Oh, they know how to pull a pint here,' he says approvingly.

'Adam!' Julie belts him. 'Spill.'

Adam nods. 'Right.' He shifts about in his seat and begins, 'When I went over, I was determined, in my mind, to tell the truth, no matter what, at this interview, wasn't I?'

'God,' Julie looks at him, 'is this going where I think it's going?'

Adam ignores her. 'So, I went into the room, and there were three blokes there, all dressed in suits and ties, the works, and they're all really impressed by my CV and my experience. And it's all going really well and I'm telling them ideas to help their store improve and they're all nodding away, really impressed. Then the middle one asks me why I left my old job.' He gives the two of us a wide grin. 'So I said that I hadn't left, I'd been sacked.'

'No!' That's me.

'You bloody idiot!' That's Julie.

'Uh-huh.' Adam smiles at the memory. 'So as you can imagine, that sort of threw them. One of them asked why I'd been fired so I told him that the staff hated me and that I'd gone absent without leave and apparently I was being blamed for losing the company fifty thousand which, for the record, was not my fault.'

Julie and I are speechless. I don't know whether to hit him or hug him.

He nudges me. 'You know the way your lot are so fond of telling your sins to a vicar?'

'Priest,' I nudge him back. 'Our lot call them priests.'

'Priest, sorry,' he says. 'Well, I can kind of understand it. It was liberating, just telling all my failures to a group of people. I told them about my childhood and my counselling and then I told them that I was telling them all this because

I was going to be myself from now on and that if they didn't like it they could ask me to leave.' He grinned. 'So they asked me to leave.'

'And that's good?' Julie whispers.

'That's great,' Adam beams. 'Don't you think so?'

'I think so,' I say, much to Julie's chagrin. 'I mean, who else can you be?'

'Exactly.' Adam slams his fist on the table. 'Good one, Hope.' He looks at Julie's concerned face and concedes, 'Unfortunately, though, Ju, I do realise that I have to earn some money so I might have to gloss over the exact truth in my next interview.'

'Good,' Julie nods vigorously. She screws up her eyes. 'You could say that the staff in your previous job resented your work ethic. Which is true.'

'And you could say,' I add excitedly, 'that the workers took the fifty thousand and blamed it on you.'

'Eh – there might be a legal issue with that,' Adam laughs. 'You know, false accusations and stuff.'

'Well, you were accused falsely,' Julie says.

'If I were you, I'd have them sued for false dismissal,' I chime in.

'If you were me, Hope,' Adam said, 'you'd know that losing that poxy job was the best thing that ever happened. In fact, and I hate to say it, you being in that plane crash made me see what was important and I realised what a shit I was.' He stands up and, holding his pint aloft, says, in a posh English accent, 'May all those who are shits suddenly wake up and smell the roses.'

'And what a lot of roses grow in a shit-pile,' Julie giggles, standing up and clinking his glass.

She's right. My shit-pile of lost jobs and aeroplane accident have shown me who my mates are. And given me a chance to be normal again.

Such a lot of roses.

As Tim might say, you can't have the roses without the thorns!

31

M Y NEXT COUNSELLING session consists mainly of Tim asking me how I am and how I feel and how the last week has gone and me telling him about every little farty thought I had during that week. It's quite exhausting, analysing everything. He comments that I seem a little down. For someone who has made such amazing progress, he says, you seem a little down.

'I lost my cool with a friend,' I tell him. 'I said some awful stuff. And when I apologised, he accepted it but he didn't really. He hasn't called me since.'

'And why do you think that is?' Tim asks.

'Because he didn't forgive me, not really,' I say. 'I hurt him too much, maybe.'

Tim nods. 'Maybe you did but you apologised. He should have met you half-way.' He stops. Nods. Pulls at his hair. 'It really is important to do that,' he says again. 'Really important.'

'So you don't think I should call over again?'

'Do you feel you did your best with the first apology?'

'Yes.' I shift about on the chair. I suppose I hadn't told Logan the *exact* truth but it probably wouldn't have made any difference.

'And do you understand why you rowed with him?'

'Unfortunately, yes. I didn't think in the way you taught me to think and I blew it.'

Tim nods. 'Well then, give him some time.' He smiles a little sadly. 'Sometimes it just takes a little time. I need lots of time after someone apologises to me,' he says. 'Your friend is probably the same. Is that the same friend who had the trouble with the women?'

'Oh God, no. It's a different friend.'

'Oh. And how's he getting on?'

I tell him about Adam. 'He's kind of stuck, he's buying drinks for girls and he says he's going to be broke.'

'So let him take it a bit further next time,' Tim says. 'He should get a number, ring a girl. Just a casual date, maybe for an hour. See how that works.'

'I'll let him know that.' I laugh. 'You should set yourself up as a relationship adviser, Tim.'

'Believe me, Hope, I could possibly be the worst person on the planet to do that.' He sounds a little down himself now. He glances at the clock on the wall. 'Anyway, you've done great this week. I think the next time we meet, we'll start tackling the accident, are you happy with that?'

My heart lurches but I nod. 'Fine. Thanks, Tim.'

'See you –' he consults his diary – 'in two weeks' time – is that OK? I've to go to a conference next week. If you want me, just ring.'

Two weeks' time, it's like a reprieve. I actually smile. 'Great. No problem.'

Julie and Adam are waiting for me when I get out. Julie has declared that today will be the day that we get some clothes for the hotel opening. Adam has wriggled out of buying anything, saying that his interview suit will do the job. Julie has called him a cheapskate and he's a little upset at this. Unfortunately the fact that she can't dress Adam means that all her attention is focused on me.

'We will make you into a real babe,' she declares. 'Wait until Logan sees you, he'll be so sorry for the way he's behaved.'

'The only way he'll be sorry is if I deck him one,' I mutter darkly.

'He'll get over it,' Adam says. 'If a girl told me she hated my life's work, I'd say I'd be a bit annoyed too.'

'Thanks for that, Adam,' I deadpan. 'That makes me feel a whole lot better.'

We arrive in Killarney, and the place is buzzing with tourists. Julie drags me into a designer shop where she immediately spots this gorgeous beaded aquamarine three-quarter-length dress. It looks great on her. Four hundred euro lighter, we leave the shop, her dress wrapped in tissue paper and resting in a bag. 'Now for you, Hope,' she sighs happily. 'Have you any idea what you'd like to wear?'

I shrug. 'No. I can't remember the last time I wore a dress, Ju.'

'So what's your favourite colour? You wear a lot of yellow, would you like a yellow dress?'

'If I wore a yellow dress, I'd look like Big Bird from *Sesame Street*.'

Adam and Julie laugh, much to my alarm. They could at least have disagreed.

'Well, let's go in here,' she says and takes my arm. 'This looks like a nice shop.'

It is a nice shop. If you're into shops like this. It's the sort of place that invites people to whisper and where the assistants look like they earn a lot more than their customers.

'Now have a look and pick something out,' Julie orders in a whisper.

Adam gives a snort of laughter as I gawp uselessly at the rails of dresses. 'See you outside,' he says merrily, winking at me and exiting.

I turn to Julie. 'I don't know if a dress is me.'

'But you have to wear a dress.' Her voice has a touch of panic in it. 'Like, what else can you wear?'

Oh God. 'Maybe I just won't go.'

'Hope, you have to go. You're the one that got invited.'

She sounds annoyed now so I grab the first dress I see. It's blue and long and has spaghetti straps.

'There you go,' Julie smiles. 'Now try it on.'

Feeling extremely self-conscious, knowing her eyes are on me, I make my way to the dressing room. 'And if you can't pay for it,' Julie shouts after me, causing just about everyone in the shop to look, 'I'll lend you the money.'

'Great,' I say weakly. 'Thanks.'

The dress is horrible on. Even Julie says it is. Spaghetti straps do nothing for my big fleshy shoulders. Scooped necks do nothing for my huge cleavage. Julie informs me that I need a dress with wide straps and a V-neck and an Empire waistline.

The shop assistant, a woman with long talons of fingers and a deep voice agrees and the two of them spend hours handing me in dresses. My confidence is on the floor when I realise how long it's actually taking them to find something I look good in. Finally Julie hands me in the ugliest dress I've ever seen. It's red and shimmery. Wide straps and a plunging V. In fact the V plunges to the waist. 'Julie, it's pornographic,' I hiss at her. 'I can't put it on.'

'Try it,' Julie hisses back.

And so I do.

The dress is like liquid the way it falls down over my body. It flows and sparkles over every curve, from my breasts to my hips, and from there it drops down to the floor in a sort of asymmetrical way.

I stare at my reflection, awestruck. Never have I looked so good. So feminine. Even with my hair shorn, I look like a proper woman, not the round basketball person I'm so used to.

'Let me see,' Julie commands.

I walk out, faintly awkward.

'Wow!' Julie walks around me, looking me up and down. I feel the heat of embarrassment breaking out all over me. I've never liked being scrutinised. I suppose I've always wanted to be invisible on account of all the lies I told as a kid, and anyone paying too much attention to me makes me acutely uncomfortable. The sudden flash of insight doesn't help alleviate my uneasiness, however. Julie says 'wow' a few more times before declaring the dress a success.

'It's fab,' she tells me. 'And I don't want you saying it's too tight – you've lovely curves, Hope, you should make the most of them.'

'You think?' I try to sound modest.

'Lovely.' The woman in the shop has come over, no doubt hoping for a sale. 'Well chosen,' she says to Julie. 'You've a good eye.'

'I know,' Julie nods. No false modesty about her.

They stand back to admire some more and I cringe.

'Well, Hope, what do you think?' Julie asks.

'It's . . . it's nice,' I say.

'Look at yourself, will you?' Julie laughs and pulls me to a mirror and once again I stare at my reflection. 'You are hot, Hope. Hot. Hot. Hot.'

And I think I actually am. A little.

That night, Julie screws up her courage and rings her mother. She'd put it off all day, which was why I reckoned she focused so much on buying clothes for us. 'OK,' she whispers as she takes out her phone and begins to dial.

I have to admit, my heart is hammering. She's a lot braver than me, I still haven't contacted my mother, much as I'd like to. I guess I'm too afraid of it all falling apart again.

'Mum,' Julie says, as Adam and I hold our breath, 'It's, eh, Julie.'

Her mother says something back.

'Nothing. Just to wish you a happy birthday.'

I give her the thumbs-up.

And then Julie is holding the phone away from her ear and a tinny voice at the other end is yammering away. Julie looks hopelessly at us.

'Hang up,' Adam says calmly, taking the phone away from her and pressing it off. 'You don't need that,' he says as he tosses the phone aside.

Julie doesn't move. 'It'd be a happy birthday for her if I did my best at work,' she says, sounding eerily calm. She shakes her head, her voice wobbles. 'Bitch!'

'Bitch!' I say too, putting my arm around her and sitting her down.

'You don't ring her again,' Adam sounds quietly furious. 'Don't let them boss you, Ju.'

'I won't,' she says. There are no tears in her voice now.

In fact, she even manages a smile, 'So, come on, who's for Scrabble?'

Adam looks at me and I look at him.

Scrabble it is.

32

EIGHT O'CLOCK. SATURDAY night. I'm standing in my silver shoes and red dress, my hair looking exactly the same, despite the blow-dry. Julie has done my make-up and I feel as if someone has caked a mask to my face. My eyes are heavy with mascara, my lips dry from the lipstick. But my two friends think I look great, which makes me feel great. Adam is being an eejit and pretending he doesn't recognise me.

'Who is this?' he keeps saying. 'Where has Hope gone? Has she been kidnapped?'

'Ha ha.' I make a face.

'And you are?'

'Adam, stop, would ya.'

He contents himself with a grin, only to say two minutes later, 'They've kidnapped Hope, you know.'

Julie, fabulous in her blue dress, leaves the room and comes back with a package. 'Here,' she thrusts it at me. 'You look lovely and I'm proud of you and this is for you. From me and Adam.'

'What is it?' I open it excitedly, I love presents. And then I stop, finding that I'm unable to take her gift out of the bag. Instead, I turn my gaze on her. 'Julie,' I whisper. Something in me breaks a little at the kindness.

She smiles and wraps her arm about my shoulder. 'That's for you,' she says softly, 'to say we're proud of you and all you've been through and that tonight, you look lovely. Now take it out, for God's sake and let me see it. I was hoping you'd go for silver shoes and you did!'

It's a beaded silver bag with a red fringe. It must have cost a fortune. Reverently, I take it out and I love it. I can't believe it's mine. I've never treated myself to beautiful bags before. 'I don't deserve this,' I mutter, touching it and running my fingertips over it.

'Of course you deserve it.' Julie gives me a playful punch. 'Everyone deserves to have something lovely.'

'Yeah, but she's got us,' Adam says, 'so technically she's had her quota.'

I stare down at myself. Prettified. Girly. Almost beautiful. And to my horror, a big fat tear rolls down my face. And then another. And another. And before I know it, I'm scrubbing my face with a tissue and I just can't stop.

Julie isn't happy. My eyes are red and swollen and my make-up had to be redone. She's kicking herself for giving me the bag. I keep telling her that I don't care what I look like, I look better than I ever have before, and she really can't argue with that.

At around eight-thirty, the taxi we've ordered pulls up. Adam hurries out to put our overnight bags into the boot and when he has finished, we all hop in; Adam in front, with Julie and me in the back.

It takes about ten minutes to get into town and then our taxi joins the line of taxis slowly crawling up the enormous curved driveway of the new hotel. It's an impressive structure. When I was a kid, we'd climb the old crumbling walls and play hide-and-seek behind enormous trees and pillars in the grounds. Now, it's transformed. It's been restored to the stately house it once was with two new wings added on to each side. As is the way with many hotels in Ireland now, it's also got its own golf course and the grounds sweep away behind it in various shades of green. Lights twinkle from the trees and lanterns light the way as the taxi pulls up in front of the wide steps which lead up to the front door. Julie hops out first and I pull myself out behind her. My leg is still quite stiff and not as nimble as it was in doing things like that. I'd never have been able to hop in and out of the cars Nelson hired, yes HIRED, when he visited Julie. Adam drags the bags from the boot.

'Do ye want help with all those bags?' the taxi driver asks as he observes Adam struggling up the steps. Julie has brought a suitcase with her. A full to the brim suitcase.

'Please.'

The taxi driver takes Julie's case, wincing at the weight. Adam carries my bag and his own. The doors to the opulent reception area are open. It's breathtaking. Huge floors, wide and expansive, in white and black marble. Up above us an enormous chandelier hangs from the vaulted ceiling. The smell of fresh, polished wood dominates.

'Dunport has arrived,' the taxi man says loudly as he dumps the case down beside the desk and peers around. 'No doubt about that.'

Oblivious to the tooting of horns outside, he has a good look around the foyer before leaving. We hear him telling the other drivers to 'chill'.

Adam checks us in. The receptionist tells us that our bags will be brought up to our rooms if we'd like to go on into the reception.

'Come on then,' Julie is breathless with excitement. 'Let's go meet the Kerry elite.'

It's packed. Chatter and noise and hum. Clinking of glasses and the tinkle of polite laughter. A big window dominates the massive room and everything seems very civilised and posh. I glance quickly about and recognise a few faces I really don't want to recognise. Neighbours and business people from the town. Jack's parents – his mother looking as snobby as ever, dressed to perfection and his father, dishevelled, trailing in her wake. Adam asks me if I want a drink and before I'm aware of it, I tell him that I want a nice large glass of white wine. It'll help me cope, I think, meeting all the people from the past.

'You're not meant to be drinking,' Julie, ever the spoilsport, intones. 'Get her some water, Adam.'

'I'll have a wine.'

Adam looks from one to the other of us in confusion. 'Eh, Hope, I think –'

'She wants water,' Julie says.

I roll my eyes. 'Right, water it is.' I'll sneak in a wine at some stage, when she's not looking. She's bound to start flirting with someone here sooner or later.

Adam grins. 'I wouldn't have got you wine anyway.'

Before I have a chance to say anything, he's gone. Bloody typical. A free bar and I can't even sample its delights.

'Hey.' The simple greeting makes me catch my breath. I'd forgotten Logan would be here. He has come up behind Julie and tapped her on the shoulder. 'What you all doing here?'

Julie shoots a look at me. We haven't heard from Logan since my apology, whether it's deliberate or not, I don't know.

Adam has met him, I think. He hasn't exactly talked about it and I haven't asked. As far as I know, he gave him a lift into Dunport a couple of times to get some shopping.

'Hiya, Logan.' Julie shoots a look at me and smiles up at him while I try to gaze into the distance beyond his shoulder. 'We're here because Hope knows Jack Dunleavy.'

'Oh, that's right.' Logan nods in my direction. 'Well, you both look great – almost didn't recognise you.'

'Thank you,' Julie smiles again.

'Yeah, thanks,' I say in an offhand manner. I still can't bring myself to look at him.

Silence descends.

'Well,' Julie says brightly, 'I'm just going to find Adam.' I gawk in disbelief at her. 'He's taking ages with the drinks. Excuse me.' Pushing past me, she has the nerve to wink and suddenly it's just me and Logan on our own. Well, I think, I'm not going to start a conversation. No way. If he thinks for one moment –

'Your bed is missing you,' he says, shoving his hands deep into the pockets of what I notice must be an incredibly expensive suit. 'Every night it asks, where has Hope gone. I liked her sleeping on me. Even if it was only once.'

'If I got you into trouble with your ex, well . . .' I pause; I had been about to apologise, then I think, why should I? I apologised enough. 'Well, I'm delighted,' I finish off.

He laughs.

Oh God, he is gorgeous, my traitorous mind says. If Logan looked good in jeans, he's about a million times handsomer in a suit. 'You couldn't get me in trouble with that woman,' he chortles, 'it's an ongoing thing. She hates me.'

His words reassure me. He doesn't sound at all put out about it, which makes me smile a little.

Another silence descends.

'About your apology –'

'About that day –'

He nods. 'You first.'

'No, you.'

'OK.' He pauses. 'Well, I'm just going to say that I'm –'

'Hey, Hope!' A tap on the back and Greg appears at my shoulder. 'I didn't know who you were at first. You look great!'

Talk about bad timing. I feel like someone who has just got five numbers instead of six in the national lottery. 'Hi, Greg.' I try to smile but it lacks enthusiasm. 'How's things?'

I hear Logan give an impatient sigh and much as I like Greg, I want to kill him for interrupting.

'Totally great,' Greg says, oblivious. 'Hey, hey, Mandy, come over here and see who it is!'

Mandy?

A tall blond woman turns to look in Greg's direction and when she sees me, the smile slides from her face. I'm sure my own face mirrors hers. Amanda Coonan. Taunter supreme.

'Come on!' Greg gestures for her to come over. God love him, he hasn't a clue about vibes and undercurrents and all that.

Amanda, wearing a very clipped smile, totters towards us on impossibly high heels. She looks as snotty and as snobby as I can remember from school. She's wearing a midnight blue silk dress that makes her look even skinnier than she is. Her highlighted hair falls softly over her shoulders and half-way down her back. I have such an urge to pull it. The biggest diamond I have ever seen sparkles on her ring finger.

Greg puts his arm around Amanda, pulling her towards

us. 'This is Mandy, my fiancée. D'you remember Hope, Mandy?'

'Yes.' Amanda gives me a stiff smile.

I give her one back. Then I realise how stupid I'm being. People change, I think. OK, I haven't, not yet, but that's just sad old me. So I hold out my hand. 'Nice to see you again, Amanda.' The lie almost chokes me.

Her handshake has all the aplomb of a flat sponge cake. 'Really?' she says, arching her eyebrows. 'Thanks.' Her voice is as clipped as her smile. She lets my hand go quickly and stares about the room. 'Come on, Greg and let's see if we can find Jack. I'm dying to talk to him after all this time.'

'Well, you haven't seen Hope in a long time either,' Greg says, a little embarrassed.

'Yes, and we've talked to her. Come on.' She starts tugging his sleeve.

Logan quirks his eyes at me, wondering, I suppose, why she's so horrible.

Adam and Julie come back then with a glass of wine each and a big pint of water for me. Adam hands it to me over my shoulder. 'Hi,' he says easily, recognising Greg. 'You're the barman, aren't you?'

Greg is thrilled that he's been remembered. 'And you're the Shamrock lover.'

'That's me!'

'This is Mandy, my fiancée.'

'Hello.' Adam proffers a hand, which she shakes. 'I'm Adam. How do you do?'

She responds to his warm tone. 'Great, thanks. Enjoying the night, are you?'

'Free drink, beautiful women, who wouldn't?'

My, but Adam has improved his line in chat, I think, feeling slightly amused.

Greg takes heart from Amanda's change in humour. 'And this is Julie.'

Julie smiles and shakes her hand too.

'And this is Logan, Mandy – he did the artwork in the hotel, didn't you?'

Logan nods. 'Uh-huh.'

'Wow!' Amanda is seriously impressed now. She touches Logan lightly and points to a massive picture which I hadn't noticed until then. 'Did you do that fantastic one opposite the window?'

'Yeah,' Logan nods. 'That was the biggest one.'

The picture is massive, measuring about ten by ten. It hangs opposite the bay window but is a picture of the view outside the bay window, minus the hotel and driveway. It really is very clever, showing how the landscape should look without a hotel in the middle of it. It's quite subversive and it makes me smile.

'It's brilliant,' Amanda says. 'Did that take you long?'

'Yeah, too long,' Logan says, mock-groaning.

'I must go and look at the other ones,' Amanda says, smiling up at him. 'Will you tell me about them?'

'Sure, be glad to,' Logan says easily, and chatting together they walk out of the room, Greg following them.

I glare at Amanda's retreating back. She was always one for the fellas. I turn back to see Julie and Adam looking expectantly at me. 'What?'

'Well,' Julie's eyes are gleaming, 'what did he say?'

'Logan? Nothing. Why?'

'It was obvious he wanted to talk to you.'

'Was it?'

'He stood there, shuffling from foot to foot and staring at you and if you'd bothered to look at him, you would have noticed that.' She pauses. 'So what did he say?'

'Nothing. Greg came along.'

The two of them groan loudly, which makes me laugh. Oh God, I hope he comes back.

But for the next couple of hours, as Julie and Adam get slowly sloshed and I remain sober, Logan stays firmly surrounded by what seem like adoring fans. I notice with some disquiet that they are mostly women and that they all seem to find him hilarious.

I try not to glance at him but my gaze is drawn time and again to his handsome profile and his laughing face. I can't seem to concentrate on what Julie and Adam are saying at all, I just want to talk to him, assure myself that we're friends again. That he likes me again.

In fact, I'm so preoccupied by Logan that I fail to notice Jack at all, until he breaks into our group and tells me I look great. I get such a shock that my water slops out all over my dress. So much for being calm and composed. 'Eh, hiya,' I stammer out. 'Thanks.'

'These must be your friends?' He's totally confident, totally in control of the conversation.

'Yes,' I try to match his tone. 'Julie you've met already and this guy here is Adam.'

'Hi, Adam.'

'Hi, Jack,' Adam nods. 'Great party.'

'Thanks. It's great to be finally back in Dunport.' His gaze sweeps me from top to toe. A pause, before he says slowly, 'I loved it here.' There is a whole other meaning in his tone, which I can't ignore.

Adam has no problem ignoring it. 'Yeah, we love it too. We're having a great time, aren't we, Hope?'

'Well you are,' I smile. 'Free booze and free parties and crappy traditional music.'

'Exactly,' Adam raises his glass. 'Nice wine, by the way.'

'Thanks.' Jack touches my arm. 'Great to see you,' he says again. He looks uncomfortable suddenly. 'D'you fancy meeting up for a chat some day? To catch up?'

Funnily enough, seeing him is not at all like I imagined it would be. This was the man I'd invested so much in when I was seventeen, the boy I'd lost my virginity to, the one I'd told things to, the one who'd discovered where my tickles were when I thought I didn't have any. But he was also the boy who had gone to college and never contacted me once. I'd written and written and he'd never replied. Meeting him again after ten years, I suddenly realise that none of that matters any more. I have moved on, I think with some surprise. Just as the world turns and you can't feel it and if it wasn't for the sun rising in the morning and setting at night, you wouldn't know that you'd just revolved three hundred and sixty degrees. Well my life had turned too without me noticing and if I hadn't met Jack again, I'd never have known I was over his rejection of me. Yeah, I'd been angry seeing him at first, but now, what did it matter?

'Well?' he asks and there is such a funny look in his eyes that it almost makes me sad for him.

'Catch up?' I say.

'Yeah.'

'There is no need,' I reply. 'I've caught up.' And I smile at him.

I don't think he understands. He looks at Julie and Adam and then at me. 'Just for a chat, some time?'

'Well, I'm going back to London so . . .'

'Maybe I could talk to you now, for a second?' He stops. 'In private?'

'OK.' I find his urgency to talk to me a bit unnerving. 'Why?'

In answer, he pulls me gently away from my curious friends, who make no attempt to follow. He leads me out into the foyer, where the first thing I notice, besides the hush, is Logan's fabulous painting of the waterfall. Jack turns to me. He takes a deep gulp of air, runs his fingers through his hair and says, half defensively, 'I'm sorry, Hope. OK. I'm sorry.'

I don't say anything. In all honesty, I can't quite believe it.

'I've felt guilty about the way I treated you for ages,' he says. 'I got your letters when I was in college and knew you'd phoned me and everything, but Jesus, Hope, I was only eighteen.'

'Yeah. I know that.'

'And you were so needy,' he goes on, 'it was like you wanted me to save you from your life and I couldn't do that. I felt like I was drowning in quicksand.'

Is this an apology?

'You were suffocating me and I just thought that the best thing to do was to not write.'

It's not like any apology I've ever had before. Now I'm the one feeling guilty.

'Eh, Jack,' I hold up my hand. 'Enough said. There's no need to do this. It doesn't matter any more, honestly.'

He doesn't seem to get that bit. 'And also,' he looks at his highly polished, highly expensive shoes, 'I had to get away too. It wasn't just you I ran away from, just in case you think it was.'

I don't say anything, not fully understanding.

'My dad,' he gulps out. 'He can be very difficult to live with. I just wanted to get away, make a clean break.'

As if he senses that he's being talked about, Jack's dad comes staggering out into the foyer, being supported by some of the waiting staff.

'Put him upstairs in his room,' Jack says wearily, before turning back to me.

My world tilts slightly. I think back to those lazy, weird, teenage days. How I'd sit on the grass on the mountain top with Jack and tell him everything, but never, I realise, ever, ask him about himself. I'd been as selfish then as he had been later. I'd been so absorbed in my awfulness that I hadn't thought about anyone else.

'Jack,' I say softly, 'it's your big night. You don't need to apologise to me. I shouldn't have expected you to look after me. I know that.'

He nods slightly.

'Now you've opened a hotel in Dunport, will you just let go and enjoy it.' I rub his arm briefly. 'I know I will.'

The sound of his dad falling up the stairs reverberates around the lobby.

He catches my hand. 'Thanks, Hope. That means a lot. It's the one thing I'm really ashamed of.'

'No need to be.' I pause, thinking of my own mother. 'Sometimes we need to be selfish just to survive. I understand that.'

He squeezes my hand and just walks away.

I watch him go and wonder if I'll ever stop being selfish. If I'll ever see my mother and not feel that I'm suffocating.

Dinner is served at around ten. Adam, Julie and I sit together. Three other people join us. Jack had obviously thought that

321

I'd like to sit with people from school, so, much to my dismay, Greg and Amanda are there and so also is a guy I barely remember from school. Dylan. He'd joined in sixth year and, as that had been a very patchy year for me, I didn't really know him. It turns out he and Jack had gone to college together and done the same course. He's chatty and funny and he sits beside me. Greg and Amanda are over the other side, beside Adam. I notice that Amanda seems to be charming Adam the way she charmed everyone in school. The teachers had loved her.

Dylan notices me looking over at her. 'I had a big crush on her in sixth year,' he says. 'I even asked her to the debs.'

'Yeah? And did she go with you?'

'Are you joking? I was skinny, spotty and scrawny. She told me she'd let me know and then she goes with him.' He nods towards Greg.

'Wow, they've been together a long time.'

'Who did you go with?' he asks. 'Or did you even go?' He laughs. 'All I can remember of you that year is your grumpy face on the days when you did turn up.'

I laugh too. 'I didn't go.'

'We all thought you'd go with Jack. You were seeing him, weren't you?'

I nod. 'Yeah. But it was over by then.'

'He liked you a lot, I think.'

I suppose he had, in his way. But for Dylan's benefit, I just snort scornfully, and then change the subject. From the corner of my eye, I see that Logan is the centre of attention at his table. He really has changed from the dour man I'd first met a few months ago. He seems to be taking a lot of business cards from people and tucking them into his pocket. I look at him and he must sense it, because at one point he stares in my direction and gives a hesitant smile. I give him one back. Then he gives me a big huge one and the feeling of happiness that washes over me makes me almost feel like crying.

I will talk to him after dinner, I decide. I'll just walk up to him and talk to him and explain what happened with the whole ex-girlfriend thing.

A gong signalling the speeches shatters that train of thought. 'And now . . .' Jack stands up at the podium, his confident manner back in place, his resonant voice filling the room. 'I hope you've all had a lovely dinner and are looking forward to our mystery guest. Ladies and gentlemen, the hotel will now be officially opened by –' he pauses for dramatic effect – 'David Dunne.'

The film star! No way! Dunport had definitely arrived!

A huge gasp, mainly it has to be said from the women, goes up and Julie, who has drunk way more than is good for her, stands up and cheers loudly, much to Adam's obvious mortification. People nearby laugh and Julie is then joined in her cheering by a few others.

David Dunne is gorgeous. Ten times nicer in the flesh than on film. He shakes Jack's hand and turning to the microphone gives his trademark wink and people whoop and whistle. All I can think is that it's not half as sexy as Logan's. I look towards him but he's laughing at Julie's antics. He has a lovely smile too. And a nice easy way of going on, when he's not glowering over something. I wish, in that moment, that he was mine.

David makes a speech but I barely hear a word of it, so busy am I telling myself sternly to be sensible. I live in London, he lives here. It'd never work. Plus there is the small matter of my cruel words.

After David's speech, all the uncool people rush up to him for his autograph. Julie is first in line, a napkin and a pen lent to her by Adam clutched firmly in her hand.

I decide to go and retouch my lipstick – lent to me by Julie – so that when I see Logan next, I'll look as good as I can look.

On the way to the bathroom, some photographer from the *Dunport News* asks me to pose for a photo. I meet Maurice, our landlord, who I wouldn't know only for the hideous hairpiece on his head. He's with a woman, presumably his wife, who's doing a feature on the opening for her paper. 'I hope to get front page,' she confides to me. Maurice stands proudly beside her and tells me that she's a top-class journalist; that she broke the Dunport story of the killer chips. 'Well, not that they'd actually kill you,' he says, 'it was just that they were reheated ones from the night before.'

I manage to look suitably impressed, while at the same time amused by the idea that that was the most dramatic thing to happen in Dunport in recent times. What a lovely place to live if that's the main problem.

Some other locals I can't avoid bumping into say hello and ask how I am after the crash. It's not as bad as I'd feared.

After what seems ages, I make it to the Ladies, which is just as fancy as the rest of the place. I stand in front of the full-length mirror and see myself in my entirety for the first time. I do look nice. Very nice, even. The dress slims me down, as do the shoes. The only odd thing is my really short hair, but there isn't a lot I could do about that. As I'm applying my lipstick, someone flushes a toilet in one of the giant cubicles and to my dismay, Amanda comes out. She flicks this disdainful glance in my direction and then ignores me. IGNORES ME. The nerve. I feel the old anger rise in me. The anger that I felt for her years ago. Unfortunately, I haven't outgrown what she did, probably because most of her bile was directed at Jamie and not at me. I begin to stare hard at her as she flicks her hair this way and that and pouts her lips and uses a big brush to sweep powder over her face.

'It's only polite to say hello,' I say witheringly, knowing I should just ignore her too.

She turns to face me. She's about three inches taller than I am. 'I don't want to say hello to you,' she says back in this ultra-polite voice.

For a second, I'm speechless. 'Really,' I reply. 'I guess that's because you're just as big a bitch as you always were.'

Oh my God, I sound like a five-year-old.

I watch in slight alarm as she slams down her make-up bag and crosses towards me. 'Where you're concerned, I guess I am.'

We are less than a foot apart. I look up at her. 'I did nothing to you. You always picked on me and Jamie. You called us names.'

For a split second, at the mention of Jamie, she looks a little ashamed, but then her arrogance reasserts itself. 'I know,' she nods. 'And you used to throw muck at me, and get Jamie to do the same. You pushed me and I ended up in hospital. But, you know, I can forget that even if you can't.'

'Oh, you can forget it by not saying hello, is that it?'

'Why would I want to say hello to someone who treats their mother the way you treat yours?'

It's as if she's slapped me. I open and close my mouth before finally spluttering out, 'I beg your pardon?'

'You should be begging your mother's pardon, not mine.'

She does a big sniff sort of thing and makes to turn away. Huh, she's not getting away that easily.

I catch her arm and squeeze it. 'My relationship with my mother is no concern of yours.'

She shakes me off. 'Oh yes it is. I visit your mother every day, did you know that? She's such a nice woman. She told me you were calling and she was so happy. I don't know what happened between you but you haven't called since and I know she's hurt over it. And I think you're being so selfish. The whole of Dunport knows you're back and you haven't called in.'

'You said it, Amanda, you don't know what happened, so keep your big nose out.' God, she is tall. I find my gaze level with her neck, so I have to stretch my head back as I say, 'And unlike you, I've never cared what the neighbours thought.'

She ignores that. Instead she snaps, 'So why did you come back? Was it to torment your mother, make a show of her? Because if it was, you're doing a wonderful job. She was sick last week, did you know that?'

I open my mouth to answer but nothing comes out.

'So don't say hello to me. Don't come near me, actually. Your mother is a great woman and you make me sick swanning about the place with your friends. Do you know how hard she has struggled to keep going after you left?'

I gawp at her.

'No, you don't, how could you, you left. But I was here and so was my family and we saw how hard she had it. She was an ill woman. She'd lost her son and been deserted by her daughter. She crawled back to life, Hope. That's what she did. And now you come breezing back into town as if nothing has happened.'

'Lots happened,' I blurt out. 'Lots.'

She pauses and says softly, 'I know lots happened, Hope. I know what happened when we were kids was wrong, I know what happened to Jamie was terrible, but staying away is not going to make things any better, for anyone.'

'You stay away from my mother,' I say stupidly, my voice shaking.

'Like you do.' She arches her eyebrows. 'No chance.' She holds my narrow-eyed gaze for a second or two before turning on her heel, grabbing her brush and bag and slamming the door of the Ladies behind her.

I stand there for ages, not able to move.

Of course, I have to go back out. But I can't face anyone now. I'm sure Amanda will tell Greg what happened and it'll get around the room, the way gossip does in a small town and everyone will be staring at me. I wonder if they all think I'm selfish. I'd lied to Amanda: of course I cared what people thought. I'd cared so much, I couldn't stay in Dunport. I place my hands against the flat of the tiles, letting their coldness shock me into clear thinking. I just have to get out. Get away. I take a deep breath and, head down, I walk from the Ladies, up the corridor and instead of going into the ballroom, go through reception and outside to the garden.

No one is about. It's a warm evening, so I totter on my heels into the shadows of some trees and sit down on the grass, not caring that my dress might get stained. I ease off my expensive shoes and rub my feet, observing the twinkling lights and the shadows of happy people in the ballroom. I just want to stay here, away from everyone so that I can't be judged, so that I can't make mistakes, so that I can just breathe. And so I stay there.

And I think about what Amanda has said, about what

327

happened with Jack, and it hurts a lot because if I look at myself from the outside, I see me as a big selfish bitch. But inside, I know I'm not. Inside, I'm just about coping. Inside, I want to ring my mother but it's too scary. Way too scary to make that initial contact and see it fall apart and both of us hurt all over again. It's way too awful. Inside I'm scrabbling about like a moth in the dark trying to find some light. And I can't seem to find the switch to turn things on.

People come out during the evening, some for a smoke, some for a snog. I watch it all from my trees. Julie and Adam come out at some stage. I think they're looking for me but I can't join them. They look well together, I think absently, from my vantage point. Both blond, both tall. Julie is very drunk. Adam holds her up. Then he puts his arm about her shoulder and begins to pull her back inside, his head resting tentatively on the top of her head.

I wait until they are out of sight, then creep from my hiding place and scurry up the stairs to my bedroom.

I spend the night lying on top of the bed, looking at the stars out of the window and trying not to think.

33

I FALL INTO a fitful sleep which is shattered by a frantic tapping on my door. Glancing at the television, which has a digital clock on it, I see that it's after ten. The sun is up and streaming through the window. I've probably missed breakfast but last night's dinner is sitting in my stomach like cement, so I wouldn't have eaten too much anyway.

'Hope! Hope!' It's Julie. 'Hope, are you in there?'

'Yeah,' I call out, then heave myself up from the bed and walk barefoot to the door.

Julie bustles in and shuts the door firmly behind her. She's about to say something when she notices what I'm wearing. 'You're still in the dress from last night,' she says. 'Have you only got back now?'

'No.' I know she's wondering if I was with anyone. 'I just fell asleep in it.'

'Oh,' she pauses. 'So, where did you get to last night? We were looking for you.'

I shrug. 'Nowhere, really. Amanda and I had a few words and I just wanted to get away for a bit. Have a think.'

'Words? Horrible words?' She looks concerned. 'What did she say?'

I sit back down on the bed. 'Nothing that wasn't true, unfortunately,' I admit. 'It was hard to hear.' Oh God, I don't want to think about it. I've thought about nothing else. 'And you,' I ask, 'did you have a good night?'

Her silence tells me more than any words. So does her rueful expression. 'What happened?' I feel momentarily fearful. I don't like the unexpected.

'Oh shit, Hope, I've done something stupid!' She presses her hands to her face and looks at me with anguished eyes. 'Really stupid.' And she sits down beside me on the bed, then winces. 'Oh, my head,' she moans, clutching it.

My heart sinks. 'What?'

'Now,' Julie looks fearfully at me. 'Promise you won't be shocked.'

'That means I will be shocked.' I gaze at her, dreading what she might say. 'What happened?'

'Oh Hope, I am so thick, I've gone and ruined everything.'

'How can you ruin everything?' I half smile at her dramatics. 'Have you killed someone or something?'

'No!' Julie says. 'It feels worse than that.' She closes her eyes and mutters, 'I kissed Adam.'

'Kissed?' For a second I am lost. 'Adam kissed you?'

'No!' Julie shakes her head, '*I* kissed *him*!'

'You kissed him?' I repeat, just so I understand properly. 'Like as in snogged?'

'Yeah.' She nods. 'Kissed, snogged. Whatever you want to call it.'

'Why?' Jesus, I am shocked. If he'd kissed her, it might make some sort of sense, but for Julie to kiss Adam, well, she must have been really drunk.

'I don't know,' she groans. 'I know I was drunk but Hope, he was up at the bar, buying some girl a drink and all I could think of was that he was going to get her number and call her and so I went up and dragged him outside to look for you and then I threw myself at him.'

'You threw yourself at him.'

'Yeah.'

'Why? D'you fancy him?'

'Hope, this is *Adam* we're talking about. He's our friend.'

'I think he fancies you,' I say slowly. 'I've sort of thought it for ages now.'

In answer, Julie turns over on the bed and buries her head in the duvet. She mutters something that I can't make out.

'What?'

'I said,' she says, turning back, 'that he told me that it wasn't a good idea and that maybe I should go to bed.'

'Well, in fairness —'

'And I said, oh God —' Julie stops as if she's only just remembered, 'I said only if he came too. Oh God. Can you believe I said that!'

'I can't, actually.'

'What am I going to do?'

'Do you fancy him, Julie?'

'You asked me that already.'

'Do you fancy him?'

She shrugs. 'I don't know. D'you know the way you have hair?'

I point to my pretty bare scalp.

Julie manages a panic-stricken giggle. 'Well, I don't mean just *you*, I mean everyone.' She touches her own blond mane. 'You know the way people have hair and they get it cut and they think it's only OK?'

'Yep.'

'And then a few weeks later the hair grows and they suddenly realise that they like it. Well, that's the way I feel about Adam. First off he was just there, he was my friend and I liked him, but this holiday, well, I think he's grown on me. I was pissed off at him last night for chatting that girl up.'

'So you do fancy him.'

'A bit, I suppose.'

'So tell him.'

'After he told me to get to bed? Are you joking? I never want to see him again.'

'That's going to be difficult, seeing as we all live together.' And even worse for me, I want to add and don't. 'Maybe, Julie, he was just being a gentleman if he stopped you from going any further last night. It shows he cares about you.'

'No,' Julie shakes her head. 'No, he didn't want me.'

Bang!

Bang!

Bang!

More knocking. This time it's Adam. 'Hope, Hope, are you in there?'

'Shit!' Julie looks at me, 'don't answer. Pretend you're not here.'

'Hope!'

'Adam, hi,' I call out. There is no way I'm taking sides in this. 'Hang on a sec.'

'I have to hide,' Julie says. 'How could you do this?' She runs madly about the room like something from a comic strip as I open the door on a very dishevelled Adam.

'Ju kissed me,' he announces, before catching sight of her and going red. 'Shit!'

He coughs slightly, 'Hi, Ju.'

'Adam, hi,' Julie stops mid-run. 'I, eh, was just explaining the situation to Hope. Like, it was all a big mistake and I apologise for being so drunk and, well, embarrassing both of us. I know I made a complete idiot out of myself.'

Adam looks as if she's just hit him full force with a cannon. His eyes linger on her for a second before meeting mine. 'Yeah,' he half laughs, 'right. OK. Good, then. As long as we're all friends, that's all that matters.'

'So you do think I made an idiot of myself?' Julie says, a little crossly. 'Is that what you really think?'

'Well, like I only —'

'Thanks.' Julie sounds hurt. 'That's great.'

'Hang on here,' I attempt to intervene. 'Let's just try to find out what we all feel.'

'Hope, there is no need for that counselling stuff.' Julie moves over to stand right in front of a bewildered-looking Adam. 'We all know how we feel. He thinks I'm an idiot.'

'I never said that,' Adam defends himself. 'You said that.'

'You led me on. You kept telling me I looked beautiful.'

Adam looks for help from me. I shrug. What am I meant to do?

'Yeah, well, you did,' Adam says clumsily. 'And you know, I liked you being an idiot, it was the best feeling I ever had.'

The words fall into dumbfounded silence.

'So why did you tell me to go to bed?' Julie asks, and her voice is not quite as cross. 'I was prepared to snog you and you told me to sober up.'

I wish I could leave but Adam is blocking the doorway. Instead, I cross over to the window and watch the two of them from that vantage point, though I don't think they're even aware I'm there any more.

Adam is running his hands up and down the leg of his jeans and audibly gulping. I know he's about to take the biggest risk of his life. 'Because,' he says, and his voice, though awkward, is so sincere and honest that I wish he was saying it to me, 'I got scared and also because I want to be with you when we're both sober and know what we're doing.' A pause while he rubs his hands together hard. 'It's all I've wanted for ages, Ju. It's not every woman I'd let take me to the hairdresser's and get my hair butchered.'

'It wasn't butchered, it was lovely.'

'As long as you thought so.'

They stare at each other as if they've never quite seen each other before.

'So, you like me?' Julie looks up at him. 'You fancy me?'

'Totally.' He laughs a little. He's embarrassed, I think.

'I'm sober now,' Julie says.

Adam looks thunderstruck. 'What?'

'I said I'm sober now. Are you?'

I wish I had her nerve.

'Well, yeah, yeah, I guess.'

'Come on then.' Julie tugs his arm. 'Show me what all the girls have been missing these long years.'

I don't know how I feel as they leave the room. It's great for them, but sad for me.

I hate it when things change.

34

JULIE AND ADAM are most definitely together in the next few days. I catch them touching and smiling at each other and despite their best efforts to be discreet, I do feel like the prize-winning gooseberry in the village fair. Adam has made a major leap in the therapy stakes. From buying women drinks to full sex is quite an achievement, and I'm glad for him. He's got a whole new air about him that is surprisingly sexy, a complete ease with who he is. A Logan air, I call it in my head. I know that when I go back to London I'm going to have to find somewhere to live on my own. It's a bleak thought. But I guess I can't go depending on the two of them for moral support for ever. There comes a moment when we all have to be self-sufficient, and mine has come.

Unfortunately Logan hasn't come. I really thought that he'd be around the day after the hotel ball but we haven't seen him at all. Still, it's probably for the best: with Julie and Adam being all lovey-dovey, just being friends with Logan would be quite difficult and yet I know there's no point in being much else if I have to leave for London.

Adam drives me to my counselling session the next week. Tim isn't in his office when I arrive and I see that for once the place is clean and organised. His desk even seems to have been polished. Adam offers to hang on until Tim arrives but I wave him off. I know he wants to get back to Julie so they can have some time together while I'm out.

'Ring me,' Adam taps his mobile, 'and I'll collect you.'

'Sure. Thanks.'

Adam leaves and five minutes later Tim arrives. 'Sorry about that.' He grins and holds up a paper. 'I just nipped out to buy this and look who I see on the front!!'

Oh God, it's me.

'You look great,' he says.

The headline screams, *Babes at the Ball*.

'The babes were pretty thin on the ground,' I shrug jokingly, 'so they used me instead.'

'Don't be so modest,' Tim grins, putting the paper away in his drawer. It's then I notice that his ponytail has gone.

'You've chopped your hair,' I say, surprised.

'Well, actually, I paid someone to do it,' Tim says wryly. 'They mustn't have done a great job if you think I chopped it myself.'

I laugh. 'That's what I meant. You got your hair chopped.'

'Yeah.' He shrugs. 'My wife made me do it. She's been at me for ages – she hates long hair.'

'Oh. Right.' So much for the hippie chick wife I thought he had.

I wonder what people think when they see me? Do they think I don't care about things when in fact, I do? Better not to try than to try and fail, that's always been my motto. I'd tried to keep a family together and failed. I hate the feeling of powerlessness that failure brings.

'Is your wife really fashion conscious?' I ask.

'No,' he shrugs. 'She just always hated my hair. But as she cleverly pointed out at the weekend, I was just letting it

336

grow to hold on to my own identity in the relationship.' He smirked. 'She's reading too many of my books.'

I wonder if that is why he had his sleeping bag with him at the office one night. I don't have time to think about it though as his tone becomes serious. 'Now Hope, you know that today might be a tough one. We're going to talk about the accident. I know you can't remember much, but once you open your mind you'll begin to remember other things. It's a case of preparing yourself and when you're ready, you will remember. OK?'

'Yeah.'

Tim asks me again about the previous two weeks – my thoughts, actions and exposure therapy.

'Good,' I answer. Then, haltingly, 'But, well, I feel I'm letting go of a lot of things when I listen to the tapes.'

'Like?'

'Jamie. And I'm not sure I want to let go of him.'

'He's already gone,' Tim says softly. 'He's been gone a long time. What you have to let go of is the feeling that any of it was your fault. That maybe his illness was something you could control. We have to see that we can't control every-thing, Hope. And we have to accept it. That's the hard part.'

He is right. But thinking like that is scary. It means that feeling powerless is something I might have to get used to. Feeling that it's normal that life can change in an instant. But what other way is there to live? I can't go on as I am – rigidly controlling myself. Losing control to have control. At least now, after listening to the tapes, I can think of what happened. I can examine it as you would a rare object, by holding it up to the light and trying to be objective. Things about that time keep popping into my head. Things that soften the image I've held on to for so long. The way my mother had told me that it wasn't my fault. The way she had held me at the funeral and said over and over again that it wasn't me. That it was her. That I mustn't feel I let Jamie down. I'd stood, frozen, unable to react as they'd buried my little brother. I blocked it all out. Held on to the anger because it had kept me going – kept me in some sort of powerful position. If just once I'd allowed myself to feel the full extent of the grief I might never have got up again. And now here I was, talking about it, listening to myself talk about it every day and remembering. And grieving. But remembering how my mother had shouldered the blame herself. Little by little the truth is getting through.

'So now,' Tim says, 'let's get cracking.'

I really don't want to do this. I know I've improved a lot since seeing Tim first. I sleep a little better at night but for months I've resisted this. 'Tim, if I didn't do this, would it be a big deal?'

He seems taken aback. 'What do you think?'

Julie and Adam come with me to the airport. I'm happy to be leaving. I'm feeling a little depressed at myself. I don't want them to know, so we joke and laugh. I don't know myself why I'm leaving unless it's to get perspective.

'Do you know now?'

I nod. 'I think I just wanted to escape more than anything. To be another person. It's what I did when I came to London first. It wouldn't have worked, I know that now.'

Tim nods. 'OK. Go on.'

I get on to the plane. It's a small one. Beige seats, I think. A child behind me. A man sits in beside me.

Then I wake up in hospital.

Adam said some man saved my life, but I don't remember.

'That's all,' I say. I sound a little defiant. 'That's it.'

'The man? The one that sat beside you, what was he like?'

'Young, I think. Friendly.'

He's not letting me away so easily. I watch as he takes a newspaper from a drawer.

'I have a paper here,' he says. 'Maybe you can recognise him?'

I hadn't known there were pictures of us in the paper. I suppose I hadn't wanted to know.

'Oh, I don't think so.' I don't hold out my hand to take it from him.

'Try.' His voice is sterner than ever before. He passes the paper across his messy desk.

Without touching it, I reluctantly study the pictures. The victims. Was the person who sat beside me a victim, then? I feel a chill as I look at it. Little did they know when these pictures were taken that one day soon they'd be used in an article about their deaths.

I scan the photos and stop at the fifth picture. Scan them again. I point at the man identified as Joe Ryan. He's handsome and looks good-humoured. 'He looks, I dunno, familiar.'

Tom nods, pleased. 'That's him, all right,' he says.

'How do you know?'

He leans across the desk. 'Haven't you read anything about the accident since? Or even at the time?'

I shrug. 'I was in a coma at first,' I say. 'And then, I suppose people tried to get me to talk about it, but I didn't want to. Then, I went on holiday and Adam talked about it once, just briefly. He told me that someone had saved my life. But I feel sick when I think about it, so we just don't mention it.'

He nods.

'So how do you know he was sitting beside me? We could sit where we liked on the plane.'

'Well,' Tim nods at the paper. 'Maybe you should read it, see if anything jogs your memory.'

My hand trembles slightly as I lift the paper from the desk. There's stuff about the flight. How it was a nice, cloudless day. How everything had been fine on take-off. Then some sort of a problem with the engine. A noise. I remember the noise now. Pop. Pop. Pop. 'A popping noise,' I say. 'I remember that. I looked out and saw smoke coming out of one of the engines.' I gulp. 'And, oh God, we started to go down and the pilot tried to turn the plane back.'

'Stop if you get too stressed,' Tim advises. 'I just want to try to kick-start the memory.'

According to the report, we'd made it back to the runway. The plane had then skidded, turning round and round at a high speed. Luggage was strewn inside and outside the craft. And people had died, including Joe Ryan. 'How do you know he was sitting beside me?' I ask.

Tim points to a small paragraph, inset into the main body of the piece.

The latest survivor is an Irish citizen identified by friends as Hope Gardner. Her survival is being described as 'miraculous' by rescue workers. It is thought that a fellow passenger shielded her from the worst of the accident by covering her body with his.

340

He has been identified as Joe Ryan originally from Dublin. He
is survived by his wife who is currently expecting their first child.

I read this paragraph again and again. And again. This man made the ultimate sacrifice and I can't even remember. I jab at the photograph. 'This was the man – he saved my life?'

'Supposedly.'

It's a blank. A black hole. I feel guilty. 'I can't remember.'

Tim looks at me. 'But I bet now you want to,' he says.

And he's right. I owe it to this man to remember. To myself to remember.

'Now close your eyes,' Tim says. 'I want you to talk it through again only this time, I'm going to try to get you to remember colours, smells, sensations, OK?'

Julie and Adam come with me to the airport. I'm wearing tracksuit bottoms. As usual. Julie is dressed up and Adam looks tall and lanky and awkward. They wave to me as I go to Departures. Julie is crying, Adam is comforting her. I get on the plane with the beige seats, definitely green and beige, and I sit beside a window. I like window seats, it makes me feel more in control. I know I sat there because later, I looked out the window and saw the black smoke coming out of the engine. A man sits beside me. Young. I think about Joe Ryan's face. Joe Ryan. Nothing. But I can remember crisps suddenly. I think he was eating crisps. Cheese and onion crisps. I think he offered me one. Then the popping sound. Yes, I remember that. I heard it before anyone else. Then it got louder and suddenly I see smoke coming out of the engine. Then the pilot said they were turning back. Then I am in hospital.

By the time I've finished, my heart is pounding. I've reached a ten on the stress scale. Tim holds up his hand, rewinds the tape and plays it back to me. I listen to my voice talking about the accident. I feel sick at every sentence. My stress is still a ten. Tim plays the tape again. And again. By the end of the session, I can bear it. My stress has gone down to an eight. Tim tells me that if I listen to it over the next two days it'll lessen even more. I believe him. I don't believe that I'll remember anything much more, though. It's like trying to blow a feather through a brick wall.

'We'll find the crack in the wall,' Tim says. 'Memory walls have unsteady foundations, you'll see.'

'Can I have that?' I indicate the paper.

'I was hoping you'd take it,' he grins.

'Thanks.' I fold it up, looking once again at the man who allegedly saved my life. How can I not remember?

35

ADAM PICKS ME up as promised and he's in great form. 'Got another interview next week,' he tells me. 'And this time it's as a supervisor in two stores for a rival chain.'

I laugh. 'How will your ex-bosses feel about that?'

'D'you know, Hope,' he grins at me, 'I don't care.'

'Well, I hope you get it.' I pat his arm. 'Serve them right. D'you have to fly over again?'

'Yeah, this job-seeking is costing me a fortune in air fares but if I get this one, it'll be worth it. At least,' he says, suddenly serious, 'it'll give me a chance to prove that I can actually be a half-decent boss.'

'Of course you will.'

He smiles and flicks on the CD player. Adam has invested in some of the Shamrocks' CDs and they are woeful. But he enjoys them, tapping his fingers to the beat on the steering wheel.

'Adam,' I ask without thinking I'm going to, 'what happened the day of the accident?'

He shoots a look at me.

'Yes,' I confirm, '*that* day. Can you tell me anything? I know I haven't wanted to talk about it but I think I have to if I'm going to remember.' I pause. 'I couldn't remember anything in counselling today.'

Adam indicates and eases the car on to a grass verge, just off the road. Then he gazes quizzically at me. 'Are you sure you need to know just now? You looked pretty upset coming out of Tim's office.'

'I'm sure.' Actually I'm not but I don't know if I'd ever get up the nerve to ask him about it again.

'D'you want to go back to the house and talk or go for a coffee?'

'Here is fine.'

'In the car?' He looks incredulously at me.

'Yeah, if that's OK.'

I know Adam will give me a better version of things than Julie. Her story would be too emotional and too descriptive and I'm definitely not ready for that.

'Well, OK,' Adam smiles a little at me. 'If you're sure.' He waits a second, then begins, 'Well, after you left, Ju and I went for something to eat. Ju was pretty upset so she didn't eat much and we didn't stay long. Then we hopped into the car to head back to the house. I was working later that day and I wanted to go over some files. Ju was going shopping to cheer herself up.' He smiles at the mention of her name.

'Anyway, we were driving along, about four miles out of the airport, when a newsflash comes on the radio about a plane crash-landing in Heathrow. I don't know, Hope, but somehow we both knew it was your plane. And Julie got completely hysterical and started ordering me to go back but we're on the wrong side of the bloody road and I think she thought I'd somehow, by some miracle, get the car to molecularly move to the other side. We had a huge row about it, but it was only because we couldn't face the fact that maybe something had happened to you. So anyway, I

344

drive and drive and find a turn and get back on the road to the airport but it's jammed. The airport is blocked off and the tailback goes for miles so we're sitting in the car, Ju is hysterical, I'm trying to drive and make calls and then the news comes on that yeah, it was the Heathrow to Boston plane and that a lot of people seem to be dead.'

I shiver and the guilt of a survivor washes over me.

'So Ju gets out, slams the car door and announces that she's walking to the airport. I drive the car to the grass verge in the middle of the road and that's what we do.'

'You walk?'

'Yeah. It takes ages. When we get there, we can't get in. We can't get any information. We're told to go to the hospital or go home. It was a nightmare, Hope. A bloody nightmare.' He looks at me and I'm stunned to see tears in his eyes. 'We thought you were dead.'

'Hard to kill a bad thing.'

'So we go home. There's nothing else to do. And we sit and watch the telly all day and feel useless and get pissed off with each other. And all the time the news is on and nothing about you. It's wall to wall, this accident. I think they thought it was terrorism at first but it was an engine fault. And then they announced that they've recovered another two bodies from the site, a young woman and a young man. And then we get a call to say that it was you and that you were alive.'

'And the man?'

'He was the guy that saved your life, or so they said.'

'Joe Ryan?'

'Yeah, that was his name.'

'I don't remember him, Adam. I feel so guilty because I can't remember anything.'

'He was young, about twenty-six or something. I think they said he was a salesman.'

Salesman? Salesman? It's blank. 'Maybe I didn't talk to him.'

Adam shrugs. 'Maybe,' he says. 'Anyway, Hope, that's all I can tell you. That's all that happened.' He pauses. 'I wish I could help you more.'

'No, that's great. Thanks.'

'No probs.' He fires the engine and gets the car going before looking at me again. 'It was the most horrible day of my life,' he says quietly.

My answer is to touch his hand and he squeezes mine back.

Julie is a lucky girl.

Julie certainly doesn't feel lucky when we arrive back. She runs out to meet us, her mobile phone held aloft as if it's about to explode. 'Where were you?' she says, her voice quite panicky. 'Oh God, since you left, Adam, I've had about ten calls.'

'So?' Adam asks, amused. 'I haven't banned you from answering your mobile phone, wench.'

'My mother and father!' Julie hisses as the phone begins its *Jaws* theme tune. 'They've been ringing all morning.'

Since the row with her mother, Julie's phone had gone silent. Julie has pretended to be cool with it, but her reaction now proves what I'd suspected. She's still not fully over it.

'Would you not answer it?' I say. 'You can always hang up. And at least they're ringing you.'

Julie stares at the phone which has gone silent but then starts up again. 'They've probably thought up some new strategy.'

'Here, give it here.' Adam holds out his hand. When Julie gives him the phone, he presses the button to switch it off. 'Now.'

'You can't do that.' Julie presses it on again. 'Say it's an emergency?'

'Then answer the bloody thing,' Adam tousles her hair. 'The sooner you know, the sooner you can get on with things.'

'Oh God,' Julie dithers as it starts to ring again. This time it's her dad. I know because the ring tone is different. I think it's from *The Omen*. *The Omen* ceases after about ten seconds to be replaced by *Jaws*.

'I'll answer it,' I say, 'and if it sounds important I'll pass it to you, OK?'

'OK. Good idea.' Julie hands me her phone. 'Good, good, Hope.'

I take it. My own heart is pounding now. Just witnessing Julie's mother and father in action has made me scared of them. 'Hello?' I say cautiously into the receiver.

'Hello? Juliet?' God, the woman sounds frantic. 'Is that you, Juliet?'

'Eh, no, it's her friend, Hope.'

Julie gives me the thumbs-up.

'Is Juliet there?' Her voice breaks a little. 'Please put her on, it's important.'

'I'll just check,' I say, feeling awful. The woman is obviously upset. I turn to Julie, point at the phone and make a tearful face while mouthing silently, 'Crying.'

Julie flips her hand at me.

'Eh, I can't seem to see her. Can I give her a message? She should be in soon.'

'Oh, well,' her mother gulps at the other end. 'I don't like you having to tell her. It should be either her father or me.'

That sounds bad. 'Oh,' I say. 'Hang on, here she is now!'

I thrust the phone into Julie's hands but she resists. 'Julie, your mother has some news for you.'

Julie takes it from me slowly and stares at it before putting it to her ear.

Adam raises his eyes at me behind Julie's back but I just shrug in reply.

'Mum,' Julie says in this false bright sarcastic voice, 'what's the occasion?'

Then her face registers shock, she pales and sways and if it wasn't for Adam behind her she'd have fallen, I think. 'No!' she says, as if she's about to cry. 'When did you find out?'

Her mother answers.

'And no one knew?'

Another reply from down the line.

'But I only saw her a while ago and she said nothing.' Then Julie does a lot of uh-huhing and nodding before hanging up with promises to keep in touch.

'What happened?' I ask.

Julie turns to me and Adam with blank eyes. 'I can't believe it.'

'Ju?' Adam gently takes the phone from her and leads her inside. 'What is it?'

'Angela's just had a baby!' she whispers. 'And my mother only just found out now.'

'Angela, your sister?'

'Yeah.' She sounds dazed. 'I can't believe it. God, you think she'd tell us! In the end, her partner rang. Apparently her baby was born this morning, he's a month early, he's very small and sick.' Julie starts to cry. 'Oh the poor baby!' She looks in bewilderment at us. 'Imagine not letting us know.'

'Maybe she thought your mother would go mad.'

'She is going mad!' Julie shakes her head. 'She's hurt and upset and angry too.'

I say nothing.

'I'll have to ring her,' Julie says and picks up the phone. Then puts it down again. 'Oh, I don't know what to say, we haven't talked in months. And she's got so much to worry about now.'

'Well, maybe Angela will want to hear from you now,' Adam says, holding out the phone.

'We're not close. Maybe if our parents had been different we might have got on better.'

'Just deal with what is, Ju,' he says. 'Ring her – would you like her to ring you if things were the other way round?'

Slowly she takes the phone from him, 'Yeah. Yeah, if it was me, I'd like my family there.' She calls but hangs up as it starts to ring at the other end. 'Oh God, I was horrible to her when we met the last time.'

'That wasn't just your fault,' I remind her. 'You made the effort. Go on, ring her.' I bite my lip. 'Don't be like me.'

They both stare at me, but it galvanises Julie. She dials again. This time she allows it to be answered. 'Hi,' she says, 'this is Julie. Is Angela there?'

The person at the other end says something and Julie winces. Another deep breath. 'Angela, it's Julie. How are you? I believe you had, had a little baby? How is he?'

Angela seems to be talking back, so Adam and I leave the room and head out the door, not wanting to earwig on the conversation.

We're sitting in the long grass at the back of the house, enjoying the air skimming over our faces. We're trying to make conversation but both of us are keenly aware that Julie's phone call has ended and she still hasn't come out.

'I'll just go in and check on her,' Adam says, standing up. 'Make sure –'

'Hi.' Julie arrives out at that moment. We scan her face for news, but she looks surprisingly OK. 'Well, that was hard.'

'How'd it go?' Adam pats the grass between us and Julie sits down.

'OK.' She looks a little guilty. 'The baby is small but they reckon he'll be fine after a while.'

'Good.' I smile. 'You're an auntie.'

'Some auntie! I feel awful for not contacting her before now. D'you remember, Hope, when she met us in the shop that time?'

'Yeah.'

'And I said I was never going to talk to her again. Well, I wish I had now.'

'Hindsight is a great thing,' Adam mutters.

'The reason she reacted like that, she said, was that she'd only found out she was pregnant and was totally shocked. She said she kept putting off going to the doctor's because she was terrified of what would happen if Mum and Dad found out.'

'Jesus.'

'I just assumed it was me, you know. I assumed that she didn't want to talk to me. If I'd only rung her to find out why she was so distant. But I assumed it was me.'

'What else were you supposed to think?'

'I should have made the effort and then at least I could have a clear conscience now.'

I decide not to pursue it. She'll have to come to terms with that herself. Instead, I ask how Angela is.

'Worried about the baby more than anything. She says

she doesn't care what Mum and Dad think any more, that the baby is what matters.'

'Too right,' I nod.

'Plus,' Adam pinches her cheek affectionately, 'you messed up a lot more than she did, so she won't get into too much trouble.'

'Thank you!' Julie slaps his hand away, but she's smiling. 'Angela said she thought it was brilliant the way I stood up to Dad. She said Dad was going mad. She said how could she tell him she was pregnant after that bombshell.'

Adam and I smile at her.

'But everything is fine otherwise.'

I marvel at how they're both so scared of what their mother thinks. I'd never been scared of my mother. Maybe a bit of fear would have been a good thing, I don't know.

'I'd never have thought that she'd be afraid of them,' Julie muses, half to herself. 'She was the golden girl.'

'She was probably more afraid than you were, which is why she was the golden girl,' Adam says.

Julie and I look in surprise at him. 'Wow!' Julie teases, 'I'd never have put you down as a psychological whiz-kid, Williams!'

'I have many talents,' Adam says. 'As you know.'

'Oh God,' I stand up. 'The big green gooseberry is getting out of here.'

'Stop!' Julie, laughing, pulls me back down. 'You are not a gooseberry and you never will be.' She taps her phone. 'Anyway, I've promised to ring her every day to get a progress report.'

'You should.'

'And,' she looks at me a bit guiltily, 'I'm going to fly over next week to see my new nephew, which means both Adam and I will be gone, is that OK? Will you be all right on your own?'

'I'll be perfect on my own,' I tell her. And at her doubtful look, I say, 'I can look after myself you know.'

'Of course you can,' she says, sounding as if she doesn't believe it for a minute. 'And you can always call on Logan, our friendly gorgeous neighbour if you need anything.'

'The way he's called in on us?'

'He's away this week, didn't you know?' Julie says. 'He got so much work offered to him the night of the hotel do that he's talking to people this week. Did you not know?'

'No, when did you find that out?' It's hard to disguise the delight I feel at the fact that he hasn't been avoiding me. THANK YOU, GOD!! And that's capitalised because that's how I feel.

'Oh yeah, you weren't there much after dinner on Saturday – we were talking to him then. He said he'd have to disappear for the week to sort all his new work out. He was looking for you actually, wasn't he, Adam?'

'Uh-huh.'

Now she tells me. 'Oh.'

'I said you probably went to bed or for a walk. But anyway, he's coming back next week, so he's there if you need him.'

'Right,' I try to say nonchalantly. 'But I'll probably be fine.'

36

O VER THE NEXT two days, I try to remember more
about the accident. Adam and Julie try to help me
by describing what I wore on the day. Well, Julie remembered that, Adam hadn't a clue. I'd worn a 'horrible pair
of tracksuit bottoms and an old faded T-shirt'. Nothing they
say jolts any memory at all and so I listen to the tape and
listen to the tape and still nothing happens. I'm in the garden,
listening to it for what must be the five-hundredth time when
Julie taps me on the shoulder. I jump about a foot in the
air and she starts to apologise. It's a legacy of the accident,
one I'm sure that will go in time. I jump at anything at all
unexpected. Anyway, Julie is grinning like a cat.

'Visitor for you,' she says.

'Where?'

'Out at the front door, he's being very polite, I must say.'

'Logan?'

'Yep.' She looks gleefully at me. 'He fancies you, he fancies
you,' she sings in a low chant. She sounds about fourteen.

'Don't be silly.' I try not to sound too thrilled.
Approaching from the back, I see Logan before he sees
me. He's leaning against the porch, his hands shoved into
the back pockets of his jeans. Julie hasn't followed me, for
which I am grateful.

'Hi,' I say, my hands shielding my eyes from the sun. 'Were you looking for me?'

He turns and, hands still in his pockets, surveys me. 'Yes,' he answers, coming towards me, 'I was.'

'Why?'

He stands about two feet away and cracks a sort of smile. It's that of a cheeky kid who knows he's in the wrong but is hoping he won't get into trouble. 'I came,' he says, dragging out the 'came', 'to apologise for the appalling way I acted when you apologised to me. I was a total wanker.'

'Well, you won't find any argument here,' I say lightly. 'But, yes, unlike you, I will behave with dignity.' I make a big production of bowing my head. 'I accept your apology.'

He smiles a little. 'Don't make me feel honoured that you've done so or anything.'

'Oh,' I smile back, 'do you not feel honoured? I must do it again.' I bow my head. 'I said, scum, that I accept your apology.' He laughs a little. 'And,' I continue, 'I also want to say that I love your paintings and I especially love the one just behind the desk in the foyer.'

A small silence before he says, 'I was wondering if you'd notice it.' His voice has gone all quiet and sends delicious shivers up and down my spine.

'Of course I did.' My own voice quivers slightly. It's the one he sketched the day we went to the waterfall. 'You did it justice.'

He seems to be closer to me now. 'Thanks.'

We stare at each other. I desperately want him to come closer and I don't know what he wants. The moment seems to go on and on, zinging with possibility. He steps even closer to me and I catch my breath. I can smell him, a mix of earth and oils and soap. I want to touch him. To feel the roughness of his jacket and the softness of his skin. The silence stretches until I ache for him to touch me too. I can feel his breath on my face, I can see the faint hint of stubble on his upper lip. I close my eyes.

'It was Maria's fault.' The tension snaps like a bit of elastic band. I don't know if I imagined it.

'Was it?' I stammer out. My mind takes time to adjust. Had he been going to kiss me or not?

'Yeah.' He shrugs, flushes, turns slightly away from me. 'She was meant to come down to sort things and she was a complete cow. Maybe I was in bad form too, I don't know, but it was a disaster. And when you came along, I took it out on you. Well, if I'm honest, I thought there wasn't much to choose between you and Maria.'

'What?'

Logan shakes his head. 'Don't get me wrong. You're much nicer than her, it's just that the way you went on at me that night was the way she used to go on at me, only her horribleness was all the time: Get a job, Logan. Your pictures are crap, Logan. Let's move back to Dublin, Logan.'

I don't know what to say. Being much nicer than his much-hated ex is not exactly a compliment.

'Anyway, sorry again.'

'Like I said, no problem.'

He looks at me and I look at him but it's gone. The time was there and he ran from it. Maybe I would have done the same. So, I manage a smile and ask him if he'd like a coffee. He's about to say no but I can't bear him to leave so I walk on by him and beckon him inside.

Julie is going shopping for her new nephew. Adam has no choice but to drive her. I'm tempted to refuse to go. I can't think of anything more boring than shopping for a baby, but I do want to buy the baby something myself, so I agree. I haven't got a lot of money left in my bank account, but there's enough for a couple of nice babygros or something. Logan says he could do with some art stuff, so we go to his house first, he grabs some money and we head off. 'I don't know what I'll do when you go back,' Logan says, clipping his seatbelt. 'You've saved me a fortune in taxi fares this summer.'

'Don't you drive?' Julie asks.

'Can't afford to,' he says. 'I think now, with all the extra work, plus the exhibitions I've been promised, I'll be able to get a car.'

'Brilliant!' Julie grins.

'It'll take time to save,' Logan says. 'But I'll get there. I just have to be patient.'

'That'll be hard for you,' I joke.

'Yeah, it'll be as hard for me to be patient as it'll be for you to be nice.'

'Folks, folks,' Adam says mildly. 'Let's try to be civil to each other.'

'Leave them alone,' Julie belts him. 'They love it.'

I can't look at Logan. Instead, I stare out the window. I think he does the same on his side.

The city isn't as busy as normal. The summer is drawing to a close. The really hot weather has changed and it is now cooler and breezier. Ten more days and it's all over. Ten more days and I have to go back to London. I don't know if I want to. I don't know what I want to do. This summer hasn't been at all like I'd imagined. It's been better in that I've finally come to some sort of peace with myself and worse because it wasn't done by meeting my mother.

'Now,' Julie is all business. 'I'm going to go to all the shops with baby things. I'm an auntie,' she says to Logan.

'Congratulations.' He sounds amused.

'Do you want to come with me, Hope?'

'Yeah.' I know she's dying to ask my advice on bibs and bottles and dummies and all sorts of stuff I haven't a clue about.

'Goody.' She hugs herself, like a little kid would. 'Let's go. Meet you boys back at the car in three hours.'

'Three?' Adam is shocked. 'But what will I do for three hours?'

'And me?' Logan says. 'I only want to get a few canvases.'

'I dunno,' Julie shrugs. 'Think of something.'

And, her arm through mine, she waltzes me away.

I'm bored. It was great at first, admiring all the tiny trousers and shoes and cute little things but after about two hours they all run into each other. Julie seems determined to buy this baby everything. I think in a way she's trying to make it up with her sister too. We're in a baby toy shop at the moment and she's rummaging through every conceivable rattle ever invented. Winnie-the-Pooh ones, Mickey Mouse ones, Dora the Explorer ones. I'm looking at a little electronic keyboard for babies of three months. Three months, I mean, come on . . .

'Hey, what about this?' Julie holds a giant rattle under my nose and gives it a shake.

My first thought is that the child would want to be Hulk Hogan . . .

And I'm back there. It's the most enormous rattle I've ever seen. Scary looking too. The child would want to be Hulk Hogan to rattle it. 'Lovely.'

357

'Yeah, I thought so too. And it's not too boyish or girlish, so it's not?'

'Nope.'

As the plane takes off, he bends down and carefully puts the rattle away.

Just then the seatbelt sign, which had gone out, flicks back on again.

'Oh,' Joe rubs his hands together. 'Turbulence, I love a bit of turbulence.'

'Will passengers please return to their seats, we are experiencing some difficulties and may have to go back to Heathrow.'

Joe is still going on about turbulence, telling me of a trip he took once where the plane dropped hundreds of feet in seconds because it hit an air pocket.

'Did the captain say we're turning back?' I ask.

'Nah,' Joe shrugs. 'Why would he say that?'

I want to believe him but I'm sure that's what I heard. I take a quick glance up the aircraft and see the air hostesses belting themselves in. Is it my imagination or do they look a little freaked out?

'All passengers remain in your seats. Keep your seatbelts on. We are experiencing difficulties and are turning back to Heathrow.'

POP!

POP!

POP!

Each bang is louder than the last.

'Oh God!' someone shrieks. 'Look!'

Smoke is pouring out of the wing on my side of the plane. I can only stare at it. I can't even scream or shout, just gawk at it in horrible fascination. It's as if I'm out of myself, just not quite able to believe this is happening.

POP-POP-POP.

More smoke.

POP-POP-POP.

The sound is louder.

The lights go off and the plane plummets. It's dark inside and bright outside. Overhead baggage starts to smash and thump. Some of it falls out. The plane is lurching about wildly.

Joe turns to me. His brown eyes are scared. I can only imagine what mine must look like. 'It was nice to meet you,' he says.

'You too.' I think I might cry. 'Will you hold my hand?'

'Sure.' He grasps my hand in his and I notice that he's holding the other lady's hand too. She's still praying.

'If you survive,' he says then, 'will you find my wife and tell her I'm sorry — Mary Ryan in Baltimore, West Cork — will you do that?'

'Tell her that you're sorry?'

'Yeah. She'll know what I mean.' He has to shout as the plane is screeching now. The poor child behind is bawling her eyes out in terror. 'Will you do it?'

'I will.' The noise is unbelievable. I clasp his hand tighter. 'And will you find my mother and tell her I'm sorry — Helen Gardner, Dunport, Kerry?'

'Will do.'

We hold each other as the plane careers downwards.

And I wonder if I'll see my life flash before my eyes.

The plane screams and lands with a bounce on the runway. We're going too fast. Joe pulls me down and makes me put my head between my legs. He makes the woman on the other side do the same. The poor little girl behind is screaming as her mother tries to get her to keep still. Everywhere, luggage is still tumbling from lockers all around us. The screech of brakes outside rips through the plane. Smashing. Banging. Thumping. And then the plane starts to spin and spin, round and round and round. So fast, it's like being on a giant chairoplane. Weirdly, the world slows down. I see everything in super-slow motion. I see everything that happens.

Thump. Thump, thump goes the luggage.

Something large hits me on the head. I can't even feel the pain. Something else hits me. Joe yells out and pushes me over. Taking off his seatbelt, he covers me with his body.

I'm suffocating. He's telling me it'll be OK.

The spinning and screaming and sound of falling things seems to last an eternity. I can't breathe. Things are still falling on top of us.

Then there is silence.

There is a crowd around me. Julie is pale-faced, crying. 'Hope. Hope, are you OK?'

I sit up shakily. In the distance I hear the siren of an ambulance. I feel sick and weak and very scared.

'I think I had a flashback,' I say. My voice trembles, but I'm smiling a little too. I catch Julie's hand. 'Ju, I remember now. I remember everything.'

37

TIM VISITS ME in hospital the next day. I'm sitting up in bed, impatient to go back to the cottage. I'm not ill. In fact, I feel quite good. I remember now and somehow, the memory is not half as scary as not knowing.

Tim tapes me telling my story and gives it to me to listen to. All I want to do, however, is contact Mary Ryan and talk to her. 'I promised him I would,' I say urgently, 'and I can't let him down.'

'I understand that,' Tim nods, 'but you've got to be able to cope with the accident yourself before you go explaining it to someone else. Someone who has been horribly affected by it.'

And of course, that makes sense, so I spend the whole day in hospital, listening to the tape. It stresses me out, but not as much as I'd expected. Not as much as talking about Jamie. In fact, what amazes me is that I also remember that I'd wanted him to say sorry to my mother for me. I don't quite know how I feel about that. What had I been thinking of?

Tim tells me that he'll see me in four days, and that if I'm up to it, he'll give me permission to talk to Mary Ryan. He'll go through what I should say. I'm not out of the woods yet, he says sternly. I've a long way to go. But I think I'm coping a lot better. Don't get me wrong, I'll probably never go on a plane again, but I can talk about being on one and almost dying. I think I can do that.

Adam and Julie take me home later on.

'I'll need post-traumatic stress counselling with what you've put me through,' Julie jokes as I climb into the car. 'God, all I did was shake a rattle and you freaked out.'

'Too much information.' I hold up my hands to ward her words off. That's another thing I'll never do – go into that shop again. Apparently I'd frightened everyone. People had run out in panic, others had frozen to the spot. Oh God, the embarrassment.

'So what now,' Adam asks. 'Are you finished with counsellors and stuff?'

'No, I have to go to someone when I get back to London. Tim's recommending a few people to me.'

'I'd love to go to counselling,' Julie announces. 'I think it must be great to understand yourself.'

'Julie, if they don't understand the whole three persons in one God concept, they're hardly likely to understand you,' Adam snorts.

I laugh at her indignant expression. Three months ago, Adam would probably not have said that to her. But if things can change in the blink of an eye, things can certainly change in three months.

It's three days later. Less than a week before we go home. I'm sitting on my own, looking out at the blue sea. The sun is setting and a blood red path has cut it right through the middle. Adam is inside, getting ready to fly out the next day for his interview. He's quietly hopeful, he says. Julie is on the same flight, only she's decided that she's leaving for good. Her sister and new nephew are expecting her. She's a bit nervous about meeting Angela but they've talked at length on the phone, discussing how they both feel about their parents and I think it'll be fine. Anyway, Julie's adoration of the baby and her piles of presents will more than make up for any awkwardness.

Adam is coming back to bring me and his car home on the ferry but I'll be on my own for six days in the cottage. I don't know if I'll like it. As I'm sitting there, I sense someone looking at me. I see Logan, standing a field away, and when I look he raises his hand in greeting and begins to stride towards me. I smile at him as he sits down.

'How's things?'

'Good.'

'Good.'

There's silence for a moment.

'If you need someone to stay with you when they're away, just ask,' he says. A week ago, I would have read all sorts of signs into that, but now, after what happened in the garden, I know Logan is not interested in a relationship. 'Thanks.'

'I mean that, OK?' He nudges me gently with his elbow.

'I know,' I smile. Then, 'I've to go to my counsellor tomorrow to see if he thinks I'll be OK to visit this Mary Ryan in Baltimore. I'll need help tracing her and, well, I'll need someone to go with me to see her.'

'Mary Ryan?'

'Yeah.' I stare at the ground. 'She's the wife of the man that saved my life on the plane and I have a message for her from him. Will you bring me? Adam's car will be there.'

Tim hasn't exactly given me the all-clear, but I think he

will. And if he tells me it's fine, then I'm going to have to find out where the woman lives. I'm not leaving it until Adam gets back. I've left it too long already.

'Consider it done.' Logan isn't looking at me. He's staring at the sea too. 'Will you miss this place when you go?' he asks.

'I won't know till I go,' I answer.

'If you miss it will you come back?'

I glance at him. He's still not looking at me.

'If someone misses something, they always come back,' I say.

He nods. 'I suppose so.'

We leave it at that.

38

'WELL, HOPE,' TIM sits back in his chair and regards me. 'You certainly don't seem as anxious as you were before when you talked about the accident.'

I had just described the whole thing to him in the most amazing detail and I only had to stop once because my anxiety level had risen to an eight. I know that if I listen to the tape in the next couple of days I'll be fine about it. Of course, I'd still be upset, but not so bad that I want to block out the whole thing or be unable to talk. It's contacting Mary Ryan that's important to me now. It's a small way to make up for the man who saved my life.

'So?' I lean across the desk. 'Can I try and find Mary now?'

He nods slowly. 'Listen to the tape, Hope. Listen to it well over the next couple of days and I'd say by Thursday, you'll be ready.'

'I will,' I promise. 'Thanks, Tim.'

'Don't thank me,' he says. 'You did all the work.'

I hop up out of my seat. Now that I've been given permission to talk to Mary, I want to get on with the job of finding out who she is. 'Can I go now?'

'Go on.' He flaps me away with a grin.

'Oh, by the way,' I fumble in the pocket of my jacket and pull out a gift. 'It's only small, but I thought you might like it.' I hand it over to him. 'It's a thank-you for giving me my life back.'

Tim has blushed, I'm delighted to see. 'Oh,' he seems genuinely touched. 'Thank you, Hope. But I didn't give you your life back, I'm not that great. You did the work yourself, I only pointed you in the right direction.'

'Oh spare me the cliché,' I groan, 'I'm sick of them.'

He laughs and pulls at the wrapping paper. Then he laughs some more. I've given him a brand new Dictaphone and some spare batteries. 'I think I wore your other one out,' I explain. 'And here.' I hand him a card and a box of chocolates. 'Enjoy.'

'I did enjoy you, Hope,' he smiles at me. 'Now good luck with the rest of your life.'

We shake hands and I know he's one person I really will miss.

Adam drives me back to the cottage armed with the Cork telephone directory. There hadn't been one in the house and so we'd asked Greg in the pub for a lend of his. I'd already been on to the airline but, unless I requested it in writing, there was no way they'd release Joe's home address to me. And that, in my opinion would take far too long.

So, telephone book at the ready, I'm going to do some detective work. Unfortunately Adam and Julie have to leave this afternoon, so they can't help me, but Logan has promised to come down and lend a hand.

The minute we pull up outside the cottage, Julie runs to meet the car. 'Well?' she asks as I get out.

'Yeah, I'm allowed to talk to her.'

'Great! I knew you would be. Oh, I wish I could still be here.'

'No you don't.' I punch her lightly on the arm. 'You're only dying to see that little nephew of yours.'

'Aw yeah, I am too.' She whips out her mobile and shoves it in front of my face. 'That's him, isn't he gorgeous?'

I can just about make out a very blurry picture of a tiny blue bundle. I take it from her and peer at it before handing it back. 'He is the cutest baby ever!'

'Andrew, that's what they're calling him. It's after my dad. I think it's to sweeten him up.'

'And has it?'

Julie giggles, 'I think so. They're buying him his pram.' Then she stops and looks serious. 'Aw Hope, they're devastated. I almost feel sorry for them. They just can't believe Angela never told them. They can't believe how scared she was.'

'That's no harm though, is it?'

'No.' She shakes her head. 'Might do them good.'

The taxi to take Julie and Adam to the airport pulls into the driveway and stops any more conversation.

Adam goes inside to get the cases, which he then hefts into the boot of the taxi.

'All ready,' Adam calls. 'Come on Ju, let's go.'

Julie turns to me. 'Time to go,' she says, a little breathlessly.

I can't believe it. Our holiday is drawing to an end. Julie won't be back at all. The next time I see her will be in London. 'I'll miss you,' I say. 'Give that baby a kiss for me.'

'Oh, I will.' She enfolds me in a hug. 'Take care. And make sure Logan minds you, especially when you go to see Mary.'

'I have to find her first.'

'Oh, you will.'

We hug for ages. It doesn't feel at all awkward. Eventually I let her go and we regard each other. 'It's been a blast,' she says. 'Every little thing, even horrible Nelson.'

'It has,' I nod. 'I'm so glad I wasn't in Boston on my own.'

The three of us gaze at each other, all of us thinking the same thing, I hope. That it was a much better holiday, the three of us together.

'Oh Adam, just let's go or I will cry.' Julie blinks hard and hops into the car.

'See ya, Hopeless,' Adam says. 'Back in five days, OK?'

'See you then and good luck with the job.'

We hug then too.

Both of us have come such a long way.

Logan is as good as his word. He arrives about thirty minutes later and can't believe that they've already left. 'I never got a chance to say goodbye to Julie,' he moans as he sits down opposite me at the kitchen table. I've the phone book open at the 'Ryan' page and all the Joe and Mary Ryans marked out.

'You'll see her again,' I say absently, wondering who to call first.

'How?' Logan peers at me. 'Unless you're all coming back next year?'

And it hits me suddenly, we might never see Logan again. Despite my guilty feelings, I haven't rung my mother. I wonder if I ever will. Phoning her is all I might do, so I might never venture here again. It seems too hard to grasp that this man opposite with his dark, sullen but incredibly sexy manner and cute grin, might be out of my life in a few short days. An episode in my life. My heart keeps thinking that he should be so much more but my head is saying no.

'Well,' Logan says and he sounds hopeful, 'are you coming back?'

'I don't know,' I laugh it off. 'So,' I take the book and push it towards him, 'what do you suggest we do?'

Logan studies it. 'Well, I suppose the best thing is to ring all the Joe Ryans and ask for Mary and if we get one, we'll just hang up.'

'Hang up?'

'Well, what else do you suggest?'

He has a point. At least if we had an address, we could go there. There was no easy way of saying over the phone who we were. No way at all, in fact.

'OK,' I said. 'There are five Joe Ryans. Will I go first?'

'I can ring them if you want,' Logan says. 'Don't sweat it. You just take it easy.'

I want to hug him for that. 'Thanks, Logan.'

He winks at me and gastric gymnastics start in my belly.

He takes out his mobile and dials. A few seconds later a tinny voice somewhere in west Cork answers. 'Hey,' Logan says, 'how's it going? I'm looking to speak to Mary Ryan?'

The person at the other end mumbles something and Logan says, 'Sorry about that.' He hangs up and shakes his head. 'One down.'

The next call proves fruitless, as does the third. The fourth, to our delight, results in a Mary Ryan and he gives me the thumbs-up. I write down the address. 'I'll ring the last one,' he says, 'just to be sure.' He dials. It's answered almost immediately. 'Hey, can I speak to Mary Ryan please?'

And he hangs up.

'Two Mary Ryans.' He looks at me, half in amusement,

half in exasperation. 'Why couldn't your rescuer have a more unusual name?'

I groan as I realise I have no idea what to do now. 'How do we find out which one it is?'

Logan shrugs. 'I don't know. We can hardly ask to speak to Joe, can we, that'd be a bit upsetting.'

'Yeah.'

We sit and stare at each other in silence; my hands are cupped about my chin, elbows on the table while Logan lies sprawled back on his chair, tapping his foot as he tries to think.

'We could pretend we're from the hospital and ask about the baby,' I suggest. 'You know, how is your baby feeding or something?'

'And what if something has happened to the baby?'

'Shit!'

More thinking. More silence. 'What would an ace detective do?' Logan asks speculatively.

'Probably spy on both of them,' I mutter. 'See who's a more likely candidate.'

'Yeah!' He grins at me. 'Genius! That's what we'll do. We'll drive down to Cork, park a little away from their houses and see who looks more like the Mary Ryan we want.'

'Oh, that's a good idea. And you wouldn't mind?'

'No, Hope,' he says, earnestly, 'I wouldn't mind.'

With that decided, Logan takes out a map and plots out our journey while I make us some sandwiches. I put a plate in front of him and without looking up, he pats the seat beside him and I sit down. 'See —' his long finger traces a path from Kerry to the outskirts of Cork, 'this looks like the shortest way. What do you think?'

'I think I haven't a clue,' I admit, taking a bite out of my sandwich. I push the plate nearer him. 'Here, eat up, you must be starving.'

We munch contentedly, enjoying the silence. We seem to be able to sit with each other and not talk. He folds up the map and shoves it into his jacket pocket. 'You eat really weird,' he remarks, 'you sort of chew a lot.'

'Thanks!'

'My sister does that.'

It's only the second time he's volunteered any information about his family. 'You have a sister,' I slag, 'and she hasn't killed you!'

He smirks. 'I'll have you know I have four sisters and they all love me. I'm the youngest.'

'Oh God, I should have known. No wonder you have a superiority complex.'

'It's not a complex, it's actually very simple. I am superior.'

'Ha di ha.'

'And you?'

'I had a brother. Younger. He died.' I find I can tell him without choking up the way I used to.

'Oh, that's hard.'

'Yep.' I chew a bit more, then become conscious of my chewing. 'He was twelve,' I add. And before I know it, I'm telling Logan everything. I don't mean I'm doing it in a needy way or a self-absorbed way, I'm just telling him and it all seems so simple and I wonder why I never told anyone before this summer.

'Christ,' Logan says when I finish. 'That was rough.' He's cross-legged on the floor; how we ended up sitting on the floor I have no idea. 'I thought it was bad when my folks died.'

'Your parents are dead?'

'Well, my mother died first, she was sick for ages. And then, about six months later, my dad just didn't feel well and went to bed.' He pauses. 'I found him the next day, he just died some time in the night.'

'Oh, that's terrible.'

Logan shrugs. 'Yeah, it was. But he was so broke up after my mother died, I reckon he would have just faded away without her anyway. It was better the way it happened.'

I nod. I can understand that. 'Yeah, I think that's what happened to my mother, she never got over Dad.' A sudden image of the four of us pops into my head. We're on a beach. Me, Jamie and Dad are splashing about in the water and my mother is telling us sternly not to splash her, that she's going to immerse herself in the water in her own time. 'Own time me arse,' Dad laughs and with one lunge, he has picked her up and ducked her under the freezing water. Jamie and I laughed and laughed . . .

'It was after that happened that I started seeing Maria,' Logan says, interrupting my train of thought. 'I think I just wanted someone to be with.' He gives a self-deprecating laugh. 'Didn't realise I'd just chosen the bride of Frankenstein.'

'Stop!' His expression makes me giggle.

'Naw, I was as bad. We were about as happy together as two cows in an abattoir.'

'Stop!'

He laughs. 'Never thought I'd joke about it,' he says and takes another sandwich. 'You have a good effect on me, Hope.'

'That's not what you said three months ago.'

'I was a fool three months ago.'

'An arrogant fool.'

'Uh-huh,' he agrees good-naturedly. 'Tell you what, though, the whole Maria experience has frightened me big time.'

'Aw, poor you.'

'I will not be going there again for a while.'

I try to keep the smile on my face. 'Probably a wise decision.'

'Well, not unless the girl is very special and loves me as much as my sisters do.'

'Logan,' I shove him gently, 'you will remain alone for the rest of your natural days.'

His answer is one of his gorgeous smiles.

I am really going to miss him too.

39

LOGAN SITS UNEASILY behind the wheel of Adam's car. He spends some time checking what all the buttons and switches do. Then, taking a deep breath, he turns the key in the ignition and the engine roars into life. The car jerks forward then cuts out.

'Way to go,' I joke.

Logan quirks his eyebrow and dangles the keys in front of my face. 'Would you like to drive? Would you?'

'Sorry,' I shrug, grinning.

'Then button that –' he points to his mouth, turns from me and tries again. This time the car surges away. And cuts out. After about five more attempts he gets the hang of it and soon we're winding our way towards the village. I feel a little sick. Tim had offered to come with me, which was pretty decent, but I'd told him I'd be fine. Now that I'm actually on my way, I'm not so sure.

'So, what's the story with your work now?' I ask Logan, once we're well clear of Dunport. 'The hotel opening obviously got you noticed.'

'Yep.' Logan nods. He doesn't talk much while driving. In fact, I don't think he's a very good driver: the car keeps surging forward one minute and stalling and juddering the next. He's staring out the windscreen now with the fierce concentration one might use when dissecting a brain. 'A lot of gallery owners seemed to be there. Your Jack Dunleavy is very well connected.'

'He's not my Jack.'

'Whatever. Oh shit!' He slams the brakes, puts on the hazard lights and attempts a U-turn. 'Wrong bloody way.'

I wince as a chorus of horn-blowing begins.

'Fuck off,' Logan mutters under his breath.

'Just keep going,' I tell him, as calmly as I can. 'We'll find a turn and go back.'

'Yeah, maybe that would be best.' He jams the gears and the car screeches but it gets into the flow of traffic again. Logan waves an apology at the driver behind, who looks like he can't believe what he just saw.

'Anyway,' Logan continues, as if nothing major had occurred, 'I've been offered three galleries, two in Dublin and one down here. They'll take the sculptures too, which is good. And I've two more commissions.'

'Brilliant.'

'Yep, I'm pleased.'

'I thought you didn't like commissions?'

He thinks for a second and says, 'Put it like this: do you mind earning money?'

'Nope.'

'Neither do I.' We come to a roundabout and after some careful negotiation, we're back on the right road. 'I used to be a bit sniffy about commissions all right –' he flicks a glance at me. 'But hell, I can't bloody rent all my life and the money from the sale of the house in Dublin plus what I earn on commissions should get me a place here. I hope to buy the cottage I'm in at the moment.'

'That'd be a great place to live, right on the mountain like that.'

'Yeah, I think so.'

It must be nice, I think, to know exactly where you want to belong.

We arrive in Baltimore a good while later. The minute I see the road sign advertising the fact that we've arrived, I want to tell Logan to turn back. But of course, I can't. I close my eyes and take deep breaths, trying to calm myself down.

'Now . . .' Logan pulls in and consults his map. It's in bits from him constantly looking at it and checking our way. He has a hopeless sense of direction too, I've discovered. 'The first Mary lives –' he peers at it for ages – 'there somewhere.' He jabs his finger at the name of the road we found in the phone book. 'So, let's go.'

It takes about thirty minutes longer than it should because Logan goes up a one-way street and blocks all the traffic for ages. Eventually he has to reverse and I know Adam would have a heart attack if he'd seen how close Logan came to scratching his highly polished car.

'I hate driving,' Logan admits as everyone on the road gawks at us. 'Especially when I haven't a clue about a place.' He acknowledges the horn-blowing and rude hand gestures from his fellow drivers with an apologetic wave.

I wisely remain silent.

We find ourselves in a cul-de-sac of eight houses arranged in a horseshoe around a tiny green. Iron gates lead up small concrete paths to houses of thick walls with net curtains hanging in the windows. Some inner instinct tells me that this is not the place but nevertheless, I have to check it out.

'I don't think this will be the right Mary,' Logan surprises me by saying. 'These houses just seem too old for the guy you described. Like I'd imagine anyone who lived here would have to be hitting ninety.'

As if we've been overheard, an old man emerges from the house two doors away from the one we're interested in and begins walking up the road towards us.

'Hang on a sec,' Logan says and he bounds out of the car and up to the old man.

After a lot of nodding and pointing and shrugging between the two Logan hops back into the car again and with a bip of his horn takes off, waving to the man as he does so.

'Bingo!' he says, smiling at me. 'That old guy knew every single person in the place. The Mary Ryan that lives in this estate is eighty, she hasn't had a baby in about forty years, her husband is still alive but he's bedridden. Our Mary Ryan, however,' he pauses for dramatic effect and my heart wallops in my chest and I suddenly feel very sick indeed, 'lives two miles from here and just had a baby boy a month ago.'

I can't even speak. The reality of meeting this woman is beginning to dawn on me. Once again, I have nothing prepared, beyond a certain point.

'You OK?' Logan looks at me in concern.

'Yeah. I'll be fine.' I smile briefly. 'You've been great. How did you find out? Did you just come straight out with it?'

'More or less. I just asked him if Mary Ryan lived around. Her husband was killed in a plane crash, I said, and you know yourself, if people didn't know her before, they'd certainly know her now. He gave me directions, I hope I can remember them.'

*   *   *

He does remember and ten minutes later, we arrive outside a bungalow, set deep into the hillside above the fishing village. It needs the grass cut and a lick of paint but otherwise it's like a small piece of heaven. We drive up the short driveway and Logan pulls the car to a stop outside the front door. He switches the engine off and turns to me. 'You OK from here?'

'Will you come in with me?' I'm terrified. I don't know why. I want him with me. I can't imagine doing it without him.

'Sure.' He looks reassuringly at me before getting out. Together we walk to the blue-painted door. Putting his hand on my shoulder, his eyes meet mine. 'You'll be fine. I couldn't think of a better person to turn up on my doorstep.'

I grin shakily, take a deep breath, fling a silent desperate prayer to Joe, wherever he is, and press the bell.

It takes a couple of minutes before we hear movement inside. The door is opened by a woman, older than I'd been expecting. She's dressed quite smartly in blue trousers and a cream T-shirt. Her hair is a mixture of grey and black and cut quite short. She peers at us; I reckon she normally wears glasses. 'Yes?' Her accent is very thick.

'Eh, Mary?' I ask, taken aback, wondering if we've got the wrong address again.

'No, I'm Rosemary. Mary's inside with the baby.'

'Well, would it be possible for us to see her?'

The woman shuffles from foot to foot. 'She's not really up to having visitors at the moment. She's had a very bad few months and she's just had a baby.'

'I, eh . . .' I lick my lips and turn to Logan, who nods encouragingly. 'Well, I know about her husband,' I stammer out.

The woman nods. 'Then you'll understand why –'

'I was with Joe on the plane.'

The woman reels back a little to look at me. Her face pales. 'Joe?' Her voice softens as her eyes fill with tears. 'My Joe?'

'Joe Ryan.'

'He was my son. Mary's husband.' She pulls the door wider. 'You'd better come in, so. Mary!'

We're ushered into a big kitchen where a woman in a dressing gown is sitting beside a Kosangas heater. Her hair straggles down in front of her face and she's clutching a big mug of tea in both hands. A baby is sleeping in a Moses basket at her feet.

'Oh, what a lovely baby,' I automatically say.

Mary takes a sip of her tea and regards us. 'Who are you?' I know her dead voice. I know that blank expression. I feel horribly sorry for the tiny baby in the basket. And for the woman sitting beside it.

'This girl says she was on the plane with Joe,' Rosemary says gently. She pulls a few papers from a sofa and nods for us to sit down. Logan sits beside me. I reach for his hand and he holds mine tight.

'Hi, Mary,' I manage weakly.

Mary lifts her head up slowly. She's so pretty, I think. And so young. 'You saw Joe?' Her voice is a whisper.

'He sat beside me,' I answer. I think I might cry and I don't want to. 'We talked.'

'That was Joe,' Mary says, nodding, almost to herself. 'He talked to everyone.'

I'm about to tell her that he saved my life, when she asks, 'What did you talk about?'

'Oh,' I try to remember, 'we talked about his job and I

379

told him I hadn't got a job. He laughed at that.' I bite my lip. 'Eh, we talked about his ironing boards.'

To my surprise, both women chuckle gently. 'He loved those ironing boards,' his mother says. 'They iron on both sides. They were his baby, weren't they, Mary?'

'Yes.' She looks at me, a small smile hovering about her lips. 'Joe was determined they were going to be the next big thing.' A small lull before she says quietly, though bitterly, 'He had so many plans, so many ideas for our life.'

'Hey, hey.' Rosemary bends down to wrap her arms about her. 'Stop now. Come on. He had a great life.' She looks at us. 'That was the only thing that kept us going, that *has* kept us going – that Joe lived life. I mean, he really lived. He'd travelled, he was successful, he did everything he wanted to do, didn't he?'

Mary just nods. A solitary tear drips down her face and plops into her tea.

'He saved my life,' I blurt out, not at all in the way I was intending. 'When the plane was going down, he threw his body over mine and saved my life.'

Both women are silent, regarding me. Mary's hands grow white on the mug.

'I'm sorry he died because of me,' I say on a sob, 'I really am.'

'Hey,' Logan wraps his arm about my shoulder. 'Hey, Hope, come on now.' He gently kisses my cheek and wipes a tear away with his thumb. 'Don't,' he says, looking right at me. 'Don't.'

'So you're Hope,' Mary says quietly. 'I read about you in the paper. I wondered who you were.'

'Well, now you know,' I respond softly.

'Don't be sorry,' Mary says. 'It wasn't your fault.'

'I know but –'

'If he saved your life, just value it.' She is quiet but firm. In the Moses basket, her little baby stirs.

'I value it, every day.'

She nods, her eyes never leaving mine. 'That's good then.'

'I've been in Kerry, recovering,' I explain, after a small silence. I swallow hard. 'And, well, I've something else to say and I'm sorry that it's only now I'm saying it, but I had trouble remembering the accident until recently.' Logan takes his arm from around me, but keeps hold of my hand. I can feel his steady gaze on me and it helps.

'What else?' Rosemary asks, almost fearfully.

'As the plane was going down, he asked me to tell you something, Mary.'

'He did?' She hunches forward in her chair and I'm afraid she'll crush her mug between her two hands. 'What?'

Rosemary lays a hand on her shoulder.

'He said –' I take a deep breath. This is the hardest thing I've ever done – 'he said "tell Mary I'm sorry". He said you'd understand.'

Her eyes widen for a second and then her face crumples up and she stifles a sob. 'He said that?' She leans further forward. 'He really did?'

'He did.'

'Oh God. Oh God.' And she starts to cry. Huge, heaving sobs that shake her body. Her tea slops out but she hardly notices.

Gently Rosemary takes the mug from her and places it on the table. In the basket the baby starts to cry.

I look at Logan. Jesus, what have I done? He looks at me as if to say that there was nothing else I could have done.

His hand tightens around mine. 'Sorry if I've upset you,' I stammer out.

'No,' Mary shakes her head. 'No, it's good. I'm glad.' She wipes her hand across her face, ridding it of tears. 'Joe had our lives all planned out,' she says shakily. 'Hush, hush,' she bends over and picks up her baby. Holding him close, she says again, 'He had our lives all planned out.'

'Mary, you don't have to explain. Joe just told me to give you that message.'

'You've come all this way,' she says, 'you deserve to know. And besides, I want you to know. He saved your life.'

'Yes, he did.'

She smiles at me and continues softly as she rocks her baby, 'Joe had big dreams for us, big dreams for his ironing board, his house, our lives. He had such energy and fun and he made me laugh a lot.' She pauses and strokes the tiny head of her son, looking at him now, instead of me. 'But he never figured on kids,' she sniffs. 'Not until we were on our feet. But this little guy,' a gentle kiss on his forehead, 'well, he didn't want to fit in with any plans, sure you didn't? When I got pregnant I didn't tell Joe for about four months.'

Rosemary silently pours the water into the teapot and swirls it about.

'And, so, when eventually I told him, he went off the deep end. Said we couldn't afford it – we had a big row the day he left on that plane.' She bites her lip. 'Just as he left to go to Departures, he said goodbye and, well, I didn't answer him. I mean, he rang me when he was in London, but it was all so strained. And I never saw him again.'

Her voice breaks.

'We all do those things,' Rosemary murmurs as she hands us each a mug of tea. 'It's just human nature.'

'He was excited about the baby when I met him,' I say. 'He, well, he'd even bought it a present.'

'He had?'

I cross over to her and hand her the baby bag I'd brought in with me. 'This is the same rattle as the one he'd bought.'

She balances the baby in one arm and peers into the bag. 'He bought a rattle?' She smiles as I take the rattle out of the bag and hand it to her. 'Oh Rosemary, look. Isn't it just like Joe to buy the biggest rattle he can find?'

Rosemary laughs, takes the rattle and shakes it. It produces a very weird sound.

'I guess he was expecting Hulk Hogan for a son.' I smile too.

'See what your daddy bought,' Mary whispers to her son, pointing at Rosemary as she rattles it in front of him.

'I told you he'd come around,' Rosemary says.

They both peer at the baby, Rosemary rattling and both of them making soft cooing sounds. Then Mary looks up. 'Did Joe say anything else?'

I tell her about him not being able to find his hotel and driving around for ages in a taxi looking for it.

'That was Joe,' she laughs. The word 'was' seems to catch her and she swallows. 'I don't know how I'll survive without him. Babies are hard work and I miss him every day.'

Rosemary looks at me hopelessly over her head. 'You'll cope,' she says. 'I know you will.'

'My dad died when I was six,' I say. 'He died and left my mother on her own.'

'Really?' Mary looks at me with a sudden hope in her face.

'Yeah. I was six and my baby brother was two and he was mentally disabled. Like, there was a lot you had to do for him and he was a lot of work for my mother.'

'And how did she manage?'

I gulp hard and go for what I know now is the truth. 'She did the best she could.'

'That's all anyone can do.' Rosemary nods, kneeling down in front of Mary and giving the rattle another shake. What a lovely mother-in-law, I think.

'It wasn't perfect,' I continue, 'but she did her best. And I'm here now. And I survived.'

'Yeah.' Mary stares at her unblinking, solemn-looking baby, its little fists curled up and cute blue eyes staring back at his mother. 'I named him Joe,' she says to me. 'After his daddy.'

I smile and touch the baby's face. 'Hello, Joe. Your mammy is going to be great.'

Mary smiles gratefully up at me.

I'm so glad I've come and I send silent thanks to Joe, wherever he is. Without realising it, he's just saved my life for the second time.

40

'ARE YOU SURE you want to?' Logan asks.

We're in a small coffee shop, about an hour from Dunport. Logan is starving and despite the fact that I'm in a hurry to do what I know I should have done a long time ago, I couldn't deny the poor guy something to eat. He is half-way through a fry and chips and has just ordered dessert.

'I'm sure.' All I have in front of me is a cup of coffee and a cake and I can't even eat the cake, though it's my favourite, a cream doughnut.

'You've had quite a stressful day already,' he says, forking about three chips into his mouth. 'I'll bring you tomorrow, if you'd prefer.'

'Logan, today was the best day I've had since the accident.'

He looks incredulously at me. I know my eyes are red and puffy, I know I'm so tired from meeting Mary, and yet, today has been such a relief.

'Honest.' I reach across the table and touch his hand. 'Thanks.'

He entwines my fingers with his and both of us look at where his long fingers cross over with mine. I am suddenly incredibly turned on, Jesus, this guy presses all my buttons. I lift my eyes to his face, but he's still staring at our joined hands. Slowly his inscrutable eyes look up. 'OK,' he nods slowly. 'Anything.'

And he lets my hand go and continues eating as if nothing just happened.

We arrive outside my mother's house and all is as it was before. The house looks clean enough, the garden is still overgrown but with a lot of brown grass due to the hot weather. The brass bell on the front door is gleaming, which is a surprise.

'So,' Logan glances at the house and then at me, 'this is where you're from.'

'This is it.'

'Nice place.'

'It's OK. Not as nice as living up the mountain, though.' I stare at my mother's house through the car window.

'And this – you want to do it on your own?'

'This – I have to do on my own.'

'OK.' He taps the steering wheel, 'I'll be back in an hour. If you're not here, waiting outside, I'll hang on for you.'

'Logan, I don't know how to thank you.'

'Oh, I'll think of something, don't worry.' He winks at me. 'Go on.'

'OK, see you.' I climb out and slam the door closed behind me.

Logan rolls down the window. 'And for what it's worth, Hope, you're doing the right thing. I'd give anything to have my mother again.' With those words, which bring tears to my eyes, he's gone.

I turn to face the house, feeling differently towards it than I had a couple of months ago. The tension inside me has gone, replaced by a sort of acceptance. I can't control events, I know that now. But I can control my response to them and what I had done to my mother, though it had seemed right at the time, was wrong.

It starts to rain as I make my way up the path. I feel a little sick and nervous, but hopeful too. I want to see her, I want to explain stuff to her, I want to have a mother again, even one that isn't perfect. And maybe she might want a less than perfect daughter again too.

I reach the front door and my hand is poised over the doorbell when I hear voices coming up the hallway from inside. Oh God, it's bloody Amanda Coonan. I don't want her to see me here. I don't need her judging me. The words she'd said to me the night of the hotel ball still have the ability to sting me with their truth. I look around for somewhere to hide. The only place is behind the big tree in the centre of the garden. I'll have to hope I'm thin enough to be hidden by the trunk. I make a dash for it and only get there as the door opens.

'See you, Mrs Gardner,' Amanda says cheerily.

Mrs Gardner? How babyish. Still, I'd probably call her mother Mrs Coonan.

'I'll order in those flowers for you,' my mother says. She doesn't sound like my mother, I think wonderingly. She sounds confident and in control. 'You'll have the nicest flowers of any bride.'

Amanda laughs. Then stops and I have the uneasy feeling she's spotted me. 'Hello?' she calls out, confirming my suspicions. 'Who's behind that tree?'

I stay very still.

'Behind the tree?' My mother sounds puzzled. 'I can't see anyone.'

'There is definitely someone there,' Amanda says. 'Look, you can see the front of their trainers. Come out, whoever you are.'

Wow, she's brave, I think with a grudging admiration.

'Out!' she shouts again. 'Are you some kind of pervert?'

Shit, she's coming closer. I close my eyes, hoping somehow that it'll make me invisible. Then realise it won't. 'It's me,' I stand out and glare at her. 'I was just looking at the tree.'

To say they look stunned would be a gross understatement.

'Do you like trees?' Amanda asks. She tries to make it sound as if hiding behind a tree in my mother's garden is perfectly normal. I suppose that's nice of her. She looks so good, all dressed to perfection, and she makes me painfully aware of my poorly co-ordinated outfit. Still, I bet I'm a lot more comfortable than she is.

'Yes, as a matter of fact I do.' I sound defensive and want to kick myself.

'Hope always had a thing for trees,' my mother says quickly. 'Didn't you?'

She's on my side. Unexpected tears spring to my eyes. Even after all this time and all that's happened, she's on my side and telling lies for me. I take a second to absorb this and to steady myself. I focus my attention on her and she nods slightly, as if encouraging me to go along with her. 'I'm here because I came to talk to you,' I say, gulping a little as I go for the truth. 'And when I heard you both coming out, I got cold feet and hid. I wasn't looking at the tree.'

'Oh,' Amanda smiles at me and I see the kindness in her eyes. And the fact that it's not her fault she looks so snooty. 'Well, I was just leaving, so I'll say goodbye, Mrs Gardner.'

'Yes, goodbye Amanda,' my mother says absently. 'Talk to you in a couple of days.'

Amanda leaves without looking back and my mother and I face each other across a swath of dried-up grass with the rain falling lightly on our faces.

The silence seems to last for ever.

'Will you come in, Hope,' my mother says at last, sounding unsure.

'Yes. I'd like that.'

She smiles at me shyly before turning around and leading the way. I follow her across the grass, wiping my feet on the doormat as I go into the hall, and from there we move into the kitchen. Everything is clean and tidy and in its place. This is the home of a woman in control of her life. When she reaches the centre of the kitchen, she turns and faces me. Her earrings jangle and flash in the light coming from the window. I'm about three feet from her. 'I'm so glad to see you,' she says earnestly.

How can she be glad when I was so horrible to her?

'I'm so glad to see you too.'

I don't know how it happens, but suddenly we're in each other's arms and for the first time in years, I feel a sense of home, of belonging, of being safe. I never want to let go. She smells of flowers and earth and grass.

'I'm sorry, Mammy,' I gulp out, not having been aware of what I was going to say until right that minute. 'Sorry for leaving you, sorry for not writing, sorry for not understanding how hard you had it and for being so difficult.'

She relaxes her grip and pulls herself back to look at me. Her hands are still on my shoulders. 'Sorry?' she says and she sounds shell-shocked. 'You're sorry?' She shakes her head and asks wonderingly, 'What on earth have you to be sorry for?'

'For –'

'You were the best little girl anyone could have had.' Her fingers tighten their grip. 'The best little girl,' she stresses 'the best' and furiously blinks back tears. 'I didn't deserve you. If you hadn't been so good, we'd all have gone under. You minded Jamie, you cooked and cleaned. I'm the one who's sorry. I let you both down. Jamie might still be alive –'

Her voice cracks.

'You were sick, Mammy. You couldn't help it.'

'I was your mother,' she says definitely. She gives my shoulders a little shake. 'Your. Mother. I was meant to protect you both. I let you down. For a long time, I found it hard to live with that failure.'

'It wasn't your fault,' I say. 'I know now that you did the best you could.'

'Oh, Hope,' she says, letting me go and walking to the window. She places her hands on the sink and looks into it, her shoulders drooping. 'I struggled badly after your daddy died. I did try but . . .' she pauses and continues, 'You have no idea how sorry I was about what happened, but nothing I could do or say could give you your childhood back, your brother back or your daddy back.'

I can't answer her. I'd wished it all back too many times.

'And the fact that I knew that made me even more depressed and more bitter and I know that's why you left.' She turns around. 'And I don't blame you.'

'I just found it hard to cope, Mammy.'

'You shouldn't have had to cope.'

I bow my head.

'Even though you left, you still rang,' she goes on, crossing towards me. 'And even then, I managed to drive you away

390

with my sadness. Hope, I knew I was doing it but I couldn't help it.'

'I shouldn't have stopped calling. I was selfish.'

'No.' She shakes her head. 'You were right. You couldn't make me better.'

'Really?'

'Really,' she confirms and my guilt at the way I've treated her dissolves like salt in hot water.

'I was glad when you stopped,' she continues, 'because you needed to get away from me. You would have gone mad otherwise. And I needed to let you go because I had to accept that there was nothing I could do to make it up to you. The only thing I had left to show you how much I cared, was to give you your freedom. That's why I didn't ring you.' She pauses and gives a hesitant smile. 'I always hoped you'd come back.'

'Well, I have.' It's a whisper.

'Thank you.'

And she hugs me again.

I remember the other times she's hugged me. The other times I've been happy in this house, the times I blanked out because to remember was so painful. I remember them the way I'd suddenly remembered them when the plane was going down. I remember that that's why I'd told Joe Ryan to apologise on my behalf. But I was lucky enough to be able to do it myself. And I know that this time the memories will stay with me for ever.

I've come home.

We talk about Daddy's death. I tell her that I can't really remember him and she finds a massive photograph album and as we turn the pages together, she tells me stories.

'When he died,' she says, as she stops at a picture of him on our very last holiday together as a family of four, 'it was such a shock. My head couldn't accept it. Every day I kept wondering where he was, why wasn't he coming home. The doctor told me that I got depressed so that I wouldn't have to face life without him.' She runs her finger up and down the picture of a man that looks like me. I've got his big build, his round face and basketball shape. 'He was such a lovely man.'

And at that, I think of Logan. Oh shit! Startling my mother, I jump up from the sofa and peer out the window. Sure enough, there he is, in Adam's car, waiting patiently for me to come out. 'Oh no!'

'What?' My mother looks alarmed. The photo album falls from her lap.

'Sorry, Mammy.' I glance at my watch. Jesus, the poor guy is out there at least two hours now. 'A friend said he'd pick me up ages ago and I forgot and he's still sitting out there.'

'Well, ask him in,' my mother says as she picks up the album. 'I'll make you both something to eat.'

'Really? That would be OK?'

'That would be fine.' She smiles at me and indicates the album. 'We've the rest of our lives to talk, haven't we?'

'Yeah.'

We smile at each other.

As I go to rescue Logan from the car, it dawns on me that this is one of the few times I've ever had a friend home.

And it feels so good.

41

I T'S TIME TO go. The summer has ended and the rain is bucketing down as Adam and Maurice put the cases into the boot of Adam's car. I'm sitting in the front of the car watching them, wondering if Logan will come to wave us off. But of course he won't, it's way too wet. The last time I'd seen him was when he'd driven me back to the cottage to get some nightwear so I could stay at my mother's. My mother had been charmed by him. Well, he had been on his best behaviour, smiling and joking and nodding. She'd asked him about his sculptures so he'd been charmed by her. The night before last, he'd picked me up to bring me back to the cottage so I could pack. He'd given me a chaste hug and told me he'd be in touch. A phone call last night to wish us a safe trip home had been all he'd done.

I don't know what I'd expected; after all, he was just a friend. That's all he wanted to be, he'd made that quite clear in subtle ways.

My mother and I had reached a peace. All my life, I realise, I'd been looking for that peace and I'd been looking in all the wrong places. I'd hoped to escape my past and fill the hole in me, but you can't fill a crack in a foundation with superglue or cotton wool. You need to try to rebuild from scratch, go back to the source and repair it in that way.

Now I am ready to begin over, though I reckon I'll still bristle if I feel I'm being taken for a ride, only now I'll be able to distinguish who is actually taking advantage of me instead of feeling permanently persecuted.

'There now.' Maurice throws a final case on the back seat. 'That's everything. Sure we'll probably be seeing you again, Hope. You'll be visiting your mother, no doubt?'

'I will.'

Adam grins at me.

'I'm glad ye are both talking again, a lovely woman your mother is,' Maurice nods approvingly.

Dunport. The home of everyone's business. 'Thanks for that, Maurice. I'm so glad to have made you happy.'

Adam splutters out a laugh.

'Oh you have,' he nods. 'Sure, no matter what happened between ye, there comes a time to let go.'

'Yeah.' I look at the house. At the view of Dunport. 'Time to let go.'

'And you?' Maurice looks at Adam. 'Will you be back?'

'Maybe.'

'Well, give me a call if you come back next summer. The cottage will still be here.'

'Will do,' Adam grins.

'OK, so.' Maurice slams the car door and as we pull away, he waves furiously after us.

'Shall we call in to Logan to say goodbye?' Adam asks. 'We've plenty of time.'

I was hoping he'd say that. I just want to see him once more.

'Yeah, why not?' I make my voice deliberately casual. 'That'd be nice.'

'Yeah, nice,' Adam scoffs as he turns the car towards Logan's house. Ten minutes later we're pulling up outside. It's quite a depressing sight in the bad weather, the whole place looks sort of run-down. Adam and I make a dash for the front door and hammer on it.

Nothing.

'Logan!' I call. 'Logan!'

It's hard to make ourselves heard above the wind, which is picking up nicely. It's going to be a horrible day for a ferry crossing. 'He could be in his studio,' I shout. So we make a dash for it. He's there all right, chipping away at some wood. His horrible cat is lying curled up at his feet. When I rap on the window, his chisel, or whatever he's using slips and seems to cut him because he jumps up and hops about the place, holding his hand.

'Oh shit,' I wince. 'I think I've just done him an injury.'

He isn't mad when he opens the door, despite the blood seeping from his wound. 'Hey,' he gives me a big bright smile and flicks his glance to Adam. 'All set for going?'

'Yes,' Adam nods. 'We just thought we'd say goodbye in person.' He holds out his hand and Logan grips it in his firm one. 'So long.'

'Yeah, safe trip.'

They nod and Adam indicates his car. 'Well, I'll leave you to it, Hope.' He saunters off and leaves me and Logan on our own in the studio.

We stare at each other for a bit. 'So,' Logan eventually says, 'you're leaving.'

'You'd better get something for that hand,' I say uneasily as blood drips on to the floor.

'What? Oh yeah.' He holds it up and, finding a piece of

dirty-looking rag, he wraps his hand in it. 'I'll shove a plaster on it in a bit.'

'What? When it gets gangrene?'

He smiles.

A pause.

'Thanks, Logan,' I stammer. 'I know I've said it before but these last few days you've been so good to me. I'd never have managed without you.'

'It was my pleasure.'

'And mine.' My voice shakes. 'I . . . I liked being with you.'

'And I with you.'

God, he's so beautiful. And it's not just his face. It's him. I love everything about him. His smile, the way he glowers when he's cross, his nonchalant way of walking, his sloppy dress sense that mirrors my own, his hair that has begun to lengthen despite its recent cut. His sallow tan that I'm sure is there all year around. I love the way he loves my mountain. My sky and sea.

I realise suddenly that neither of us has said anything for the past minute or so. He seems to be looking at me the way I'm looking at him. He crosses the space between us and my body liquefies as he wraps his arms about me and hugs me to him hard.

'My pleasure,' he says again.

I entwine my arms through his and feel the broadness of his back under his green T-shirt. His chin is resting on my head and I can smell him. All clean and gorgeous. I rest my head on his chest and press his body to me. Very slowly he begins to rub my back and my senses spin into erotic heaven. His face lowers itself to mine and oh my God, he kisses me. Right on the lips. I feel as if I can't quite breathe. I respond and my heartbeat goes off the Richter scale. His lips are hungry, insistent and I can hear his ragged breathing. His hand caresses the back of my head as he presses my mouth to his.

And then, he pulls away.

'Shit!' he says, rubbing his hand over his face and looking at me in exasperation. 'Sorry, Hope.'

My poor body doesn't know what hit it. 'Sorry?' I mouth. 'For what?'

'I shouldn't have.' He shakes his head. 'That was stupid of me.'

'I liked it.' I don't care now. He likes me, I like him. 'I really did, Logan.'

'So did I,' he says almost angrily, 'but does that mean you're going to stay around?'

I shrug. 'Well,' I indicate the door. 'No. But so?'

'So?' he says. He pulls the cloth tighter on his hand. 'I had a girlfriend once who didn't want to live here, I'm not going to have another.'

Point taken. I'm not as important to him as his art. As this place. 'I see what you mean,' I say, more calmly than I feel. My heart, which had been singing, drops in my chest like a stone in a pond. Only the ripples remain to remind me what has just happened. 'But couldn't we –'

'Call in when you visit your mother, won't you?'

His interruption is to stop me making a complete fool of myself.

'Won't you?' he asks again gently.

'Yeah.' I don't know if I will. I don't know how I could bear to hear about his life if I'm not in it.

He smiles, lovely white teeth. 'Good. I'll look forward to that.' Pause. 'Well,' he says slowly, as if he doesn't want the words to come out, 'So long, Hope.'

397

'Yeah, so long.'

He doesn't attempt to shake hands. Neither do I. Instead he turns briefly away to look for something for his hand. The rag is pretty soaked. I wish he'd say something to me. I wish he'd go for a long distance relationship, just for a bit. Just to see how it'll pan out. But he doesn't. Instead, he finds another equally vile rag, then we look at each other again. The silence seems to zing with what I find I can't say.

'Bye, so,' I mutter and my voice is small.

His answer is to chew his lower lip and wave his hand.

It's not much fun being on the ferry with Adam. I'm morose and grumpy. I thought we'd have a laugh going home but I find I can't get Logan out of my head.

Eventually Adam asks, 'What's the matter?'

I stare into my orange. 'Nothing.'

'Oh, come on. You've been more miserable than this weather since you left Logan this morning.'

I sigh, dip my finger in my drink and suck it for a bit before answering, 'He kissed me. Then he told me he didn't want me.'

'What?' Adam gawks at me, his mouth open. 'He kissed you?'

I shrug.

'Then he said he didn't want you?'

I shrug again. It hurts too much to say it twice.

'Well, that's bollix,' Adam pronounces, to the horror of some older women sitting nearby. They cough loudly and look in our direction. 'Bollix,' Adam says again, unintimidated. 'The guy – and take this from me, Hope – is crazy about you.'

I laugh. 'Adam, no offence, but you're hardly an expert on relationships.'

'Offence taken,' Adam says back good-naturedly. 'Look, the time you had that row, you know the row where you were very mean to him and then you went to apologise and he was very mean back to you, d'you remember that?'

'Eh, yeah.' It's not something I could forget in a hurry. I don't think I've ever been as nasty to anyone, ever.

'Well, I gave him a few lifts in the car during that time. He wanted to get stuff in town and I swear, Hope, all he talked about was you.'

'He did?'

Adam nods. 'In a sort of indirect way,' he explains. 'Blokes don't do the sort of things girls do, but I got his vibe.'

Adam got his vibe. That's not exactly what I was hoping for. 'Well,' I shrug, 'his vibe has obviously changed. He likes me but not enough to have a long distance relationship.'

'So, move back.' He says it like it's so obvious.

'Move back?'

'Yeah.' Now he's making it sound like I'm a moron. 'I mean you love that place. Anyone can see that. You'll never settle in London again, Hope.'

'Of course I will. London is my home now.'

He shakes his head. 'London was never your home.'

'Yes it was.' I feel like crying. 'Anyway, you're only saying that so I won't be around to cramp your and Julie's style.'

He doesn't reply and I know I've been mean and horrible.

'Sorry,' I mutter meekly. 'You know I didn't mean that.'

His hand finds mine. 'You know Julie and I love you to bits, don't you?'

'Just like I love you two.'

'So, that's why I'm going to say this and you can take it or leave it or think about it. Remember you told me about Tim, your counsellor and the problems he and his wife were having?'

'Yeah.'

'Well, that's you and Logan. One of you has to give way. One of you has to say OK, I will give in and move to where you are.'

'But why me?'

'Because you love those mountains, that's why. Forget about preserving control of your identity and just go for it.'

'It's not as easy as that. He wouldn't do it for me.'

'So do it for yourself.' He pauses. 'Meet him half-way.'

'Oh, so what?' I smile a little. 'I meet him half-way and we live in the middle of the ocean?'

'Oh, don't be so smart.' But he says it affectionately. Standing up, he stretches. 'I'm going for a walk – want to join me?'

'No, I'll stay here.' I watch him leave.

There is no way that I want to see the Irish coastline recede into the grey day.

42

'AND HE SMILED at me today. He's very intelligent.'

Julie has about a hundred snapshots of her baby nephew and is showing them to me and Adam. Each photo has a ten-minute history and each story has to be 'oohed' and 'ahhed' by both of us.

'You're not listening,' Julie says suddenly.

'We are,' both of us say simultaneously.

'So, what did I just tell you that his first word was, then?'

Adam looks at me and I look at Adam.

'Eh – hello?' Adam says lamely.

Even I know that's a long shot.

'He's two months, he can't talk yet,' Julie says annoyed. 'Now if you're not interested, just tell me. I'd hate to bore you both.'

'I am interested,' Adam lies.

'No you are not!' Julie pouts. 'All you care about is that you've got promotion again.'

Adam laughs. 'My arse!'

'Your arse,' Julie scrunches up her nose. 'Well, if I were you I wouldn't go boasting about it.'

'That's not what you said last night.'

I pretend to puke and stand up from the table. 'Too much information,' I grin. God, I think to myself, I have to get out of here. I've been looking at a few places to move to in London, but so far, nothing has appealed. Even though I have money to buy a place, since compensation for the accident is in the pipeline, I can't see anything I want. 'I'm just going out for a bit. I've another apartment viewing.'

'Oh, by the way,' Julie shouts after me, 'your mother rang.'

'My mother?'

'Yeah, she said to tell you that she's expecting you next week and that your bed is all made up.'

'Oh right. Ta.'

'So, you're flying, are you?' Julie asks.

'Yeah. Nervous about it but I think I have to do it.'

'Good for you.' She gives a little cheer. 'Will you be seeing Logan?' she asks teasingly.

I shrug. I'd been home last month, on the ferry, and I hadn't called in to him. I just hadn't been able to face it. 'I don't know,' I answer. 'If he's around, I might.' Even the mention of his name makes me feel a little sick. I miss him more than I thought I would. I go over and over our kiss every night in bed, bringing it to what should have been its conclusion.

Julie turns to Adam. 'Despite what you thought, Adam, Hope and Logan never got it together.'

'Not yet,' Adam says confidently.

'Still, probably for the best.' Julie picks up a photo and smiles at it. 'Aw, look at that one. He was in his bath there.'

'Why is it for the best?' I can't help sounding cross at her assumption.

'Well, you know, if you didn't love him enough to stay, you mustn't have really liked him all that much.'

'I did so like him.'

'Not enough, though.' Julie dismisses me and turns back to her photos.

The estate agent is a bit pissed off with me. So far, she's shown me at least twenty new homes. So far, I haven't been interested in any of them.

'You again,' she says, and she can hardly contain the weariness in her voice. It's as if she recognises that showing me around this salubrious new penthouse is a waste of her time.

'Yes, me again,' I smile at her. I had been hoping it wouldn't be her, that it would be someone else from the company. 'I hope this one is for me.'

She doesn't reply, her silence saying everything. Instead she walks into the foyer of the newly constructed building. It's all very plush. Wood and chrome, carpeted elevators that hardly make any noise as they whoosh us up to the top floor. The agent click-clacks her way along the polished wooden floor of the corridor, her clip-board in hand. 'Right,' she says, as she unlocks the door of an enormous apartment, 'have a look around.'

Up to this, she'd been doing a hard sell, telling me all the features that this flat or apartment or house had. Now, I think she's given up on me. I'm determined to show interest. Only, as I look about, my heart sinks. It's just not . . . well, it's not cosy, for a start. And it's too new. And expensive. I give everything a quick glance, just to be polite before telling the woman that I'm finished looking around.

'Well?' she asks.

I shrug. 'I'll let you know.'

She sighs. 'Look, Ms Gardner, I've shown you our best properties. There is nothing finer in London. Have you thought that maybe London isn't for you?'

And that's when, as the sun dips its face into the sprawl of the city beyond the huge glass window of the penthouse, it hits me. It's not that London isn't for me, it's that I'm no longer for London. Adam was right and it's taken me two months to realise it, but London was only ever an escape for me. I think, though I don't voice it aloud, Dunport is where I truly belong. And I belong there whether or not Logan wants me. Maybe seeing him and going for what I want is better than not seeing him and saving myself from hurt.

I'll call in to see him this time, I vow. I'll call in to him and ask him if we have a future.

43

THE LETTER AND parcel arrive on my desk in work, the next day. The letter is in a plain white envelope with just my name on the front. The parcel is wrapped in brown paper and tied up with twine. Very classy.

My boss, who I hate, because he's bossy and grumpy and he keeps getting me to make his tea, has thrown it across my desk. 'For you. From reception.'

'Oh right. Thanks.' I finger the envelope. 'Who's it from? Is it a message?'

'Eh, I'm the boss, not ya secretary.'

'Oh, yeah, I forget sometimes.'

He glowers at me and I smile sweetly back at him. He 'harrumphs', rolls his eyes and stalks out of my cubicle. I'll resign next week probably because I'm going home. I'll write a nice letter and hand it to him. I won't storm out and get fired like I used to do. I've sort of grown up now. I'll resign and get another job in Kerry.

I open the envelope, wondering who's sending me letters in work. Inside is a plain white sheet of paper with the most bizarre words.

O. O. Shame! U dope! Miss Lovely gon.

What?

I peer at it again. *O. O. Shame*? Have I a stalker? I stare at the parcel, almost scared to open it now.

Did the boss say he'd got it from reception?

I dial down. 'Hi, is that Carrie?'

'Yes. Who's that?'

'This is Hope in web design. Did you just get an envelope and parcel for me?'

'Yes. I gave it to Gary, your boss, he said he'd give it to you.'

'He did. I don't know what it's about.'

There's silence at the other end.

'Who gave it to you?'

'Some guy, I buzzed him up.'

And then I get the weirdest sensation. I feel I'm being watched. I glance up and what I see makes me drop the phone to the floor. Carrie's tinny voice saying 'Hope, Hope' over and over is soon replaced by the dial tone.

'Hiya.' He's lounging in the doorway, his head against the frame and a sardonic grin on his face.

'Hi yourself.' My voice is a whisper. God, he looks so good.

'Knew all that *Countdown*, I'm such a genius was a load of crap.' He nods to the paper.

'Sorry?'

'It took me ages to do the "O. O. Shame" stuff and you never even copped it.'

'Copped what?' And then I do cop it. I pick the letter up and just by thinking it's an anagram, all the words rearrange themselves in my mind. A small flutter starts up in my stomach.

Unaware of my flutterings, Logan straightens himself up and regards me. 'It took me this long, Hope, to figure out that I missed you.'

'I missed you too.' My eyes are drinking him in. I don't even know what I'm saying. I just want to stare at him.

'You couldn't have missed me that much. You visited your mother a few weeks ago and never came to see me.' He sounds hurt.

'I thought it would hurt to see you.'

'Hurts me more when I don't see you.'

His blunt honesty makes me unable to answer.

He nods in the direction of the letter. 'Thick, that's what you are. Will I explain it to you?'

'Do you miss me. Logan loves Hope.'

'Impressive.' But his voice has lost its cockiness. 'Well?' he pauses, 'Do you miss me? I miss you.' He crosses towards me and sits on the edge of my desk. 'I can't work any more.' He indicates the box. 'That's the last thing I was able to finish.'

My hands are shaking as I untie it. It's just a simple bow but it takes me longer than it should. Inside is a white cardboard box. Opening it, I take out a small wood carving. The bust of a woman.

'You,' Logan says, 'that day on the mountain.'

I hardly recognise myself. The lady he has carved is beautiful. Full lipped, slanted eyes and a shaved head. 'Me?' I whisper.

'That's how you look to me,' he says.

'I look gorgeous.'

'Yeah.' He says it matter-of-factly.

'It's . . . it's,' I touch the wood, it's alive and vibrant. 'Thanks.'

'I'll even move over here to be with you,' he says earnestly. 'Honest, Hope, I don't need anything except you.'

Without taking my eyes off him, I pull open my desk

drawer. 'Well,' I say, 'you don't have to. I booked a flight to see you this weekend.'

'A plane?'

'Uh-huh. The quicker the better.' I place the tickets where he can see them. 'I was going to move back home and I thought I'd let you know.'

'Really?'

'Yeah,' I smile, and stand in front of him, where he sits on my desk. He puts his hands lightly on my waist and my heart flip-flops as he pulls me to him. 'If you miss something,' I whisper as his first kiss lands on my lips, 'you always go back.'